Voi

He was lurking when she bought throat pastilles at the pharmacist, prowling at another card carousel as she chose her postcards. He was nearby as she took note of a dry-cleaner's address.

His persistence deserved a medal, thought Julia wryly, but not from her. 'Come on then, pinch me,' she muttered, humour and irritation blending. She wondered if she were being unfair. Had she perhaps smiled at the man in one of their coincidental meetings, sent the wrong signal? She wished he would make his move. 'Let's get it over with.' Checking her step, she turned.

Twenty paces back on the pavement, the man had stopped. Ignoring frowns and gestures from people who shoved past, he was cleaning under his fingernails with a knife – not a penknife: Julia knew that at once. This was something heavier, surely much larger than any normal person would wish to carry.

Telling herself that she was over-reacting, Julia lengthened her stride. Suddenly she felt very alone.

Behind her the beat of footsteps increased.

About the author

Born in Huddersfield, West Yorkshire in 1960, Lindsay Townsend worked in libraries for several years after taking a first-class history degree at Bangor. She is now a full-time writer. *Voices in the Dark* is her first novel.

Voices
in the Dark

Lindsay Townsend

CORONET BOOKS
Hodder and Stoughton

First published in Great Britain in 1995 by Hodder and Stoughton
A division of Hodder Headline PLC
First published in paperback in 1995 by Hodder and Stoughton
A Coronet Paperback

British Library Cataloguing in Publication Data

Townsend, Lindsay
Voices in the Dark
I.Title
823.914 [F]

ISBN 0-340-62297-0

Typeset by Avon Dataset Ltd, Bidford-on-Avon

Printed and bound in Great Britain by
Cox & Wyman Ltd, Reading, Berks

Hodder and Stoughton
A division of Hodder Headline PLC
338 Euston Road
London NW1 3BH

You need no specialised equipment to torture someone, only imagination and patience.
I have always had both.

Scarpia

GENERAL
ACKNOWLEDGEMENTS

The characters in this book are all of my invention, except for the Kochs and Luisa Ferida, whose activities are documented in English and Italian sources. There were real fascists in wartime Bologna, Italian and German, but the people mentioned in my work are fictitious and any resemblance to anyone living or dead is entirely coincidental.

The villages of Mutta, San Martino della Croce, Castel San Martino and Ponte Maggiore do not exist. Sadly, real wartime massacres of civilians did occur: one of the worst was the slaughter by the Waffen SS of over 1000 men, women and children at Marzabotto near Bologna in late September, 1944.

During the war, many real partisan units lived rough in the hills for months. The partisans' intelligence gathering, sabotage missions and pitched battles with the Nazis were acts of great heroism. For the purposes of my novel, I deliberately made my characters' group a small affair, operating from their own homes in support of bigger, more 'military' units. Anyone wishing to learn more of the courage of the real partisans and civilians who helped to liberate Italy should consult Italian and English historical sources.

In the present-day parts of the novel the singers' lives, performances in certain named and unnamed operas and schedules are fictitious, although I have tried to convey something of the often hectic lives of international performers in their very demanding art. In the opera *Don Carlos*, the character Eboli is sometimes played wearing an eye-patch. In the production in this book, Eboli's wound – legend says she sustained it saving the King from an attacker – is represented by a scar.

The local 'legend' surrounding the corncockle flower is made up. The cities in which some of the novel's events take place are real, but private houses, some shops, Plini's café, the temporary archives in Naples, the dance hall in Bologna, the hospital in Florence, the recording studios in Edinburgh and Pisa and the stage and backstage interiors of the opera houses are my invention.

I owe a special debt of gratitude to my family, who have always supported and encouraged me, especially to my husband Alan and my mother Joan, who have read and re-read this novel and whose insights were always invaluable. Also to my father Gordon, for his practical answers to problems. Special thanks go to my agent Teresa, who first gave me the inspiration for this novel, and my editor Carolyn: their support, patience and criticism have been vital, and I cannot thank them enough. Any mistakes in the following pages are entirely my own.

Thanks finally to my friends and fellow-writers, especially Muriel Best of the Huddersfield Choral Society, David Glover, Veronica Gabanski, Ted Best and Jim MacDonald.

Lindsay Townsend

PROLOGUE

26th November, London

She had foreseen his revenge, but the attack when it came was brutal. Impossible to avoid, she watched the knife slicing towards her heart, her features betraying a mixture of anger and agonised suspense. Too late – she would never know love now, only obsession.

He struck, and a dull throbbing bloomed in her chest. The blow smashed her to her knees and the wooden floor seemed to jackknife upwards, sucking her into a cool embrace. She lay still, horror and fear fading as a warm languor swept through her body. Dying was easy.

Dimly, she heard the man standing over her chant something; a lament, a name, then he too was silent.

The main lights snapped on and she coughed.

'Sorry, it's the dust,' Julia murmured, coming out of the role and her character, rising to her feet. The Maestro seized her hand.

'Marvellous,' he was saying over the applause. 'Bravo!'

The masterclass for *Carmen* was over.

The Maestro caught up with her as she was hurrying from the hall. 'Is it tomorrow you're going?'

Julia nodded, pushing Carmen's veil down in her bag.

'Good luck – take care.'

Julia smiled, thinking of another promise. 'I will,' she said.

* * *

Summer 1944, Italy

The terror began with the music. As they wound up the gramophone, the youth moaned and thrashed, trying hopelessly to break free. He lay in chains, a blindfold cutting into his eyes. The walls of the underground chamber were wet: blood or water he did not know. Sometimes he touched the stones with his broken fingers, desperate to invoke their silence in himself.

This time would he break? The record needle dropped onto the seventy-eight, the chamber rang. A finger glided down the boy's calf – he tensed, but the pain did not come at the music's climax. A lighted cigarette was thrust against his right foot and allowed to burn, spitting in the open wounds.

'Tell me!' The whisper carried over the chords, over his scream, piercing the moment when he felt he could bear no more.

'Know nothing . . .' He shuddered. 'Don't.' He lifted his head, pleading with the Whisperer, the voice he most feared.

There was a moment's silence. And then a man, another captive, suddenly began shouting.

'I'll have you! Not one of your family will be safe! I'll have your wives, your children – their children . . . I promise you – you'll see . . .'

GENERAL 1

28th November, Florence, Italy

Her search would begin tomorrow – tonight she could keep for herself.

The wind, sweeping through the funnel of jewellers' shops, thrust Julia along the Ponte Vecchio. She sped across Florence's oldest bridge, watching the faces of the local people, fascinated by their every nuance of expression, at once familiar and exotic. Winter sunlight flashed on her earrings as she turned her head, determined to miss nothing.

Polished windows tossed back reflections of a young woman in jeans, trainers and duffel coat. With glowing skin, bright, grey eyes, animated features and a headful of black curls, she attracted attention even in the bustle of the pre-festive rush. She could be taken for a teenage daughter of the Italian matrons cutting over the bridge with their bags of vegetables, yet she had the surface confidence of someone older, unafraid to show feeling in an age of fashionable cynicism.

That same commitment marked Julia Rochfort as a rising force in British opera. She was twenty-six, and this was her first time in Italy since childhood.

English, English-speaking, yet also fluent in Italian, Julia had always intended to return to the country where she had been born. She found herself at ease within the swarms of dark-haired Christmas shoppers and black street traders

hawking bangles and carpets. Out of the crush a jeweller sat
relaxing beside his window, drinking from a china saucer.
Julia smiled at him as she passed.

The wind swept on, grit-blasting the eastern edge of the
City of Flowers, cleaning and brightening its face. The golden
orb at the top of the dome of the cathedral gleamed, like a
star pointing the way she should go.

Julia knew where she was going. She was taking part in a
singing competition, the springboard, she hoped, to an
international career. In four days she would be performing to
her first Italian audience. She was apprehensive yet
exhilarated, opened-out by the challenge. She was in Florence,
amongst people who spoke the same language as herself, who
were dark as she was; people with whom she felt she belonged.

The sharp tang of the river drew her to the loggia set
in the middle of the medieval bridge. Wind flicking her
face, she passed a gaggle of school children, arguing – with
the same extravagant face-pulling she had made herself as a
child – over whose turn it was on a pocket-sized games
machine, and leaned out over the Arno. The tip of her tongue
played between her teeth, as always when she was
concentrating.

Looking across the muddy waters to the biscuit-coloured
apartments opposite put Julia in mind of her own family. Enrico
and her mother Angelica would be boarding their plane now,
to spend Christmas in Tenerife.

The holiday was her gift. In October, her mother went into
hospital for an operation – not serious, but Julia was on tour
and unable to visit. Now, with Angelica fully recovered, a long
stay on a warm island would set her parents up for the new
year.

It had made a hole in her savings, but she had been glad to
spend it. She just wished she and her mother—

Julia laughed at herself and shook her head, cutting off the
thought. She watched two youths bump over the stone sets
on a scooter, black slicked hair gleaming more than their
leathers. Across the river, above the snarl of rush-hour cars
came the sudden ringing of bells, a clock striking the hour: it

would soon be evening. In the meantime she would enjoy this
mirage-like dusk of fading sun and coloured lights, the music
of people's voices, the throaty chatter of roosting pigeons.

Julia smiled, absented-mindedly winding a curl of hair round
her thumb. It was ironic that she, so much a creature of light,
should spend most of her life working at night.

Enough, she thought, stifling old fears with a twist of her
hand. Tomorrow she was going to Bologna, to see where
Enrico had lived. Her stepfather had always talked about his
life in Bologna, but was afraid to go back in case he or the city
had changed. His widowed mother and sister had been killed
during the Allies' bombardment: Enrico, then a prisoner of
war, had seen no reason to return. He had stayed in England,
eventually marrying a woman fifteen years younger than
himself and with a small child – Julia.

Tomorrow she was going to Bologna to trace her mother's
surviving Italian family.

This search was as important to her as the competition.
Whatever happened, Julia had decided to spend three weeks
in Italy. Surely in that time she would find something.

She pushed away from the chill parapet. Seeing a beggar
crouching under the third arch of the loggia, Julia crossed
over to give him money, then hurried on. Enrico knew virtually
nothing about his wife's past: she had promised her stepfather
she would find out something. The journey to Bologna was
partly for his sake, an attempt to discover who Angelica's
family were, but mostly, Julia had to admit, the trip was for
herself, filling a gap in her life.

'You think Rochfort is Italian?' her mother would say
whenever Julia attempted to question Angelica about where
they had both come from, 'I'm English. *You're* English. Forget
Italy.'

Julia could not forget. Perhaps if her beautiful, auburn-
haired, English-rose complexioned mother had told her of
the Rochforts, of her real father, Julia might have been able
to dismiss Italy, yet Angelica had remained stubbornly silent
on these too. Throughout her childhood, Julia felt she
belonged nowhere: she had often wished she looked as

English as her mother, yet she did not.

Now, as an adult, Julia recognised that whatever her mother's claims, Angelica was also Italian. She had married Enrico, given up 'Rochfort' and taken his name. She was Angelica Varisi; she was linked to someone with a past. Enrico had snapshots of his family, Julia had none of the Rochforts. Or of the others, the mysterious Italian side that her mother always denied. It was not enough to have a name and nothing more.

She had been born in Emilia Romagna – Angelica had told her that much. Bologna was the capital of the region. Somewhere in that city there would be her birth records, people she could talk to, a family to discover.

Julia wished the days were longer, so that she could start at once.

Glancing back, she noticed a man in a grey woollen coat and scarlet scarf approaching. He was eating almond macaroons from a paper bag. A few crumbs showed pale against his lapels.

Julia swung round into the wind, pausing to fiddle with the loose bracelet of her watch. The man was speaking to the beggar, who gestured in her direction. She recalled seeing him earlier, hearing snatches of that staccato tread as she crossed the flags of the Straw Market and later along the stone corridor linking the Uffizi gallery to the Ponte Vecchio. Her musician's training gave her a good ear, a good memory.

Licking her lips, Julia decided to return to the jeweller's to have her watch repaired. It was something she should have had done weeks ago, except she had never had time.

Fifteen minutes later, the bracelet of her watch tightened and snug against her wrist – 'No charge,' the jeweller told her, with a smile – she emerged back onto the street.

The man in the grey coat was still there, scowling at the prices in the window across from her. Tossing a crumpled paper bag into the gutter, where the breeze spun it along, he moved when she did. Another tourist, taking in the same sights.

Julia stiffened, irritated at herself. This was already her

country. She strode over the last cobbles off the Ponte Vecchio without looking back.

He was lurking when she bought throat pastilles at the pharmacist, prowling at another card carousel as she chose her postcards. He was nearby as she took note of a dry-cleaner's address.

His persistence deserved a medal, thought Julia wryly, but not from her. She decided she would leave finding a launderette for another time. Her thumb wound in her hair as she walked on. Now that she thought about it, this fellow was interested in linen, too. Why else had he been lingering near the market stall where she had bought her sewing silk?

'Come on then, pinch me,' she muttered, humour and irritation blending. She wondered if she were being unfair. Had she perhaps smiled at the man in one of their coincidental meetings, sent the wrong signal? She wished he would make his move. 'Let's get it over with.' Checking her step, she turned.

Twenty paces back on the pavement, the man had stopped. Ignoring frowns and gestures from people who shoved past, he was cleaning under his fingernails with a knife – not a penknife: Julia knew that at once. This was something heavier, surely much larger than any normal person would wish to carry.

Telling herself that she was over-reacting, Julia lengthened her stride. Suddenly she felt very alone.

Behind her the beat of footsteps increased.

A few moments later, whipping down twisting, car-echoing side streets back to the river, she was convinced she had lost him. Humming a competition piece, Julia crossed a road lined with Vespas and turned down another alley, hoping to find a short cut to the rank of bus stops outside Florence station. Her hotel was in the suburbs.

He was waiting up ahead in the piazza, one of several men leaning against a column. She saw him detach from the group: the blood-red scarf separating him from a hundred other strollers. He wasn't a tourist. He knew the city better than she. Her knowledge came from maps; his from experience.

The red scarf bothered her more than the knife. It suggested impulse, a man who had spotted her in the street and was wondering whether to try an approach to ask her out. Yet the stranger was stalking her with a determination which seemed out of all proportion to such a casual interest. But if he were trailing her – as he obviously was – then why would he wish to draw attention to his pursuit? Was the scarf a signal to others?

Even compared with opera plots the idea was bizarre, but then this was Italy, home of the kidnapper. Only last month a certain soprano – famous but hardly a great star – had been snatched from her hotel in Padova and held for ransom.

Dammit, thought Julia, yanking her hood over her head then immediately tugging it back, she wasn't going to allow this man to worry her. Nor under any circumstances would she lead him to her hotel.

Cutting through office cleaners streaming from a bank at the corner of another small, bustling square, Julia stepped briskly along the Via de' Tornabuoni. Florence's smartest street thronged with fashionable locals – easy to distinguish from visitors by their designer sunglasses worn even in winter, and those loose, taupe-coloured suits. Choosing the brighter, wind-blown half, she made great play of studying the ultramodern clothes displayed in the new Galatea salon. The mirrors gave her a chance to observe more closely.

There he was, walking straight past, scowling at the strobe light. Small and slight, with a jerky gait. Definitely not what she thought of as a mugger or the kind of prowler who preyed on lone women. He was older than his close-cropped brown hair and animated walk suggested – fifty at least. Expensive grey suit, close-fitting coat, conservative tie – clothes which should have given him presence. The red scarf was incongruous with such an outfit, yet somehow fitted the man.

No, he was nothing more sinister than a pest, Julia decided. The knife was probably bravado. There was no need for her to search for a police station, nor disturb the two carabinieri striking a movie-star pose on the street corner. Their guns

made her nervous of approaching them, especially in so trivial
a matter. She did not want to be mocked or pitied by those
tough young men because of one ageing Romeo.

Julia stuck to that conclusion even in her more paranoid
moments, when, between gusts of swirling air, she imagined
she could hear that busy tread both behind and coming
towards her. She hurried along, planning what she would do,
counting her steps under her breath to keep wilder fancies in
check. No one could possibly be interested in her. She had
two assets, a strong voice and stamina, neither of which could
be sold – not yet, anyway, not as a performer unknown outside
England and without a recording contract. So who would pay
for her release?

She dismissed the idea, letting out a sigh as she passed
the obelisk outside the black and white patterned front of Santa
Maria Novella. Cutting through a bumper to bumper line of
traffic, she entered the building, forgetting to cover her head.
She had remembered that this church backed onto the road
opposite to the Station. Soon there would be a bus leaving for
the outskirts. She would wait inside, then make a run.

The man would not accost her here: even Cosa Nostra drew
a line at attacking people in the sanctuary of church.

Julia's prayers were swift. She checked her watch by the
candle light: twenty minutes left.

At the end of the time she burst out of the great church,
darting round two sides of the long building before her eyes
had fully adjusted to the twilight. Her bus was waiting along
the Piazza della Stazione, revving its engine. Julia pitched into
the mêlée – Italians never queue when they can shove – and
was fighting for a place when a prickling between her
shoulders made her swing about.

The man had joined the crowd and was elbowing closer.

Julia felt a blaze of anger – she did not want this creep
trailing her all the way to Bologna. She had been wrong to be
discreet: the best way to deal with a threat was to confront it.

She stopped dead in the heaving mass, letting people flow
past, and pitched her voice so everyone could hear.

'I really think this has gone far enough,' she said coolly,

her narrow hand pointing unerringly to its target. 'I'm talking
to the gentleman with the red scarf. If you don't stop following
me, I'm calling the police.'

The smallest of gaps opened for an instant around the man
in the red scarf and several more innocent businessmen, their
expressions such that Julia was almost sorry.

Seizing the moment before the press closed up again, she
leapt onto the bus as its doors were closing. The driver roared
off as she squeezed past other standing passengers to punch
her ticket, her hands not quite co-ordinated as she glimpsed
the man staring after her from the pavement.

The man's name was Tommaso and he answered to it,
although in his own mind he was Tom. Now he was angry at
himself for giving way to impulse. Seeing the girl by chance
in the street, he had lost his head.

And how, Tom thought, scowling into his unsugared brandy
coffee. His left hand was aching: he'd had to dig out a splinter
from under the nail – he got a lot of splinters in his line of
work and nearly always missed a couple until they were really
hurting. He hadn't considered what the girl might think,
catching him using a knife in the street.

Shaking his head, Tom took a sip of coffee, savouring the
bitter drink whilst he stared out at the emptying square from
his bar stool. In the tobacco stand opposite, a crumpled stack
of papers flapped the day's stale news: another collaborator
exposed and brought to trial. With the World War Two fiftieth
anniversary commemoration due in the new year, prosecuting
magistrates had switched their attentions away from the Mafia.
These days anyone who wanted to get on in the judiciary was
rooting out war criminals: it was seen as part of the new
democracy, a clearing of the decks.

Tom snorted, signalling to the barman. Only Italians could
get excited about ancient witch hunts.

The bearded barman brought him another coffee, poured
in brandy without asking. Tom always drank brandy coffee at
this bar: the place and indeed the city had many special
memories for him. Of course had it not been for the business

he would not have moved here two years ago after his wife's death. He wasn't sentimental, although he had his weaknesses.

He had kept his promise to his wife over the years, but that hadn't stopped him from being curious. When he had read the article in *Oggi* and learned that the girl was coming to Italy, Tom had seen it as fate. He was a believer in fate.

Tom lifted his grey coat from the next stool, leaving a few coins on the bar. He'd been undecided about Julia. Maybe if she hadn't confronted him he might not have bothered, let the whole thing slide. As it was, he had been offered a challenge.

Planning their next encounter, he stepped into the dark street, tucking the scarf round his throat to keep out the wind.

2

Sherry eyes fixed on his fellow-singer, Roberto pursued Isabel
Alvarez across the stage through rows of peasant dancers.

He was a tall, vigorous figure. The sword at his belt seemed
freshly forged for him, the long athletic lines of the eighteenth-
century costume breeches suited him. A thin white shirt
defined every muscle of his torso as he sang.

His face, that square forehead and chin and hawkish nose,
was as telling as a Roman portrait bust, but his dark brown
hair was a war zone of untamed spiky curls.

Isabel, the Spanish-American soprano singing Zerlina in
Mozart's *Don Giovanni* was as beguiled as the audience of
the San Francisco opera house. Roberto Padovano could have
any woman he wanted, Isabel thought, and I wish it were me.
She wished she and Padovano were more intimate than just
colleagues. The Italian bass was just *so* convincing as the Don.

But the conductor was glaring at her from the orchestra
pit: she was losing concentration. Isabel began and finished a
heated duet with another singer and tried to conceal her
impatience as the stage emptied. In a few moments, she would
be in Padovano's arms as much as Don Giovanni's.

Now they were alone. If only this was more than acting,
she thought, her voice almost stopping as he approached.

He caught her at the edge of the stage. His actor's kisses
covered her eyes and cheeks and lips. He played at untying

the strings on the bodice of her costume. He wrapped his arms tenderly around her middle – singing all the while, it seemed, only to her.

It was better than sex – almost. No man could sing like this one: the love song poured from him, a living caress in sound. Closing her eyes, Isabel leaned against him, breathing in music, answering not because she remembered the words but because she wanted them to become real.

Their duet drawing to a close, Roberto whirled her off her feet, carrying her towards the back of the stage as they sang.

Isabel shivered. A warm hand stroked along her flank, the touch light yet firm.

'You're doing fine.' His low speaking voice steadied her. Roberto smiled, absently wiping a trickle of moisture from the side of his nose, brown hair spiralling across his forehead.

As he set her down on her feet, Isabel let out a shriek.

Roberto glanced up. A light fitting directly above them tilted wildly, then snapped with a loud crack. The heavy mass plummeted downwards.

With one hand, Roberto thrust Isabel Alvarez out of harm's way. His own momentum had them both on the floor, where they skidded violently into a laden props table. Disregarding a sudden fire in his left foot, Roberto gathered Isabel Alvarez gently into his arms, cradling her as the curtain finally swung down over the wreck of the light.

The doctor at the state hospital glanced from the X-ray to the tall impassive man seated in his consulting room.

'You finished the performance with this?' the doctor asked, tapping the X-ray sheet with his finger.

'After a break to restore a little calm.'

'Just as well it was the last night. Must have hurt like hell.'

Roberto smiled, thinking already of his flat in Milan, of local bars, familiar evening strolls and the fountains in the park across the road. 'Not as much as it could have. Accidents happen.' Glancing at his watch, he knew he would still make it to the airport for his flight home.

3

Julia gazed steadily at the manager of the pensione, then glanced through the mock rococo archway at the man in the shabby sitting-room. 'Him?'

The manager nodded. 'He came this afternoon, asking for you. He's been waiting ever since.'

The stranger rose hesitantly. Behind him, the televised crowds at the Rome – Fiorentina match booed as a Rome player missed a penalty. Her visitor looked back over his shoulder to see the replay.

Because of the position of the lights, the man was not able to see her clearly, but she could see him. Dressed in grey chauffeur's uniform, cap on another chair in the deserted public room, he seemed as anonymous as the wallpaper. A spry man in his sixties, of average height, he had grey curly hair and shiny black shoes. No scarf, Julia noted with relief, no red.

But she was allowing this evening's excitement to assume too much significance: no wonder other musicians grumbled that singers had an exaggerated idea of their own worth.

You're not important enough to be a target, lady. She smiled reassuringly at the manager. 'Thank you.' She crossed swiftly from the desk to meet the stranger.

Other impressions crowded in as she closed on the man. The oil-stained fingernails, the steel-grey watch. The gleam of an embossed tie-pin, a personal touch to the well-pressed uniform. Red ears, hollow cheeks, small nose, neat grey moustache.

'You wish to speak to me, Signore?'

The man turned. His features showed a welter of feelings: disquiet, shame, relief. Colour lit his face as he touched the tip of his nose in surprise. Julia, who knew how difficult it was to produce a blush to order, to reveal a rapid play of emotions, felt reassured. If the stranger were acting, it would have to be a virtuoso performance.

He held out a hand, apologising for not recognising her at once. 'I'm sorry ... the match ... you know how men are football crazy.' Leaning back, the man rummaged under his cap and retrieved a small parcel.

His pale grey eyes had never left her face. Feeling slightly ridiculous, Julia wondered if she had a smut on her nose. Why should he have recognised her? From a publicity shot? What was all this about?

In the corner, the television roared as Fiorentina scored.

'Please—' The goal seemed to give the man confidence. 'The Contessa told me to wait, to deliver her things into your hands.' He held out the package, coming a step closer.

It was not sealed: someone had anticipated her suspicions. Julia raised an eyebrow in acknowledgement as she took the parcel, suggesting the chauffeur watch the game. With her unexpected guest absorbed in the second half of the match, she settled on a chair arm to study what 'the Contessa' had sent.

There were a dozen black and white prints. One had an album tab attached to a corner. This picture showed a family picnic: man, woman and child.

Julia held the photograph up to the light. Despite the intervening years the little girl had not changed so much as to be unrecognisable. Gently, she touched the smiling face. She had never seen any pictures of her mother as a child.

Sitting beside Angelica was a young woman. Julia leaned sideways against the armchair. Dark curly hair, high cheekbones, long nose – she could have been looking at her double.

No wonder the messenger had been disconcerted. Julia shivered, putting that picture aside.

The remaining black and white pictures were mainly of the same man and Angelica; two showed Angelica with the young woman. The final photograph was in colour: another family group, taken indoors. Red flash filled their eyes, clashing with Angelica's auburn hair, making the widow in her long black dress appear rather forbidding. The toddler jouncing on the widow's knee was blurred.

'But it's me,' Julia murmured, tongue between teeth again as she brought the photograph closer, 'It has to be!' This must have been taken just before her mother had left Italy for good, bringing her away too.

The old lady, easily recognisable as the young woman of the earlier black and white photographs, looked not only frailer in this final picture but very different. The eyes were wrong, Julia decided. Perhaps it was the effect of the flash.

Clutching the photograph, her head full of questions, she leaned forward on the edge of the chair arm. Her mind seemed frozen: she did not know what she felt. Angelica had said nothing about this. Her mother would never talk about Italy.

Beside her, the chauffeur shook his fist as one of the forwards was ruled offside. The small sitting-room throbbed with the noise of the stadium. She would get no answers from him right now. Quickly Julia leafed through the rest of the papers.

A birth certificate for a girl, born to Guy Rochfort and Clara Rochfort-Scudieri. The father's profession was given as vintner, the child's name as Angelica. *Rochfort, her own name.*

There was a coat of arms on the document: the Scudieri badge. Julia smoothed out a crease in the gold leaf with a finger, thinking of her parents' modest terrace house in Leeds.

A batch of letters, unopened and marked, 'Not known at this address, return to sender.' Julia recognised her mother's handwriting. She glanced at the postmarks. All were dated to within the previous six months.

Her past, her Italian family. She had tried for years to find out about them from Angelica and now, laid out before her—

'You are very alike, you and the Contessa.' From being too loud the room was suddenly quiet. The football had finished.

'Even though I was prepared, the likeness between you is uncanny,' the man continued in a nasal accent, coming to stand at the other side of the armchair. 'You will probably not remember me. I am Andrea. When you were tiny you used to watch me washing the Contessa's Mercedes: we still have the same car. Of course you will not remember me, you were only a baby.' He cleared his throat. 'I knew then that you would grow to be more like the Contessa.'

He spoke quietly, yet with a sincerity which unnerved her. There was nothing she could say, unless she be unkind or flippant. Looking away, Julia found herself staring at her mother's birth certificate and the father's name: Guy Valentine Rochfort. *Guy.* Not an Italian name, for sure: very very English.

Slipping onto the dusty parquet tiles was a note. Catching it before it fell, she read:

Andrea, my chauffeur, is waiting for you in the hotel. I am waiting at the family house. Please come.

Your grandmother, Clara Rochfort-Scudieri.

To the point, thought Julia, fighting her desire to belong, wary because of it. Part of her, now that the first shock had passed, was deeply suspicious and – she admitted it – resentful. Why had this woman waited so long before getting in touch? Again, it seemed, she had been rejected.

Fighting these childish feelings, Julia rose and stepped round Andrea to the sitting-room window. An old Mercedes was standing under the hotel's security light, the insignia of the Scudieri clearly visible on its doors.

Julia, conscious of Andrea watching, leaned against the glass. She must choose what she would do. Scanning the note again in her hand, she found herself no wiser. She was walking into the dark.

Yet someone was asking for her company. She could not turn away. The car was here, waiting, as the Contessa – Julia could not think of her as grandmother – said it would be.

In the end it came down to whether she was willing to trust messenger and message, whether she thought the risk worthwhile.

She glanced again at the grey chauffeur. Unless her intuition was totally wrong, Andrea was as he seemed, a loyal, honest employee and a gentle man. It was the woman waiting ahead who was the mystery.

Turning from the window, Julia walked swiftly back to the chair. 'Very well.' She nodded to the chauffeur as she gathered photographs and documents, 'Let me fetch my coat.'

Their shoes crunching on the gravel, Julia and Andrea left the glare of the entrance. Filling two parking spaces, the Mercedes loomed before her in the twilight, dark as a hearse.

Disturbed by the association Julia checked her step. Angelica had never told her why she left Italy. By leaving with this stranger, could she be embroiling Angelica in an old vendetta? Was 'the Contessa' making her the bait to force her mother's return?

'What is it?' Andrea sounded so surprised at her hesitation that Julia almost laughed: the man was either a superb actor or completely genuine.

'You – this.' She would not speak of her mother to a go-between, even one who claimed he knew her, but kept to the more obvious threat. 'In 1993 the Uffizi was bombed. Last month a chorus member in an opera house was shot. Musicians have been kidnapped. The arts have become a target. Can I trust you?'

'Ah! I forgot!' Andrea reached into his jacket. 'The Contessa told me to show you this.' Something flashed in his hand.

A delicate gold locket, engraved with flowers: pretty, something her mother would have liked. Julia gently sprung the catch.

A tiny, blurred photograph of Angelica, taken when her mother was in her mid teens, smiled up at her. Drawing out the deeply folded paper in the facing side of the locket, she saw the dedication, written in her mother's round hand: 'Happy birthday, Mamma. Love from Angelica.'

Carefully replacing the paper, Julia closed the locket, seeing how the back was shiny with wear, the clasp recently repaired. She thought of revenge: 'A dish best served cold,' according to one saying. Yet this locket had not been flung in a drawer and forgotten; it had been worn, touched. She could not see it as a device in a coldly contemplated vendetta.

Andrea cleared his throat again. 'The Contessa also instructed me to ask if Signora Angelica likes candied fruit.'

'Yes, but only apricots,' replied Julia promptly. She threw Andrea a questioning look. 'Was that a test?'

The chauffeur gave a disclaiming smile. Julia closed her fingers round the locket. 'May I keep this for a while?'

'Of course.' Andrea went ahead to open the car door.

Entombed in the Mercedes, Julia knew an instant of panic. Sweating, she crossed her legs and leaned against the cream leather upholstery, concentrating on the scenes flashing past the window as Andrea dexterously swung the vintage car onto the Bologna – Florence road. The locket, cool against her palm, gave her confidence. Whatever the risk, she was committed.

She licked her lips and settled back. Andrea, more assured now he was behind a wheel, began a voluble commentary which revealed quite a different character from that of the reticent employee waiting at her hotel. Julia, a non-driver, could only marvel at the transformation – one she had seen in others – of mild man to car man.

'Right! This is Francesco Redi road. Now we're on Belfiore road, the place to come if you need a taxi. Those lights over there are the railway station. Can't you smell the diesel! See this piazza? Twenty and more years ago I had a puncture here by the Porta al Prato. You and your mother were travelling in the car and you were over an hour late for your feed. You sang out then, I can tell you!'

The Mercedes swung round another hairpin bend, its bumper missing the curb by inches. Andrea was ruthless in his use of the horn and the car's bulk to bully scooters, pedestrians and once even a horse-drawn carriage, crammed with red-cheeked tourists. Sweeping a cavalier hand towards

Florence's music theatre on their left – where Julia would be performing – the chauffeur accelerated through a red light onto the Vittorio bridge. The river flashed beneath them and the swirl of headlights clashed with the lights in the apartments on the western side of the city.

Yet she must not be seduced by the glamour of the vintage car, nor by the dazzle of a sickle moon breathing silver over the Arno. She would not be won as cheaply as that.

Andrea, pointing out a gross example of neon signing on a renaissance palazzo, said, 'The Contessa won't have a town-house in Florence. She thinks the city's common: dirty, smelly . . .'

Julia chuckled, and hung on to the doorhandle as the Mercedes hurtled towards the Roman gate. 'What do you say, Andrea? Do you like Florence?'

'Sure! I've lived here all my life.' Andrea's pale eyes regarded her in the driving mirror. 'But the Contessa's right; the city's too full of foreigners, too hectic for her. She likes the country, somewhere with gardens.'

Somewhere with gardens, thought Julia. She might have said the same thing herself. Her mother and stepfather were not interested in the countryside, but one of her strongest wishes was to have a garden some day. She felt a momentary rapport with the stranger waiting ahead.

'Of course, the Contessa has a house in Bologna. She stays there sometimes in winter: the Florentine fogs aren't so good for her health. And she has the seaside place at Bari. There was a villa at San Martino della Croce . . . but that's another matter.'

Andrea closed his mouth with a snap and stepped on the gas.

'I see,' said Julia. Any brief identity with 'the Contessa' was shattered as the woman's wealth was flung in her face.

Angelica must have missed this way of living – here perhaps the reason why her mother was sometimes unaccountably depressed.

Yet Clara *Rochfort*-Scudieri had seemingly washed her aristocratic hands of her daughter, at least until six months ago. Why? thought Julia, fingers tightening on the locket. And again: why, if the woman had broken with Angelica, had she clung to this simple trinket?

Julia shook her head. Her present journey was full of contradictions. 'Have you always worked for the lady?'

'Since I was a boy.' Andrea changed down a gear. They were climbing out of the suburbs into Tuscan hills dotted with vineyards and olive trees. Looking back, Julia caught a glimpse of the cathedral, a golden silhouette floating above an arc of floodlights, and was once again entranced by the city.

Andrea, unimpressed by the landscape behind or the silence of the country ahead, asked if he could smoke. When Julia said yes if he kept the window open, the chauffeur lit a Toscana.

'1946, the year my mother died, I started work for the Contessa,' he went on, blowing cigar smoke into the swirling wind. 'It's a debt, you understand.'

'For what?' Julia leaned forward as the Mercedes ran along an avenue of cypress. There was a light directly ahead.

'My life,' said Andrea, bringing the car to a smooth stop outside a small, classically fronted villa.

'We're here,' he said.

4

28th November, Milan, Italy

Roberto Padovano was pouring engine oil into an empty fuel can. Even by the dim light of the underground garage, he could see that it was black as tar.

Roberto snorted in exasperated amusement. 'One of these fine days this engine's going to get so overheated it'll weld together,' he muttered, flicking off the last droplets from the roasting tin which served as a collecting tray. Fine musician his father might be; when it came to nuts and bolts, Simone had the manual dexterity of a cow.

Next time he was on tour, Roberto reflected, he would pay for people to collect and service his father's Fiat at regular intervals. Changing engine oil was not quite the way he had planned to spend his first evening in Milan after flying back from California.

Simone had met him at the airport. Roberto was surprised, touched by the older man's kindness, but his father's first words were: 'There's a funny smell in my car. Will you look at it? I'm not paying for garage labour if it's nothing.'

'Nothing' turned out to be back brakes worn to bare metal, a blocked air filter and filthy engine oil. Returning to his apartment, Roberto suggested that Simone might like to drive the Fiat to a garage, only to be told that his father needed the car by eight that evening.

'Take mine,' said Roberto evenly. Simone, with the finely

tuned nerves of an instrumental musician, was becoming agitated.

'Sandro's borrowed it for a family trip to Venice – I told him he could.' Simone rubbed his chest. 'My indigestion's terrible.'

'I'm not surprised.' Roberto suppressed a flash of irritation against his younger brother. Knowing Simone's impractical nature he should have checked over their father's car himself before now. Simone, preferring independence, never travelled on the orchestra coach.

'Where are you working tonight?' he asked.

'Piacenza – and the trains are on strike.' The planes of Simone's classically featured face seemed to grow sharper. His hazel eyes bulged slightly. 'I'm not going to get there! After not missing a performance in twenty years—'

'Take Sandro's sardine can.' Roberto, stretching muscular arms, cracked his fingers above his head. 'I'd drive you, except—' He indicated the plaster cast on his foot.

But Sandro's 2CV was in for a gearbox fault, and when Roberto phoned round Milan, every garage said the same thing: they couldn't book in Simone's Fiat today and have it ready by evening. When Roberto suggested a taxi Simone had been horrified: had Roberto any idea for how long this concert would go on? Did he want his father to be wandering round Piacenza in the middle of the night looking for transport? And all the decent hotels were probably full . . .

'Go with Otto,' suggested Roberto, stifling a yawn. He had been singing in that bizarre *Don Giovanni* less than forty-eight hours ago. After reassuring his singing partner for that evening that she really would be OK, he'd had to spend an hour in casualty and then a long time explaining to the press what had happened.

'He can't take me.' His father's voice returned Roberto to Italy and the present problem. Otto, a cellist, was indisposed. Sofia the flautist was going with three more musicians; there was no room in their car. He would not travel with a horn player . . .

Listening, Roberto smiled. During these last twelve months

their relationship had changed. Increasingly, it was as though Simone were the son and he the parent. Roberto even found himself speaking to his father as though he was a child.

'I have to go out.' Interrupting the list of musicians Simone could not travel with, Roberto checked that his wallet was in his jeans pocket. 'I'll be back in an hour.'

'Where are you going? What are you doing?'

Buying you a decent car, thought Roberto, but he did not say that. He respected Simone's pride. 'I won't be long.'

Simone glared. 'I won't have it.' He spoke with the old imperiousness which had terrorised Roberto as a boy. He jabbed a finger at his tall son. 'You can't buy yourself out of everything. I want help, not your charity.' Suddenly they were talking about more than a faulty car.

'Look, I'll come with you tonight. I'll get our taxis—'

'If Sandro were here, he'd want to help his father.'

'OK.' Throwing out his hands, Roberto conceded defeat. Never mind that it made no sense, his father *needed* him to fix the wretched car. Though whatever he did, it was never enough.

So, after a cold shower to stave off jet lag, Roberto Padovano, world famous singer, went to buy car parts and, lying under his father's Fiat in a draughty underground garage (plaster cast and all), set about a little car maintenance. Now he was almost finished.

Whistling through his teeth, Roberto spun the top fast on the fuel can and skidded it along the floor to join the rest of the rubbish. The hazy white lights of this place reminded him of the subdued spotlights of a certain nightclub in Milan.

He smiled and rolled onto his back, thumping his forehead on the Fiat axle and receiving an eyeful of rust.

'Hell and damnation!' Roberto hurled the meat tin into the darkness and struck the cobwebbed garage wall with a fist: his head smarted like hell but what he hated was the indignity. 'Why am I so clumsy?'

He never barged into things on stage. Glad that no one had been around to see him, Roberto wormed towards the raised rear end of the Fiat. Only the wheel nuts were to tighten.

When he'd done, he'd make a quick circuit in the park; he
liked walking at night and no one would see the state of his
clothes.

A hurrying step made him raise his head.

'My God,' said Simone, taking in his son's grease-spattered
square chin, the rugged brown hair, the warm, compelling
gaze. 'You look like a farm labourer.'

Roberto laughed and returned to tightening wheel nuts.

'OK. All done.' He rose to his feet in an ungainly if efficient
manner. The task completed, jet lag hit like a hammer between
the eyes. The dim lights of the garage drummed in his skull
as he waved his father off.

Any nights on the town would have to wait, thought
Roberto, limping to the lift. Right now he was going to bed.

Hours later, a car backfiring outside his apartment in the Via
Manin brought Roberto stark awake. He lay in the blessed
blackness in an icy sweat, strong hands clenching into fists
as he told himself not to scream. No one expected someone
of his size to be scared of a little noise.

Roberto hated faulty car exhausts and air rifles. At six years
old he heard grandfather Padovano blowing his brains out.
Running into the orchard to save grandpapa, the boy found a
corpse.

Even at six he knew that grandfather was dead, although
he did not know then and did not know now why Aurelio
Padovano had committed suicide. Years later, any sudden
booming noise could still affect him.

Roberto scowled into the dark. Whereas the sight of a gun
did not paralyse him, its sound was another matter.

Roberto never told anyone his problem, especially not
Sandro. Sandro was a traffic policeman, married, with a young
son and a life which was totally in order. If not exactly used to
gunfire, he would certainly be sympathetic, but it was the elder
brother's job to look after the younger, not vice versa.

Now Roberto eased himself from the bed and walked
awkwardly across to the window to close it. Looking out, his
eyes were caught not by the tail lights of the disappearing car

but by the tall sycamores of the park. He had chosen this apartment because it overlooked grass and trees. When Roberto was fifteen, the family had moved from Fiesole to Milan. Sandro had taken to big city life, but he missed the country. Whenever he tried to paint the Tuscan landscape from memory, the light was never right.

Ah, he was going back there tomorrow. Roberto scratched his itching foot against the wall, realised the itch was beneath the plaster cast and swore. Any discomfort was worth it. A broken foot gave him three weeks free of opera, since La Scala hadn't wanted him clumping around the stage. A plaster cast hardly fitted the image of an assassin like Sparafucile. He was looking forward to getting back to Fiesole, his home town, to Florence, his home city, and to judging the Galatea competition.

At the competition he was a stand-in for another judge, a substitution made possible by his injury and arranged only at the last minute, after he arrived in Milan. He knew nothing about the competitors, but that didn't matter. The voice and personality were more important than any CV. It was exciting to see new talent, people he might be working with soon.

He could hear amplified breathing and a clock ticking. The rest of the apartment was quiet.

Roberto turned and set his broad back to the window. He was alone tonight and missed a woman in his bed. He and Carlotta had been apart seven years, but nine years of marriage weren't so easily forgotten. He remembered the early days when they were eighteen, how obsessed they'd been with each other's bodies.

'You give me everything and tell me nothing,' Carlotta once said. She also accused him of being both too solemn and not serious enough: looking 'grim as a coffin-plate', and yet laughing too loudly, 'like a crazy boy'. Carlotta had wanted him to mirror her hopes, desires and aspirations, whilst at the same time have him, 'the great singer', to cast lustre on Carlotta.

Fuelled by the superb sex their marriage survived for almost a decade, of which they spent less than four years

together. He had to tour, a thing Carlotta hated and never
understood. It wasn't surprising really if in the end she had
turned to someone else for consolation, a Piedmontese like
herself. The results of his fertility test had merely given his
wife the final justification to leave.

'You want a divorce?' he asked, when he found her packing.
'A divorce, when we were married in church?' Roberto
regretted his outburst at once: the words made him sound
simple for twenty-six; worse than that a pious bigot, the sort
of man he detested. He was a believer – that should not make
him a fool.

Carlotta in answer had thrown him a pitying look. 'There
are times, Roberto, when you're actually medieval,' she had
said, snapping the locks on her suitcase.

So their marriage had ended. It had been unfair to marry
her, their divorce had been the usual mess, but how he envied
her now! How he envied Sandro. Sometimes when he lay
awake in the middle of the night he would ask What next? He
was thirty-four. What was he doing with his life? Professionally
it was good, but when was the last time he'd held a
conversation with a woman out of bed that wasn't about opera?
He lacked a focus.

A cry, amplified by baby alarms in the electric sockets,
sounded throughout the room. *Not again.*

Roberto limped quickly through the living-cum-music-room
to the room at the back of the apartment, away from traffic
noise.

He opened the door. Simone, safely back from his concert
in Piacenza, was sitting up in bed, craggy, clean-shaven face
wet with tears. Kneeling down, Roberto held the older man
for a long time. 'Another bad dream?' he asked finally.

'One of the worst,' whispered Simone. He was even colder
than Roberto had felt when woken by the backfiring car.

'It's over now.' Lowering his father, Roberto drew the covers
up to his chin and tucked Simone in, just as he remembered
his mother doing to him when he was little. 'Go back to sleep.
I'll sit with you. I won't leave.'

'That's what your mother said.' Maria Padovano had died

last year of a heart attack. Her sudden death had shocked the family, none more so than Simone. Robbed of any certainty in his life, Roberto's father had fallen prey to mysterious nightmares.

Remembering Aurelio Padovano, Roberto had opened his apartment to his father. A year on, Simone was still living with him, an anxious, carping house-guest who expected his eldest son to take care of him whilst at the same time refusing to acknowledge that his child was now adult, with strong drives. Roberto, accepting that any compromise would have to come from him, throttled back at home. He might be amused at the need to be discreet, but he remembered Aurelio.

'Do you want to talk?' he asked now. 'Sometimes it's easier if you do.' How many times had he himself been on the point of blurting out to Sandro about their grandfather's suicide? 'Come on, Dad, tell me.' He had to get his father to talk, to stop him bottling up everything inside . . .

Simone reached across to the bedside table and took a drink from the glass, a spoonful of stomach-medicine from the bottle. His hands shook, but Roberto knew better than to help.

He sat back on the floor, ignoring the dart of agony which seared down his left leg as he twisted his broken foot out of the way. If he was built like a labourer, then Simone was formed on more aristocratic lines. He was the same height, one metre ninety, but slimmer; standing together Simone appeared the taller. His features were longer, his chin less jutting. His nose, more aquiline than his son's, was distinguished. Simone's fine pewter-coloured hair did not spike. It would stay as he combed it, full of restrained elegance. He had a politician's aura of competence, not a performer's flashy dramatics.

His father played the viola at La Scala. It was perhaps inevitable that there would be rivalry between them, although Roberto was sensitive to Simone's musicianship and laughed off parental jibes to the orchestra regarding his son's clumsiness. It was true anyway. At home, it was Roberto, never Simone, who had embarrassing accidents with door-handles, or cracked his head on the stairwell. On stage was different.

There Roberto was spectacularly public, and with the room
to play it. He knew that he was good.

'I could have been as good as you,' said Simone, almost as
though he read his son's thoughts.

'Of course you could.'

'Better, with the chances you've had.'

'I know. The war got in the way.' Roberto, unhappy with
the way the conversation was heading, rubbed a hand on the
back of his neck. He wondered if other old complaints would
emerge: how Sandro – 'the clever one' – should have been a
priest, not a roughneck policeman; how he, Roberto, had
always been a disappointment to his father.

'In any opera, who remembers the bass?' – *Yes, they were
going down this well-worn track* – 'Now a baritone like me . . .'

Roberto inhaled through his nose and thought about his
mother. Was it selfishness which made him realise at times
like this how sharply he missed her? And what about Simone?

'Tell me, Dad,' he said, 'Tell me about the war, when you
were in the south. Where was it again, Naples?' Obeying an
impulse of comfort – both by virtue of what he did and as part
of his essential nature Roberto was an intensely physical,
affectionate man – he leaned over and kissed his father.

Maybe the kiss did it. He had asked Simone the same
question on other midnight occasions, similar to this one, and
got nowhere. This time, perhaps because he really was
shaken, perhaps because he remembered Aurelio Padovano
putting a gun to his head and pulling the trigger, his father
began to talk.

5

The door closed behind Julia. Listening to fallen leaves scraping the stone steps as wind surged against the house, she was reminded of the fairy stories her stepfather had told her when she was a little girl. In those too there were mysterious women, family secrets, miraculous returns. She was not a princess, nor any longer a child, yet there was a glamour about this evening. Julia was intrigued, and honest enough to admit that the glamour was appealing.

'The Contessa is waiting for you in the dining-room.' Andrea took her coat, spiriting it away into an old walnut wardrobe. 'There is a good fire. Please, go on ahead.' He pointed across the ante-room to a pair of gilded doors.

Julia ran her hands through her hair, straightened her collar, brushed her shoulders, then crouched and checked the laces of her trainers. For a meeting with an aristocrat she was seriously underdressed; worse, she felt young. She frowned, running her tongue over her teeth. There was no help for it: her two concert gowns were hanging out their travel creases in her room, she had no other dresses. Had she known she was to be entertained by the nobility, she reflected, she would have brought less music and more clothes.

'Shouldn't you announce me?' she asked quizzically, tilting her head up to Andrea.

'Please,' said the chauffeur in his nasal Italian, 'she has been waiting a long time.' Formal again, he held out his hand.

'Thank you.' Julia rose to her feet.

'In twenty minutes I will bring the champagne.'

Andrea slipped out of a side door, leaving her alone. Taking a deep breath, Julia walked to the gilded doors and opened them.

She felt her eyes widening. This was not the dining-room she had expected but instead a brightly lit gallery, dominated by huge terra-cotta urns filled with plants. In a single delighted sweep, Julia took in pink camellias flowering cheek-by-jowl with scarlet poinsettias, double begonias frothing over the edges of their pot like whipped cream, stately blue iris in vases and great pompoms of standard roses, winter blooms in bud for Christmas. Here was a garden.

She cupped a damask rose lightly for a moment, inhaling its musky perfume. She liked this room, its clash of colours and meld of scents, the antique mirrors hung to reflect the beauty of the flowers. Again the thread of enchantment touched her. It was as though she were walking in a forest.

Catching a glimpse of herself in an oval silver-gilt glass, Julia was surprised. She looked graceful and dignified crossing the tiled floor, not young and foolish, as she felt. It was not her performance 'mask', she was glad to see, but something different, almost as though she was a stranger to herself.

She reached the second rank of doors, pushed on the golden handles and walked into a host of lights.

Julia gasped. Tilting her head back, she stared at the dazzle of crystal and flame. A candle chandelier, straight from a scene in *La Traviata*, only here it was real.

Here too were flowers and plants: pots of basil on shuttered window ledges; vases of fully opened yellow roses on the heavy oak dining table, and all along the marble mantelpiece a single horizontal flower arrangement whose bits of green-stuff were swayed by the heat of the blaze beneath.

'Do you like it?'

Spoken in careful English, the question issued from a leather armchair, one of two placed before the fire.

Between the two chairs ran a low lacquer table, its top littered with silk flowers, crumbling bits of oasis, and a swathe of silk floral arrangements, each no larger than a coffee saucer. As Julia skirted the dining table and a dark blue Chinese rug, a gnarled white hand extended past the studded chair back to deposit a pair of scissors on the low table. A face now appeared above the crook of the chair arm.

'Well?' the face demanded, 'Do you?'

Julia nodded. 'I like it very much.' She saw no reason to lie. 'What is that scent?'

'Apple-wood.' The white hand indicated the blazing fire. 'When it burns it is sweet.' The woman stumbled slightly over the English words. 'Please, sit,' she said, not offering to shake hands.

Julia took the other chair. She watched her hostess in the flexing light, struck afresh by their likeness to each other.

This was the Clara of the photographs. A widow still in black, the only brightness a golden crucifix and a probing, direct gaze. Her hair was as black as Julia's but her eyebrows and lashes were thinner, her oval face lined.

'You will have questions.' Her tongue battled through the treacle of an unfamiliar language. 'Forgive me. My English is not used for years. You must be patient.' Her hands, marooned in her lap, wrung against each other. 'Bah! Look at me. An old woman fidgeting!' Disgusted with herself, she used the Italian word.

Julia laughed softly. How many times through childhood had she heard her mother's instruction, 'Don't fidget!' followed by a hard slap? Her heart began to warm to the Contessa. 'Why don't we speak in Italian?' she asked, switching to that language.

The widow pursed her lips. 'You will not smile at me behind your hand?' she said, suspicious as an old market woman. 'I am from the South. My accent will sound uncouth to you.'

Julia shook her head, disarmed by the direct approach. She liked this woman. Whatever she had anticipated, it was not this surprise, that she should take to Clara Rochfort-Scudieri at once, after two decades of neglect. She had come

expecting to be courted and charmed, but had found instead
a simple frankness. Julia had sung often enough of instant
alliances, now she was realising such things were possible.

Her feeling of rapport increased as Clara Rochfort-Scudieri
switched to her native tongue. Hearing the broad southern
vowels, Julia was hard put not to smile. Not at Clara – suddenly
'the Contessa' seemed too formal a title – but with her.

'Tell me,' said Clara. 'How is Angelica now? Is she well?'

'She is very well.'

'Excellent!' Clara looked away. 'I am glad you have come,'
she said, staring at the fire. 'That shows you have courage.
That you are worthy.'

It was disconcerting for Julia to discover that her old
resentments were not buried after all. 'I wasn't aware I had to
prove myself to you,' she answered, sitting back in the leather
armchair and crossing one leg over the other. 'Is that the
reason you didn't contact or help my mother for twenty years,
because she wasn't worthy?'

To her astonishment, Clara laughed. 'How very fair-minded
you are! How very English!'

She laughed again. Her laughter was of the same quality
as Julia's, warm, compelling. Despite herself, Julia's own lips
twitched: this was a game old bird. Her grandmother?

'To answer you honestly,' Clara went on, 'I never stopped
offering assistance or cash to my daughter. *You* would have
more money now if you hadn't bought those airline tickets,'
she added drily.

How did she know about Tenerife? 'Maybe I wouldn't have
needed to treat my parents to a long-overdue holiday if you'd
helped them more – cared more – years ago.'

'No, you don't understand. Angelica didn't want my *care*:
she never opened my letters. She would not even speak to me
on the telephone.'

There was a bleakness in these statements which struck a
further chord in Julia, but she was still determined to be wary.
'Why didn't you get in touch earlier than six months ago?'

'I tried. Believe me.' Clara plucked her scissors from the
table, and balanced an unfinished arrangement on her knee.

'I tried to find my daughter, to make sure she and her baby were safe.'

She broke off, mouth trembling slightly before she resumed. 'Newspaper adverts, private investigators, rewards for information . . . It was as though Angelica had disappeared from the earth. Several detectives traced her as far as England, a young mother and infant travelling to Heathrow on her passport, but after that they lost her. One told me Angelica must have changed your names, obtained false papers: there was no way of knowing even if you were still in the same country. I wanted to watch you growing up in our house,' she finished softly.

Julia watched a miniature silk yellow rose being thrust into the oasis, steel wire piercing its heart. She was very still. 'Surely when my mother married Enrico?'

'She probably gave a false name.'

Julia thought this in character, although she had never seen her mother's hidden marriage certificate. Knowing Angelica, Julia guessed that her mother would have told Enrico nothing until after they were married. Enrico loved Angelica very much; he would have respected her wishes not to delve into her past. This hadn't prevented Enrico from being curious: hence Julia's promise to him to find out something. The strange thing was that Angelica had brought Julia herself up with a true family name: such openness seemed odd after such secrecy.

'So how did you find me?' she asked after a moment.

'A magazine ran a piece – they said you were someone to watch out for.' Clara smiled, shedding ten years. 'I was so proud of you. And now I had two names: your stepfather's and your own – *my* married name, Rochfort. I'd never thought of looking for *you* with *my* name. The article said you came from Leeds. A telephone call to international directory enquiries was all it took. No Julia Rochfort was found in Leeds, but your stepfather's name gave me a telephone number.'

And Angelica had refused to speak to her. Julia sighed. What had happened? Had they quarrelled? Could anyone get close enough to Angelica to fight with her?

Clara was still explaining. 'Flying has never appealed to me, so I wrote letters. As you see, they were all returned unopened. My own daughter . . .

'I had your parents' address now, but not yours. No way of knowing if you still lived with them, if you were married – or anything about you except that you sang. You were a mystery.

'I wrote one more letter, on a postcard, begging Angelica to tell me something about my granddaughter. Your stepfather Enrico received it whilst Angelica was in hospital and telephoned. Angelica had hidden my other letters from him. We spoke for a long time. He told me about their holiday, by the way.'

Clara paused to clip another flower – was this ceaseless activity her way of coping with their meeting? Julia wondered. She sat deep in thought, breathing in the apple-wood fragrance of the room, finding Clara's nimble, birdlike movements strangely relaxing. As she sat, watching the old lady create a fragile beauty which seemed alive, bitterness gave way to pity. She could only imagine the years of anxious waiting, the dashed hopes, the fear. The courage needed to communicate with someone whom you do not know.

It was Angelica and herself all over again, but worse. Her mother had been withdrawn but she had not cut her daughter completely from her life. 'What happened then?' she asked.

Clara turned the arrangement on her knee and glanced up, meeting Julia's gaze. An oddness in her eyes revealed itself, one grey orb too fixed. There was an old scar near her right temple.

Unaware that she did so, Julia touched her own face. Clara had lost an eye and needed surgery to repair the damage. What had happened?

'What happened?' Clara repeated the phrase, only to a different question. 'Enrico told me about *you*. I already knew from the magazine article that you were coming to Italy to enter a singing competition. After that phone call I decided that the choice should be yours as to whether we met. My approach would be by letter: you would be the one to come to me.'

'Besides, waiting in a dingy hotel lobby isn't very stylish for an aristocrat,' remarked Julia blandly.

Clara chuckled: 'You are like me.' Her eyes glittered in the flashing firelight. 'Tell me, why didn't you marry this James? Did he resent your success? Or did he perhaps throw you over? Your stepfather said there have been no other men since.'

Julia laughed, enjoying their sparring as much as the old lady. 'James was a pianist: there was never any professional rivalry between us.' There had been none on her part at least. Julia stopped for a moment, suddenly four years younger again. James with his easy charm, chestnut hair and deep blue eyes, like Angelica. James who, after they became engaged, showed his true colours, resenting even her help.

'I left him because he was lazy, unreliable and feckless,' she said, returning to the present, her eyes running along the length of the mantelpiece flower chain as she raised her head to drive home the point.

'Not to mention being unfaithful with one of your fellow singers.'

Enrico had been frank, thought Julia, blinking away the unwelcome memory. Yet even without discovering James and Portia in bed (something she had told no one) she would have finished with the pianist. At twenty-two she had been innocent, softer, more long-suffering, but not that naive. Now she concentrated on her career and could reply honestly, 'It wasn't important. I'd already made up my mind.'

'Not worthy, eh?'

Julia, amused by Clara's joke, shook her head. Dismissing the recent past, she thought instead of Enrico, as dark and warm as James and her mother were pale and cold. She wondered aloud why her stepfather had not mentioned the telephone call to her.

'Because I asked him not to,' was the response. 'I wanted to be the one to tell you.'

Julia smiled at this forthright statement. Despite the flashes of sarcasm and temper she liked her grandmother.

Meeting the southern aristocrat's fierce look, seeing it soften with understanding, with a sympathy even for her resentment, Julia was struck by another startling fact. Clara liked her.

Clara liked her: it was that simple.

'You smile like me, too.'

'I know.'

For a moment neither spoke. It was a comfortable silence, broken only by the ticking of the fern-entwined mantelpiece clock and the distant sounds of a night-time road-sweeper.

'Good. Now, to begin again, my name is Clara Rochfort-Scudieri and Angelica, your mother, is my daughter. I was born a long way south of here in 1913. At fifteen I was married to a pig of a man called Antonio – his nickname "Black-face" was more appropriate. He died, and I met and married your English grandfather, Guy Valentine Rochfort, in 1936. He turned the estates over to producing vermouth and saved me my properties.'

Julia raised a hand against this catalogue of events and dates. 'I really am part-English.' Despite the Rochfort name she had never quite believed in Angelica's assertive 'Englishness'. She had been proud to be all Italian: pride born in reaction to her mother's rejection of everything Mediterranean. Suddenly this ground had been cut from under her feet: she was truly *Anglo*-Italian. 'Valentine – my middle name is Valentina.'

'I insisted on it,' replied Clara. 'Angelica was determined to give you a purely English name: I wanted some part to be Italian. And it honoured your grandfather, Guy.'

Clara stared again at the fire. 'That was the last thing Angelica did for me before she turned her back on the family and ran away to England.'

'Family?' Julia slid forward on the leather armchair, 'There are more?'

'A few cousins in Naples. No one important.'

'I see.' This did not sound promising. Julia's throat went dry. Putting off her most important question, she asked after Guy's family. The Rochforts, whom Julia – again as an adult reacting against her mother's 'Englishness' – had never tried to trace in England.

Clara knew little. The Rochforts had lived in Bristol. There were two brothers older than Guy, but when Guy married 'that foreigner' and remained abroad, his relatives made no effort to keep in touch.

'For the last six years of our marriage there was a war on, you know,' Clara finished drily.

'Yes, I realise that.' Julia coughed. She was caught between her desire to know, her sense of loyalty to Enrico and an old bitterness at having been abandoned.

There was no way over it except to be blunt. 'Do you know anything about my father?' she demanded, and with that question came a torrent: 'Do you know who he was – Have you a picture of him? Do you know why he left my mother?'

Waiting for an answer, Julia bit down hard, making herself stop before she asked, 'Was it because she was pregnant with me?' She sat back so rapidly that she struck her knee against the low table, jarring her body.

Clara sighed, shaking her head. 'I know nothing.' She leaned forward to rake together the fire with a pair of brass tongs. 'Angelica was always – how can I put this? – rather wild. Through her twenties there were many men. Sometimes we quarrelled over it. She said I was old-fashioned: "Out of touch" was how she put it. She did bring a few of her young men home, although there never seemed to be one she particularly cared for, one I could say for certain . . . But surely, if you asked her?'

'I've tried.' *And got nowhere*, Julia added in thought. But then maybe she had been asking the impossible: maybe her mother wasn't sure. She sucked in a long breath, turning so that Clara would not see her eyes. She did not want Clara to think she was crying over a little knock.

Besides which, Julia reminded herself sharply, she was not the one who had suffered most. Her mysterious absent father was not the same as a lifetime partner or an only child, and Clara had lost both.

She cleared her throat. 'I'm sorry about your husband. I presume—'

'Dead,' said Clara flatly, replacing the tongs on the stand. 'Dead these fifty years. A war hero who will be honoured in next year's "anniversary". You fidget as much as I do.'

'I'm sorry.' Julia knew she wasn't expressing herself clearly, but there was, after all, so much to take in. After years of being regarded by her mother as a nuisance or a rival, she had found acceptance in the house of an Italian aristocrat. Clara liked her. She frowned. 'I am truly sorry about Guy. I would like to have met him, too.'

'I am sure you would.' – Clara threw her an unfathomable look with her good eye – 'But your grandfather is dead. I warned him against siding with partisans: a child could see how that would end. But he wouldn't listen. He was tortured by Scarpia's agents, but what really killed him was his own idealism.'

Scarpia. This was the first time Julia heard Clara say the name which would cost her and others so much. Not knowing the future, she thought for a moment she had misheard. Scarpia to her was a character from Puccini's *Tosca*, not a real man.

In the opera, Scarpia was a torturer. Amongst other things.

Clara was fiddling with her scissors. 'I would like you to stay here with me at my house, stay for as long as you can,' she said. Amazingly to Julia she coloured like a young girl. 'There is a music room here – I would love to hear you sing.' She plucked at the chair arm. 'Will you stay?'

Julia, overwhelmed by a surge of affection for this proud, anxious old lady, threw back her head and laughed. 'Of course I'll stay,' she said, rising to her feet as Andrea entered, bringing champagne glasses and black grapes on a silver tray. 'Thank you.'

They talked, eating sweet grapes, sipping dry champagne. Andrea stayed for a toast, then retired to bed, at which point Clara gave Julia a mischievous look.

'I'm not tired. Are you?'

'Certainly not!'

They talked on into the night, sharing the last drops of premier cru between them. The candles in the chandelier began to sputter and slowly burn down, the apple-wood fire collapsed in on itself, and still they talked. Clara was hungry for news of her family, interested in everything.

Julia for her part felt the comfort of acceptance. With her grandmother, this southern Italian aristocrat over fifty years her senior, she did not have to measure her words, hide her gestures, or suppress her responses. She could share her achievements and touch on her fears, secure in the knowledge that she would not be called a show off or a coward. Her intended trip to Bologna after her next rehearsal tomorrow, to search for the Italian side of her family, was not needed. With Clara, curiosity was not forbidden, as it had been with Angelica, but encouraged.

So, when she said in an unguarded moment, 'Why did you and my mother fall out?' and then automatically began to withdraw the question, Clara said softly:

'No, you need not apologise, it is your right to know. For myself, I cannot say why she left. One day Angelica was with me, the next –' She spread her hands in a helpless gesture, her grey eyes strained in bewilderment, '– my daughter was gone. She has been lost to me ever since.

'Listen, I will tell of the day she left. Perhaps you will see a reason for her action: she is your mother.'

Julia, flinching as the wind blew down the chimney, stirring the glowing embers, leaned forward, her chin on her hand. Clara, speaking in a low voice, began to explain.

'It was Assumption Day, August 1970. Your mother had just returned from the Bologna palazzo where she had gone to paint – a holiday in oils, as she called it. You were with me and Andrea.

'There were no harsh words between us, no real quarrel. Angelica came into the gallery where we were, lifted you in her arms and retired to her room. She said nothing, but at the time I thought little of it: the day was hot and we were all fractious – you especially.'

Clara's smile faded. 'That was the last time I saw her. When Andrea called Angelica to lunch he found her room empty. We searched the grounds, waited and in the evening phoned the police.'

Clara sat cradling her empty champagne flute, her face drawn with memories. 'She took very little, you know,' she said. 'Nothing except the holiday suitcase which she had not unpacked and a few clothes and toys for you. For weeks I was obsessed by the fear that my child had committed suicide. Even when the private investigators told me of her flight to England and showed me copies of airline records, I was still afraid.'

As she spoke, Clara seemed to withdraw into herself. The champagne flute trembled in her hands. 'It was a degrading, sweating kind of terror,' she murmured. 'It was worse than anything Scarpia could devise, and I did it to myself.'

There it was again, that name. Scarpia. Suddenly Julia felt as though something touched her. She shivered, rubbing the pricked hairs on her arms. 'Who is Scarpia?'

Clara closed her eyes. 'There! And I promised myself that I would not say his name tonight.'

'Who is he?' Julia persisted. 'Why did he torture my grandfather?' Her *English* grandfather, Julia added in thought.

Clara opened her eyes and her hands, careless of the glass in her lap. 'Are you sure you want to know?'

Despite the fire, the room had grown cold. Julia stared down at the lacquered table, at her grandmother's arrangements, the stiffened leaves and wired roseheads.

'Tell me about Scarpia.'

6

10th June, 1944. The village of San Martino della Croce, Italy
Clara was standing in the doorway of the villa at San Martino
della Croce. She twirled slowly, watching her silk dress
shimmer back the light. The rising sun blazed between the
mountains like a fire opal. The cicadas sang, as they had fifteen
years earlier at her first wedding. Below, the gardens were
hung with dew and scents: rosemary, vine flowers, orange
blossom.

She had been married twice in this gown, once by force
and once by choice. It was the best thing she owned.

Like the dress, still white and unblemished on its flounced
surfaces, Clara was outwardly untouched by the years. As
with the dress, one had to look beneath to find the scars. The
repairs to the ripped underskirt clinging to her bare legs were
a constant reminder of that first wedding night. Next morning
and following mornings for two never-ending years, Antonio
Scudieri, cousin and husband, had smiled handsomely at the
maids and they in return had redoubled their efforts, never
suspecting what hurts those manicured hands and gleaming
teeth inflicted on his wife. Antonio had been good at leaving
no obvious marks.

Clara circled again. She had survived. She had watched
her husband and his parents brought into the villa on doors,
riddled with gunshot. They had been driving to a dance when
bandits had murdered them. Clara would have been with them,

except she pleaded off, feigning sickness. She had wanted to be free for one night.

And now she was free. Nothing would trap or touch her again.

'Mamma!' Seven-year-old Angelica, a skinny cherub with titian hair and grubby fingers came galloping up the steps from the herb garden. 'Let me ride with you in your soft dress.'

Clara laughed and swung the child up. 'Round we go!' She spun them. Angelica, in a daze of squealing excitement, kicked her bare heels against her mother.

'Daddy! Look at me!' Angelica's sun-reddened face was wide in smiles as Clara swung her one final time. The instant she was set down, the little girl was running towards the tall figure striding up from the cellars. Clara watched the man's arms open, the child hurl herself into them. For an instant the two red heads, auburn and dark chestnut, seemed to mingle and then two pairs of cobalt eyes were trained onto her – almost like a gun-sight, thought Clara. She could never get over the startling colour of Guy's and Angelica's eyes.

'I see you're ready for a day in the fields.' Guy's voice rippled with amusement.

Clara shrugged. 'I wanted to see if I could still get into it.' She gave a slow, provocative twirl. 'Do you like?'

Glancing at the slim, sinewy body, the flushed fair complexion of her second husband, she had her answer.

'Come here.' Guy put down Angelica. 'Your mamma married me in this dress.' He rumpled his daughter's ragged hair, dragging Clara closer.

'You'll crease my dress,' warned Clara. Sometimes she could scarcely believe that he was forty-four years old. 'I must go and change. This is for later.' She tickled him to make him release her.

Guy laughed and let her go. 'We'll wait for you by the apricot trees.' He lifted Angelica onto his shoulders. 'The place where we met – do you remember?' He tilted his head back to look up at his daughter. 'Mamma was picking apricots because she couldn't afford to hire any help that week.'

Clara smiled. 'Your papa wanted a bed for the night. He was on a—'

' "Walking Holiday".' Clara and Guy both finished the sentence, erupting into laughter at the English words.

'Please!' Angelica, ignoring family history, was squirming to be let down. Clara rescued the child from her high perch and Angelica trotted off to try to catch a cicada. Alone for a moment, Guy kissed the top of Clara's head and she stepped back to him, drawing his arms around her middle. They stood quietly together, remembering.

Clara and Guy had met in 1936 when Mussolini was at the height of his powers and voices were being raised in Europe against Adolf Hitler. Guy had come to Italy to buy wine stocks for his flourishing liqueur business. Tramping round the country, alone and unannounced, he could see for himself which estates were managed well or badly.

His reasoning was typical and showed the kind of man he was: practical, little interested in ideas. His experience as a young man of eighteen fighting in the trenches for a year had left him disillusioned with politics and with a taste for solitude. He did not join groups, or clubs.

The Great War had another profound effect on Guy. It woke in him a craving for light and strong sun. Guy, for all his fair colouring, loved the Italian sun.

He loved Clara too and in the same way, completely and at once. Seeing her pale, anxious face as he strode towards her through the apricot trees, Guy had been struck. Her bold strong voice had been the final spell.

For Clara, their first meeting was a shock. This man was so different from the people she was accustomed to, so strange. He was dressed in shabby tweeds, with different-coloured laces in his brogues, yet he carried himself with the ease of an aristocrat. His smooth, fair-skinned face gave him a youthful look, yet his eyes were clear and shrewd. Unable to place him as either a nobleman or a farmer, Clara had been afraid that Guy was a tax-collector.

His Italian was good and her fear had not lasted, especially when Guy let fall that he was a vintner. Questioning him, Clara

found him knowledgeable. With her own vine stocks
diminishing through lack of money and skill, she invited Guy
into her home. At the end of one week, in a calculated risk,
she invited herself into his room.

By the end of the month they were married; each delighted
with the other. Though Clara had known that all men could
not be as bad as Antonio Scudieri, Guy's patient, tender
lovemaking had been a revelation.

The villagers of Croce, the people on her estates in Bologna
and Tuscany, had been slower to accept the Englishman –
but only by six months. After that they took him as their own.
The Contessa, who had always provided them with work, and
had lived an exemplary life as a widow for six years, had
chosen well. Guy knew how to grow vines. He was no fool.

Practical as he was, Guy was prudent when it came to the
melting pot of Italian politics. He did not often make the long
winding journey down from San Martino della Croce into
Bologna, but when he did, Guy held himself aloof from both
the left and right wing in the cafés and public places of the
city. He concentrated on raising estate and village workers'
standards of living: building a school, paying their doctors'
bills . . .

A small English plane buzzed over, breaking into Clara's
reflections as it whirred above the hills.

'I wish this damnable war would end,' said Guy. 'I really
hoped last year with the armistice that it would finish.' His
hands tightened around her, the right hand, the one with three
fingers missing, gripping harder than the left. When Guy had
fought in the last war, he had lost his fingers to a detonator: it
meant he couldn't use a gun.

When war had broken out again between Germany and
England, Guy, unable to join up for active service, remained
in Italy with his wife and baby daughter. Italy, though allied
to Nazi Germany by the Berlin – Rome Axis, had not entered
the war and would not do so for another year. On that day,
10th June, 1940, the local head of the carabinieri had
summoned Clara and Guy to his office in Ponte Maggiore,
the small plains town.

The Marshal, a small, neat man in his late forties with light brown wispy hair and slightly protruding upper front teeth, introduced himself then settled back in his chair. Planting his heels on top of his desk, he squinted at them over bulging trays of paper.

'We have not met officially before, my friend; we do not move in the same circles. Yet I know you. You are an English gentleman married to an Italian aristocrat. Though not active in society, you have allies amongst the great in Bologna and more importantly have made no enemies. You have held yourself apart from factions – very wise! You have taken the trouble to learn the local dialect of the people who work on your estates and they have repaid you with their loyalty. You have an Italian child. To move against you would stir up a hornets' nest which, since I am a lazy fellow, I am not inclined to do. Besides, it would mean more paperwork.'

The Marshall brushed a heel against one of the trays heaped with manila folders and stared at the cracks on his office ceiling. 'Subversives, Communists and anti-Fascists: all young hotheads. My superiors want these first before they remember one Guy Rochfort, respected middle-aged family man who takes no interest in politics, sends them Christmas boxes of superb vermouth and whose wife is the godchild of Prince Zeno.' His eyes left off studying the ceiling. 'Have you guns in any of your houses?'

Clara started at the question. Guy smiled and leaned forward in his chair. 'May I smoke?' He offered the Marshal a cigarette, and the business of lighting up occupied his hands.

'My wife has a small pistol for her protection.' He blew out the match. 'We have no need for guns on our estates.'

The Marshal watched Guy's right hand. He expelled a stream of smoke from his nostrils and observed, 'Of course spies do not need fingers, only their eyes.'

Guy threw back his red head and laughed. 'If I'm a spy then to whom have I been reporting all these years? And what should I be saying, "The grape harvest was good this year?" '

'A man came to see you last week, did he not?' remarked the Marshal, crossing one foot over the other on top of his desk. 'An English man. What did he want?'

Guy flushed and Clara frowned. She had never seen her
husband so angry as he had been on that day. The pale
Englishman who had introduced himself as Mr Smith had
refused to talk in front of her. He and Guy had been closeted
in the wine cellars for an hour, after which Mr Smith had
walked away with the doom-laden warning, 'Then we can do
nothing for you, *Signore.*'

'He wanted me to return to England,' said Guy. 'With or
without my family, that was up to me. Of course there could
be no guarantee that my wife, as an enemy alien, might not
be placed in "protective custody".' Guy's blue eyes hardened.
'I told him to get out.'

'He did not ask you to use your special knowledge and
position to root out secrets for the British?' said the Marshal.

Guy drew hard on his cigarette. 'Mr Smith said that my
"obviously divided loyalties" made me a suspect source.'

'Ah, that bit hard, did it not?' The Marshal tapped ash onto
the sand floor, inviting Guy to do the same. 'What is this man:
a bloodless little bureaucrat who has lived in the British
embassy compound in Rome for a month and thinks he knows
Italy? But you can do something for me, my friend. Any
suspicious groups springing up amongst your workers, anyone
voicing anti-government propaganda, I want to know.'

Guy rose to his feet, grinding out his cigarette. 'No,
Marshal,' he said quietly, 'you are asking me to spy on my
own people. I will not do it.' He picked up his panama. 'I wish
you good day. My wife and I will be in the café across the
square if you wish to arrest me.'

Clara, lightheaded, midsummer heat sticking her cheap
print dress to her body, clutched at the handbag on her knee,
feeling the gold coins she had brought as a bribe biting into
her hands through the leather. She knew Guy was right and
yet—

The Marshal whipped his heels off the desk and stood up.
'That will not be necessary, Signore. You are both having
coffee with me.' He pressed a button on his desk. 'Come, sit
down,' he continued, in a less strident voice. 'You have proved

yourself. Had you accepted those terms for your freedom I would have imprisoned you on the spot. Now we must see about means to keep you out of internment. Fortunately most of my men are lazy fellows like me, so it should not be so difficult.'

It turned out to be surprisingly easy. Guy remained living openly as an English-born naturalised Italian. In the early days of June 1940 there had been a few zealous Fascist officials who wanted to whisk him off to their Bologna headquarters, but a phone call by Clara to her godfather Prince Zeno prevented that. The Prince, a grizzled ex-army man, was a powerful figure in the Emilia Romagna region. Courted by Fascists, respected by left-wing opponents, Zeno was rumoured to have the ear of Mussolini.

Guy meanwhile continued to grow vines and busy himself with the affairs of his tenants. He moved rarely from San Martino della Croce. He went with Clara to the opera, but otherwise did not appear in society. Soon he was forgotten. A middle-aged vintner who could not shoot was of little interest when there were greater threats.

The war was going badly. Mussolini was no longer popular. In a country where there was only one officially recognised party – Fascist – an increasing number of people were voicing different opinions in secret. Communists and Liberals joined forces. Soldiers began to desert, selling their weapons to anyone who wished to buy. Food was becoming increasingly scarce.

It was about this time that Guy began going out at night. He told Clara that it was to 'trade' on the black market.

Then, on the 25th July, 1943, fifteen days after the Allies had invaded Sicily, Mussolini was deposed in Rome. In September, the new Italian government, led by Marshal Badoglio, asked the Allies for an armistice.

Italy's 'peace' was short-lived. As soon as the armistice was announced, the Germans moved into the country in force. Northern and central Italy became part of the Nazi state.

Clara and Guy soon learned the difference between Italian and German fascism. On the second evening after the

Germans had invaded, the Marshal of Ponte Maggiore drove
to their remote mountain villa in San Martino della Croce. He
came with grim news.

'It's terrible,' he said, sitting with them on the steps to the
herb garden. 'All the Jews are being deported to a place called
Auschwitz. Young men are being rounded up to work in
German factories; if they try to escape they are shot as
deserters. My own boy is missing with the rest of his unit in
Russia: I don't know if he's alive or dead, but it was German
foreign policy which sent him there.'

The Marshal reached into his jacket pocket. 'It's time for
you to have a new identity, my friend!' he told Guy. 'I did not
shoot you as a spy, but the Germans might. This is the address
of a forger, the best in Bologna. I've burned any papers at my
headquarters which refer to Guy Rochfort. My advice would
be to lie low here: let village loyalty work for you. The Germans
will have to come through Ponte Maggiore, Castel San Martino
and the three hamlets in the foothills before they reach San
Martino della Croce. No one in the lower villages is likely to
give you away; you're not an escaped prisoner of war, so
there's no tempting reward on your head.'

The Marshal grinned but his eyes were shadowed and
strained. He had not shaved and his previously immaculate
uniform had dark patches under both arms.

Clara, taking in the older man's appearance with a searching glance was careful. 'We're grateful for everything you've
done,' she began slowly, 'and we know you took a great
risk in destroying official documents. Yet why are you helping
us?'

The Marshal whistled through his prominent front teeth,
glanced at Guy, then stood up. 'I don't really know why.'
He stared into the darkness, then added, 'The Germans are
doing terrible things. You're lucky that you have been
forgotten.'

Clara, remembering, shivered. They had indeed been
lucky. Guy, complete with his new identity and papers as
Mario Scudieri, one of her cousins, had been able to remain
at San Martino della Croce. The villagers, even the children,

accepted him as Mario. Never having called the Contessa's husband by either his Christian name or surname, they had nothing to unlearn.

'Bugger Hitler and bugger Il Duce,' he said now.

Clara was silent. On moonlit nights she could see the fires clearly from this hilltop villa as the Allies bombed Bologna.

'I really must go,' she said, and Guy nodded.

On her way into the villa she felt his gaze and turned: he and Angelica waved from the shade of a wizened apricot tree.

'I wish I knew how he did that trick of making people look round,' muttered Clara. Perhaps it was some quality of those blue eyes.

She shrugged and went on inside.

A few moments later, in wooden sandals and wine-stained dungarees cut down from Guy's overalls, she joined her husband and daughter at the boundary to the orange grove. Swinging Angelica along between them, Clara and Guy walked through the sweetly scented trees. Trestle tables were already set out: at midday the estate workers and a few friends and neighbours would be here to celebrate the midsummer feast of San Martino della Croce's own Madonna: 'Our Lady of the Vines'.

Her 'shrine' was set in the longer outer wall of the church nave. There a piece of low relief sculpture, half life-size, taken possibly from a forgotten temple, had been incorporated into the church wall. Once painted, the sculpture's bright colours had faded over the years to odd flaking patches of blue and gold, but the relief itself remained clear-cut. It showed a woman, possibly a goddess, dressed in long flowing robes, surrounded by hanging branches of grape-laden vines. In one hand she held a spray of poppies and wheat, near her feet a wine cup.

This pagan figure had in the Middle Ages taken on a significance which might have surprised the earlier church builders. From being a prettily decorated piece of useful stone, the low relief sculpture became the focus of a local cult of the Virgin Mother. All the villagers' pagan superstitions, denied by the masculine conventions of the church, now centred on this figure with her grapes and wheat, the two staples of the region.

Wine and bread: the Croce Madonna ensured both of these for the village, and fertility for its animals and people. On a June day in the seventeenth century the Croce Madonna had appeared in a vision to a shepherd as he passed through the churchyard. Touching the hand of the low relief figure of Our Lady for luck, the shepherd found his fingers clasped in return and the Virgin standing straight in front of him, her golden hair wreathed with flowers and her other hand full of poppies and wheat stems.

Ever after, the 10th June had been her day. The villagers of Croce all looked to their own Virgin to protect them and increase their vines. Her shrine had been decorated with wreaths of vine flowers that morning and the priest and his curate had already celebrated mass in the church to 'Our Lady of the Vines,' the ceremony starting last night and lasting right through until dawn: services which Clara and Guy had attended.

These sacred duties done, it was time to relax before preparing the feast itself – a feast the villagers looked forward to as a welcome break. Besides, if they did not honour 'Our Lady of the Vines,' she would send them barrenness instead of bounty: crops and vintage would fail, springs would run dry.

Faced with such fears, Clara and Guy knew the festival had to take place. Both were determined that the war would not deprive the local people of this annual celebration to their Madonna.

Now Clara went ahead and opened the gate onto the terraces, taking one of the hoes leaning against the stone wall. 'Here, little one, put your hat on.' She brought out a faded cap from her dungarees pocket. 'What about you, Guy?'

'I'm working under shade this morning.' Guy patted the knife at his belt. 'Bleeding the mastic trees.' Despite Clara's appeals that he stop at least some of his jobs on the estate, Guy refused to allow the war to dictate his daily life. 'If someone sees me, what of it?' he would say. 'I've been part of the landscape here for almost ten years. It would be more suspicious if I started skulking indoors.'

'Can I come?' Angelica squinted up at her father.

'I'll be working with sharp tools . . .'

'Oh, let her,' Clara interrupted him. Sometimes Guy was overprotective. 'Go on.' Clara set the cap on her daughter's head, tweaking it over her eyes. 'Be seeing you.'

Out on the terraces it was blisteringly hot. The few women gathering strawberries two tiers down moved slowly, their patched clothes blending with the rough scrub of the hillside. Shading her eyes, Clara looked out over her land. Starting at the top, forests of beech and holm oak near where Guy would be working; below them high pasture with the small village of San Martino della Croce clinging onto one of the broader rock outcrops. Below the village were terraces of olives and grapes: this was Clara's land too, and the three lower hamlets on the twisting dirt road was where many of her tenants lived, although the villagers at Croce were always the closest, both in distance and in loyalty.

The lowest village of Castel San Martino and the valley floor with its groves of poplars, narrow fields of wheat, maize and sugar beet was a different country. Down there somewhere amidst the corn a dog was barking.

A distant chanting floated to her. Clara's eyes tracked the sound back to the monastery church on the opposite ridge, lingering a moment on the long barn where cheeses would be ripening in the darkness.

How long had it been since she tasted proper cheese? How long since Angelica had eaten white bread? At least before the Germans came she had been able to feed her family in some style.

Ignoring smoke from the charcoal burners in the woods, the skimming shadow of a hunting goshawk, Clara braced her shoulders and set to work hoeing. Several moments passed before she realised that someone was watching her.

'Stop!' She swung round but the youth was a fleeing blur, skidding down the hill. At her feet a bunch of corncockles tied with a rag, a slip of brown paper tucked between the long stems. Fingers trembling slightly, Clara looked for a message on the paper: there was none.

'Good day to you. A beautiful morning, is it not?'

Startled a second time, Clara dropped the bunch of corncockles. It fell in a heap at the German officer's feet.

'Good day, Signor Krusak,' she replied, refusing to use the man's ugly-sounding rank, 'It is indeed a lovely day, unless of course you are working in it.'

She stared at him steadily. The Germans had begun to investigate San Martino della Croce and the surrounding villages as part of their unceasing clamp-down against an increasingly active Italian resistance, many of whose partisans were operating from the mountains. She and Krusak had met before, in the village church, where the tall, grave young man had offered Clara holy water. He had commented on Guy's colouring.

'Yes, it is unusual, but then my cousin is not really Italian, but Etruscan; fair like a Celt,' Clara had replied, touching her fingers into Krusak's cupped palm before the holy water ran away. 'I regret you cannot converse with him, but Mario understands very little Italian, only the local dialect.'

By this time Guy was completely fluent in the native dialect: a tongue so different from written Italian as to be almost another language. But then he also spoke a purer Italian than she did, and Clara had no intention of allowing Krusak to spend time alone with her husband. Krusak was Croatian, a subtler race in her experience than English or German.

Now she could only marvel at the young man's self-possession as, with a flick of his boot, he retrieved the bunch without stooping. 'How apt for today,' he remarked, removing the strip of paper and placing that in his pocket, 'But your youthful admirer is mistaken: it should be a crown.'

Skilfully his hands wove the required shape, and before Clara could prevent him, Krusak stepped forward and set the flower coronet upon her head.

'Flora crowned for the feast. You look now as your Roman ancestors must have appeared at their banquets.' He was too polite to add that this was true only from the neck up, but his eyes were not idle.

He was ten years younger than her at least, and Clara chose to be amused. It never occurred to her to be alarmed, although she and Krusak were alone. She was only concerned that he might make mischief for Guy or her people. 'Young man,' she replied, 'I should be grateful if you would state your business.'

If she hoped to remind him of his place she was not successful. Krusak gave her a smile which transformed his narrow face and continued, 'I believe that in this part of the world the flower holds a special significance, one of betrayal. Because it flourishes amongst corn and yet is poisonous. Perhaps you should inform your admirer of that fact.'

Clara adjusted the coronet and answered straight-faced, 'Perhaps he wanted to warn me of your approach.'

Krusak's deep brown eyes widened. 'Because I am an early guest for your party?'

Clara laughed at this dissembling. 'But no one knew you were invited, Commendatore.' She ironically gave Krusak the rank of knight. 'Not even myself. And I manage everything on my estate.'

They smiled at each other, gazes bristling in silent combat. Who would have given way in the end was never to be discovered: from the hill above came a shout.

'Ah, your cousin,' Krusak replaced his cap and wheeled about. 'And your daughter with him – strange isn't it, how her hair is almost exactly the same shade as his.'

'I was auburn as a child,' murmured Clara.

'You were? Well that explains it.' He bowed his head. 'Farewell for the present, Princess.' Matching her irony, Krusak gave Clara this higher-ranking title rather than her true title of Contessa. 'I shall be bringing a guest to your festival, I hope you don't think it too presumptuous. He's from a village outside your estate, a wine grower called Vittorio, a charming man.'

'Of course.' Clara hid her fury with a brilliant smile. 'I shall look forward to your arrival, young man.' She watched him ambling down the mountain and waved when he did. Guy, coming alongside with Angelica perched on his shoulders, also waved.

'Don't say anything,' hissed Clara, lifting her daughter down and smoothing the child's skirt, 'He might hear. He's coming back at midday.'

'It'll be all right,' whispered Guy in dialect, taking the hoe from Clara. 'Here, cousin, let me do that,' he said aloud.

Angelica shrank closer to her mother – she had learned to be afraid of men in uniforms. Clara laid a work-roughened hand on the child's head, sick with rage against this war which had aged them all. She waited until she was sure Krusak was out of earshot. 'He's bringing Vittorio.'

'Oh, God.' Guy turned and began pummelling the soil with the hoe, 'What a mess.' He threw the hoe down, his face taut. 'I could murder a cigarette. What's that in your hair?'

'A crown of corncockles,' answered Clara. 'Krusak made it for me, so I thought I'd better wear it.' She removed the crown, spun it on her wrist. The purple flowers were wilting.

'A village boy – someone from Croce – brought me the flowers this morning.'

Guy, as superstitious as the locals about the beautiful yet deadly corncockle, swore softly, in English. 'Was there anything else with them?'

'No.' Clara had forgotten the brown paper.

'So what do you think that means?' Guy retrieved the hoe, working on without looking at her.

'I don't know.' Clara tossed the crown aside and sat down on the hillside: suddenly she felt tired. 'Unless Vittorio has talked.'

Guy grunted. 'That's unlikely, considering where he's from. They'd skin him alive.'

'Don't say such things.' Clara rubbed the standing hairs on her forearms. 'Must you keep going out at night after curfew?' she burst out. 'If the Germans catch you, you could be shot. Guy – you're not involved in something else besides the black market, are you?'

Guy swung round; she could hear him chuckling. 'Of course not,' he answered mildly, blue eyes open as the sky above them. He was going to get burned working in this heat without a hat, reflected Clara. The thought thrust in from a maze of others.

'I think you should disappear for a while, Mario.' She gave Guy his alias to emphasise her words. Her husband stared.

'What, now? Do you know how much there is to do on the estate at this time of year?' Guy shook his head, his face set. 'I need to be at the feast. There are people I need to see. There's a rumour that Rome has fallen to the Allies.'

Clara knew that expression: he would not be moved. 'Promise you'll take care,' she said, hugging her knees.

Guy leaned on the hoe. 'I think Krusak's really rattled you, my sweet,' he announced, 'And I must admit he's strange. I'm certain he's even younger than he claims to be, and he looks as though a breath of air would blow him over. Yet there's something about him . . .'

'Promise me,' begged Clara. In her anxiety, she slipped into her own southern dialect.

Guy flung up a hand in an Italian gesture. 'All right!' he exclaimed, stabbing the discarded crown with the hoe. 'I'll be careful. Does that satisfy you?'

'I suppose it must.' Clara rubbed at her forehead. 'What a morning,' she muttered.

'You worry too much,' said Guy.

7

Clara disliked the people from Castel San Martino, the village at the bottom of the mountain. The women thumbed their noses at her because she came from Calabria, in the southern 'foot' of Italy – Clara knew that they laughed at her accent. Behind her back. No one, not even the smirking men of Castel San Martino – several of whom boasted openly of being Communist – would dare be insolent to her face.

Now the mayor, Vittorio, smacked his greasy lips, smiling at her with shrewd bean-black eyes whilst he complimented her cuisine. The feast was onto the fruit, but Vittorio harked back to the antipasti.

'Exquisitely well-cured,' he was saying. 'Even better than the hams produced by your establishments, Father.' He waved a spoonful of strawberries at the young neat priest seated beside Clara. The priest, intent on a plateful of pastry twists, merely nodded and continued to chew. Vittorio lifted his glass, winking at the women passing along the table with jugs of wine. He crammed the scarlet berries into his wide mouth.

'I am pleased that you are enjoying our rustic hospitality, Mayor,' remarked Clara, seeing her precious food – gathered together by weeks of hoarding and black market 'deals' – disappearing down the man's cavernous throat. She watched in cold fury as Vittorio pinched the young matron who returned to serve him. Celeste's husband, an Italian infantryman, had not dared to show his face at the feast. He and a dozen other young men were in hiding, avoiding Krusak and his guards. Even now, the occupying force might still pick up any Italian servicemen they found and deport them to Germany to work for the Reich. Vittorio knew it, just as he knew that Celeste would not dare protest. It infuriated Clara that she could do nothing to protect her people.

'I will have wine.' Directly opposite from her, Krusak drained his glass. Celeste left Vittorio and moved along to serve him, but Krusak did not look at Celeste.

He has beautiful eyes, thought Clara, feeling that sombre gaze drawing her own, like an icon's. The contrast between her two uninvited guests could not have been greater. Vittorio was brown, badly shaven, stocky, sweating in a faded, tight-fitting suit. Krusak was young, elegant, wire-slim and immaculately groomed, his every movement precise. Unlike the Italian, the Croatian had eaten sparingly. Throughout the meal he had questioned Guy about the progress of the harvest and Guy had smiled and glanced at Clara, waiting for the translation into the local dialect, giving his answer in dialect.

It was a charade of course. Most of the Italians round that table, including Vittorio, knew who Guy was. And Vittorio was with Krusak, and six German guards.

Clara smiled at the Croatian, trying to read him. There was a gloss on the young man, nothing like the complacency which Vittorio made no effort to disguise, but none the less real. How much did he know? she thought. Was he planning to return to the villa tonight, when she and her family were alone?

Whatever Vittorio had told him, it wasn't much. Clara was certain that Guy would have been picked up already if the Croatian had suspected him of being English.

A muscle in her face was jumping, making her right eye twitch. Clara covered the eye with her hand. She stared past Krusak at the blood-red patches of fading sunlight, struggling to think.

The estate workers, the people of San Martino della Croce and the three lower hamlets were loyal, weren't they? Guy was well-regarded in the district. It took a large leap of imagination to consider that even the men and women from the rival village 'under the hill' would breathe a word to a German officer. Since the Allies were rumoured to have started another big offensive in the south of the country, everyone was waiting to see what would happen. The most ardent Fascist, faced with a possible Allied victory, was tempering his beliefs until it was clear which side was going to win. For many more Italians, with sons deserting from the Italian army and on the run, the choice was already made. The Germans were the enemy now.

Remembering this, Clara was comforted. She glanced round the people at her table, feeling a pang of regret as she looked to Prince Zeno's place and found it filled by another man. The Prince, her godfather, had died in his sleep last month. Her trip into Bologna for the old warrior's funeral had confirmed how much the Germans were hated. At every checkpoint other eyes as well as hers had watched as the tall, angular foreigners bullied, screaming at people in their harsh language.

On the road outside the cathedral members of the German SS had cornered a suspected Italian Jew. Clara remembered the man's cry as they slammed him against the huge red stone façade of the building: his groans as they kicked him to the ground added a ghastly counterpoint to the requiem music pouring from the cathedral doors. People hissed when the man was dragged away.

Clara, stepping over the bloodstains, had been late in attending the final mass for her godfather. Another reason, if one were needed, to hate the invaders.

Pietro, the young man sitting in Prince Zeno's place, bobbed his head, giving her a nervous smile. Funny Pietro. She had known him a month. They had met on the day of Prince Zeno's funeral: he was one of the less ragged-voiced members of the depleted choir. Appearing at her elbow after the service, he whispered that he needed help.

Clara took in the small, portly, blushing stranger and asked coolly who he was.

The man shot her a look of supplication through a liquid brown eye. 'Please!' he begged in an agonised whisper as Clara drew her veil over her face, 'Someone told me that you live in the country. You could hide me – I could be one of your estate workers.'

'Not with those hands.' Clara drew back. Seeing one of the German officers who had sat through the entire mass crossing the dim nave in their direction, she turned sharply and knelt at one of the side chapels to pray.

The round-faced stranger slumped onto the wooden rail beside her, white hands twitching as he crossed himself. 'Please!' he whispered, 'I've lived here in Bologna all my life. I'm a performer – not a brilliant one but I love my work. Now the Nazis want to take me away: Italian artistes are being rounded up, sent to Germany to entertain.'

The man swallowed. A trickle of sweat ran down his small Grecian nose which he mopped away fussily with a lace hand-kerchief. 'One of my stage props,' he murmured, stuffing the lace into a threadbare coat pocket, 'the proper ones are rags by now. You know how it is, everything's short these days.'

Clara tilted her head and regarded him keenly. An Italian blond, crinkled hair the colour of dark wheat, greying at the temples. Clean shaven. Sagging, pouched cheeks. A laughing mouth. Anxious wide-open eyes. Round shouldered and with a paunch.

She indicated his stomach. There was something both comic and pitiful about the man's disguise, although until one came close it was really quite good. 'Your padding's slipping,' she murmured. The German officer was admiring the sixteenth-century painting of the Annunciation in the nearby presbytery: a few stragglers from the funeral lingered in the echoing nave. She smiled as the stranger hurriedly patted himself back into shape.

'It seemed a good idea to disguise myself as older.' He indicated his dyed temples.

'If the Germans are after you, why did you come to the requiem mass today?' The answer Clara received was disappointingly commonplace.

'I was told we'd be paid. I needed the money. Look!' The man hooked one of the uncomfortable cheek-pads out of his mouth and slipped it into his black trouser pocket. 'I know I'm not the heroic type. I'm small and fat and I've flat feet: the army didn't want me. Even so, I don't think I've done anything so bad as to deserve being transported out of the country. Mauro the forger told me about you, said you were one of the people who helped others. Please say you'll help me. I'll do anything to earn my keep.'

Tears were standing in those wide brown eyes.

'You've forgotten to wring your hands,' said Clara, but then she smiled. The stranger grinned back.

'I've always been a frightful ham,' he admitted. 'That's why I need to get out of Bologna soon.' His grin folded and the roguish sparkle faded from his eye. Suddenly he looked dog-tired, and young.

Though irritated at Mauro – at least the forger had not mentioned Guy to the stranger – Clara was touched by the young man's story. Why should the Germans have him? She pushed herself up from the altar rail. 'How are you with horses?'

'I don't know.' The man fell into bustling step beside her, 'But I can learn. My name's Pietro, by the way. Pietro Terni. That's my real name. If you want to, you can give me away now.'

Clara threw him an old-fashioned look. 'What, and lose a groom? Certainly not.'

Pietro Terni had turned out to be good with animals, reflected Clara, smiling across her feast day table at the blond young man. He lived with Giacomo the farrier and mucked out Clara's carriage horses every day. In a month his hands had hardened and his jaunty round face was peppered with freckles, yet he never lost his slack stomach. He looked Italian, but never a countryman. Funny Pietro. With five Pietros in the village he was called Pietro Simone on his false papers.

Not that his name was used much. Giacomo was a deaf-mute and slow-witted besides, and the people of San Martino della Croce had little inclination for conversation. Pietro was largely ignorant of the affairs of her estate. For his own sake it seemed wisest that the young Bolognese remain uninformed.

By contrast the Marshal of Ponte Maggiore, seated alongside Pietro, knew more than anyone about Guy. He wore a black armband for his son, missing presumed dead on the Russian front. His narrow face, even on this festival day, was lined with private grief. He hated the Germans.

Clara's restless gaze fixed now on Stefano, the shock-haired, clubfooted farmer from the first of the foothill hamlets, the region's herbalist. Very thin, tall, his skeletal appearance was at variance with his prodigious appetite. He would sell anything, even poison, for a bowlful of pasta. Clara nodded across the table to the gaunt giant, reflecting that if Stefano sold Guy she would certainly suggest to the police that they investigate Stefano's illegal still. Always nervous of police poking into his affairs, was Stefano.

The Fioretti twins of Castel San Martino – seated next to the herbalist and surrounded by a pile of spent wine bottles – knew Guy solely as Mario. If they suspected anything else they would not care. For fifty years the Fiorettis and a Croce family, the Patuzzis, had been involved in a feud over some long-forgotten insult. Even as Clara studied them the twins were glaring at wiry, toothless Signor Patuzzi, who glowered back. His younger cousin Davide, the coffin maker from the second hamlet, sat stroking his stubble with a silver fork, measuring the twins with slanting black eyes. Occasionally the coffin maker cleared his throat and spat in the dust – though never anywhere near the Fiorettis. On saints' days feuds were supposed to be forgotten, yet everyone had something they wished to remain hidden from the outside world. Clara as the Contessa, the one with power in the region, knew more secrets than the parish priest.

The priest. Her charity – really wages – helped him to live as a gentleman in the country. There were others too who were grateful to Clara. Meeting the glowing, arabic-looking features of one such man, she was rewarded with a solemn bow of the head. Umberto Gasparini from the third hamlet remembered how Clara had refused all rents due on his tenant

farm during 1937, a year of bad harvests for the Gasparinis
when their vines had failed. Guy had told them how to clear
and disinfect their land. Clara could reel off the names of
another three families whom her husband had helped in the
same way. And, she reminded herself, Davide Patuzzi was a
tenant for whom she had waived due rents for *this* year. For
any of these to turn against Guy would be a great dishonour.
They would never be trusted again by anyone in the five
settlements.

Vittorio, Mayor of Castel San Martino, was different.
Honour had no meaning for him; he took bribes shamelessly.
His was the name which occurred in every crooked deal in
the region, but he was shrewd enough to cover his tracks so
that there would be no proof. He even managed to be popular.

The richest man in Castel, Vittorio was a man who aspired
to the good things in life. There would be a price to pay for
his silence. How much? She needed to know.

Clara motioned to two women to refill the German guards'
glasses. If Krusak could play a waiting game, so could she.
Sometime before the party broke up, when the guards had
more wine and food in them, Guy would be able to slip away.
He could take Angelica and go to the charcoal burners' camp
in the woods. Then whatever happened, whatever Krusak had
learned from Vittorio, Guy and Angelica would be free.

Clara glanced down the trestle. This year, on her advice,
mothers with young children had stayed away. Angelica, the
only little girl at the feast, was with the strawberry pickers,
out of range of Krusak's hearing, and being fussed over to
her heart's content. With her hair brushed into gleaming
waves and in her new blue dress – cut from three pillow-slips
– Angelica shone in the late afternoon light. A person would
need to be made of stone not to be moved by her, thought
Clara. She would do everything necessary to protect her.

'You should congratulate me, Princess.' Krusak's measured
voice, his continued ironic use of that title, made Clara look
across at him again – Guy was also looking and she nudged
him under the table, a reminder to her husband that he
understood no Italian. As Guy's face lost its blaze of interest

and settled back into an appearance of pleasant, drunken
reverie – a look he had maintained for most of the feast –
Clara asked Krusak why he should be complimented. 'You
must allow me to thank you for the fresh coffee,' she went on.
'It was a kind thought.'

Krusak dismissed his gift with a turn of his glass. 'It was
nothing.' He watched the dark vermouth sticking to the sides
of the glass. 'This is excellent. You must have a master vintner
on your estate.'

Guy, draining his vermouth in a single swallow, was looking
hot. Clara tapped on the table. 'Your news, Signor Krusak?'

'Two days ago, we captured fifteen partisans and ten Italian
deserters. I believe that when we have finished questioning
them, it will finally be possible to make this area safe.'

'Indeed,' murmured Clara, rubbing her twitching right eye.
Her head was aching: this feast was going on too long.

'Do you doubt me, Princess?' Krusak stretched in his seat,
lighting a cigar from one of the lanterns hanging in the trees.
These had just been lit and a smell of oil tainted the air. Krusak
inhaled, as though enjoying the scent, or his cigar, or the
situation: possibly all three. He leaned forward, pushing his
plate away with his elbows as a small boy might, but the pistol
on his belt struck the trestle with a heavy thud.

'People in this region appreciate what we are doing,' he
remarked, breathing smoke through delicately flared nostrils,
'They understand the strong arm as a bulwark against
anarchy.'

The young officer drew his gun. 'Allow me to demonstrate.'

The force of the pointblank blast hurled Vittorio and his
chair backwards. His scream was a shriek of total shock and
horror, the sound starting high and ratcheting higher, filling
the cold silence. The chair legs twitched as Vittorio jerked,
blood frothing from his mouth and a raw hole in his belly.

Without rising from his chair or relinquishing his cigar,
Krusak fired a second time. Vittorio's screams were cut short,
stopping before the echoes of the gunshot had faded.

Krusak motioned to his standing guards to remove the
body.

'Your pardon, Princess.' He clipped the pistol back into its holster, 'The man was a traitor to the Reich and to his country. I learned today that he collaborated with Communists and partisans: anyone in fact for the right price.'

If a gun had been within reach Clara might have used it: instead she had to make do with words. 'You kill a guest of my house, abuse all laws of decency, and speak of traitors?'

Krusak smiled. 'Let us not be hasty . . .'

Guy, who had leapt to his feet, took a swing at the smug young face. Clara grabbed his arm. 'No!' she shouted.

A spasm passed over Guy's regular features and then he relaxed sufficiently to throw off Clara's hand and push past the hovering German guard. Clara found herself holding her breath until he reached Angelica.

The child, face doll-blank in shock, allowed herself to be picked up. 'Is he dead?' she whispered. Guy cuddled her close and carried her away, throwing a final glance to his wife.

Clara sat down again, hearing the priest mumble the prayer for the dead. No one else moved or spoke.

Clara closed her eyes. She felt sick.

'It was necessary. These hill dwellers must be taught not to obstruct progress.' Krusak poured wine from his glass into her own, held out the glass. 'Come. Do not distress yourself. He was not one of your men.'

'Do you think that makes a difference?' Clara glared at the guards: she could not bear to look at Krusak. A movement from one of the tables arrested her gaze. It was the blond youth, the one who had thrown her the flowers. He was being sick.

Clara promised herself that the Croatian would inflict nothing else on them. She would do everything necessary to keep San Martino della Croce free of Germans, Allies, or partisans. Let others kill; up here they would not be drawn in to this never-ending blood-bath.

'You disgust me.' Clara extracted the glass from Krusak's fingers and pointedly set it down without drinking. She was so furious that her Italian deserted her. 'You shoot a man like a dog on my property, in front of my servants, in front of my child—' Clara switched to German, determined that Krusak and his guards should understand: 'You are monsters!'

For an instant Krusak's poise was pierced: he coloured. Then the blinkered look of self-confidence flowed over his features again and he drew thoughtfully on his cigar. 'If I seek to bring order out of chaos by unusual means, what of it?' he demanded. 'Was it not Machiavelli who said the end justified the means?'

That does not mean one should enjoy it, thought Clara, but shock had come at last and she shuddered.

'Go,' she said. 'No one will move until you leave.' She motioned down the table at her petrified guests. 'You have achieved your purpose, now get out.'

Krusak got up from the table. *We have not finished yet*, his look told her.

Finally it was over. The guests had gone, the trestles taken down, the plates and glasses washed and put away. Clara, rubbing at a bloodstain on the sash of her dress, closed the door to Angelica's bedroom, said goodnight to Dolores, the child's nurse, and walked downstairs to her husband.

'Sound asleep.' Clara yawned herself. She glanced at the elderly footman near the front door, fingering his collar, bald head beaded with sweat and no doubt itching under the powdered wig. Tonight Luigi, like herself, would be glad to get out of his formal clothes. Clara motioned him away, waiting until she could no longer hear his wooden shoes clicking on the tiles. When she heard the door to Luigi's small downstairs chamber close, she spoke. 'You should be in bed, too, Guy. Why not snatch an hour before you leave?'

'I'm not going anywhere.'

Clara, freed of the presence of servants, sat down on the bottom step. 'Please.' She tugged at her husband's jacket to emphasise the point, 'This isn't the time for heroics. Krusak's not only cruel, he's cunning: he'll want to lull us into a sense of false security, catch us in bed—'

'You perhaps.' Guy took her hands between his, breathing on her wedding ring and polishing it gently with his thumb.

'I've seen the way he looks at you.'

'Don't!' With Vittorio dead, Guy's semi-caress, the glimpse of that white throat through his open collar, were almost obscene. 'Listen, Guy, you must go tonight. Take Angelica; the villagers will look after her. Don't tell me where you're going and then Krusak won't be able to force it from me. I'll tell him you had to return to Calabria unexpectedly; then after a few days when everything's died down you can come back . . .'

He stood looking down at her, smiling with his dark blue eyes, chestnut hair pressed into damp coils by the sultry June night. 'And how would I have got through the British lines?' he asked. 'You know it won't do, Clara. What sort of man would I be, to leave my wife behind to face the music?'

'Sensible for one thing,' snapped Clara, wringing her hands from his. 'Why do you English make a joke of everything?' She threw all the pleading she knew into her voice. 'Please, Guy.'

'If I smile, it's not because I'm laughing at you.' Guy crouched on the step beside her. 'I'm frightened, Clara,' he said. 'Frightened for you and Angelica. I'd like you and her to cross over the mountains into Switzerland. Tonight would be a good time to start.'

'And how would you live if I left? No, Guy, we leave as a family or not at all. Besides, I have responsibilities here. I cannot simply desert my tenants.' They had held this conversation, or something similar, over and over in the last few months until Clara was sick of it. She reached round behind herself, plucking wearily at the buttons on her dress, when Guy's next words jolted her completely.

'Not even if I come with you?'

He was deadly serious: she could tell by the way his eyes made her look at him. He knelt before her, unbuttoning his shirt, her Etruscan come to life. 'Well?' he said.

'I don't understand,' said Clara, blinking as the rising evening star shone in on them through the open door. Guy was as attached to the land he worked as any Italian peasant. 'You've always rejected the idea before.' Her heart was hammering, bursting the barriers of custom and obligation. No one could blame her if she left with her husband. This was a way out for them both, an escape . . .

Guy was still a moment. Starlight moved over him from the door and windows, bars of radiance and shade. He was as unreal as Orion, the stuff of fantasy, thought Clara. Sometimes she wished she did not love him so much, then maybe she would not worry so much.

Her husband cursed again in English, dragged savagely at his right ear with his left hand. 'Times change,' he said. 'Rome's fallen to the Allies – No!' he cut short her exclamation of hope. 'The Germans are falling back to regroup behind the Apennine mountains; it'll take months to dislodge them. There'll be no quick end, and the Germans are desperate. This isn't their country, they won't care what they do to it or the people. Tonight showed that things are getting even worse.'

Clara knew what Guy meant by 'things'. 'Things' were the punishments the Germans visited upon families discovered helping escaped Allied prisoners, 'things' were the shootings and deportations which occurred in villages after the partisans had blown up a road or bridge or sabotaged a train.

'Things have been getting worse since the Germans invaded,' she said, 'and no one has talked. People here have known you for almost ten years. You are one of us. Your child plays with the village children. Why should you be denounced now?'

'You know why.' Guy and Clara looked at each other, not speaking for a moment, knowledge passing silently between them.

Guy sighed. 'And then the Blackshirts have been threatening for some time to burn villages, shoot everyone in them, unless all aliens are handed over.' He lowered his hands. 'You know they mean it, Clara.' Since the Germans had established the Salò Republic, governing the north and centre of the country as a puppet state with Mussolini at its head, the Italian Fascist party had been re-formed. Drawn from the most right-wing of Mussolini's supporters, its members, called

Blackshirts, were often more fanatical than the Nazis.

'Yes, I know these new Fascists are worse than the Germans,' said Clara, 'But then no one is innocent in war.' She broke off, frowning. 'Would they trouble us here? It's not as though we were down on the plain, these villages are remote. And I've done what I can to discourage political extremists of any kind.'

Guy's blue eyes turned cold. 'Usually it's better to allow others to decide for themselves.' He knelt looking at her, his gaze softening as he traced his wife's maternal curves, the suggestion of a double chin. He sighed and shook his head.

'The Germans have known for months that several resistance groups are in these mountains. Vittorio tells me – told me – that they and the Blackshirts are probably going to move against the partisans again soon in another round-up . . .'

'*Vittorio* was the one that warned you? When?'

'When he arrived. You don't have to look so worried: Krusak wasn't in earshot and Vittorio said it in dialect.'

'Yes, but Vittorio . . . What if Krusak knows? Maybe this is their way to make you break cover.'

Guy licked his lips: the laughter was back in his voice again. 'You worry too much.' He drew her close, letting her feel his skin as his shirt folds enveloped them both, and began kissing the vestiges of lipstick from her mouth.

8

When the alarm woke her she was in bed, naked and languid after their lovemaking. Perhaps it had been a mistake for Guy to kiss her, but she did not think so. Besides, war made you do crazy things.

Knocking off the officious little bell with a sleepy hand which sent the alarm spinning onto the floor tiles, Clara squinted at the English grandfather clock set in the recess opposite the four-poster. It was not yet three, still early for any escape. She rolled over, propping herself on an elbow. 'We'll need to dress warmly, it'll be cold on the mountains . . .' She stopped. The rest of the bed was empty, the sheets crumpled but cool.

Lying on the bolster was a note. Clara lit a candle and read. 'Had to go out. Be ready for five. Burn this.'

Where had he gone? thought Clara, watching the flame shrivel the paper. Why had he gone? Why tonight, of all nights?

She could no longer stay in bed. Clara kicked aside a pillow and flung back the doors to Guy's wardrobe. He had taken his boots, warmest trousers and jacket, his water flask, hunting knife and compass. Not the rucksack.

A pile of underclothes and socks lay on the bottom of the wardrobe; Clara scooped these out and bundled them into the rucksack. Everything they could take must be fitted into this pack: they would need their hands to climb.

She dressed, packed the essentials, then crossed the landing to Angelica's room. In the next room Dolores was snoring. Her daughter was asleep and Clara could not bear to wake her; let Angelica rest whilst she could, she thought, bending over the snuffling child and kissing the sunburnt forehead. Slowly, giving each item a small caress, she spread out her daughter's clothes on the end of the bed, the tiny boots, trews and coat she would wear on their escape.

Angelica's best dress, which she had worn for her first confession, would have to be left. Clara lifted the long frilled dress from the chest, laid her cheek against the white folds, remembering how serious Angelica had looked when wearing it. Had that been only this summer? Clara let the dress go and replaced the lid.

She glanced at her wristwatch: three-thirty. Where was Guy now? What was he doing? Perhaps if she went out onto the balcony of their bedroom she would see him returning.

A knock on the outer door froze her between landing, bedroom and stairs, and then she was running downstairs, ahead of Luigi, the elderly retainer, ahead of Dolores, the plump nurse. Their faces, puckered and foolish in sleep, made Clara want to strike them in frustration. These people, they were so slow.

She flung open the door. Outside was a blond boy – not the one who had thrown her the flowers, this youth was older. It was a clear night and he carried a lantern. This was unlit because of the sign it might give to enemy aircraft. In the distance was the dull thunder of an Allied bombing raid.

Clara could never remember his name, only his nickname, Sprint. Six months ago in a bar in Bologna, Sprint's father had been forced to drink castor oil by a hooded man wielding a shot-gun. This humiliating 'punishment', used by Blackshirts to 'purge' their victims of impure thoughts or words against Mussolini, had a dramatic effect on Sprint himself. He became withdrawn, dropped out of school and looked with cold-eyed hatred on any possible sympathiser with the Duce.

If Sprint had come then it could only be bad news. Clara dragged the youth inside. 'What is it?'

'Mario's been hurt,' Sprint told her, without so much as a greeting or glance at the shivering Luigi or sulky Dolores, standing on the bottom step of the stairs, her hips straining the seams of one of Clara's old night-dresses.

'How badly is he hurt?' demanded Clara.

At seventeen, the boy was as impenetrable as stone. 'He's badly stunned, but he'll live. He's been taken somewhere safe. He must be moved tomorrow because of the German patrols.'

From the corner of her eye Clara saw Dolores suppress a yawn of tiredness and tension. Guy was lying hurt somewhere – in a barn, a ditch, on somebody's kitchen table: the boy had not said where – and all Angelica's nurse could do was rub her eyes. For an instant Clara hated her.

'What happened?'

Sprint, showing a touch of feeling, lowered his cold green eyes. 'Blackshirts almost caught us.'

He continued in a rapid whisper. 'Your cousin Mario,' – the boy was scrupulous in using Guy's alias – 'met four of us late tonight at the Inn. I can't give the names of our group: the less you know, the better for you and yourself. There was a cache of small arms collected from disbanded Italian servicemen buried in the Inn yard: it was our job to get the guns to our supporters in the mountains.'

'A partisan group?' asked Clara faintly. She had long suspected that Guy was involved in something of the kind, although whenever she asked he said it was nothing except straight black-market trading, which after all, one had to do in secret, preferably after curfew . . . He usually brought coffee or cigarettes back with him after such midnight scrambles, displaying them as proof. She had learned not to inquire too closely after Guy's absences, which had been growing even more frequent of late—

Sprint coughed and nodded. 'Yes, partisans,' he murmured. 'We helped them whenever we could, brought them weapons and food. Tonight it was guns. But we were betrayed.'

Clara thought of the bundle of corncockles, symbol of betrayal. Someone had tried to warn Guy. Why had he not heeded the warning? Despite her desperate worry, she felt a flash of anger against her husband. Why had he had to leave her and Angelica on the very night they'd planned to escape?

'. . . So we were in the Inn yard with a sack each,' Sprint was saying, 'when suddenly there were lights, men in black uniforms, dogs. We ran back through the barns and into the vines. We lost them there, but then Mario collapsed. He was ahead of me when suddenly he disappeared. When I reached him his speech was thick: he'd stumbled over an old vine stump, struck his head when he fell. He couldn't walk very well.'

Sprint jabbed a bony arm in the direction of the village and finished tersely. 'We got him somewhere safe, but Mario's still dazed.'

'Take me to him.' Clara turned to her servants. 'Luigi, fetch my sponge, a towel, soap and smelling salts from my dressing table. Hurry! Dolores, go back upstairs and stay with Angelica. Don't leave her! Lock the door to the nursery and leave Luigi to answer the bell. Understand?'

'Yes, Contessa.' Dolores was nodding vigorously. 'I will sleep with the little girl.' She was devoted to Angelica. Simple peasant woman as she was, Dolores would sacrifice herself before her charge. Clara's features softened.

'God keep you,' she said in a low voice. She took the little bundle of toilet things from the returning Luigi, touching the old retainer's hand.

'I will pray for the Signore,' said Luigi.

Sprint, taking that as a signal, slipped out into the darkness. Clara paused, watching Dolores return to the nursery, then she followed.

They scrambled through the grounds and across one corner of the hillside of vines, but not quickly enough for Clara. 'Wait,' she gasped. Grabbing Sprint's arm – he was taller than she was – she kicked off her wooden shoes, leaving them where they fell. 'Now we run.'

The village was in darkness. They skirted the cross of Saint Martin which gave the place its name, sprinted across the little square and out onto the dirt track that was San Martino della Croce's main road. Already out of breath, Clara forced herself to run faster. Until she saw Guy for herself she mustn't think. She mustn't imagine . . .

The youth streaming ahead suddenly dived off the road into the fields, making for a covered truck parked in the middle of newly planted sugar beet. He wriggled under the truck's tarpaulin and then the flap was lifted for Clara. Inside the truck a sudden bruising light as someone flicked a torch directly into her face.

'Clara!'

She recognised Guy's voice, but not his form. Quick as the light had appeared, it was extinguished; there were the sounds of scuffling, repeated blows.

'No!' Blinded by the torch-flash, Clara pitched herself forward towards the moving, hooded shadows, begging whoever it was who held her husband to stop.

Amazingly, it did. And then she heard another voice say, 'Blindfold them. Take them to the usual place.'

The fire had almost gone out. The fern-entwined mantelpiece clock had stopped. Clara completed her final floral arrangement for that evening before she spoke again. She surveyed it, then pushed it across the lacquer table to Julia. 'You can take this with you to your room when you retire.'

Julia cupped a wired pink between her fingers and sat very still in her armchair, feeling the clammy leather against her back. She had joined Clara in this flower-filled, rococo room hours ago: now the apple-wood scent had faded. The amazing candle chandelier – left burning at Clara's insistence when Andrea had retired – wept wax from its polished brass candle holders all the way down the brass stems. It hung above them like a crown of branches dipped in hoar.

Julia shivered, listening to a tree branch whipping against the shutters. She had no idea what time it was – evening, midnight, dawn – nor even any longer what time she was part of.

'Was that Scarpia?' Her mouth seemed to burn with the name. 'Or Krusak?'

'We were driven around.' Clara continued as though Julia

had not spoken. 'I kept hearing the sound of anti-aircraft guns and so knew it was late, but I lost all sense of where we might be going. Then finally the truck stopped and we were hauled into some kind of underground shelter – I knew it was underground because it was so cold. There were two rooms: Guy was thrown into one and I was thrown into the other. I banged on the metal door that separated us; I struck it so hard it rang like a gong. And then someone whispered in the other room, "Unless you tell me the names of your group, your 'cousin' – or should I say wife – will be next after the music."

'That was Scarpia, that whisper, that threat! Scarpia thrived on mental cruelty. Spoletta did the torturing but Scarpia gave the orders.'

'Spoletta – Scarpia's second?' Rising from her seat, Julia plucked the fire tongs from their holder. Clara seemed oblivious of what she was doing, although when Julia had found some chopped pine in a silver plated fuel-box and set some to burn, the old lady leaned forward to warm her hands.

'That was his nickname,' she answered. 'I never knew his true name. Something I do remember of him, a thing that could not be hidden by a blindfold, was that he was young. Sixteen, certainly no more than seventeen.'

'And Scarpia?' asked Julia, settling in the chair again, 'He was older?'

Clara did not hear: she was reliving that night. In the spitting flames of the burning pine her profile was as pale and rigid as a cameo.

The tree branch outside resumed its tapping on the shutters. Julia, sensing that Clara needed to talk but at her own pace, fed the fire to keep them warm. When her grandmother spoke again, the scene had changed.

'There were six of them in that vile chamber where they took me next. I never knew their names, only that they were Blackshirts, the kind that looked to the Nazis for inspiration.' She shrugged her bony shoulders. 'Krusak may have been one of them, though if he was he never spoke. I do not believe he was there. Other men were in control, *Italian* men.'

Julia stiffened, thinking of Clara and Guy being at the mercy of such men. And Angelica, her mother, perhaps waking in the middle of the night and wondering why her nurse was sleeping with her . . .

'They strapped me to a table,' Clara was saying. 'My blindfold was loose. I caught glimpses of them as they moved. They had removed their hoods.' She had picked up the flower scissors again and was opening and closing the blades in dull, repetitive movements. 'One – a youth, I think – had a mole on his right cheek, close to the jaw. One had dark stubble and a deep cleft in his chin. Another, who was blond, had an earring in his left ear. All were from the mountains. All spoke – whispered – the same dialect, the one used in San Martino della Croce, Castel San Martino and the three hamlets.'

'The partisan village? Your own people?' This was horrible: men Clara and Guy might have known, at least by sight, probably more than that. But then, as Clara's account had implied, Sprint, the blond youth who had led her to the truck, must have betrayed both her and her husband.

Perversely, Clara seemed to find this amusing. 'Of course some were involved. Guy and I were popular in the region – Guy I think more than me – but someone informed on us. Local men – who could only have been part-timers in some kind of militia, not regular soldiers – tortured us. Who and why I don't know, even though some of them must have been from my estate.'

Clara touched her mouth and face with her fingers, as though exploring an old injury. 'I knew at the time I should question people, ask around, but after Guy's death none of that seemed important. Discovering who had betrayed Guy would not bring him back to life, and I wanted to get Angelica away.' She sighed and shook her head. 'It is only now, when it is almost too late, that I feel I must know.'

Julia found herself wondering how Guy had died. 'How did you escape that night?'

'Air-raid,' answered Clara bluntly. 'A direct hit. Guy was killed, and I managed to run away whilst they were trying to put out the fires and escape themselves. They didn't expect me to be able to walk, you understand, let alone run. Not after this.' Clara felt under the low table and brought out a crocodile handbag, opened it and produced an old, passport-sized photograph.

The kindness of candle-light, Andrea had said, referring to the chandelier. But now it was not kind; it showed the ruined eye, the scarred cheek. The face, the eyes in the hazy photograph were Julia's own, but on one side frightful.

Scarpia had done that – Julia recoiled at the thought and was instantly ashamed, guessing that Clara might believe her appearance had revolted her. It did, but not in the way Clara might think.

Unfortunately her grandmother had spotted her instinctive movement. Her lips twisted in a smile.

'I see that you appreciate the effect,' she said. 'Angelica, when she saw me for the first time after I'd escaped, ran away into the gardens screaming for her father.'

Seven years old, her mother had seen that. Julia was appalled. 'No wonder—' she stopped.

Clara looked at her coolly through her good eye. 'Children will accept anything, Julia,' she said, using her granddaughter's name for the first time. 'Angelica accepted that I had been hurt, and that it would take a while for me to get better.' She paused and then resumed. 'As soon as I was fit to travel, I covered myself with a veil and moved us from the villa to this house. Pietro helped me.'

'Pietro Terni?' Julia remembered the five other Pietros from Clara's estate. The older woman nodded.

'Pietro Terni found me.' Realising further explanation was needed, Clara added, 'After the air-raid I don't remember much – I knew Guy was dead; I knew I had to get away. Where I ran, I don't know.'

She dropped the handbag onto the marble hearth at her feet. 'Snatches, that's all I can tell you. My feet pounding dirt, slipping on grass. My face and hands sticky with blood. And then for a long time nothing except thirst. The doctors told me later that I lost a day.

'Pietro was out with the horses when he found me. It was

on the track to Ponte Maggiore at the bottom of the mountain; I was crawling towards a stream. I remember that moment vividly: he brought me water in the horse pail.'

Clara's mouth twitched. 'He was crying, young Pietro.' Her voice was as dry as the fire. 'He burst into tears as soon as he saw me.'

A pine log spat and both of them jumped. They sat quietly for a moment.

'I'm glad you left San Martino della Croce,' said Julia then. Taking the photograph from Clara, she stared at it.

'I should never have fallen asleep. I should have stopped Guy from leaving,' Clara was saying. 'Why did he go out that night? My fault.' She was trembling.

'I wish I could help,' said Julia.

Clara, to her amazement, laughed. 'You look so much like me and you act so much like Guy.' She leaned forward, running a finger down Julia's cold cheek before she kissed her.

The easy kiss shook Julia, though not half as much as the evening's revelations. 'You're family,' she said seriously.

Clara patted her hand. 'I think it is more than that,' she answered. 'I know how many concerts you give for charity. When I said you are like Guy, it is because the plight of others moves you.' She stroked the right side of her face, smoother now than the left because of the plastic surgery. '*That* is why you want to help—'

Clara broke off. 'I am in torment,' she whispered. 'The thought of him and the others free, enjoying life, while I rot here and Guy rots underground. Justice is what I want. To find Scarpia. To find all of them. If they are still alive I want to look into their faces when the magistrate sends them to prison.'

'If they're alive,' said Julia, '*I'll* find them.'

Her grandmother sighed and sat back in her chair. 'You will not like what I tell you now,' she began hesitantly. 'I never saw them properly, you understand, but they made sure I heard them. Each time before they began ... music. One of the young men – I think it was Spoletta – was a good singer. The guards and Spoletta rarely *said* anything and when they did they always *spoke* in whispers, disguising their voices.

Scarpia himself spoke in whispers, but then sometimes . . .'

Clara shuddered. 'It must have been Scarpia,' she muttered. 'The sound was fuller, more mature. Trained, you understand?' She sagged in her chair.

Julia for a ghastly moment thought she might laugh, the idea was so bizarre. Was this what Scarpia had meant by the phrase 'after the music'? Singing torturers – yet why else the nicknames? 'It's impossible.'

'Why?' snapped Clara. 'You think saints inhabit your precious musical universe? I know he is out there, somewhere in your world. He must be: that voice was too good to waste – it was exceptional. Even I knew that. And what better place to hide oneself than a public stage where you are always on view yet buried behind a mask of character?'

Would these men still be performing? thought Julia. Her mind was moving slowly; she forced it to work, to go forward, for Clara's sake. Certainly not Scarpia himself, she decided, unless for occasional masterclasses. As for the other, if sixteen or seventeen in 1944 Spoletta would be in his mid-sixties now – late for a singer, but possible. Yet would his voice be recognisable? Voices change over time and to a man or woman in pain . . .

'Of course I have been to the opera since the war.' Clara's voice was quiet again. 'But on stage it sounds so different. Besides, opera was Guy's passion. I have listened on the radio and it sounds like so much noise – beautiful noise, I grant you, but to me many voices blur into one.'

She flinched, as though in pain. 'Do you understand now? Scarpia is someone like you.'

9

29th November, Milan

'Sandro, can you come over? I want to be in Florence by ten, spend the day free before that competition. Dad's sleeping now, but I don't want him left alone too long. Sorry to ask—'

'Dad having his nightmares again? Thought so . . . Don't mention it, Roberto. Margherita and I are happy to help. Yes, we've a key. Go and enjoy the ruins and galleries. Driving yourself, you madman?'

'I've hired an automatic, should be no problem. Sandro, I need another favour. Can you give me a contact in the Naples Police? There are a few things I want to look into when I'm down there.'

'Nothing to do with the men of honour, I hope.'

'No, nothing like that. Just something Dad mentioned about his wartime experience in Naples that I'd like to check . . . Thanks, Sandro. Be seeing you.'

The hire company had brought the Alfa Romeo to the door. As Roberto finished his phone call to his brother it was waiting, sleek in a typically Milanese early morning mist. Flinging his case in the boot, Roberto shunted back the driver's seat, climbed in and accelerated along the Via Manin.

Milan's lethal traffic system kept all thoughts except survival at bay, but once on the Autostrada heading for Florence he could leave his foot on the accelerator and concentrate on his father's story.

* * *

'I was there,' Simone had kept repeating, 'in that chamber of horrors. Nothing was too cruel. And always music . . .'

Roberto could only watch as his father wept. 'What music?' he asked, when Simone was quieter. 'What do you mean?'

'Singing. A man's voice; sometimes a record, sometimes not. Always the same role: the Chief of Police from *Tosca*; the signal that torment would soon resume . . . Someone, maybe the Englishman, called it "The Whisperer's Entrance". Yes, it was the Englishman, although he was held for only a few hours . . .'

Roberto had a soft spot for the English: they were polite to him at Covent Garden, fair-minded. That thought flashed through as his mind ran ahead, taking in the full implications of what his father was saying. It confirmed his worst suspicions.

He had been uneasy for some time, particularly these last two months. Simone's nightmares, beginning after his wife's death, had been infrequent at first: lately they had been becoming more regular, growing more vivid. Staying with him until Simone slept soundly again, Roberto had guessed from things which his father muttered in his sleep that he was troubled by some wartime recollection, some memory which was resurfacing after many years' dormancy.

Now, conscious of the older man's pride, Roberto resisted the impulse to embrace him. Such obscenities as torture went on in war, were even to be expected, yet why did his father, the most sensitive of men, have to be a victim? The worst was that Simone would have been very young.

'Always the helpless,' he murmured.

'No, the man was given tea!' Simone, catching Roberto's darkening expression and misunderstanding it, snapped his fingers in front of his son's face. 'Maybe he wasn't touched: I never heard him cry out. Does that make you feel better, salve your precious conscience? Pah, what would you know? Partisans, Fascists, they were as bad as each other.'

'And the Englishman?' asked Roberto softly.

'He was one of the leaders of the partisans.'

'Such men accepted him?' Given the narrow loyalty of Italian villagers, Roberto was immediately sceptical. 'Who was he – a spy parachuted in to help some resistance movement?'

Simone shook his head. 'The Englishman was already well-known in the district; he married a local girl before the war. *She* was tortured in his hearing, to make him talk.'

Roberto felt his guts grow cold. There were questions he would have to ask, but not yet. 'Who was the Whisperer?'

He watched his father shudder. 'No one ever saw his face. Prisoners were blindfolded. It was always dark. No one saw him.'

Simone was moving in the bed, a strange sideways rocking, like a baby in a crib. 'Always dark. Always underground. And the singing—' He shut his eyes and the rocking grew fiercer. Suddenly his lashes snapped apart. 'Have you never wondered why I studied the viola after the war instead of the voice? Sandro asked me once, but I couldn't tell him: your mother was alive then and I wanted to bury the past. Now, with her gone, with all these show trials, I can't stop remembering.

'You don't want to ask what they did to me, do you, Roberto? You don't want to know about the burning, the beatings, the water. But it's too late.'

His father began to laugh. Simone was still laughing when he told Roberto what had happened to him on those summer evenings fifty years before, when he was just fourteen . . .

Thinking back, speeding through Florence and past the Porta al Prato with the invincibility of a local, Roberto felt again the rage and frustration that had overwhelmed him in the face of Simone's suffering: pain which had not ended with the cessation of war. Simone's horror of water, his hatred of *Tosca* – these strange manias were explained. As a child, Roberto had not understood why Daddy would never paddle in the sea like other fathers; now he knew better. Last night, Simone had shown him the soles of his feet, scars which had made walking a torment.

Glancing in the driving mirror, Roberto saw himself white with anger, wide, almost Slavic eyes glinting. If the bastard responsible for hurting his father were still alive, he'd find him. And when he did . . . That was why he wanted to keep Sandro out of it: his younger brother had a wife and son to consider.

Swerving up to the modest front entrance of the Teatro Comunale, parking in a space marked for competition judges, Roberto limped rapidly away from the music theatre.

Until he reached Naples there was nothing more he could do. Now he had time to kill and he knew where he would spend part of it. In that most medieval of places – church.

10

'Less draughty, isn't it?'

The question was addressed to her. Yawning, Julia raised her head from her music score. 'I beg your pardon?'

'This modern opera house. It's not draughty like the old ones. Have you seen the dressing-rooms? They're comfortable!'

The man slid into the next seat. 'You're Julia Rochfort.'

The orchestra was gathering for the first full-blown rehearsal of the opera competition, but Julia resigned herself to the fact that she would not be able to study her pieces one last time before she was called onto the stage.

'Guilty as charged.' She closed her score. Turning in her stall seat, she was disconcerted to find a pair of dark brown eyes fixed on her open coat. Sticky with nerves and her vocal warm-up in a practice room, Julia wondered for a dreadful moment if other buttons were undone. She decided to brazen it out, smiling in guileless fashion whilst she buried her hands in her pockets and cut down the view.

'What time are you on?' She indicated the stage with her foot.

'After you. Around ten-thirty.' The young man realised he was staring and coloured from his prominent cheekbones and Grecian nose to his narrow chin. Jerking his head aside, he almost collided with the wall.

It seemed clear why he had come so much earlier than necessary to his rehearsal. Julia was touched and flattered. On-stage she courted admiration, off-stage was different.

She was also puzzled. She thought she knew every competitor: she had met them yesterday morning at the first piano-accompanied rehearsals before her dramatic evening in Florence, but this fine-boned man was a stranger. How had he seen her when she had missed him? She tried to set him at ease. 'You're a tenor?' She guessed the pitch from his clearly articulated voice.

'Right!' The young man grinned. 'The new Pavarotti!' He bounced to his feet, whipping a handkerchief from his jeans pocket. 'Without the beard.'

Or the body, Julia thought. He was small for a singer, as she was.

'One metre sixty-five, if you're wondering.' The tenor touched the top of his dark blond, straight hair.

Julia smiled. Five foot five, she thought. She had decided that he was all right, that she liked him. An underlying shyness, despite odd moments of bravado, brought out the protective in her. 'I didn't see you here yesterday.' Keeping an eye on the platform, Julia saw the orchestra taking off coats and readjusting music stands.

'That's because of my engagements. I've been standing in for someone at Lucca.' He revealed this information with just the right amount of casualness, Julia noticed. 'Yesterday I came in late – that's how I caught a glimpse of you, when your rehearsal over-ran.' The tenor's brown eyes widened. 'You're very dramatic.'

'I hope that's a compliment!' laughed Julia. On the stage, the first violin had emerged. The rest of the orchestra broke into ironic applause. Julia rose to her feet.

'I have to go,' she said, gathering her music. 'Good luck with your performance, – ?'

'Francesco,' said the slim young man. 'Francesco Terni. Do you know what we have in common?' he added, keeping her a few moments longer as the orchestra began to tune up, 'My father comes from Bologna, like you.'

The same name. The same city. Julia was too struck by the force of coincidence to contradict Francesco Terni's assumption of her birthplace. 'What's your father called?'

With a dazzling smile, Francesco Terni handed Julia her final score. 'He's called Pietro,' he said. 'And I'll be very jealous if you say you know him.'

'No,' said Julia hurriedly. 'I don't.'

Her appallingly early rehearsal went well. After that, the morning had gone downhill. Julia wasted half an hour in the public library, attempting to extract information from a moody librarian.

Recalling the encounter as she walked, Julia closed her mouth with a snap, biting her tongue, an accident not designed to improve her temper. The man – it had to be a man – had been pleasant at first: it was her clumsiness which had made him otherwise.

She had approached the desk. 'Could you tell me where I'll find the historical archive collections?'

'You could try Rome: I'm afraid that's where most of them are these days.' The librarian, a darkly handsome man in his fifties, smiled and rose to his feet.

'What kind of information are you looking for?' He booted up the computer reserved for staff use.

'Local history, records dealing with the last war. I'm particularly interested in any Fascist groups operating in Tuscany or Emilia.' Julia knew she was covering old ground explored by Clara, but she hoped that with the passage of time more information would have emerged. She also needed to check for herself: Clara could easily have missed a music term which might be a vital lead in her search for Scarpia.

'It's not the Koch gang you want?' The librarian tapped the keys of the glowing screen.

'I'm not sure,' Julia answered. 'Who were they?'

Wanting to learn about the kind of men she was after, Julia didn't interrupt the librarian's explanation, even when it became clear that the cocaine-sniffing Koch and his band of thugs were not the men she was after. They had certainly

indulged in torture – to an extent that even the Gestapo were
revolted by their activities – but had operated in Milan, from
a house known as the Sad Villa.

Julia, leading over the librarian's shoulder as he called up
the names of the gang on the staff computer, drew in a sharp
breath when she read what was on the screen.

'Yes, a woman was with them.' The librarian touched the
name with his pen. 'Luisa Ferida was an actress: it's said she
found her finest role at the Villa Triste.'

Julia shook off her horror at a woman being involved. 'I'm
searching for someone who lived near a village in Emilia
Romagna called San Martino della Croce,' she explained more
fully. 'Someone who collaborated with the Germans during
the war.'

The librarian reached over to the wall socket, pulled the
plug, and the screen blinked off. 'Try another library, then.'
He pushed past, stalking to his desk.

What had she said? He had been so helpful, yet now – Julia
raised her chin. 'Are there no records for that village?'

'Not here.' He glared up at her from his swivel seat, all the
ease stripped from his dark face. 'You another journalist, or
are you just looking for kicks?'

'I don't think I deserved that.' Julia was shaken not so much
by the man's sudden, inexplicable hostility, but by her own
desire to justify herself. It was a bad trait for a performer; she
didn't have to explain to anyone.

She approached the desk for the last time. 'Goodbye.' The
man did not answer. It had been a frustrating exchange, yet
she had learned one important fact.

The war threw a long shadow. She would have to be careful.

The National Library had been closed at 11.15 a.m. – no reason
given. Stalking away from the colonnaded building in a rage,
Julia escaped over the river. Taking any street without a troupe
of admiring visitors on its pavements, or battalions of horn-
happy drivers on its roads, she made her way to the less
fashionable San Frediano district.

Even as she cooled off she could not escape. Clara's voice

kept recurring in her mind, and when she closed her eyes she saw shadows, shadow-faces half-revealed.

By now she had reached Santa Maria del Carmine. Several stone sets in front of the church steps and side entrance had been taken up – why Julia had no idea. She assumed some connection with the drains, and spent no more thought on it other than to skirt carefully past the slim metal posts, cemented into old paint cans, strung with red and white plastic and placed haphazardly around the hole. Glancing at the bare façade of the church, she was surprised to see a figure well-known to her from photographs limping from the building. He stopped in front of the Carmine's shadowy entrance, standing only a few yards from her, a few feet away from the gaping road.

Not that Roberto Padovano, newest judge of the Galatea competition, was interested in drains. He was scrutinising the Carmine's car-filled piazza at his eye level – right over her head. He would not know who she was anyhow. Good: she could steal away. She had a horror of imposing on people.

Pity, she thought, turning aside to go back the way she had come. Even in shabby denims and with a plaster cast on one foot, he was attractive. She liked big, long-legged men. It was a shame he was so dark and decisive-looking, she preferred fair, amenable men. This one, with his shaggy hair and stark, closed-in features, his 'look but do not touch' expression, carried himself as though he knew what he wanted and was not afraid to pursue it. She would have put him in a white shirt instead of that faded black jacket, but then in certain male operatic circles denim seemed to be almost compulsory casual wear. And perhaps he was right to dress in sober colours. White or cream would make him look lumbering, show off more of that chest and shoulders, the thick band of muscle under the ribcage.

Pity, she thought again. Acting on her first impulse to slip away, Julia stepped farther into the street.

'Watch it!'

She started, stopping altogether. A Vespa rider, skidding past with only a foot to spare, lashed at her with one of his gloves – he couldn't do more, because he had a tinsel Christmas tree balanced precariously across the handlebars. He had been forced to brake sharply and swerve to avoid her.

Naturally the man was upset, but Julia did not care if he was. She flashed him a return gesture with her fist, a reaction which enraged the rider so much that he slammed on his illegal klaxon.

'Holy Mother of Christ!' The loud oath was audible even above the resulting cacophony. Whipping round, Julia saw that Roberto Padovano wasn't one to be inhibited by injury; he was bearing down on the Vespa. He looked as though he wanted to strangle someone, and the Christmas-tree rider had decided that it wouldn't be him. Much to Julia's amusement, he took off.

'Oh, so you think that funny do you?' The injured man had misinterpreted her reaction. 'Well maybe if you weren't such an idiot that Vespa wouldn't—'

The rest of this tirade was abruptly cut short. A small dog, streaking through from the nearby green-shuttered Machiavelli School, launched itself in a frenzied attack against Roberto's cast, teeth and jaws worrying at the dirty-white plaster for a grip. With another barrage of curses, the singer shook off the growling dog with a violent kick, sending it hurtling back where it had come from, but together noise, dog, and his own sudden movement had thrown him too far off-balance. As the terrier turned tail and fled, Roberto stumbled, falling towards those metal rods.

Julia never stopped to think; she simply reacted, running forward to grab him. Roberto couldn't avoid her: she put herself in his path.

The resulting collision was like being hit by a toppling statue. The wave of weight and force broke over her and then she could breathe. 'I've got you,' she whispered, still with her arms around him, waiting for the world to stop tilting.

Suddenly the man shook her.

'How long have you been in Florence? Stunts like that can get you killed! And what if the man had been a handbag snatcher? Anything—'

Not a word of thanks. He just stood there, towering over her by a foot, spitting complaints at her. Julia's Italian temper was aroused.

'Oh yes, a handbag snatcher with a Christmas tree, I can just see it. And next time I'll let you splatter yourself all over the piazza. What was I supposed to do, watch you rolling into the gutter like a slab of salami?'

The image was too funny – both of them started to laugh. 'My God.' Roberto's eye fell on the jutting metal scarcely a yard from them. 'I'd have been kebabbed salami. I'm sorry.' He couldn't tell her why he had been so angry, or how alarmed, seeing her almost run down, but he drew his arms tighter about the young woman, supporting her as her head sagged briefly against his chest. He must have hurt her, and indeed, when she raised her face to his a second time, she was frowning.

'Are you hurt? Your leg . . .'

Roberto shook his head. 'I'm fine.' Other throwaway words were forgotten as she looked at him.

Her grey eyes, containing many contradictions – brilliance yet warmth, trust yet wariness, determination yet humour – were the first shock. This woman really saw you.

Her vivid smile made him feel so good that he didn't notice anything else. As it faltered the painter in Roberto recognised an artist's ideal: strong lines, good skin. When she blushed her face didn't mottle but took on an attractive colour, defining that long nose and ample mouth.

'Beautiful,' he murmured spontaneously. He brushed back a wispy curl falling across her forehead; her hand hovered towards his chin where a small bruise was forming.

'Hazards of shaving,' he said, for no particular reason.

He felt her stand on tiptoe and for one glorious instant – that kind of wondering delight he thought he had lost with his youth – Roberto believed she might actually touch him.

Julia shied sideways, banging her head against his shoulder. Roberto Padovano falling on her must have knocked sense as well as breath from her, she thought. What was she doing? Here was one of her competition judges; she was compromising herself and him. Yet she had never felt so safe. Especially now, with the past hanging over her like a sword. With less than a decade between them, this man was of her time, her generation. Francesco Terni might be her contemporary, but Roberto seemed to belong even more to the here and now.

She knew he was looking at her, regarding her with those clear light-brown eyes, the colour of a Tuscan roof-tile but with the shine of sherry. His thick, brown collar-length hair of spiky curls had a kind of side parting – there was no grey in it, nor in the strong black eyebrows, but his sideburns were flecked and he was already getting the two long singer's lines from the side of the nose down to the mouth. He had a strong wide chin and a high broad forehead and his nose was long, aquiline. Roman Emperor, thought Julia giddily, feeling power and danger and attraction all at once.

How was she going to get out of this?

11

Sometimes prosaic things save us. Julia's stomach rumbled.

It broke the spell: they laughed again, released each other.

'You come with me to a late breakfast,' said Roberto, introducing himself whilst stooping carefully to retrieve Julia's bag, knocked from her shoulder. 'Or if you prefer it can be an early lunch: I know a good place.' He held out the bag. 'What—?'

Julia shook her head. She would have to tell him. 'I can't have lunch with you. I'm singing—'

'Ah, this week.' He understood at once. 'And you are?'

'Julia Rochfort.'

'So, Julia Rochfort, you think we shouldn't associate with each other because of the competition?'

Julia, looking directly at him, finally took the bag. 'Would it be appropriate or fair?'

'Is it fair my falling on you? At least let me buy you coffee and brioches. I promise not to talk about opera.'

Roberto lifted her hand in his, cradling her fingers. 'Would you like to see the Masaccio frescos first?' he went on. 'In my opinion they're not as good post-restoration as pre, but it's still a genius at work.'

Julia smiled: it was going to be easy. Conversation was not going to dry up. And although Clara had said time was of the essence in her search for Scarpia, there was little she could do until after the competition. Clara might be happy to live in the past, but she should not.

Besides which, thought Julia, concealing her black curls with her hood to enter church, this man was already established in the opera world. She might be able to pick his brains – discreetly of course – and discover clues that would lead her to the sadist who had, in effect, murdered her grandfather.

'I'd like that,' she said.

Over creamy cappuccino and a sweet brioche at Plini's – the small white-walled café which, according to Roberto, served the best cappuccino in Florence – the two singers discovered common passions in Italian painting, common interests in non-vocal music and literature. When Julia produced her precious copy of Lampedusa's *The Leopard* from her shoulderbag, Roberto laughed.

'Mine's as battered,' he said, running a finger over the faded cover. 'I take it with me on every foreign tour as a good luck charm. Sometimes I even read it.'

Julia, watching him, remembered those same fingers resting gently on her back to guide her into the coffee house. Even for an Italian, Roberto used his hands a great deal: big sweeping cuts, shrugs, raised fingers, open palms, all carried off with natural aplomb. She could understand his reputation as an exciting performer: no gesture would seem too large for him. She wondered why his hands were faintly scarred.

'Is this your first time in Florence?' Roberto's deep voice broke her reverie and she scrambled to retrieve the rest of his question. Following her grandmother's disclosures, she had not slept well at Clara's villa.

'Yes, it's my first time, and yes I like it. People here are alive; they've refused to be buried by the weight of the past.'

'You have to take them on their own terms,' put in Roberto.

'Yes.'

'And you don't find that disconcerting?'

'I'd be a fool if I said I didn't sometimes, but then you have to rise to it, don't you?'

Roberto, who liked his home city for similar reasons, grunted an acknowledgement. 'I think you'll find New York interesting when you go to the States,' he said, returning the wave of a local woman he knew as she passed the café's gleaming windows. 'It's harder to meet people there, but once you do you'll find them very Italian.'

The singer stirred the last of the chocolate grounds vigorously into his coffee, giving the saucer a ringing tap for good measure. 'And the food's nearly as good as in your town,' he added, nodding to a carabiniere, an old school-friend, standing at Plini's mirror-topped bar.

'Oh, I'm not from Bologna,' said Julia. 'That is, my stepfather Enrico was, or is, but I was taken from the country as a baby and brought up in Leeds.'

Aware it must sound confusing, Julia spread her own hands in the same helpless gesture her grandmother had used to her.

'Leeds in England? Where they hold the piano contest?'

Julia nodded. Finding the rest of her brioche suddenly unappetising, she laid it on her plate.

'You speak our language like an Emilian – I assumed you were from Bologna.'

Julia, unable to deny the burst of pleasure and pride this answer gave, nodded again. 'Enrico always spoke Italian with me.'

'But not your mother?'

'No,' she said, 'Angelica preferred English.' Setting down her cup, Julia heard Angelica's voice in her head, saying, as she had on many occasions, 'My life began here in England, why should I think about the boot of Europe? A land of polenta-eaters, corruption and tomatoes, forget Italy.'

'Your parents left Italy to start a new life?'

'I think that's why Angelica emigrated – she met Enrico in Leeds.' Julia regarded Roberto steadily, wanting to see how he took the next sentence. 'I don't know who my natural father is.'

He didn't look away or duck in his reply: 'That must have been tough for you as a child.' Across the small round table,

one of those expressive hands reached for hers. Julia was
ashamed, feeling she had been angling for sympathy.

'Not really,' she answered quickly as Roberto squeezed her
fingers. 'My stepfather was always kind.' She smiled at him,
trying to cover her tracks. There was something about the
man that threw her off-guard, made her want to talk.

Old memories, her own and now Clara's were flooding
back, but Roberto's warm, secure grip kept her hooked to
the present. She felt the pads on his fingers of his left hand
and recalled reading in a magazine that he played the cello.

'How long are you here for?' he asked, changing the subject.

'I've a ticket to go back on the eighteenth, but it all depends
on what happens next week – I might be staying longer.'

Julia frowned. Aside from taking part in the competition,
this was her first holiday in five years. She had been looking
forward to both, but now, with Clara's hopes as well as her
own pinned to her winning, she felt a double obligation to
succeed.

Roberto had released her hand. 'I'm tied up tonight with a
formal reception,' he was saying, 'and of course this week
and next . . .' His hands spoke for him. Biting deep into his
brioche, he got a blob of custard on his chin, and grinned
when Julia touched her own face. 'I know I'm a pig – ' He
wiped his mouth with his napkin – 'and since the boar is one
of the emblems of Florence, I think it only appropriate if I
were to show you around for the rest of today.' He wiped his
mouth again. 'Of course, you may wish to practise or have
other plans . . . I understand this.'

What's wrong with me? thought Roberto. I'm stammering
like a schoolboy. Is time with this woman so important?

He was slightly gap-toothed when he grinned – it was an
unexpected, boyish contrast to his rather forbidding
appearance. Julia had no doubt that Roberto Padovano would
make full use of that contrast when he wanted to, but there
was an honesty in him that made him more than a simple
charmer.

'No – I've two more rehearsals tomorrow: I'm up to here
with practice.' She touched her throat. 'But you're sure it would

be no trouble?' She started rooting in her bag for a wrapped sweet. Like many singers, Julia was concerned about all aspects of her breath. She had once been on the receiving end of an aria where the tenor had eaten garlic.

'Here,' Roberto rolled a packet of mints over the blue table-cloth. 'Not Caruso's brand of digestive aid, I grant you, but very mild.'

He rose to draw back her chair for her – his manners were a touch old-fashioned for thirty-four, Julia thought, but she didn't mind. Picking up her bag, she remembered Francesco Terni staring at her breasts. The man with her now was more subtle in his approach, more dangerous, but she trusted him.

'Can I make a request?' she asked, as he held the door for them. Roberto gave another of his large gestures, putting a potted plant in peril as he invited her to speak.

'Somewhere green. I want to go to a place where there are trees. I'm beginning to feel shut-in with all these buildings.'

'Then we'll go to the Boboli Gardens,' said Roberto, smiling because in this way too they were alike.

Returning with her new companion to the Ponte Vecchio, the bridge she was driven from only yesterday by the man in the red scarf, Julia was soon glad that Roberto was impeded by a plaster cast. His flowing stride was deceptive: he covered a lot of ground.

'I need you to have a handicap,' she exclaimed at one point, dragging at his denim jacket to make him slow down. 'I realise what Eurydice must have felt like, toiling through the underworld watching Orpheus' retreating back.'

Roberto laughed and held out his arm. 'I'm sorry. I forgot how women like to linger over sights.'

'Be thankful I'm not taking you shopping,' answered Julia, laughing herself at Roberto shielding his head with his hands, his expression of mock-horror. She linked arms without even thinking about it. 'You were telling me about Russia . . .'

They moved on through the crowds over the covered bridge, through the Pitti palace, and entered a green quiet scented by damp herbs. There, strolling on gravelled paths between avenues of cypress and disgruntled-looking statues, the two singers spent most of the afternoon. When they returned to the bustle of the city, the passeggiata was in full swing.

This evening walk, in which Italians of all ages saunter through a town's main streets, was something known to Julia but never before experienced. On her first day she had been alone, apprehensive because of being followed, now it was different.

Now she and Roberto joined the throngs viewing the Christmas lights. Skirting cars, street sellers, musicians, patient crocodiles of Japanese, they kept close to the river, weaving between families with pushchairs, the ubiquitous scooter riders, and young couples throwing pebbles into the sun-flashed water.

Roberto glanced at his watch. He hesitated to mention so mundane a subject as food, but they'd had no lunch, it was long past five and he was hungry – besides which, reception catering was always dire. He ducked into the side streets near Santa Croce. 'Fancy a snack?' he tossed back over his shoulder. They were passing a man roasting chestnuts on a bed of coals.

It smelt delicious but Julia hesitated, not having much money on her and reluctant to let Roberto buy everything. 'Do you want me thrown out of parts because of my weight, like that Moscow dancer?' she asked lightly, referring to one of their earlier conversations.

Roberto shook a finger at her. 'Singers must eat. You're too slim as it is.'

'My mother doesn't think so.' The words were out before Julia could stop them. Roberto was studying her with that look peculiar to male singers: how this woman will look playing beside them, how she will increase their stature, show off their strength, virility, machismo.

Being small, Julia was used to such chauvinism, and laughed at it – she never had any problems matching tenors, baritones or basses – but Roberto's look was more than that. He touched her forehead and shoulders lightly with his fingers, almost making the sign of the cross. 'You're just right,' he said softly.

They were staring at each other again, daring themselves to deny or to admit the spark of mutual recognition and attraction which fizzed between them. Julia knew she should laugh, make a joke. The sounding bells of Santa Croce's campanile were her sanctuary: 'How beautiful,' she murmured, arrested by the music. Deftly side-stepping her companion, she hastened into the square to catch the ringing echoes.

Roberto's look changed to one of exasperated amusement. 'Enough of this spirituality, I'm starving.' He caught hold of her hand. 'My treat. You pay next time.'

Later, juggling and eating pizza, Roberto talked about the other countries he had toured. It seemed natural to admit that so far he liked England the best, that he would like to improve his English.

'Why not write to someone?' suggested Julia, scandalised at how much Roberto managed to devour in one mouthful. She finished her smaller cheese and tomato pizza and wiped her greasy fingers on a statue, silently apologising to the sculptor. Turning her head quickly, she added, 'Instead of ice-cream, could I have one of those herbal teas that everyone seems to be drinking?' She indicated two elderly women in furs, tripping down the pavement, sipping from coloured paper cups.

Seeing them reminded Julia sharply of Clara. Much as she wanted to ignore the past for today she found she could not.

'How do you look for someone in Italy?' She began obliquely, reluctant to come to the point. 'How would I trace relatives?'

'How far do you want to go back?' asked Roberto.

'The 1940s. To my grandparents.'

Roberto bought her camomile tea at a roadside stall. 'Well, it depends on how much you already know,' he said, handing her the tea. 'If you have names and a rough idea of where they came from, it should be easy. The historical institutes have records, and the churches – births, marriages, deaths . . .'
Roberto mentioned the Italian war office, the state archives.

'My brother Sandro can help – he can look up police records.'

No police, Clara had said, when Julia left that morning. *No private investigators. Both are riddled with corruption*. If Julia did search, Clara had continued, she must work alone: for Scarpia to remain hidden for so long could be chance, but some ex-Fascists had powerful allies. Julia would have to be careful.

After her confrontation in the library, Julia appreciated Clara's warning. There was a simpler reason why she wanted no police or detectives involved, she thought, smiling as Roberto smiled. This was a family matter, not something to be dismissed as fifty-year-old history by some official. She wanted to find Scarpia for herself.

Julia shook her head. 'No, Roberto, I don't think that'll be necessary. One thing that does intrigue me though is a family story – it's almost a tradition – that a maternal uncle or cousin started as an opera singer in Northern Italy during the war. He may be still working today.' There, she thought, she'd said it.

'Ah, and you are continuing the family business.'

Roberto looked so pleased for her that Julia experienced a tide of disgust at what she was doing. When he added, 'Do you want me to ask around my contacts to see if any of them know anything?' her first instinct was to shout No! Instead of which, she found herself forced to say, 'The only thing I can tell you for certain is that whoever he was, he came from near a village in the foothills south of Bologna: San Martino della Croce.'

'How strange,' remarked Roberto. 'That village doesn't exist any more. It was abandoned after the war; the people from it scattered.' He looked at her quizzically and Julia's heart began to pound. She hated lying to this man. Clara had sworn her to secrecy, but Roberto would be rightly disappointed, angry, if he discovered she was using him.

Roberto put out a hand. 'Could I have a drink of that tea?'

The rest of the early evening passed too quickly. In no time Roberto was leaving Julia at the station where Andrea had arranged to meet her with the Mercedes.

'Do you want me to wait with you until he comes?' Roberto asked, regretting he couldn't take her home. Julia shook her head.

'No thanks,' she said. 'Enjoy your judges' reception and thank you for a lovely day.' It hadn't been a full day, but no matter.

'My pleasure,' answered Roberto, stopping his hand stealing to one of those earrings, drops of light suspended beside that fascinating long neck. It had been his pleasure. They had known each other as people, not singers. And of course it was not going to end. 'Shall I pick you up next Saturday morning at eleven? I'd like you to see the town where I was born. It has a Roman theatre and Etruscan walls and when you have seen enough of San Francesco church maybe we can stop later at Monte Senario? You can try the pine liqueur at the monastery.'

For a heart-stopping moment he wondered if he had said too much, moved too quickly. He rubbed his fist uneasily at the back of his neck, feeling about twelve years old.

Julia's half-smothered yawn of relaxation vanished in a burst of anticipation. Roberto's comment about her paying now made perfect sense.

'Eleven o'clock, Saturday the tenth,' she said, holding out her hand. By then the competition would be well and truly over.

'No, eight p.m., Thursday the first,' said Roberto, easy again as he shook her hand, 'Our joint anonymous engagement for the evening.' He did not insult her by adding that his adjudication would be impartial: he realised Julia knew that. Turning away, Roberto began to limp back to the music theatre.

Her first heat, thought Julia, her stomach clenching in on itself. She had to win it, and the finals. A season working in Italian opera was the Galatea-sponsored prize for the top three winners. She needed that prize to gain admittance into Scarpia's world. To bring him – if still alive – to justice.

12

At the last rehearsal before the finals, threading through
competitors in the foyer, Julia heard Francesco Terni say to a
baritone, 'It's easy for *him*. He walks onto the platform and
women melt.'

'It's the plaster cast. Brings out the protective in them.'

'So that's why Ruth makes a grab for my arm when he
comes within two metres of her! Women enjoy being
intimidated, it turns them on. Julia!' Francesco grabbed her
arm as she tried to slide past. 'You were wonderful!'

Julia stiffened and her grey eyes flashed. 'Ruth was better.'
She nodded to the tallest female singer. She liked Ruth
Marlow, despite the American soprano's description of
Roberto as 'gorgeously grim'. Ruth now turned and waved.

'She'll be over here soon: Ruth likes you.' The baritone
nudged Francesco. He looked Julia up and down. 'Leaving us
already?'

'Excuse me.' Julia detached herself. She'd had enough of
male posturing for one evening. 'My chauffeur's waiting.'

'Damn them.' Julia stabbed her sole in marsala.

Clara shot her an affectionate look. 'I presume you're not
referring to the fish.'

Julia put down her knife and fork. 'Singers have to be
confident but sometimes they're just arrogant.' She reached

for her glass. 'I've fallen out for tonight with Francesco.'

'Ah, Pietro's boy.' Clara picked up the handbell. The cook would again be disappointed, but she understood Julia's lack of appetite. After she won her heat last Thursday, the girl had practised for hours in the panelled music room, disdaining meals, showing a determination which reminded Clara sharply of Guy. Clara, Andrea and the cook now took their pre-dinner aperitifs in the flower gallery to listen to the 'performance'.

'I'm going to miss this,' Andrea had said, puffing out his chest. He had expected the Contessa's granddaughter to be good, but Julia exceeded his expectations. Clara nodded, her feelings more tangled.

'Guy would have loved her,' she said softly.

Not that Julia was satisfied.

'It's not a question of money,' she said, when Clara tentatively broached the subject. 'I need to win to get at Scarpia.'

Clara was always astonished at the ease with which Julia said that name. She herself had the same urgency but not the energy: once she'd had it, but no longer. She was old. Everything was an effort, even revenge.

Andrea entered, bearing fruit on a silver tray, clutching a bottle in his free hand. Clara, glad of the distraction, watched as he cleared their main course. Meeting Julia's gaze as the chauffeur tutted over the awkward cork, she smiled. 'Francesco's a tenor, isn't he?'

'He is.' Julia, relaxing as Andrea poured the sweet Recioto, had begun to wind a curl of hair. Now she stopped. 'I haven't mentioned that before.'

Clara mentally cursed her slip. Now that whole sorry affair would have to be accounted for.

Julia was looking at her. 'You implied that Pietro Terni was an actor who sang a little.' Her voice was completely neutral. 'Was he more?'

Clara sighed. 'Pietro was an actor of sorts. He was in the Bologna opera chorus; a tenor, like his son . . .'

'Then he was not so young in 1944,' said Julia, taking her hand from her hair.

'He was twenty-five.'

'And a trained singer-actor.'

'It's not what you think, Julia.'

Julia coloured slightly. 'I'm sorry if I seem sharp. I know it was a long time ago.' Her expression softened. 'I know he was a friend.' She took a glass of wine from Andrea, carrying it the length of the oak table.

As she walked she spoke. 'I'm sorry to say this, but I must. By how you describe him, here is someone who will do anything to avoid being deported to Germany, perhaps collaborate, actively spy for the Fascists, maybe even worse things. Why not? He's exactly the kind of small, unassuming man who gets overlooked. And he's someone used to acting, used to learning parts quickly. He's someone who in his work would have to be able to absorb new languages, including dialects.' She placed the full glass before Clara's place. 'Is it possible, do you think, that Terni was not the ham he claimed to be?'

'No!' Clara, adamant, swept a hand upwards towards the fiery chandelier, bright with fresh candles. 'What do you mean by "worse things"? Pietro was a gentle man. He was a bit of a coward, really. Not the kind others would follow.'

Julia leaned against the table, fingers pointing towards a bowl of yellow roses. 'Yet Terni was not so terrified that he avoided your June feast, where he had to sit with Krusak and the Germans. Surely a coward would have stayed away.'

'Even frightened men have their moments.' Clara found the Recioto cloying, but she nodded to Andrea so that the man would leave.

Julia, sensitive to Clara's action, waited until Andrea had closed the gilded doors on them. 'Terni was the first person to see you—' She paused, seeking the right phrase, her hand brushing the roses. 'After the air-raid.'

'When he brought me home. From where he later helped me to escape. Why would he do that, Julia, if he was not a friend?'

'I don't know.' Julia ran a hand down the front of the beaded, drop-waisted dress she was wearing, a gown rescued from the back of a wardrobe where it had languished in crepe paper for sixty years.

'That dress suits you,' remarked Clara, trying another sip of the Recioto. The blue cocktail gown had belonged to her mother, but she had never looked so beautiful in it as Julia, with her creamy skin, vivid eyes and dark hair.

'Thank you.' Julia flicked a bead with her thumb. 'Of course, friendships can drift apart,' she observed, returning to more serious matters. 'You didn't know about Terni's son.'

Clara shook her head. 'After the war we found we had nothing in common. I was a widow, a mother; Pietro a young man with no ties. I was undergoing surgery, I needed privacy and quiet. Pietro was gregarious.' She shrugged. 'Quite simply, he had his own life. We saw each other occasionally after the war; later I heard that he'd eventually married and had a son and a daughter, but I haven't seen him in years.'

Sometimes Clara's missing eye ached. It gave her a stab now, deep in the socket. She was beginning to have a headache. 'You're wrong, Julia,' she finished wearily. 'Pietro couldn't have been a collaborator in any real sense.'

'Why not?'

'Because I know!' Clara burst out. 'Because if you'd seen what I'd seen—' She struck her palm on the table.

Her granddaughter, in a fluid movement of sparkling blue beads, crouched by her chair. 'I'm an idiot.' She took Clara's hand. 'Forget what I've been saying. It doesn't matter. Will you be coming tomorrow night?'

'No. It goes on too late; I would be exhausted.' She could say this to Julia, sure that she would not take offence. Her granddaughter squeezed her hand and rose, collecting Clara's plate.

'What fruit would you like?' She slid the fruit bowl deftly past the flower arrangement on the polished table.

Clara discovered that she did not like being indulged as an old woman. 'Julia!' When the girl turned, Clara experienced a sense of déjà vu. She was a living portrait.

'I know.' Julia gave a soft laugh to dispel ghosts. 'Sometimes it unnerves me, too. What is it? You don't have to say anything more. I was crass a moment ago, too impatient.'

'That's me in you.' Clara smiled. To her relief, Julia's smile in return held no shadows; it was simply a pleasure to look on her, see her own youth again. 'Shall we have coffee by the fire? Andrea will finish the wine, it's his favourite.' Clara pushed back her carved dining chair.

'There's something I need to tell you.'

13

17th June, 1944, San Martino della Croce
Kneeling by the bed, Clara stroked the bright head resting
on the pillow. Tonight Angelica, no longer afraid of her
mother's altered appearance, had fallen asleep in her arms.

'Does your face hurt very much?' she had asked, clinging
to Clara's neck. 'Sometimes,' Clara had answered, 'but that
means it's getting better.' She hoped this was so. She had
never been vain, but to carry such visible scars for the rest of
her life, to be the object of scorn, or worse, of pity – Clara had
recoiled at the thought.

Now the young woman tucked the covers round her
sleeping daughter. Under the bandages her ruined face
burned, the blinded eye wept. *'You won't be so pretty when
we've finished.'* Even in memory the whisper turned her sick.
She shuddered whilst her child slept; Angelica, who did not
yet understand that she would never see her father again.

Clara rose to her feet, walked mechanically to the door,
closing it softly on the other side.

'You should leave.'

The voice was low, insistent. Clara ignored it.

'It's not safe for you here any more. You should go.'

'I must bury my cousin,' said Clara. She leaned against the
doorjamb, wondering why she was continuing with that fiction.
Guy, her husband, Mario her cousin, it made no difference
now. He was dead.

Dolores, hovering on the stairs, started at Clara's voice.
Pietro Terni, the young man who had found her, brought her
home, stopped his odd, stiff-jointed pacing on the landing.

'And do you know where to look for the body?' he
demanded, standing balanced on the edges of his feet, his
legs bowed: a childish stance at odds with his uncompromising
manner.

The question pierced her: she did not know. The blast
which freed her had killed her husband. No one in that second
chamber could have survived: the bomb demolished half the
building, set a fire blazing through the rest. She remembered
the screams, the scuffling rush of feet, the slap of bodies as
the torturers, confused by the smoke, collided with each other.
She could not forget the smell of the blast, acrid yet sweet,
masking the scent of burning wood and skin.

'The door's on fire! The whole lot's going to come down!
We've got to get out!'

She remembered that voice, the raw panic and frantic
search for sacking or other bits of cloth to beat out the rising
flames. She remembered screaming for Guy, fear for his safety
obliterating everything, even the pain.

Clara shook at the memory. She lifted a trembling hand
and touched her cheek. She had been tortured whilst
blindfolded, the knife stabbing through the cloth to the soft
flesh beneath. She had been blinded, blindfolded.

Sleeping or awake, the memory of that moment was with
her. Nothing mattered any more.

'From what you've told us there'd be nothing left,' said
Pietro Terni brutally.

'Leave me alone!' Guy was dead. A voice had told her he
was dead; the same voice that had told her to run. Not Scarpia.
Not Spoletta. No one from Croce. Perhaps her own voice, the
voice of instinct, of survival.

'Could you find your way back there?' Pietro again, rough
Bolognese accent setting her teeth on edge.

Clara strained to remember how she had got out of the
underground chamber. The blindfold had been torn from her
eyes: she must have done it herself. She remembered lurching

from the table, the straps giving as she moved, almost as though she were being lifted by some invisible force. She remembered the sick shuddering cold that had swept through her as her blurred, unsteady sight took in the mangled metal doors and gaping crater. She could remember thinking quite coolly: *No one could possibly have survived that*. She remembered the relief that Guy must have died instantly, without suffering. She remembered feeling the fresh night air on her face . . .

But that was when she had escaped. How had she got out?

'I can't remember!' Suddenly she was weeping. The first real tears since Guy's death fell unchecked from her good eye. Clara slid down the doorjamb, put her head on her knees and cried.

Pietro squatted down on the tiles and gathered the frail-looking, bandaged figure into his burly arms. 'That's right,' he was saying, 'There now, let it come.'

Dolores, unbidden, brought a glass of water from the master bedroom. Pietro held it steady for Clara to drink. 'There now.' He stroked her hair, avoiding the bandages. 'Dolores will help you to bed and tomorrow we'll see about leaving, eh?'

'He's dead,' Clara was saying. Guy was gone. There was nothing of him left.

'Angelica's alive,' said Pietro. He took her chin between his hands, made her look at him. 'Your daughter needs you.'

Funny Pietro. And yet how wise. Looking back, Clara recognised that moment as a turning point, an acceptance of and return to life. She slept soundly that night, without dreams, and in the morning woke hungry.

Breakfasting on the balcony of the master bedroom, Clara reviewed her position at San Martino della Croce and decided that Pietro was right. However many people from the village and three lower hamlets called at the villa to pay their respects, to pass on messages of concern at Guy's 'disappearance' (and there had been a great number) the fact remained that she and Guy had been betrayed. She looked out over a landscape which a week ago she had believed to be hers and Guy's home and found it was an alien country.

There was a knock on the door. Pietro entered at her invitation, still with that odd, shuffling walk.

'Ah!' He rubbed his small Grecian nose and blushed. 'You look more your old self this morning.'

As do you, reflected Clara, surprising herself with this flash of humour. 'I've decided you're right, Pietrò,' she said, drinking carefully from her cup. Her injuries made it difficult for her to eat: she was glad he had not witnessed her performance with a bowl of bread soaked in milk. 'I'm going to move Angelica and Dolores to my mother's estate in Tuscany. Luigi can manage my affairs here.' She motioned for him to draw up a chair. 'Now, how should I go about it?'

Again, small, plump Pietro had surprised her. Not only did he know which trains might be running and which papers Clara would need for the journey, he offered to go with them.

They set off at midday in a baking heat haze. As Pietro observed, even the Allies and Germans had to eat and their train should escape being strafed from the air. Travelling to Florence had been incredible. At Bologna station platforms which had so far escaped the bombing were crowded with Blackshirts. Their bags were searched three times for illegal contraband. There were huge queues where documents had to be checked. In the midst of this heaving, sullen mass of people, Dolores fainted, overcome by heat. She would have fallen, but the crowds made it impossible.

Pietro coped with Dolores whilst Clara took care of Angelica. They made their train with three minutes to spare, losing a bag on the way through the crush but finding seats in one of the dusty compartments. Their carriage had no glass left in the windows, only wooden slats: 'Cattle trucks!' muttered Dolores. Angelica clambered onto her seat to poke a hand through a jagged tear in the roof. 'Where the Germans tried to get in!' the child proclaimed, an announcement not conducive to calming Dolores' nerves.

Clara, injuries hidden behind a black veil, prepared herself mentally for the journey south. Pietro said he knew someone in Florence who would be able to restore her looks, if not her sight. With that bleak comfort, and lulled by Angelica's happy chatter, she fell asleep on the slowly moving train.

It was evening before they had fought – and in one case bribed – their way out of Florence station. Dolores was at her most stubborn, carrying both Angelica and a suitcase and refusing to allow the Contessa to tire herself by taking either from her. Clara, weary despite sleeping, her face burning and in pain, tottered unsteadily beside a limping Pietro.

There were no taxis – petrol had been requisitioned. The trams were packed. They would have to walk the eight kilometres to her mother's villa.

'Was there no one you could have written to, to let them know we were coming?' Pietro demanded petulantly at one point, stumbling as he tried to duck under swarms of stinging mosquitoes around the house lights on the Ponte Vecchio.

Clara shook her head, her throat too dry to talk. Reaching the water tap in the middle of the bridge, she cupped her hands for Angelica to drink from and then slaked her own raging thirst, oblivious to the whirring insects. Pietro, burnt after a day spent largely in the sun, thrust his blond head under the tap and let the water run down the back of his sweat-stained shirt. They sat down, their backs against the cooling walls of the loggia. The Arno rustled beneath them, the mosquitoes whined above. A few local women, clutching bundles of precious rations, were scurrying over the bridge, wanting to get home before darkness and curfew. One noticed Clara in the shadows and made the sign against the evil eye. There was a smell of salt and sulphur, the sound of Allied gunfire.

Sitting beside her, Pietro suddenly gave a stifled gasp, clutching his instep as Clara's foot accidentally brushed his own. 'Have you hurt yourself?' she asked. Leaning towards the tap, Clara soaked her handkerchief and offered it to the young man. 'Sorry, I didn't realise.' She recalled his strange way of standing, his recent, stiff-jointed walk. Hadn't he been limping slightly a week ago, when he had found her by the stream? 'What's happened to you?'

Pietro, lips pressed tightly together, waved question and handkerchief away. A group of young German officers, off-duty but still in uniform, were wandering over the bridge making a tremendous din: shouting and rapping on the shuttered jewellers' windows. One wore a pair of waders and clutched a fishing rod: Clara was absurdly glad to see that he had caught nothing. For members of an army which had just been thrown out of Rome and were on the run the Germans seemed over-confident, but perhaps that was a front. Certainly none of the five made any attempt to approach or to question them.

Clara took Angelica on her knee until the soldiers were gone, when she turned again to Pietro.

'Show me your foot.' She waited as Pietro slowly untied his right boot, then motioned to Dolores to lift Angelica up to look out over the river.

She lifted her veil and drew Pietro's foot into the sinking sunlight. His sole from instep to toes was a mass of festering sores.

Neither spoke. Clara did what she could with her scrap of handkerchief and the warm tapwater, then sat back on her heels. 'Will you be able to walk the rest of the way?'

Pietro threw her an ironic glance with his twinkling brown eyes. 'What choice is there? The Germans or Blackshirts will be patrolling here again soon.'

Clara nodded. 'I'll do what I can for you.' She had a pair of silk camiknickers in her suitcase, they at least would be smooth. 'Who did this to you?' she asked, keeping her gaze on her work as she tore the silk and staunched and bound. She was amazed at how calm she felt: she had been tortured, so why not Pietro? Torture, it seemed, was now an everyday event.

'It was Krusak.' Pietro's face was in shadow but Clara felt him stiffen. 'Several hours after your feast for Our Lady, he returned to Croce from Bologna and came to Giacomo's house. He was asking questions about deserters and partisans; when

I said I knew nothing he took me down to the German headquarters. They worked on me there.'

Behind them, Angelica hurled a pebble into the river and laughed. Above them, someone in one of the shuttered houses began to sing a popular song. Ordinary, everyday things. Clara clung to them.

'I was held for nine hours.' Pietro's voice was immeasurably weary. 'And then they let me go. Just opened the cell door and told me to get out; I was no use to them.'

'Why did you return to the village?' Clara whispered.

Pietro shrugged. 'Where else could I have gone?' he asked. 'Besides, I wanted to warn you. I came up to the villa, found Luigi and Dolores there, but no . . .'

Clara began to laugh. *I wanted to warn you.* The absurdity beat on the raw wounds of Guy's loss and her own disfigurement. *I wanted to warn you.* She laughed until tears came and then she wept.

14

8th December, Florence

Julia was the last contestant. Six other singers, including Ruth and Francesco, had already delighted the audience and impressed the judges.

The finals were being televised. Julia made a rapid scan of the men and women who would decide whether she should stay on in Italy. Her body was vibrating like a tuning fork.

The Chairman of the judges smiled at her. The black-jacketed, powerfully built Italian seated at the end did not. His left foot, encased in plaster, jutted over the judges' platform. His brown hair had been raked into submission but, encouraged by beads of perspiration on his forehead, was beginning to spike. He was clearly uncomfortable, poor man.

Julia's nerve returned. The conductor was ready, the audience quiet. Julia took a deep breath as the orchestra played and launched herself, tenderly, into the seductive aria, 'Softly awakes my heart'.

For Roberto.

During the ecstatic applause, the Chairman leaned towards Roberto. 'What a big instrument for such a body, eh? And our youngest competitor.'

And the most elegant, thought Roberto, approving Julia's simple ruby dress. She wore a slim string of pearls, but no other jewellery. Roberto missed her long earrings, but appreciated the overall effect. 'Cutting a fine figure' was important in Italy, and Julia achieved it by pure style.

'Pity she's so sturdily built, that face would look great on fashion posters,' lamented the Galatea official, one of the judges. 'Now the tall blonde soprano . . .'

The man was an idiot. Roberto, shifting his aching foot so brusquely that it struck the official's chair, filtered out the light voice.

Julia was thanking conductor and orchestra. Roberto smiled to see her step forward on stage to gather up flowers thrown by the audience. She was blushing, hesitant, where before, when singing a role, she had been all life and fire.

What a fool that Galatea judge was. Julia was revealed as surprisingly full-figured, which he supposed might appear to the undiscriminating as sturdy. Full-hipped, with firm waist and good back, she would never need to wear shoulder pads. Her hands and feet were slender, her breasts superb, voluptuous in a woman of her height.

God, he wished he wasn't stuck on this platform.

Rubbing the back of his neck, Roberto ran a finger over the sketch he had made, then turned it over, dissatisfied. Julia had a sexy figure any painter would be proud to record in oils.

He felt a tap on his shoulder from the Chairman. It was time for the judges to retire to choose the winners.

'And in first place . . . Julia Rochfort!' announced the Chairman of the judges to the hall. A cheer went up. Already on stage, Ruth and Francesco, third and second respectively, joined in the applause.

Julia stood a moment unmoving. Apart from her first song she had not been satisfied with her performance, yet somehow, for some incredible reason, she had won.

'Sorry you didn't make it . . .' She shook hands with the other competitors. The conductor was beckoning: Julia was to come.

Flashes exploded as she returned to the platform. Julia knew she had a silly grin on her face but didn't care. Dazzled,

she kissed Ruth, linked hands with her and Francesco and
bowed. Farther along the stage, standing with the other judges
waiting to greet her and the finalists, Roberto was smiling,
showing his gap-teeth. Strange, how Ruth and the other female
singers found him 'gorgeously grim', a touch intimidating.
The lights revealed a mesh of laughter-lines round his eyes.

The applause continued. Someone tossed her a rose.
Releasing her hand from her bemused companions', Julia
stepped forward.

As she moved, patches of shadow cast onto the audience
by the stage lights retreated. Plucking the rose from the
boards, Julia found herself staring at the man who had thrown
it.

She hid fear well, thought Tom, scowling and shading his
eyes. He liked the way she glared, the provocative flourish
as, bending, she threw him a flower in return. A nice touch,
that; something a connoisseur of stressful situations (as he
was) could appreciate. And she had won.

With a practised flick of her gown, Julia turned from him
and Tom dropped back into his seat. His feelings were mixed:
he was pleased she remembered him, but regretted that she
should be frightened. Her winning made an approach more
difficult – he was used to teenage boys, cocksure men; he'd
never had to deal with a mature young woman like Julia,
someone with her kind of presence. Where had that come
from? Tom wondered, digging round the seat for his scarf.
From her mother?

One thing was certain. Somehow, he must get to her.

'Julia!'

'Papà, I've won!'

'She's done it, Angelica! Well done! Here, you must speak
to your mother . . . Come and talk to your clever daughter.'

Angelica's cool voice: 'How are you?'

'Fine.' A beat of breathing silence. 'How's Tenerife?'

'Very nice.'

'Good!' Julia touched the white rose balanced between the

horns of the receiver. The flower was perfect, but much as she loved living green things she wondered why she had kept it. 'Did you get my letter?' She had written telling her parents where she was staying. And with whom.

'Enrico says thank you for the postcards of Bologna.'

'No problem.' Julia had bought the cards in Florence. She had kept her promise to her stepfather too: found out more about Angelica's Italian past and her family. She had shared that knowledge with Enrico in her letter, but still Angelica wasn't going to mention Clara. 'Mother, about where I'm staying—'

'What? Are you in a hole? Do you need cash?'

Julia almost laughed. Never, ever had she borrowed money from her parents. 'I'm fine. Mamma—'

'Please, dear – "Mamma" makes me feel antique.' Angelica muttered to Enrico and then her voice rang down the line. 'We're pleased for you. Now is there anything else?'

Indeed there is, thought Julia. What would you say, *Mother*, if I told you that a man who's as big as a door, who scares half my peers, doesn't frighten me at all (I like him, and he likes me, which considering we're singers could play havoc with our careers) but then a little fellow who throws roses terrifies me?

'No, there's nothing.' Only why had Angelica broken from her family: why had her mother changed from the loving child Clara had known to the blank, cool woman she now was.

Suddenly at a loss for words, Julia watched the backstage door open. Limping towards her, Roberto's name was called and he turned, arms outstretched to receive whoever wanted him.

'Mother, I've got to go,' she said. 'I'll ring again.' She picked up the rose and cut the connection.

A male singer surrounded by female fans – Julia had seen it in England, but this was hero-worship Italian-style: lots of touching and posing with the 'macho' man for pictures. All of them got a kiss, she noticed.

'You looked comfortable, being mobbed,' she remarked, when Roberto detached himself from the final glowing autograph hunter, kissed the last blushing woman for the video cameras. 'And why should tenors have all the fun?'

The bass laughed: jealous already? his look said. He seemed pleased if she was. What children men and women are with each other, thought Julia, none the less reassured.

Roberto, by contrast, close enough to see the sheen of moisture on her face and body, the performance-flushed cheeks and breasts, found coherent thought shattered. His hands advanced on the flimsy dress, those superb breasts—

A door banged: Roberto, guts churning, stepped back. This was ridiculous. He was reacting like some sex-starved adolescent, not a man. 'You still OK for Saturday?' At least his voice was under control.

'I am.' Julia touched his arm. 'It's all right.'

She knew then, the effect she was having on him. Which was disconcerting, or made things simpler, depending on the way you looked at it. Always able to laugh at himself, Roberto could appreciate the irony of the established star being fazed by the newcomer. But then that was Julia.

'Your agent's turned up.' He offered her his arm. 'Now you've won, things will be different. She wants to talk about your engagements.'

All the way back to the hall, conscious of the bulge in his trousers, the bang of heat in his body and endless pictures of him and Julia making love running round his head, Roberto kept thinking about the single white rose she was carrying. Why had Julia kept it? Roberto had not been fooled by her laughing acceptance of the flower: he had seen the stiffening of her body, the over-generous smile following her single piercing glance at the stranger who had thrown it. She had been unnerved by the man. Why?

Staring at the TV screen he had silenced, Jan Krusak punched a telephone number. 'Tonight's Galatea competition. I want to know everything about Julia Rochfort.'

'Usual terms?' said the woman he knew as Anna.

Krusak named a figure. Anna registered the importance of the assignment by a sharp intake of breath.

'Is it anything to do with Ravenna?' Rochfort would soon be speaking to him in that soft, respectful manner, thought Krusak, savouring his cigar.

'This isn't business. Di Salvo isn't to be troubled. Start tonight.' Krusak killed the call, redialled. A major opera sponsor, tonight he was going to use his music contacts to get what he wanted.

Julia Rochfort. Even the name was the same. There was no doubt that she was a close relative – very close – of a woman who had obsessed him for fifty of his sixty-eight years. 'Come on,' he muttered, listening to the ringing at the other end of the line. Fifty years . . .

Clara. He remembered that midsummer feast day, 10th June, 1944. After questioning various suspects he had been set to return to the villa to arrest Clara Rochfort-Scudieri on suspicion of harbouring Italian deserters on her estate, but was overruled by his commanding officer.

Krusak drew on his cigar. The officer, a German from Munich, came from a family which traced its lineage back to the Hohenstaufens: another member of that exclusive club, the European aristocracy. Krusak, a middle-class Croatian who had dared to move against one of its lesser Italian members, was punished for not knowing his place. Transferred to the front line, he had been kept on the run by the Allied advance.

Clara, cause of his removal to the front line, went into hiding and vanished. Returning to Italy after the war, Krusak found her villa deserted, its doors and windows boarded up. San Martino della Croce was a ghost village; wild dogs prowled the hovels. Pigeons roosted in the church. He remembered the flurry of their wings, like the sound of a satin dress against wood.

In Bologna, his inquiries were rebuffed: too many people remembered Krusak as a keen young officer in the German army. Soon he himself had been under scrutiny in connection with a certain so-called atrocity. He had been forced to leave. The Scudieri woman had got the better of him.

'Come on!' Fifty years is a long time to wait. Krusak, as impatient at sixty-eight as he had been at eighteen – when he had joined the army pretending to be twenty-one – ground the cigar butt into the middle of the glass ashtray. He hated loose ends. Perhaps if he had been able to see Clara, see her growing old, he might not have nursed his hatred.

'Answer the phone, will you?' So far he had not taken his eyes off the TV. The head of the Galatea fashion house beckoning the three winners back onto the stage. Krusak covered the girl's curly dark head with his thumb.

The telephone burped into life. 'Good evening.' Krusak smiled into the receiver. Trapped under his hand, Julia Rochfort seemed to writhe as she moved on stage. He would commission a portrait: 'Nude without a head.' He was past needing any woman but possession was another thing.

'Signor Krusak! Always a pleasure.' Bazzini's lisping voice flowed like a vintage port, smoothing excuses. 'Forgive me for taking so long to answer, I was detained . . .'

'Leering at Francesco Terni no doubt.' Krusak permitted himself to press a finger between the folds of Rochfort's wine-coloured gown, bisecting the point of joining between her thighs. Sex, except in rare cases, had always been distasteful. He had been a virgin when he encountered Clara.

'Signore! I appreciate male beauty as I appreciate music . . .'

The credits had begun to roll. Time to state his demands, thought Krusak. First he sweetened the pill. 'The funding for next season at La Scala; I have decided to supply any shortfalls. Is our Italian diva still proving difficult?'

'Yes,' stammered Bazzini, too stunned to express gratitude. Krusak's offer, worth millions of lire, was fabulous. 'Last week she threw a music stand at the conductor.'

'Get rid of the woman,' said Krusak. 'Pay her off – I'll supply the money.' The news was beginning. Seeing the picture of a man recently exposed as a war criminal Krusak frowned. 'Wait.' He covered the receiver with his hand and turned up the sound.

The report, concerned with the wartime activities of a Fascist cell in Naples, contained no new revelations. With a tap on the remote switch, Krusak turned off the newscaster.

'Forgive me, Bazzini. Now, as I was saying, I may want

tonight's winner to be given star billing in Milan . . . I don't
care if it's controversial. And, Bazzini – ' Here Krusak showed
his claws – 'your group better respond exactly as I want.
Otherwise certain business documents will find their way to
the public prosecutor's office.'

Cutting off the man's promises, Krusak put down the phone.
Catching a glimpse of his dark, narrow features in the ashtray
he smiled. Nothing more need be done tonight. Bazzini was
an old gossip, but he was a power behind the scenes in opera
and knew everyone. By tomorrow word of Krusak's generosity
would be all over Milan. The excitement generated by
Bazzini's news would make it impossible for La Scala to turn
his offer down, or to ignore the special conditions which went
with it.

Clara had been out of his reach, separated by age, class
and money; now such advantages were on his side. Jan Krusak,
entrepreneur and art collector, was about to take a new
mistress.

And then the girl would pay. For all of Clara's slights,
deceptions and trickery. Indeed she would pay.

15

When Krusak phoned, Anna, alias Bianca Terni, had not only been watching the Galatea concert, she was in the second row of the audience. Flicking the transmit button on her portable phone, she killed the bell and, ignoring glares from those nearby, slid from her seat. In the relative privacy of the main exit corridor, shielded from audience din, she took the call and made a deal, returning to her seat several million lire richer.

Resuming her place, Bianca waved to her brother on stage, who didn't notice –Frankie was grabbing an eyeful of Julia Rochfort. From the dopey expression on his open face, Bianca guessed that the tall American blonde flashing those sideways glances at him – and for good measure, at Roberto Padovano too – would be out of luck. Granted, Ruth Marlow showed great discrimination in picking out one of the sexiest men in the place, but judging by paparazzi snapshots, Padovano's taste in women seemed to run to the well-stacked starlet type and as for Francesco . . . When Frankie fell for someone, he fell hard. Anyone else just wasn't real.

Bianca knew the feeling. She'd been fighting it for years. As a teenager she'd assumed it was something to do with spectacles, always having that gap between reality and herself, but contact lenses had made no difference. By the time she'd changed her eye-wear she was working in the States. Waking

up to the fact that people world-wide are all the same, Bianca
regarded them and their Byzantine emotional problems with
resigned indulgence.

Money was real. The sum Krusak had mentioned – one
hundred percent real. Double what she was getting for tonight.

Bianca glanced at the rubicund, soft-mouthed man next to
her. His hair, once dark blond like his son's, receded from
his forehead in a series of sweeping waves. He had a prophet's
brow, an illusion instantly routed by a squashed strawberry
of a nose – once Grecian – and a round face. His twinkling
eyes were riveted to the carpet, which meant that he was
crying. Papà always broke up at moments of emotion – one
reason why he had never made it as a singer. He was happy
tonight though, with both his handsome children close, his
son an acknowledged success and a thousand million lire art
deal about to be signed between himself, di Salvo and Krusak.

Which was where she came in. 'There must be no breath
of scandal,' di Salvo had said, lowering his grey-blond head
close to hers. 'I look to you, as Pietro's assistant, as his eldest
child, to remove anything which might be an embarrassment
to your father – *or to me.*' This last di Salvo had emphasised,
just before he gave Bianca her final instructions . . .

She was paid – not as much as she deserved, but it was
time for her to start earning her fee. She, as much as Tancredi
di Salvo, her boss, wanted the reputations of di Salvo and her
father to remain spotless.

'Papà, I have to go. I'll leave you the car, OK?'

Pietro, used to her unexpected departures, accepted her
excuses. He would be all right, Bianca decided, threading her
long legs between people's feet and the plush seating. Her
father had Francesco to latch on to tonight. Winking at a man
who ran an appreciative eye over her clinging short skirt and
boots she put family matters out of her mind and eased her
way through concert-goers to the ladies'.

Striding down Via Garibaldi, Bianca was a tall young woman
going places. Fur coat – the jacket was reversible – with
English-cut trousers slipped over her skirt. Shingled black
hair – her least favourite wig – and court shoes. The boots

were tucked behind a street shrine, from where she'd later recover them.

Bianca entered the Borgo San Frediano, reviewing her instructions. Tonight's competition and the evening spent with her father might not have existed; her concentration was fixed on that ochre-washed house ... the one with the green shutters. Court shoes tapping the cobbles, Bianca crossed the half-lit street.

'Signore! It's Anna,' she breathed into the intercom, giving her alias – her photograph never appeared in any of the papers where she used her real name, so even without her disguise the man would not know her as Bianca Terni – 'Can I come in?' As she waited, head bowed out of the light, Bianca schooled herself to be patient. She'd worked on this old man for two days already, winning his trust in early and late meetings, stimulating his greed ...

'You brought the money this time?' barked the intercom. Bianca smiled and put her mouth close to the metal plate.

'Please! I can hardly talk out here. If *Oggi* finds out about this, I'll lose my journalist's card.' On she gushed, about how the paper she worked for would dump her if rival *Oggi* found out that she'd been trying to cut in to one of *their* exclusive interviews. She was pleased at the note of genuine alarm in her voice.

The door buzzed and Bianca was inside, pocket recorder already out as, in her guise of an eager young reporter, she did not wait for the lift, but tripped up the winding stairs. As usual there was no one about on the stairway. She heard televisions through thin walls and then she was on the third floor landing.

The old man had the flat door open and was waiting: once tall, now stooped, a spare man with hard green eyes and yellowed wrinkled skin. He had not troubled to change from a dingy pair of pyjamas and threadbare dressing-gown to receive her: all the man cared about was clawing together enough money to get out of his crumbling apartment. Bianca had spent many weary hours listening to the old man's complaints. He claimed he had been ignored by those 'who ought to show more gratitude after everything I did for them'

'Where's the cash?' he demanded instantly.

Bianca tapped her yellow belly bag. 'Here,' she whispered casting an anxious glance towards the deserted stairwell. 'Can I record the interview?'

'Show me the money.'

Prepared for this, Bianca unzipped the small bag, displaying a roll of banknotes. This time the old man looked round anxiously.

'Come in.' He beckoned.

'Can I record?' asked Bianca plaintively.

The old man shrugged. 'You can do what you like as long as you pay me.' He bustled her into his fusty flat. 'You look different tonight.' He kicked the door shut with a slippered heel and jutted a bristled chin. 'Dressing up for me?' This said with a laugh as she turned her head aside and would not answer.

Bianca sat primly on the sofa beside a box of Christmas decorations and refused a drink. The old man took a whisky scooped the box onto the floor and sat beside her, leering, rheumy eyes up and down her long legs.

'Double, that's what you said your editor would pay.'

'He will, if you tell our paper what you know about this Nazi collaborator.' Bianca switched on the recorder, laid it on the sofa between them. 'What did the man look like?'

'Not so fast.' The old man punched the stop button. 'Before we go any further I want guaranteed anonymity.' He motioned to the window overlooking the street. 'This fella may still have friends out there. In fact – ' The old man removed the small cassette from the recorder and slipped it into his dressing gown pocket – 'I'll take that if you don't mind. They might recognise my voice.'

'Hey!' Bianca made a futile grab for the disappearing cassette, 'I've another interview on that. You'll get me into trouble.'

'Not too much trouble for one little tape. Not if you bring in your big story.' His voice sharpened. 'That's what you want isn't it?'

Bianca lowered her head. 'I can take notes?' she asked tartly, swivelling her hips to get at her back trouser pocket.

The old man watched with amusement. 'Just don't expect me to sign anything,' he answered, relaxing again as greed overcame anxiety. 'And let's have the money now, shall we?'

'Half.' Bianca laid a bundle on the seat. 'The rest at the end of this interview.'

'OK.' The man put a grimy paw over the cash and, wetting his fingers, began to count. 'Suppose I told the hack from *Oggi* about you?'

Bianca decided that things had gone far enough. She wouldn't be bullied. 'Suppose we get on and you tell me about this Blackshirt?'

'I never said he was that.' The old man was suddenly indignant. 'He wasn't a thug, he was a gentleman; always the smart clothes. A natty dresser, you know? Reminded me of Caruso – no, not him, the other one.'

'Gigli?' suggested Bianca.

'That's the one. Only this guy was fair.' The old man gagged on his whisky and took another swig direct from the bottle.

'What was his name?'

The old man threw her a pained look at such naivety. 'Please! This was war, no real names were ever given, or known. We used codenames.'

'Where do you think he was from?' asked Bianca, scribbling furiously.

'Fairly posh accent, definitely northern. Not as far as Milan, though.'

'Where did he operate from?' asked Bianca.

'Bologna to begin with, I think, but he didn't always stay in the city.' The old man took another drink. 'More remote country places gave his group more scope.'

'More privacy, you mean?' prompted Bianca. There was a silence. 'How did he recruit those in his group?' she asked then.

'Always in person, a direct approach. That way he could sound them out, get a feel of the kind of man he was dealing with . . .' He broke off. 'You're not writing any more.'

Bianca sniffed. 'Need a hankie,' she explained apologetically, feeling in her coat pocket. Her fingers closed on something smooth and cold. 'Did you get a buzz from it?' she asked, taking out a handkerchief and dabbing her nose. 'You know, that life or death power over prisoners?'

'I don't know what you're talking about. I'd nothing to do with that group. I was just small fry; a messenger earning a bit of money for my mother.' The old man reddened and Bianca smiled.

'You said "*we* used codenames",' she reminded him sweetly.

'A slip of the tongue! If you were as old as I am, you'd know how easy it is to make a mistake.' The old man was beginning to sweat. 'Jesus, you think I joined a bunch of collaborators? I told you what the Blackshirts did to my father!'

Bianca shook her head. 'I don't believe you, Sprint,' she said, thrusting the handkerchief back into her pocket.

The silenced shot took the old man in the face: he died instantly, slumping sideways onto the sofa. With her pencil, Bianca fished the tape from his dressing-gown pocket and zipped it into her belly bag. She stuffed the money into her coat pocket along with the gun.

She didn't bother with any kind of tidying up, she knew she hadn't left any prints. The clothes she'd dump later. The gun she'd clean and maybe use again: Cosa Nostra liked this kind of piece. The cops, when they found the bullet, would assume a gangland connection and either back off or take their investigations in completely the wrong direction.

Di Salvo's tip-off had been right, thought Bianca as she let herself out of the flat. The old man had been about to spill his guts to the media: she'd paid him that final visit just in time.

Bianca walked out into the deserted street.

16

'Interesting letter?'

Julia nodded. She hoped to be left in peace, but Francesco was not put off.

'Must be good, you've read it enough. Can't be another recording contract,' he went on, smudging a finger along glitter-marked eyebrows, 'Can it?'

The make-up girl would be after him, thought Julia, disarmed. He, Ruth and herself were at a fashion 'shoot' in Galatea's warehouse-like studios in the outskirts of Florence. Through the hours of posing and waiting the tenor had been irrepressible. No wonder Ruth found him attractive.

To her, aware as she was of Pietro Terni's past, Francesco was also in an odd way connected to herself. Both of them had close relations who had been tortured in the war.

'Not this time,' she answered, tracing the letter's broad signature with her thumb. 'A note from a friend.'

Their trip to Fiesole had been a week ago. Julia was fascinated to see where Roberto had been brought up as a boy, whilst for his part, walking with her under the leafless orchard where, years before, he had discovered his grandfather's body, Roberto found the place strangely peaceful. Julia made it easy for him to remember the good things: to share happy childhood memories and ignore the rest.

Talking, pointing out landmarks, sometimes touching each other's hands to guide or emphasise, they made their way through Fiesole's hilly streets. They paused in the ruined Roman theatre. After a series of climbs, Roberto was limping, but the instant they settled on the stone seats, he muttered about the light and produced notebook and pencils from his jacket pocket. Julia put her head back and enjoyed the winter sun, relaxing after the competition.

Disliking the idea of being indoors on such a day, she left Roberto sketching and walked back into the little town. She bought lunch: food and bottles of mineral water, paper napkins.

'As well your lady fans can't see, they'd be disappointed,' she remarked, watching Roberto eat cheese with his fingers, balancing a ham roll on one knee and sketchpad on the other. He laughed and flicked an olive stone at her.

'We're only doing what Roman audiences would have done.' He motioned to the empty tiers of seats. 'Brought in a few supplies to see us through to the end of the performance.'

'I wonder if they threw their food at actors they didn't like.' Julia helped herself to a salty black olive.

'Ah, just like a Parma audience! We Italians have always been very active spectators.' Roberto laid his notepad aside, bent his brown head to regard her more closely.

'Which reminds me,' he said equably. 'I guess now would be a good time to tell you.'

Roberto leaned forward, thigh muscles straining the seams of his black jeans. 'Last week's competition drew a lot of retired musicians and singers into Florence. I've been asking round. Your missing relative, remember?' he added, as Julia's face became drained of expression, 'The mystery singer from San Martino della Croce who might turn out to be one of your forebears?'

He had done what she asked, taken trouble to look up old contacts. Meeting his steady gaze, Julia passed her tongue over her teeth and produced a smile. 'I wasn't thinking straight.'

'I'll ignore that remark,' said Roberto drily. 'But you may

>e interested to learn that Terni's father comes from north
taly. His name's Pietro, and he was a singer before the war.'

'Really? I didn't know that.' Julia began wiping her hands
)n her napkin. She was too naive. It wasn't as though she was
njuring Roberto by not telling him the truth; that she was
searching not for a relation but a war criminal.

Roberto took another big bite off the ham roll on his knee.
An old pianist told me,' he explained between mouthfuls,
1ands mirroring the main actions of the scene he was
describing, 'Terni was singing at Parma in the late 1930s and
;omeone in the audience threw an egg at him. The pianist
1ever forgot.'

'No, he wouldn't.' Julia could easily have seemed more
enthusiastic, but then she didn't want to play roles off-stage.
She disliked secrecy: it reminded her of her mother.

Roberto flashed Julia one of his quizzical glances at her
ukewarm response, but said evenly, 'I know it seems too much
)f a coincidence that he's the man you're looking for, but it's
)ossible. Perhaps you could talk to Francesco Terni. You'll
)e seeing a lot of him.' He threw her a probing look to see
1ow she took that idea. His stark features were not softened
)y animation but intensified.

Julia cleared her throat. 'Did the pianist remember anyone
lse?'

'One or two. The Emilia region has always produced fine
ingers.' Impossible to tell whether Roberto was laughing at
1er. 'And a mother and son: Gina and Giovanni Respini. The
nother was a soprano who sang mostly in Bologna. Her son
vas a treble. He was a boy during the war. They came from
hat other village you spoke of, Castel San Martino. Here.'
{oberto dug round his denim jacket pockets, 'I found Giovanni
{espini's address in the Parma phone book. You could write
o him. He should remember any singers from his old village.
3efore you ask, the rest of the names the pianist mentioned
re on the back.'

Julia thrust the paper into her bag and thanked him.

Jow, conscious of the Spanish comb pinned in her hair, Julia

glanced up at Francesco. The three opera winners were being
photographed separately before a group session.

'Haven't they finished grilling Ruth?' They were used to
sweltering under stage lights, but the lights of Galatea's studio
were even hotter.

'No chance! You know what Ruth's like, soft as Ricotta
cheese. Puts up with anything.'

Julia put Roberto's latest letter in her pocket. 'You forget,'
she reminded Francesco, 'Ruth's having to struggle along in
another language.'

Francesco had the grace to blush. 'Hey, it's no big deal—'

'Yet look how Galatea are using us,' said Julia. 'At their
"suggestion" we're going to be singing as principals in Verdi's
Don Carlos at Lucca this winter: an opera that fits in with
Galatea's Spanish theme for their spring collections. We're
giving Galatea free publicity.'

Francesco shrugged, kneeling to rub his right foot. 'These
croc shoes are killing.'

'Excellent.' Julia tapped the top of Francesco's blond head
with her fan. 'I don't approve of the skin trade.'

'Neither do I – but these looked too good.' Francesco had
the most amazing grin: American dazzle, Italian charm, Swiss
dentistry. Encouraged by Julia's smile, he surged to his feet
and caught her round the middle. 'Mind you, my journalist
sister wouldn't agree – Bianca's crazy about furs.'

'Francesco!' Hampered by having to protect the Spanish
comb, Julia was a moment before she absorbed what
Francesco had said.

'What sort of journalist? I've a reason for asking,' she added,
withdrawing from his grasp. 'Your sister might be able to help
me.' It was easier to lie to Francesco than Roberto, but still
shabby. Julia spoilt her elaborate coiffure by a thumb-twist of
a curl. 'I'd like some advice on how to trace a relative. Someone
who may have worked in opera.'

'Like my father, eh?'

Julia yawned, appearing casual. She really needed help:
her search for Scarpia seemed blocked. The war records she
had found were incomplete. Books and journals had no

reference to a wartime torture cell controlled by anyone of that name, or habits.

The archives of opera houses contained posters, letters and photographs of only the more famous musicians. So far she had seen a picture of Gina Respini, the soprano Roberto had mentioned, and a poster for Nino Dontini, a name also on Roberto's list, but often the detail and addresses she needed could not be found. She had not had time to look through old newspapers and the like.

Besides which, officials were bored, or, as the librarian in Florence had been, actively discouraging. After several fraught encounters Julia decided that a direct approach over Scarpia was unwise. She returned to the fiction she had told Roberto, that she was attempting to trace a missing relative.

Not that this approach seemed at the moment to be any more successful. Giovanni Respini, writing in response to Julia's inquiry about her opera-singing 'cousin' in wartime north Italy, said he would only talk with a lawyer present and money up front. She had looked up in phone books and telephoned several names on the list Roberto had given her, finding that some had died (although the entry in the phone book was unchanged), others had moved away and no one knew where to, others would not talk to her – to a journalist, maybe, but not to a complete stranger.

Francesco's brown eyes sparkled: he could hardly believe his luck. Here was a perfect opportunity to whisk Julia away for a few days. Papà would just love Julia and as for Bianca – he'd have a word with his big sister.

'Come to my place today after the shoot – stay the weekend.'

Julia, seeing the burst of colour in Francesco's face, was touched. She deflated his bubble of pleasure as gently as she could. 'I'm sorry, Frankie, but I can't come this weekend. Roberto's flying back from Edinburgh today. He's promised to show me Milan.'

Francesco accepted this gracefully, as Julia hoped he would. 'Oh, yes, I think Ruth may have mentioned something.' He had only half-listened: that would teach him, thought the tenor. Having Padovano as a rival was a nuisance, but also increased

Julia's appeal, confirmed her attractiveness.

He smiled. 'No one but Bianca calls me Frankie.'

'I'll try to remember in future.' Julia's mobile features transformed themselves into a woebegone look.

Francesco laughed. 'You can call me Frankie as a special favour. What's he doing in Edinburgh?'

'Recording. And the night before last he had a live performance: Beethoven's *Missa Solemnis.*'

'With a plaster cast on his foot?'

'It's oratorio, idiot.' Julia gave the tenor an indulgent push in the chest with her fingers. 'He just stands there and sings.' She crinkled her eyes. 'He's singing the same piece tomorrow night in Milan.'

As she spoke, Julia felt a burst of energy buzzing through her body, an anticipation of future pleasures. After their day in Fiesole, Roberto had dropped her off at Clara's and then had to race to the airport for his flight to Scotland. Today, six days, seventeen hours later, she and Roberto would have an evening together, a night . . .

'Then it's off to O Sole Mio land, isn't it?' Francesco remembered Ruth saying *that*: with Padovano away in Naples it would be a perfect Christmas.

'On Tuesday,' said Julia. 'Three days' time.' The doctors said that Roberto's cast could come off by then and that he would be able to fulfil the rest of his winter opera engagements. At Christmas, he would be in Naples and she would be in Lucca.

'So next Saturday you're free.' Francesco interrupted Julia's thoughts.

'I am at the moment.' Not a very gracious answer; she wasn't helping this exchange along. Julia frowned: Francesco deserved better. She smiled. 'Surely that's Christmas Eve. What about your family?'

'It's Papà's house I'm inviting you to. He's broad-minded – has to be, with my sister.' Francesco leaned towards her. 'Bianca will be there if I'm not a sufficient lure.'

'I didn't say that.' Julia's dimples faded as her face grew serious. She didn't want Ruth left stranded over Christmas.

'She's coming too,' said Francesco. If he later 'forgot' Ruth's invitation that would be too bad. 'Now – your answer.'

'Yes.'

'Is that all you're going to say?'

'Yes please?'

'How about a kiss to seal the deal?'

Julia laughed, gliding closer. With Francesco she didn't need a stepladder to reach past his chin, but then she and Roberto had not yet kissed on the mouth, not even lightly.

Francesco's lips met hers: their kiss, with his hand in her hair, his arm pressing against her back, was a long one. Not unpleasant, but definitely not intended – at least not by her. Julia knew Francesco found her attractive: she found him very appealing, but there was Roberto . . .

Julia's eyes widened as over Francesco's shoulder she saw the door move. *Ruth*, she thought, trying to draw back from the embrace.

The door opened and Roberto walked in.

17

The fashion shoot was over. Roberto could feel electricity ruffling off Julia as she strode to the passenger side of the hire car and he unlocked the doors.

'Toss the music back – here.' From the driver's side Roberto scooped scores into his arms, dumping them on the rear seats.

Julia took her place. 'Thanks for the tips about Eboli,' she remarked, fastening her seatbelt. Eboli was the character she was playing in the Galatea *Don Carlos*: the make-up was tricky, since in this production Eboli was supposed to be both beautiful yet facially scarred. Roberto had sketched her some ideas; deft touches of make-up that would enhance her, add a suggestion of a darkly violent past. 'It'll make the role very sexy,' she said.

Her eyes were as fiercely luminous as a merlin's. Whenever he was close to Julia, it wasn't only sinews which were stiffened. Apart from an initial half-amused, half-angry instant when he'd felt like knocking Terni's teeth down his throat for taking advantage of a social convention, Roberto could pity the tenor. In the singing world, a kiss was only a kiss – except when it was more.

He had seen too much of the opera trade not to be wary. In this business of constant jet-setting and emotional discharge on stage, it was easy for performers to drift in and out of affairs, to believe their acted parts were for real. He didn't want that

to happen to Julia and him. As the English and Americans put
it, he wanted a relationship . . .

Julia, he thought, naked on the back seat of the Alfa Romeo,
dark hair pressed against the leather, eyes, lips, breasts
demanding attention, slender fingers thrusting at his fly zip,
dragging down his jeans . . .

So much for relationships. Roberto rubbed the back of his
neck. If it hadn't been daylight in a public place he'd have
dropped the car seats, taken her in his arms.

Julia turned her head aside. He wasn't going to touch her.
They had never kissed properly. She knew that Roberto liked
her so what was the problem? They were both adult, and in
three days' time he would be gone. Earlier hopes regarding
their night in Milan began to look farcical. Maybe she should
have packed her pyjamas, thought Julia, repressing a sigh.

Twenty-six, thought Roberto, fumbling for his ignition key.
Terni was twenty-seven: maybe more of an age for Julia. He
was thirty-four, already once married. Trying to be decent
and feeling like a shit, Roberto started the Alfa.

'I thought I was meeting you in Milan,' said Julia coolly as
the engine fired.

'I got in last night on an earlier flight.' Roberto rapped a
finger on the windscreen, his hand executing a cutting signal.
'There's your eager associate.' Francesco, with Ruth a little
behind, was weaving through the car park.

'He took me by surprise,' Julia muttered.

'Should I find a stepladder to put him on so I can hit him?'

Julia was struck by the stepladder analogy. 'Certainly not –
I'm visiting his family next week.'

It broke the tension – they laughed. Flooring the
accelerator, Roberto made the Alfa leap from the car park,
beating Francesco's convertible to the way out. Julia laughed
again and suddenly they could talk.

'I've a surprise for you in the car boot.' Roberto swung into
a stream of traffic.

'Big one, I hope,' said Julia, grabbing the handle above the
door. Roberto shot her a look which made her forget to
breathe.

Black curls, flashing grey eyes, knowing expression – she looked like a Caravaggio angel on probation, thought Roberto. He wanted her so much it hurt. Leaving every other car on the block for dead wasn't a substitute; it wasn't even a distraction.

Beside him Julia liked the speed: a non-driver, she didn't know the risks he was taking and he didn't want her hurt. Not in any way. Opera stars lived in a public world. He was still trying to live down and forget that final, highly publicised reason which Carlotta had given to every newspaper in Italy as her justification for divorcing him.

' . . . Pietro's no connection but Bianca Terni's going to help me to trace my relative . . .'

Bianca, thought Roberto, allowing the automatic to change down a gear to negotiate the snarled junction of the Florence – Bologna road. Bianca T. He'd seen that name recently.

' . . . she's a journalist.'

'I know. I read one of her pieces this morning.' Unable to resist Julia's look of surprise, he caught hold of her hand, nipping her thumb lightly between his teeth.

'Ow!' The shock set up a disturbing ripple of pleasure between her thighs. She saw the gleam in Roberto's eyes deepen. 'Shouldn't you be watching the road?'

Roberto gave her a big juicy wink and turned his head. The outskirts of Florence skidded past as she admired his profile.

'What was she writing about?'

'Some poor old codger gunned down in his flat last night in San Frediano. The police think it may be a gangland killing.'

Roberto slowed to a stop to collect a ticket for the autostrada. After a friendly word with the ticket man he flicked the card into Julia's lap.

'The funny thing is that Cesare Celere came from San Martino della Croce,' he continued, accelerating away from the toll booth, 'And in *Oggi* this morning, an editorial claims the dead man was about to reveal a sensational wartime scoop: you know, collaborators and the like. Don't worry – Cesare can't be *your* relative. He was only about seventeen when the war ended.'

Celere: the name meant 'quick', 'rapid'. Julia, removing her finger from the electric window panel, brought her hand up to her hair. 'Sprint,' she murmured.

'What is it?' asked Roberto. She was almost white. He switched the fan on to give her air.

'Sorry, it's been meltdown temperatures in the studio.' Sprint, one of the men she had hoped to trace, had been murdered. Rubbing her forehead, trying to absorb the news, feeling frustrated, strangely shocked, Julia seized the first different subject which came to mind. 'Did I tell you that a French house wants me to do a Wagner season in '97?'

'That's way too soon for you to be attempting Wagner. It'll burn out your voice.'

'I'm not a complete idiot,' answered Julia sharply. She shrugged her shoulders and smiled. 'Still it's wonderful to be asked, even though I hate to turn anyone down.'

The sun clashed into his eyes. Roberto tugged down the visor and poured on the power. 'You must never be afraid to say no, Julia.' His words meant many things, but Julia at that moment chose to see only one.

'Afraid? I've engagements booked up to 1999!'

Roberto took a breath. This was coming out wrong; Julia seemed to regard his concern as over-protectiveness. 'I only meant that you should be careful – as you're being now.'

'Don't patronise me.' Julia was thoroughly irritated. One of the penalties of her small size was that people would keep treating her as a child; it was disappointing that Roberto had fallen into the same trap. Maybe that was why he never made any real advances, she thought, crossing her legs, head held rigidly forward. Even Francesco's long kiss had been a touch reverential.

Beside her she felt the man tense then suddenly relax, as though some mystery had been explained. A smothered laugh escaped him and she twisted her head to glare.

Roberto was looking at the road. His faintly stubbled cheek was creased by a smile; his right hand cupping the steering wheel stroked a half-circle along it. 'All the five-star suites in Florence were booked for tonight,' he remarked, smoothly overtaking a lorry-load of Christmas whisky.

'So were the ones in Bologna,' answered Julia quickly. 'I know because I checked.'

He looked at her then, and his fingers touched one of her long earrings, pressing the cool silver against her neck. They regarded each other for an instant before Roberto returned his attention to the road and Julia lifted a miniature score of *Don Carlos* from her duffel coat pocket.

Without words they had decided to skip sightseeing in Milan.

'Here it is.' Roberto held the door open. He was interested to see where Julia would go, what her first words would be.

'How beautiful!' She was in the music-living-room before he had locked the door. As Roberto threw his jacket over the lobby bookshelf, Julia walked up to the picture over the mantelpiece, darted to the window to tug the curtain fully open and stepped back. For a moment only her eyes moved, then he saw the tip of her tongue sneaking between her teeth. She did that when she was concentrating.

Fighting the need to touch her, Roberto looked at the picture, one which Simone had pleaded for him to frame and hang properly. A summer scene at Fiesole, a reasonable attempt when it came to lighting and composition although the sitter's hands were embarrassingly wrong.

'The sun and trees are perfect.' Julia came and stood beside him. 'Is that your mother? You have her eyes. She looks happy.'

'She was.' He had painted her into the landscape two summers back, when she was still alive.

'What's she holding? Her fingers close over most of it.'

Roberto cleared his throat. 'A crucifix.' He hoped Julia wouldn't ask if he missed his mother.

She didn't. Running a finger lightly over his chest, she passed him and went to the piano. She opened the lid, struck a soft middle C, then lifted her head. 'Sorry to ask this but could I have a glass of water? Oh, and where's your toilet?'

'Through that door, second on the left. My room's next

door, you can leave your coat on the bed.' Roberto, conscious
of the thump of his plaster cast on the tiles and a dryness in
his mouth, moved back to the lobby. 'Make yourself
comfortable, I'll fetch your surprise from the car. I think you'll
find it more palatable than tapwater.'

'Have you noticed?' Julia's voice drifted to him a few
moments later as he remounted the stairs, 'Have you noticed
how it's always food with us?'

'As I told you, singers need to eat.' Roberto had said
'surprise', but there were three packages and he closed the
outer door with his heel. A delicious smell of freshly ground
coffee drew him to the kitchen where he found Julia without
her coat, barefoot, her curly hair fluffed out, eating segments
of tangerine. 'Found it in the fruit bowl. Hope you don't mind.'

Roberto dumped the champagne in the freezer, tossed the
roses in the sink, skidded the mini CD-player on the table,
and pulled her against himself. She was trembling slightly,
but then so was he.

God, he was so hard, so strong it was exhilarating. He was
kissing her as she had always wanted to be kissed, fierce and
deep and tender. His tongue inside her mouth explored every
tiny crease of flesh. He lifted her to kiss her breasts and she
wrapped her legs around him.

Somebody's shirt button pinged onto the floortiles.

There was a rapping on the outer door.

'Ignore it,' growled Roberto, grabbing her tighter as Julia
arched her back and pressed her right breast closer against
his curved fingers. His hands seemed to be everywhere at
once.

'I know you're there, your key's in the lock.'

If Ruth thought he had looked grim before she should see
him now, thought Julia: Roberto didn't so much stiffen as
solidify, seeming broader as his shoulders snapped back. His
eyes raked the twisting doorknob. 'What's he doing back?' he
rumbled. 'He's supposed to be in Perugia today and tomorrow.
Right now he's meant to be with the rest of the orchestra,
talking to foreign students!'

'Tidy yourself up a bit.' Julia tried to tuck in his shirt;

difficult, since he would not release her. 'You'd better let him in, Roberto.'

'Go on through.' He set her down, touched her cheek with his fingertips then whirled away; a large man stomping to the door, attempting to smooth down his clothes.

Julia finished making coffee and carried it on a tray to the living-room. Roberto and his father were in the lobby, speaking in low voices. When Roberto brought him through, it was obvious that Simone had been given some kind of shock. He did not acknowledge Julia, but slumped into the nearest armchair.

'Today was terrible.' His face was as slack and cold as ash.

'Come on, Dad. Julia's made coffee.' Squatting stiffly by the tray set on the carpet square, Roberto heaped sugar into Simone's cup. 'Drink this. You'll feel better.'

'Terrible, I tell you.'

Over Simone's chair, Julia's eyes met Roberto's. 'I'll get my coat, then. If I don't move now, the shops will be shut.'

'There's no need.' Roberto, gripping cup and saucer, pivoted awkwardly to his feet. His open hand gestured to the outer twilight, but seeing Julia's expression he quickly swallowed any further remarks.

Julia's eyes rested sympathetically on the lowered grey head. 'It was good to meet you, Signore. I look forward to talking with you later.'

She did not expect and did not receive a reply.

After Julia had gone, Roberto said quietly, 'Don't ever do that again, do you hear?' He set Simone's coffee down so violently on the mantelpiece that half sloshed into the saucer.

Simone met his son's set face with a look of apathy. 'What?'

Was Simone deliberately trying to provoke him? 'That lady is my guest,' answered Roberto. 'She's staying here tonight.' He was tired of having to pretend he was a child.

'Your mother wouldn't have approved,' said Simone wearily.

Roberto, standing by the mantelpiece, drank his own coffee – cold. Grimacing, he leaned sideways and flicked on a light. His father's face was in shadow; outside was darker still. He knew it was chauvinistic, but he hated the idea of Julia alone in Milan, a city she didn't know.

'It was terrible.'

His father wanted to talk and Julia had given Simone the space to do so. He mustn't waste her gift, thought Roberto. He settled in the second armchair.

Simone was deep in the past, and the past was his enemy. It had crept up on Simone that morning at Perugia: a German music student had found out somehow that he had once trained as a singer. The boy just hadn't left him alone. 'Why had Signor Padovano decided to concentrate on the viola instead of his vocal studies?' 'What were his favourite vocal roles?' 'Did Signore Padovano agree that Scarpia was *the* dramatic part for baritone voice?'

'Enough!' Simone had wanted to shout, when instead he had been forced to answer. Then there had been a horror of a masterclass. Inevitably, the German student had chosen to sing Scarpia with the Scala players.

'I know you've always said you detested *Tosca*, but you've rehearsed and performed it hundreds of times,' said Roberto at that point. His steadiness was both lifeline and irritation.

'Of course.'

'So playing the opera itself is not that disturbing to you?'

'No – or at least not until recently – until today in fact.'

'What was different about today?'

Simone rubbed at his breastbone. 'You wouldn't understand. You've never been in an orchestra pit.'

'Make me understand.'

'Roberto, I've only just got in.'

'Off a short flight. You want to tell me. Make me understand.'

Simone, embarrassed, searched for words to explain what he meant without losing face. Whenever he played at La Scala, he was out of sight, out of reach. The orchestra was round him, blocking out the more troublesome vocal resonances. He was with colleagues in familiar surroundings. Most importantly they were facing the conductor, their backs to the stage.

'The sound was different, more immediate. I could hear everything, *see* everything. As I watched that student it wasn't just my job any more, it was real.'

He rubbed at his eyes. 'Then there was this morning's news, that man murdered in his apartment. Today it was all too much.' Simone shuddered, long fingers clenching the chair arms. 'The student had a young voice. Like the Whisperer.'

'Ah, Dad.' Roberto was already on his feet, stepping towards him. He gave Simone a fierce hug. 'It's over. You don't ever have to go back to Perugia. It's all in the past.'

Simone's head lay against his son's shoulder: Roberto, the child he had wronged. Yet his boy never blamed him. 'Can I tell you something?'

'That's why I'm here.'

Simone took a deep breath. 'It's about the war . . .'

In the lobby, the telephone began to ring. Simone shook himself, drew back. 'Aren't you going to answer that?'

The moment was lost. Simone wasn't going to talk. Walking into the lobby, Roberto picked up the receiver. The answer-machine would have tripped on, but now it no longer mattered.

It was Galatea. They had learned Julia was with him from Francesco Terni. They wanted her for a video: there was a time 'window' at the TV station at six tomorrow morning, so she needed to fly down to Florence tonight. A car would be round to collect her in an hour to take her to the airport.

'I'll make sure she's ready,' said Roberto, putting down the phone. No afternoon together, and now no night.

'Dammit!' said Julia ten minutes later, when she returned and heard the news. She was glowing from her walk.

'What's that?' called Simone from the sitting-room. Roberto and Julia walked in from the lobby, Roberto explaining that his guest would soon be leaving.

When she had gone, Simone turned to Roberto. 'Who is that girl?'

'You should know, Dad; you've been flirting with her for the past hour.' Roberto sounded amused, or maybe relieved.

'Yes, but who is she really?'

'She's really Julia Rochfort. In other words no one you know,' answered Roberto casually.

Simone said nothing. As yet there appeared to be no need for more words, no need for any kind of action to prevent this person from establishing herself in his son's affections. But he did not like her, Julia Rochfort. He did not like her at all. She reminded him of something.

18

The big deal was in the bag. Krusak and her father were discussing new projects, walking around Pietro's Bologna gallery. Bianca slunk along behind, bearing a tray of nibbles and revelling in the hit her platinum hair, short blue suit and high heels was making. The art world was so wonderfully chauvinistic: apart from the distraction supplied by a few madonnas she had the place by the balls.

'That virgin and child cartoon by Titian's daughter?' Krusak, Pietro in tow, stopped before the drawing.

Pietro dabbed his strawberry nose with a handkerchief. 'Not one I'd recommend, Signore. The idiot who tried to clean it has wiped away its value. I purchased it as a personal favour . . .'

To the artist, thought Bianca, mentally applauding her father. Krusak was too big a fish to draw into the fake cartoon net, even though her boss di Salvo wished Papà to expand in this area.

'This, on the other hand, you would consider a work worthy of your gallery?' Krusak tipped his wine flute towards the main wall, where the Renaissance painting of Saint Sebastian was shown off to best advantage. Several dealers had gathered round this picture. Bianca went among them, offering her dainty bites.

'Undoubtedly.' A nervous tic was dragging at Pietro's mouth.

'Here, Papà.' Bianca presented her tray beneath his nose. It came to Bianca that this was the first time her father had stood anywhere within two metres of the picture. She gave him a maternal smile as he accepted her well-timed distraction and took a canapé.

Krusak, dismissing food with one languid wave of a narrow wrist, approached to examine Saint Sebastian's brushwork. Bianca noted how the dealers smoothed themselves out of his way, noticed too the bulge in the businessman's immaculate dinner jacket. A man so old should not wear his clothes so tight, she reflected, amused by Krusak's vanity. He had her report on Julia Rochfort, with those late additions supplied by kid-brother Francesco in his pocket – the envelope she had sent through the post exactly matched that bulge. It always creased Bianca that Krusak had not the slightest notion that she was the Anna who took his money.

Beside her, nose level with her shoulder, Pietro was talking to another customer – softly, because Krusak always demanded exclusive attention as a right. Papà still was not looking at the picture. Bianca, despite the fact that his spicy aftershave and her Chanel clashed, remained close as a moral support. Well, maybe not so much of the moral . . .

Below in the foyer the revolving door whooshed as a late viewer entered. Bianca was trying to see the big canvas through her father's eyes: what was it he disliked about the picture? The colours? The realistic blood? The fact the Saint was bound to a post, stuck full of arrows and looked as though he had been tortured? Those dark creeping figures?

For a mad instant she thought the new creeping figure had somehow detached itself from the oils. It was dripping, though from Bologna rain, not paint.

'So it's champagne? Used to be this stuff.'

"Castor Oil." The skeletal middle-aged man had obligingly stuck a label on the bottle. Water flew off his military-style greatcoat as he thrust the bottle out.

The dealers had drawn back: Krusak and Pietro held their ground. The tall skinny man seemed unable to decide which to address and harangued both. 'Fascist pigs! Thanks to you my father was ruined! You never went after the right people—'

'That man's drunk,' said Krusak. 'Get him a glass of water.'

Nobody moved. The tall skinny man flipped the cap off his shock of brown hair and, swaying on his feet, lurched a step nearer to his two victims. His eyes were swivelling, as though still uncertain on which man to fix.

'Year after year I've seen you prosper as you've built on the bones of the dead. And now, fifty years on, when you think it's all over, you're going to have a dance on people's graves!'

'This is a private showing,' cut in Pietro. 'Unless you leave I shall have no choice but to call the police.'

'Sprint's dead. You bastards killed him!' The thin man wiped his eyes with his sleeve. 'After all this time . . .' He lapsed into incoherence.

'Who's Sprint?' asked Pietro. Compared to the abnormally tall, black-coated intruder, he looked like a bewildered cherub beside the figure of death.

Krusak was pale with anger. 'I'll sue you for this. I'm a respected businessman.'

'Fascist!' shouted the intruder.

Krusak made to move forward, but Bianca, giving her tray to the nearest dealer, was there. Gliding up, she put her arm around the man's bony shoulder.

'You ought to be at home. You know you shouldn't drink so much.' Her warm brown eyes smiled into his as she turned him towards the door. 'Let me get you a taxi.' She removed the bottle from his slack grasp, gave that to a dealer.

The thin man blinked. 'You're an angel.' He was at the maudlin stage. Bianca, smelling his breath, marched him outside into the rain.

She stayed with him whilst someone inside the gallery ordered a taxi, and when it came, made the driver repeat the address to be sure he had it right.

'Glad that's over.' Pietro settled into Bianca's car with a sigh: the showing had broken up quickly tonight.

'Those gallery doors should have been locked.' Bianca kicked off her heels to drive in bare feet.

'You dealt wonderfully with our emergency, my darling. But then you always do.' Pietro patted her hand.

'Who's Sprint?' Bianca had this mischievous streak.

'Don't know.' Pietro yawned. His face held no knowledge, only sleep. So, thought Bianca, reversing up a one-way street, Sprint had been one of di Salvo's wartime 'indiscretions'. Unless Sprint and the drunk tonight were somehow connected with Jan Krusak – Krusak who was now one of di Salvo's closest legitimate business associates and a personal friend. That was interesting . . .

'Krusak's a cold bastard.'

Pietro's sudden statement made Bianca almost stall the car. She slammed in the clutch and braked. 'What?'

'I knew him during the war.'

'You never told me that.'

'No reason to, it's a long time ago.'

Another car, headlights flashing, bore down on them. Bianca let the clutch out again and carried on reversing. The driver flashed them all the way out into Via dell'Indipendenza.

'Prick,' muttered Bianca. They drove past the brightly lit main square. Bianca thought about her father and Krusak.

'If you don't like him why do you associate with him?' Papà was staring into the arcades; she began to repeat the question.

'The same reason he comes to me. Mutual profit. Also he may know . . . something.' Pietro turned to her. A blue and gold lighted star of David hanging beneath one of the colonnades was reflected in his right eye. 'Better you don't ask, angel.'

Bianca suppressed a smile. Papà was so cut up about his wartime 'collaboration' as he termed it that even referring to it caused him deep shame. She knew the story anyway: di Salvo had told her. All Papà's 'collaboration' amounted to was to 'shop' a POW to the authorities – an Englishman who knew no Italian and wouldn't have lasted five minutes outside the prison camp. Of course Pietro didn't want Francesco, *his son*, to know anything about it, but then who would want idealistic, immature Frankie to know anything the slightest bit unpleasant? Her brother was as judgemental as the public.

Not like di Salvo and herself, Bianca thought. They understood such matters, even though they might take steps to prevent such knowledge from reaching other, less informed ears.

Relaxing, Bianca stepped on the gas to wing the car through Saragozza gate and up the steep hill to the family home.

What a bore Pietro Terni was, always flicking him those sideways glances. Their paths had crossed in the war and Terni made sure that he never forgot it. He regretted having to deal with the man, but the Bolognese always had something he wanted. That Saint Sebastian, for example.

Krusak had booked into Bologna's grandest hotel. Now in the main suite he phoned down for a manicurist: afterwards he would have a light supper. Sitting on the four-poster bed, Krusak removed his jacket. Almost without conscious will, his fingers found Anna's report, smoothed out the expensive paper.

'Julia Valentina Rochfort, twenty-six years old, Anglo-Italian descent, father unknown, mother Angelica Varisi, grandmother Clara Rochfort-Scudieri.' *No surprises so far.*

'Presently engaged in a search for a missing relative from the region of the old village of San Martino della Croce.'

I don't believe that. The girl was an opera singer; if she played all her opportunities in the right way, Julia would soon have enough money to hire a private detective for such a sentimental chore. No, she was looking for someone else.

Who? Krusak lifted the paper to his lips. Was it anything to do with him? That idea was both dangerous and appealing: it was gratifying to think Clara's grandchild might be seeking him, but there were aspects of his past which were better hidden.

A knock interrupted these reflections. 'Come!' He slipped the report away.

The manicurist was small and dark. Soothed by the girl's chatter, Krusak permitted himself the luxury of an indiscretion. When she asked if he was staying long in Bologna he said unfortunately not. Christmas would be in Milan and the New Year in Lucca. He was booked to see the opera there.

'Lovely!' said the girl, hoping for a tip, 'Which one?'

'Verdi's *Don Carlos*.' Krusak smiled. The little fool didn't know what he'd planned to happen during that opera, the forces which, with a little prompting from Bazzini, could make or break a singer.

Including, if he wished it, Julia Rochfort.

19

His father was still having nightmares. Roberto had hoped after Simone had talked to him about his wartime experiences that his father would begin to feel easier. Instead, Simone appeared more fretful, starting almost every time a door opened.

Roberto, killing time in a bar before a visit to hospital for the plaster cast to be removed, considered meeting a psychologist. Dad thought therapy a fool's business, but if it helped him to come to terms with what had happened to him, fifty years before . . .

That was the puzzle. True, Simone had lost his wife comparatively recently: no doubt he felt guilty sometimes about Maria; Roberto knew that *he* did. The 'If only' syndrome. Yet had that event really been a trigger to his father's boyhood memories? Simone himself had given a clue: 'All those war trials,' he had said. 'I can't stop remembering.'

After a gap of fifty years . . .

Not trusting the fragile-looking stools, Roberto was leaning against the wooden bar. He had the place to himself: Milan was at the panic-buying for Christmas phase. He finished his coffee, staring at the dregs.

At least Simone would be busy from now until June. The opera season was in top gear. This month, La Scala was doing *Barber of Seville*.

Nothing in that joyful work to distress his father. And
Sandro and Margherita would stay over at the flat if he asked
them to: they'd done so on previous occasions when he was
abroad for a long time. Simone seemed delighted to have them
– he flirted with red-haired Margherita and spoiled his
grandson Paolo. The arrangement suited everyone, since the
younger couple were delighted to move in to an apartment
twice the size of theirs.

And, according to Sandro, Simone never had nightmares
when they were staying with him. Sandro didn't know what
Simone's nightmares were about.

Sandro and their father had always been close. Maybe he
was the trigger. Maybe Simone had something he wanted to
tell him, not Sandro: he knew that his father was keeping
something back.

Roberto frowned and raised his head. Outside the tinselled
bar door Milan bustled. He peered through the misted
windows. A woman caught his attention through the grinding
masses of people; small and dark, he tracked her till she
disappeared.

He didn't want his younger brother to know about Simone
being tortured. Sandro's little family gave Simone a slice of
normal life, one undisturbed by dark undercurrents.

He would have a discreet word with Simone's doctor,
thought Roberto. From his reading, scrambled whenever he
had a spare moment, he knew that torture could have
profound, long-lasting effects. Victims could feel ashamed even
for having survived. What was important for his father was
that someone would be there for him, whenever he needed to
talk. Simone was not persistently anxious but he was in a
vulnerable state.

Roberto scratched his throat. He would be away half of
next year.

Still, his father was not alone. He had a close family, a
satisfying job. The vital thing was to ensure Simone had
support without feeling smothered or that he was in any way
a burden. The best way to do that was to continue as usual,
thought Roberto, to get on with his own life whilst being aware

of this stress in Simone's life. When his father wanted to talk, he would be there. Sandro would keep looking in whenever he was on tour.

Christmas was sorted out: Simone would spend the rest of the month with Sandro and Margherita in their cramped but sunny little flat. All of which meant that he, Roberto, should be able to relax today and go on to Naples tomorrow night with a clear mind.

Naples. He had some business in Naples, something he would not share with any confessor. Again, Roberto swore to himself that he would find the man responsible for torturing his father. He would find him and when he did . . .

'Ten-thirty, Signore. You asked me to remind you.'

The bald barman jolted him back to Milan. In an hour's time he would be on the plane to Florence. Thoughts of revenge were blotted out in a blaze of energy as he strode from the bar. 'Relax' was the wrong word to use where Julia was concerned, in fact the idea was so incongruous . . .

Roberto whistled through the gap in his teeth.

Clara looked up as Julia entered the gallery. Her face was difficult to read, although her poise was a clue. Clara propped her book against a terra-cotta urn sprouting a pink camellia. 'You've been talking to Francesco.'

Julia nodded.

'So? What gems did he let fall this time?'

Julia came to the mahogany table. 'Would you like some fresh tea?' she asked, gathering spent crockery.

Clara rapped her wrist. 'You're not a servant.' She picked up a handbell. 'Andrea will bring us coffee. Don't pretend you haven't time to drink it, you've another twenty minutes before Roberto arrives . . . I like him.'

'So do I.' Julia made no secret of it. Today she sported a clinging silk dress and heels instead of jeans and trainers.

Clara nodded approval. 'Guy would have gone wild if he'd seen me like that.' She gave her throaty chuckle. 'Now how about filling me in on Francesco?'

'It's about his father.' Careful not to ladder her stockings,

Julia curled up in the wicker chair next to her grandmother's. 'Someone barged into Pietro's gallery last night during a private showing and accused him of being a Fascist.' Francesco had found that amusing; Julia less so, especially when Clara, tilting her head, observed: 'Well I suppose he was. Guy always knew that Pietro reported to the authorities in Bologna. He was a member of the party: that was known in Croce.'

Julia leaned forward. 'And you let him stay on your estate?'

'The authorities had their eye on the region. Guy thought better a devil we recognised than one we might not see. Besides, Pietro passed on harmless information.'

'The man in the gallery didn't think so.'

'Did Francesco describe what he looked like?'

'Very tall. Thin . . .'

'A bit like a skeleton in fact? That would be Stefano's boy. Of course I'd forgotten – Pietro told the Blackshirts about Stefano's hoard of "English gold" buried under his still. So it really existed? Well, well.'

Clara seemed remarkably sanguine about the whole affair, thought Julia. 'You didn't mind that he was a collaborator?'

'Pietro was doing what we all did in the war, trying to survive.'

'At the cost of his neighbours.'

'It's easy to be judgemental when you're safe.' Clara's tone hardened. Her living eye became as blank as the false one. 'Pietro never killed anyone. What if he did talk about the gold? A bit of money, which probably wasn't Stefano's in the first place. And he only admitted that much after he'd been tortured by Krusak. Week after week, Pietro gave them nothing – he reported because he had to, because if he hadn't, the Germans would have suspected my village of partisan activities. In the end the Germans and Blackshirts suspected *him* and Krusak had him interrogated – that was Pietro's collaboration! He confessed as much to me on the very day we escaped: he admitted everything whilst we were resting on the Ponte Vecchio. Do you remember what I told you about that day, Julia? How Pietro helped me? War is not as simple as you seem to think.'

Clara broke off as Andrea appeared in the doorway, cafetière and china set out on a tray. Maybe it was telepathy, Julia thought, still smarting. She flicked a hand through her hair, tugging out a knot she had missed. 'You didn't mention that Terni was a Fascist because of my naivety?'

'Maybe.' Clara's fingers flexed in her lap. 'So I forgot!' she burst out. 'Fifty years is a long time to remember.'

Julia flushed. She was allowing frustration over a lack of progress in her search for Scarpia to colour her common sense.

Andrea – grey, nimble, lean – gave her a wink as he left. As he got to know her, the chauffeur was becoming less formal. She must ask him about his wartime experiences. Julia had not forgotten Andrea's claim that Clara had saved his life.

They drank their coffee, Julia reflecting uncomfortably that her grandmother's reprimand was timely.

She had decided to concentrate her search city by city, beginning with the one closest to Croce, Bologna. One of the retired singers on Roberto's list who had played at the Bologna opera house had actually replied to her letter. Mario Felici declared himself a 'loyal admirer' of Clara Rochfort-Scudieri. Clara, whom Mario referred to as 'The Countess', had done him the honour of attending his opening night at the Bologna opera in December 1943. 'The Countess,' he reported, 'surrounded by her phalanx of German officers, had applauded generously.' As to the matter of her missing relative, Mario regretted he knew nothing . . .

German officers. Julia read that several times. Clara had said she and Guy made no contact with Germans, yet here, Clara had been seen at the opera with a group of Nazi officers.

'I remember that, December '43,' Clara confirmed when Julia, after draining her coffee, began to talk. 'But if I was surrounded by Germans then so was everyone else in the place.' She smiled. 'Mario always was a groveller.'

Julia frowned. 'I wish he'd told us something useful.'

'Give it time. You found out about Sprint.'

'That was in the newspapers.'

'Well, *I'd* missed the report.' Clara tapped her skull with a bony knuckle. 'Or maybe I saw it but forgot.'

They were laughing when Andrea announced Roberto.

20

Venice. Neither Julia nor Roberto had ever been to the floating city. Free of memories and ghosts, deserted by tourists in a day of freezing fog, Venice was theirs.

Leaning out on the Bridge of Sighs, Julia spoke their united thought. 'Glad we came.' Time, their constant harrier, glided like the mist-gilded streams under their feet as they regarded each other.

They kissed on the Bridge of Sighs, the silver fog rising from the water hiding them and the city in a secret embrace.

'I wish we could stay,' said Roberto, when they surfaced a little from the kiss. Julia turned a dreamy open face sidelong and ran her eyes over him. She wanted this rippling quiet, this day of misted sun glinting on the tops of suspended marble palaces, to go on for ever. No more struggle for success, no more troubles. No more Scarpia.

'I can't get used to you without that plaster cast,' she murmured, obliterating the world as she pressed her cheek against his chest. 'I like the suit.' Dark grey, classically cut, worn with eye-grabbing panache, the suit had been a revelation. She already had designs for borrowing the waistcoat. She hugged him tight. 'You look great.'

'And you are truly gorgeous.' Roberto stroked a hand down her back. 'Why do you hide those legs?'

His hand, and even more his eyes were doing things to her.

'Shall we?' he said.
'Yes.'

They took a gondola. Paying the gondolier not to sing, they
settled against the heart-shaped backrest, Roberto giving Julia
his cushion. Whilst he chatted to the gondolier about the latest
football scores, Julia trailed her fingers through mist to cold
silken, softly grey-green waters. Both were too aware of each
other to need more than the lightest touch of their bodies
side by side as they floated on the cradle of Venice's canals.

Venice in a shimmering winter mist was as one of its more
extravagant glass creations, cloudy and baroque at the base
its marble statues and wrought-iron house-grills looming
through the mist like porcelain flowers stuck on Venetian
chandeliers. Then halfway up the narrow buildings – just over
the top of Roberto's brown spiky curls, Julia calculated – the
mist thinned and sunshine dusted each white campanile.

'We're here,' Roberto said softly. The gondola swayed
against a painted landing post; a doorstep floated inches above
the water. This was his surprise to her: a home, not a hotel
their own private place. He had booked it, along with a few
extras, at Florence airport before they made their flight.

He opened the front door. The gondolier, paid and tipped
was gossiping into his portable phone about having met
Roberto Padovano. ' . . . and you know he's really normal . .
great bloke . . . asked about the big match, you know, Roma
versus Inter-Milan . . .'

Someone in the Romanesque palace opposite shook their
shoes out of the balcony window. Hidden by a curve of
buildings, muted by fog, two waterbuses honked as they
passed on the Grand Canal.

Julia rose circumspectly to her feet. The last thing she
wanted to do was spoil the moment, shatter the delicious
tension by an ungainly lurch off the boat. In jeans and trainers
she would not have thought twice, but high heels and a fitted
coat were a different matter.

Roberto did not offer his hand but merely plucked her from
the gondola, swinging her lightly off her feet into his arms

hey entered the Venetian house that way, Roberto crossing
e threshold carrying Julia. Closing the door on the grinning
ondolier, he continued an unhurried advance to the bedroom.

'Didn't I see a piano as we whisked through the living-room?'
ked Julia. 'And a log fire and a Christmas hamper?'

'You did,' answered Roberto, unbuttoning her coat, 'This
as once a composer's house. Now it's a luxury holiday home.'
owly, he unfastened her shoes.

Julia closed her eyes as his strong fingers brushed her
akles. 'Which composer?' she asked softly, as her high heels
ent skating across the mosaic floor to the big sunlit window.

'A German. He wrote many beautiful hymns – but then
erman is a spiritual language.' Spirit was not what Roberto
as feeling at that moment. He swept her out of her coat onto
e gold satin sheets.

Julia helped him to shrug off his jacket and loosen his tie.
Vhat kind of language is English?' she asked, her nimble
agers undoing his waistcoat as his hands deftly slid into her
ess, dispatching the fastenings. Her fingers brushed warm
sh as his thumbs circled the engorged nipples of her
easts.

'Definitely pastoral.' Roberto's hands slipped gently
etween her thighs. 'Country matters.' As she gasped he
ssed her.

Off came the rest of the clothes, in silent, feverish haste.
ne pleasure of seeing each other naked was to be fully
ijoyed in a later, less urgent moment; now it was contact,
e mutual desire for possession. They burned in each other's
ms.

'What about French?' Julia murmured several long
oments later, fingers teasing an intimate caress. He was so
m, so good to touch; she wanted all of him.

'Intellectual.' Her hand guided. Her body enfolded. It was
etter than anything he had known before. Sweating, rigid in
elight, Roberto forced himself to be slow.

Julia felt him moving deep inside her. The virtues of Spanish
d Italian must keep. She kissed his throat. His arms
ghtened around her. The spikes of pleasure intensified as

his hips ground against hers. She writhed beneath him. As he came he shouted her name. As she came she kissed him on the mouth.

For both, it had been worth the wait.

21

'You'll like her.'

Bianca slid the contact lens in place and Francesco popped into view in the mirror, straddling the threshold of her bedroom, crowing his pitch like a rooster.

'Stop fussing – you'll need another shower.' Bianca pouted. 'What shade of lipstick?'

'Carrot.'

'Hey! If you want me to be good you'd better be kind.' She slipped into her steepest heels and rumba'd over. 'Love your ass in those tweeds, little brother.'

Francesco laughed, growing up again to twenty-seven, not seventeen. 'I've been spoiled. For years women have fallen into my lap. I'm discovering the pleasures of the chase.'

Below the intercom buzzed. Francesco brushed a speck off his tweeds, glanced at his sleek appearance in the mirror.

'Let her get in,' said Bianca but her brother was down the stairs. Bianca checked her sedge green suit, fastened an Aztec-style choker round her throat. She adored big costume jewellery.

Skipping lipstick, Bianca paused on the landing, letting Francesco and Elizabetta, their unassuming mother, get their 'hellos' over with. They were rhapsodising about Julia's gift of chocolates. Julia had an amazing voice: deep, throaty Bolognese accent; a siren sound in any language.

'I suggested to Andrea we pick up Ruth, save you a trip.'

Ruth, thought Bianca. It seemed Francesco had done his trick of inviting someone and then conveniently forgetting. Bianca hoped he was embarrassed, although mother said nothing, vanishing into the kitchen to tell the staff there was another guest.

A car turned in the gravelled drive: Andrea was leaving. Bianca had to walk downstairs to greet her brother's *two* guests. She hadn't decided what persona she was going to be.

The door of the master bedroom clicked open. 'Come down with me, duchess?'

Bianca smiled. In his handstitched Monetti suit, a brown cashmere, cream silk shirt and stylish tie, Papà was a smaller-made version of Tancredi di Salvo. Not sophisticated, not with those saucy eyes, but successful. She was proud of him.

'Sure.' Bianca hooked her arm in his.

'Goodness.' Pietro bobbed down to peep under the arm of the brass statue gracing the hall beneath, 'She's so like Clara – as Clara used to be.'

Julia was a sell-out: Bianca didn't need the signal of having to match Pietro's quickened step on the oak staircase to know that. No state-of-the-art fashion for this daughter of the aristocracy, she wore a beaded dress in a cerulean blue, matched by silver earrings, clutch bag and shoes. Her black hair curled round her oval face and her make-up was immaculate. Her brilliant grey eyes held them as Bianca and Pietro advanced.

'My dears!' Papà broke ahead to kiss cheeks. He had to stretch to kiss Ruth, and as he did, Bianca pounced. Conscious of Francesco hovering to draw Julia off into the sitting-room, she decided to give him a fright.

'Delighted to meet you. Hope you don't mind me saying, but a fur would look sensational with that dress.'

Frankie tried to step on her foot. Julia smiled. 'I'll bear that in mind.'

'I thought Italian women liked furs.'

'Ah, but I'm English.' And before Bianca could react Julia

defused the whole build-up by two swift kisses on Bianca's cheeks. 'Happy end, happy beginning.' She gave the New Year greeting. Early, reflected Bianca, but appropriate.

And then it happened.

A woman yelled from the kitchen. Her cry was overwhelmed by shouting, but then her yell became a scream. Francesco dashed towards the archway but Julia, with the quickness which seemed part of her nature, was ahead, light footfalls drumming on the tiles, dress floating round her running body. By the time Bianca and Ruth reached the kitchen, Julia had the woman's hand thrust under the pulsing cold tap whilst the cook still scolded. Elizabetta turned to her husband, now standing in the doorway.

'She's burnt her hand,' she said. Her thin lips were moist. The cook was volubly shaken. The woman, a Sicilian hired to help out over Christmas, was sobbing against Julia's shoulder.

The polenta, braziered on a sizzling grill – cause of this excitement – was over the floor.

'Signor Terni, she was careless.'

Julia threw the cook a glance and the man subsided. 'It's all right,' she repeated to the Sicilian. 'You'll be fine.' She hooked a chair with her foot and made the woman sit down whilst the stream of healing water poured over her burnt palm.

Bianca, breaking from the frozen tableau clustered in the door, hustled to fetch a dressing. When she returned to the kitchen, Elizabetta had vanished. Francesco and Ruth stood uncertainly together – they made a good-looking pair: the thought struck Bianca as she trod over yellow blobs of polenta towards the metal sink.

'You'll need this.' She handed Julia the dressing. Julia nodded and turned off the tap.

'Thanks, Bianca. Do you think you could . . . ?' Her eyes, shooting away from Bianca for an instant, opened wide. 'Nothing.' She bent her head again to the Sicilian.

Bianca knew she was lying. Julia had seen what she had seen: Pietro staring at the woman's livid hand.

Reaction overtook Julia at lunch, when the scene appeared to have been forgotten by everyone else. Bianca and Ruth were chatting about Galatea, with Francesco breaking in with pithy observations about fashion houses. Julia, despising herself for acting, switched on her listening face and made herself eat a good part of each course laid before her.

'You mustn't blame them.' Pietro's voice caused Julia to drop her spoon into her half-finished champagne sorbet. The meal had been a mixture of Italian and international cuisines. She swallowed the chilly mouthful and twisted in her seat.

'Shock causes people to react in different ways.' Pietro Terni was smiling. 'Many freeze.'

'It's a perfectly natural response.' Did he want her to apologise for rushing into the kitchen? Was he explaining the behaviour of Elizabetta, who since the incident had retired to her room? Julia shrugged. 'Nerves make me speed up – you should see me before I go on stage.'

'That would be an English stage?' Down the table as though in response to Pietro's question, Bianca laughed.

Julia smiled uncertainly. Did Pietro think she denied her Italian side? It wasn't like that at all. Rather because of her grandfather Guy she had discovered a new pride in being English. 'Only some of the time,' she answered. 'From now on any pre-performance hysterics are going to be in Italian surroundings.'

Pietro chuckled, rubbing his hands. 'Watch out, some of our audiences are lethal. I had an egg thrown at me in the Teatro Regio when I "cracked" a note.'

Julia warmed to him. 'Grandmother said you were in opera.' She was vividly aware that Pietro would know other singers from the 1940s. In a moment she would ask—

'Francesco Vincenti!' Pietro's reply was definite. 'I'll never forget him, he was the best baritone I ever heard, although young, my age. A big man with hands like a blacksmith's. He said he came from Bologna but his accent was that of the mountain villages: Francesco was embarrassed by his peasant background.

'I named my boy after him.' Pietro motioned to his son as the cook, serving at table because the Sicilian help could not, gathered sorbet dishes. 'It's a pity no recordings were made, but then Francesco had a short career and retired right after the war: he didn't like the travelling. Of course he's dead now.'

Pietro smiled and Julia smiled, covering her disappointment. Vincenti was a new name to her but, if Vincenti were Scarpia, then Scarpia was dead.

'Hadn't he a birthmark on his chin?' she asked, recalling the little of what Clara knew of her tormentors. 'Grandmother mentioned something of the kind.'

'Then she must have mixed him up with another man, Francesco's face at twenty-five was as smooth as a baby's. He did have an earring: thought it made him look tough. But how is Clara?'

The main course was being served. Francesco was helping Ruth to vegetables. Pietro did Julia the same service.

'Thank you.' Julia, feeling she could not eat another bite, picked up her fork. Her heart was thumping: Clara had said that one of the men in the underground chamber wore an earring. Of course it could mean nothing. Francesco Vincenti. She could find him through death records.

'Your grandmother, how is she?' Pietro repeated; she was forgetting her manners.

'Grandmother is amazingly well. She sends her good wishes.' Clara had also sent a floral arrangement, but Ruth, climbing into the Mercedes, had accidentally tipped the basket off the back seat onto the floor. Poor Ruth. Julia was glad she seemed to be enjoying herself now.

'You must send my apologies for not keeping in touch. I was always an appalling letter writer – even to the most beautiful of women.' Pietro crinkled an amiable wink at her.

'I believe you're a bit of a rogue, Signore.'

'All I can be at my age.' But Pietro had straightened in his chair, preening over her remark.

'Tell me, as a neutral observer, what do you think of our war trials? Late in the day, eh?'

The change of subject was so startling that Julia had another mouthful of duck in white wine to cover herself whilst she thought. She was sensitive to how she must seem to Pietro, coming as a living image of her grandmother. It was a long time ago, but her face was part of his past. Perhaps it had been unkind for her to come, and yet she needed to see Bianca. Her first loyalty was to Clara and her wishes.

'If it allows those victims who want to be heard to tell their stories then I can't believe it's too late. Of course many may prefer to forget, and their wishes should be respected.' Julia stared at her silver napkin ring. 'As for bringing men to trial after so long a gap, do you remember that case in Israel a few years back? Nothing was resolved and yet the man accused of being a concentration camp guard will have to live the rest of his life with people wondering, was he, did he? I think you need to be very sure you have the right man.'

'Don't you think the victims would know who abused them?'

Pietro had known of course. Krusak, the Nazi officer. Clara had been captured by Italian men, people she knew and yet did not know. Could Clara, Guy and Pietro have been imprisoned in the same place, unaware of each other? No, thought Julia, shaking her head. Pietro had been taken to Bologna, then released; the place he'd been held had not been bombed. Yet still the question remained: could it have been Krusak who had ordered the torturing of her grandparents? If so, where did the opera connection fit?

'You shake your head. You don't think that's possible?'

'Oh no,' answered Julia. 'Or rather yes, yes, I do. Some will have no doubts, and for them . . .' Julia paused, wanting to say this right. 'For them justice must be served, and soon.'

Pietro raised his water glass and sluiced a mouthful to clear his palate for the next wine. His twinkling eyes watched Julia as he put down his glass. 'But do you really believe that will happen? Look what's been happening in Bosnia, the atrocities going unpunished – that's now. What chance then for fifty-year-old war crimes, especially when the perpetrators are today successful, respected?'

'Not all, Papà,' broke in Bianca, 'only fifty per cent.'

'Naughty girl!' Pietro leaned down the table and pinched Bianca's arm. He turned to Julia. 'You know this one is a journalist, always stirring that nose of her in things.'

'What are you two talking about?' Francesco nudged Ruth sitting next to him. 'Don't they look serious for Christmas?'

Julia jerked back her chair. 'If you'll excuse me.'

She escaped to the Ternis' vast marble bathroom. Francesco Vincenti, Sprint, Guy, Respini, Krusak, Clara, Pietro: the names spun in her head. Her time with Roberto in Venice seemed almost in the future now, so much of this lunch was haunted by the shadows of the past.

Drops of blood spattered into the basin as she dashed water over her face. A nose bleed. Usually she only had those when she was pushing herself too hard. She hadn't time for a nose bleed.

Someone was singing. A tenor. Not Francesco: Pietro. The sound was clean and pleasant, like the man himself. Julia nipped the bridge of her nose.

'Stop, won't you?' she muttered, frustrated at her body's weakness. There was a knock at the door.

'Coming!' she called, flushing a bloodied tissue down the toilet, rapidly washing her hands.

'You OK?' Francesco tried the door as Julia opened it.

'I'm fine.' She smiled as his dark eyes scanned her face, aware of how handsome he looked in his English tweeds. She enjoyed the easy companionship which existed between them, although always aware that Francesco would be happy to make that more than friendship . . . On the whole, the male Ternis seemed more agreeable than the women, but perhaps that was a sexist thought. She still had to talk to Bianca. 'Let's go listen to your dad.'

Papà never could resist showing off, reflected Bianca as she finished her duck. A moment between the main course and the fruit and he was out of his chair and at the piano in the living-room next door, accompanying his own high notes. All because Ruth had asked what kind of music he liked.

'Go and listen,' she told Ruth. 'He'll love you for it.'

Ruth regarded Bianca through her slightly prominent blue eyes and then slipped from her chair. A tall girl in a red dress cut to show off a trim waist and disguise full hips, her only flaw was that she moved badly, shoulders slightly stooped.

Still, she wasn't bad, thought Bianca, coolly assessing Ruth as she disappeared through the door. Her fair skin with its subtle tan looked great and her hair was her best feature; a natural honey blonde, long and heavy. It was a pity she wore it loose around a face whose even features tended to be lost behind two gold curtains.

Ruth, she had learned through lunch, was twenty-seven. Her father worked as a librarian at the Getty Center in Santa Monica and her mother was a sculptor. Ruth was the eldest of three sisters. After a sheltered upbringing in Culver City, she'd moved to Rome to complete her vocal studies. She spoke Italian with a Roman accent and English with a soft Californian accent. Francesco liked the accent, and he liked Ruth.

Bianca liked Ruth, even if she was shy, that kind of clam-up-then-gush shyness which Bianca had seen in a few other Californian women. When introduced, Ruth had said, 'But Francesco said you were blonde!' At which Bianca had laughed.

'I was when he saw me last. I like to keep him guessing.' Bianca changed her hair colour so often that she wasn't sure of its natural shade: dull mouse, she reckoned.

With the song birds out of the room, Bianca lit a slim cigar. She heard Francesco and Julia enter the living-room. Julia's mixed responses to her brother were interesting, nicely ambivalent, Bianca thought. If she hadn't known better she would have concluded that this warm and cool treatment was part of a ploy, but Julia was unusual. When a woman doesn't give you the sweeping glance, the head to toe once-over as you say 'Hi' for the first time, she's an original.

Papà's recital seemed to be reaching a climax. They would be back soon. Rising from her seat, Bianca stepped along to the kitchen to order fruit and coffee.

When she returned, the performance next door was still going on. Ruth and Frankie had struck up a duet from *Don Carlos*.

Should she mention the rumours she'd been hearing about that opera production? Bianca was debating the point when the door opened and Julia sped in.

'Looking for my handbag.'

'Wait,' said Bianca, as Julia plucked her clutch bag from the side of her dining chair and made to leave. 'My little brother tells me you're after my advice.'

Julia's expression didn't change but she hesitated before sitting down. *She doesn't like doing this,* thought Bianca. Julia reminded her of herself at the same age, when she still had scruples. She was thirty-six now.

Julia was talking about a missing relative, the idea Bianca had heard parroted by Francesco and which she had included in her report to Krusak. She decided to test this alibi.

'A private detective might be more useful than I can be.'

'And expensive.' Julia's answer was crisp. The truth was that Clara did not trust private investigators. Her dealings with the various men she had hired to try to trace Angelica had left Clara with a low opinion of freelance operators. 'Such people can always be bought off,' her grandmother had said.

Bianca was almost convinced, but not quite. There was a story here: her journalist's instincts were buzzing, and not only because of Julia's and Pietro's lunch-time conversation about war criminals. She decided that it would be worth her while to do some digging of her own for this 'relative'.

'Here's what I'll do. First, get you a press card: that should open some doors. Second, I can give you two names right now. Number one is Emilio Gucci – no relation of the fashion outlet, this guy's a carabiniere.'

'The police.'

'Ex-police. He's retired. Used to be the Marshal of Ponte Maggiore.' Bianca thought she detected a flicker of interest, but wasn't sure. 'Emilio still has contacts in the force and he owes me. I wrote a sympathetic piece on his arrest of a Mafia suspect when every other reporter was sending in copy about police brutality. Emilio's a rough one but he's never hurt a woman. I think he'd help. Do you want me to set up a meeting?'

Julia nodded.

'Do you want me to come with you?'

Julia laughed. 'Thanks, but you'll have already done enough. I don't want to waste your time on my family history.'

'Fair enough.' Bianca let it go: she could do her own following up after Julia had visited. 'The other person who might prove useful is a woman. She'll talk if you offer money. Calls herself Rita. She was a child prostitute in Bologna during the war, knew all kinds of weird people.'

Julia flushed and looked at the big painting at the end of the room. At the other side of the wall Francesco and Ruth were warbling away.

Bianca stubbed her cigar onto a china sideplate and rose, smoothing down her suit. 'What do you think of it?' she asked, coming alongside the younger woman. 'The water-colour.'

'The colours are vivid for an Impressionist picture.'

Julia recovered her poise fast, thought Bianca. 'That's because it's a fake.' She laughed as Julia started up, stepping closer to the painting. 'You were right about Papà; he is a rogue.' Bianca, reflecting on di Salvo's command that Papà's gallery expand in the fake cartoon area, concluded that her father was not alone.

Julia smiled. 'It's still a good picture.'

Bianca nodded. Close-to Julia looked drawn: Francesco said that between her rehearsals and practice Galatea had been working her hard. They were developing a line of clothes for the smaller woman, with Julia as a model.

She deserved a warning, Bianca decided.

'Sounds good.' She motioned to the door.

'Yes, they sing well together.'

'Don't expect it to be this easy in the opera house.'

Julia shot her a piercing look. 'Am I right in assuming that you mean more than the usual performance difficulties?'

'You better brace yourself for some Mediterranean venom. The Galatea *Don Carlos* has stirred up bad feeling: too many non-Italians in the cast. Audiences don't like it.'

'Well.' Julia flicked a bead on her dress, 'Ruth and I will just have to change that.'

Bianca nodded, wondering exactly which 'relation' Julia was looking for, and why. It should prove interesting to find out more.

22

'See Naples and die,' ran the expression. Death could be by asphyxiation, gunshot or fireworks, concluded Roberto. The opera crowds were gloriously warm and enveloping, so too the yellow smog which he could smell even in this fourth-storey apartment. Out of the window, Vesuvius was blanketed by the stuff. Down at street level in the Piazza Mercato feline street kids badgered passers-by for cigarettes and, with Neapolitan insouciance, chucked firecrackers into the mêlée of clapped-out Fiats.

'Traffic's worse every year.' Umberto Grazzi thrust a full glass into Roberto's hand. 'What a place!'

'I like it,' said Roberto. Naples was noisy, dirty, vivid. Through the grimy pane the southern sun was a balled fist on the back of his neck. 'Salute.' He tossed back the rough Gragnano wine and smacked his lips.

The grey-suited police official, who had begun to thaw when Roberto dropped a brown-envelope bribe on the top of his TV, relaxed his heavy features into a genuine smile. The accent might be hard to follow, but this Northerner knew the ropes.

'So you want me to lift a few files for you, ask certain people certain questions.' He dropped onto a saggy bed, leaving his guest standing. 'What for? And I don't mean what information.'

'My reasons are my own.'

Looking up at the dark closed face Umberto said quickly,
'I don't want any trouble.'

'It's nothing to do with the Camorra. I'm after a different
criminal breed. The kind that supported Mussolini.'

Umberto finished his drink, rolling the glass into the pillow.
'Old men, huh?'

So is my father, thought Roberto. As Cesare Celere's murder
showed, age made no difference. Old or not, the men he was
after were still the same ones who had tortured.

'Will you do it?'

'You know it's illegal?'

Thanks for the warning.' Roberto put his glass on the
window-sill. 'You haven't answered my question.'

'You haven't told me what you want.'

Simone had said he was fourteen when captured by Scarpia,
which meant the months after 19th March, 1943, through that
summer up to autumn. Roberto frowned. 'Records and
recollections from spring 1943 up to October first when the
city was liberated by the Allies.' Following his conversation
with Simone, Roberto had re-read his history. Now he counted
off on his fingers. 'Known Fascists operating in the Naples
area. Members of any partisan units here, particularly one
led by an Englishman—'

'Unusual.'

'This Englishman married a local girl. She was tortured by
one of these groups, probably a pro-German outfit. They
played chunks of opera to add a certain frisson to the occasion.'

'Jesus! And you a singer . . .'

'I want the leader. Known as the Whisperer. This would be
a young man, though probably a long-time member of the
Fascist party.'

'I'll see what I can do, although we never had as many
Fascists down here as you in the North.' Umberto levered
himself to his feet and crossed the painted concrete floor to
the telephone. 'Give me today, and meet me on the waterfront
at midnight.' He shook a cigarette from the packet on top of
his cooker and lit it on the antiquated gas ring.

'Wear something old,' he advised. 'We may have to do a

little breaking and entering if the records you're after are in storage – I could ask for them through official channels, but that could alert the very men you want: besides, it could take weeks.' He regarded Roberto through luminous, thickly lashed black eyes. 'I don't think you have the time.'

Roberto shrugged his shoulders, saying nothing.

The midnight air was softly warm as Roberto walked out of the Naples opera house and past the marble splendours of the royal palace. Pursued by autograph hunters, he had strolled down most of Via Partenope past his hotel and along the sea-front before he could call himself alone. The lights of the Castel dell'Ovo blinked at him across the petrol-coated waters of the bay.

Roberto turned his back on the boat-bobbing darkness and watched women cruising on foot for customers, the lighted tips of their cigarettes pulsing like fireflies whilst they cracked jokes with each other in ringing voices.

'I hope she's worth your saving it, honey,' one luscious brunette called to him. '*I'd* give you a fuck for free.'

Roberto grinned. 'She is, and you wouldn't,' he said, turning to go.

In the dark he heard a man cough.

'It was more expensive than I thought.'

Umberto Grazzi had suddenly materialised beside him. For an ungainly man, Grazzi could move with uncanny quiet when it suited him.

'The 1943 files covering the areas you mentioned – it cost more to get them than I expected.'

'How much?' Roberto had anticipated something of the kind and counted out the sum without comment.

The cash disappeared into the policeman's jacket pocket and he lifted six bulging plastic bags, three each hand. 'I've put these in order, but we need to get through them tonight.'

'What about public documents?'

'Ah, now there we're in luck.' Umberto picked his hairy nose reflectively before he explained.

'The records *you* want. They were in the usual place, see?'

His grey-suited arm flapped in the general direction of two huge towers looming over the roof-tops. 'Except now they've been moved. Doesn't matter why; the main thing is they're in a building in the Spaccanapoli district. What they're doing there is anyone's guess, but we can get at them.'

'Now?' Roberto asked.

'As good a time as any.'

Whoever had decided to deposit any public records – however old and unused – in the warren of tenements which formed the Spaccanapoli district was an idiot or a genius, thought Roberto, kicking his way through rubbish and ducking under lines of washing.

'I've been asking round, as I said I would.' Umberto's voice, muffled by the close buildings, drifted back to Roberto. 'No one's heard of the Whisperer. No one knows anything about an Englishman.'

'They may have been known by other names,' began Roberto, stopping when the policeman motioned him to silence.

'This is the place.' Umberto crouched by a paint-peeling door and began to pick the locks. A prowling cat ignored him, the old drunk at the end of the alley, pissing under a shop window full of violins, was more interested.

'Hey! You're not from round here.'

He waddled forward, trousers still unzipped, and made to grab Umberto's shoulder. Roberto caught him and swung him, not hard, against the wall. 'You've never seen us.'

He let the man drop and the drunk scarpered.

'Here we go,' said Umberto over his shoulder. They stepped through into a cone of dim light shed by a bare bulb.

Ranks of filing cabinets, shelves of dusty tomes, a child's umbrella, greeted them. Umberto switched on his flash light and began to walk the corridors of shelves in the stuffy, windowless room.

'What about upstairs?'

The policeman shook his head. 'It's all here. Ah! Now we're coming to it.' Jamming the torch between his teeth, he rapidly picked the padlock of one of the filing cabinets and dragged open the metal drawer.

'Want to look?'

'Sure.' Roberto, wishing he'd had the sense to bring a torch, groped through the bundles of documents for the letter P. Whilst he was here he might as well look up his father's old records.

Umberto finished picking another padlock and heaved open a whole series of drawers. 'These are some of the city archives. Help yourself. I'll start on the war files in my plastic bags.'

Roberto searched for hours but every public record showed the same thing: Simone Padovano had not been in Naples during the war, nor anywhere near Naples until *after* the war. According to city archives, the Padovanos – Aurelio, his wife Lucilla and their son Simone – had appeared in the Vomero district in 1946. They had lived in Naples for four years before moving to Fiesole.

According to *these* papers, they had come from a village in northern Italy. Roberto read the name of the village with a growing sense of disbelief.

Simone Padovano had been born in Castel San Martino.

'Nothing here about a wartime torturer called Whisperer,' said Umberto.

They were back in the policeman's apartment, sitting on the floor with papers strewn everywhere. It was four in the morning and Roberto had a plane to catch by breakfast.

Roberto rubbed the back of his neck. 'What about the other references I suggested?'

Umberto flicked his pen at a brown file. 'Nothing under "opera", "Tosca", "Puccini" or "Cesare Celere". But the last couple of names you gave me, they were useful.' He held out a sheet of paper. 'Here. I've written you a copy of what I found.'

Roberto glanced at the sheet before folding it and putting it safely in his wallet. 'Thanks.'

'Sorry there wasn't more.'

Roberto nodded. Simone had lied to him and Sandro. He didn't feel angry or cheated, but he did wonder why.

Later, he looked at the copy of the paper on the plane. An Allied war document, how it had come into the hands of the Naples policeman was likely to remain a mystery.

Umberto, copying the paper, had underlined parts:

'Scarpia: code-name for the leader of a pro-Nazi cell which operated for a few months in 1944 behind the German lines in northern Italy. Nationality of Scarpia unknown. Known to have used extreme ruthlessness against Italian partisans and those suspected of spying for the Allies. Captives were tortured, then killed by a single shot in the back of the neck.'

Reading that again, Roberto found the statement as chilling as he had done the first time. A vivid image of Simone sitting up in bed, tears running down his cheeks, reared up at him from the maze of words. Thinking of his father, Roberto read on.

'Spoletta: code-name for the second in command of a pro-Nazi cell (see reference to Scarpia above).'

Scarpia, not Whisperer, 1944, not 1943, North, not South. What was going on here?

He put away the paper and tried to snatch some sleep – nothing doing.

Admitting defeat, Roberto lifted a miniature score of *Don Carlos* from his jacket pocket and settled down with it.

Should he phone Julia to tell her he was coming to her first performance? he wondered, trying to block out more disturbing thoughts.

No, he decided. Let it be a surprise.

23

Two letters for Julia. The first from Roberto – they were writing to each other daily. The second from Signora Dontini, widow of Nino, the final name on Roberto's list whom Julia had found in the Bologna phone book. Julia had written to her, as she had written to so many others without result, and was surprised when Signora Dontini replied. The lady had invited Julia to her house. Her sister would also be there.

Eleven-thirty in central Bologna. Then another two meetings at seven p.m. and midnight the same day, organised by Bianca.

The train was stopping. Julia slipped her correspondence into her pocket, the coat she had worn in Venice. From his letters, Roberto remembered Venice as vividly as she did.

But today it was Bologna. She was going to be busy.

Cutting through the waiting-room where neo-Fascist bombers had once killed eighty-five people, Julia reminded herself to be careful. This first meeting would be safe but the others were a different matter. Julia suspected that Bianca had an impish streak; the later meetings she'd go to early, maybe hire a taxi and pay the driver to wait.

Julia passed quickly along Via dell'Indipendenza, with its cinemas and modern shop fronts. Despite its arcades, Bologna was more open than Florence, not yet choked by cars, Vespas or tourists. The smell of icing sugar drifted from shop doorways.

'Bitter as '46,' the old man in the florist's remarked as Julia paid for two poinsettias. 'Mind how you go.'

Frost sparked up the marble arcade floors, polishing some to a lethal smoothness. Julia rushed to help an elderly man who, stepping up from the market, slithered on an icy patch and spilled his ham into the gutter. Julia retrieved the ham. Carrying it to him, she had a shock.

Pietro Terni's round face glowed. 'A pleasure!'

'Will you be wanting your usual, Signore?' A passing Sicilian street trader interrupted Pietro's greeting.

'Go away!' muttered Pietro. 'No sense of style, these southerners. The government ought to ship them back where they came from.' He patted Julia's arm. His grip was unexpectedly firm, Julia thought, blinking at the man's aside.

'What brings you to Bologna? Fresh tortellini? Fresh suspects?' He laughed. 'Forgive me, I can't resist a mystery. Francesco told me about your looking for a relative. Clara never said she had any cousins in opera.'

'Ah, this is for my stepfather,' answered Julia. 'His mother's family's from Bologna.' Glancing over Pietro, making sure he was none the worse for his skating, Julia noticed a Communist newspaper tucked into his bag. After what had happened to him in the war, Pietro had been put off right-wing parties.

Pietro, natty in his chunky overcoat, offered her his arm. 'Would you do me a favour and come with me to Atti's? My wife wants a cake and I always choose the wrong one.'

Julia was early to see the Dontini sisters. 'My pleasure.'

They glided through frosty arcades, Pietro remarking on how music ran in families. 'I'd have loved to do what you and Francesco are doing, but I couldn't stand for the time required on stage.'

Julia remembered Krusak, how the Croatian had burned Pietro's feet, interrogating him on the night Guy and Clara had been captured by Scarpia. From Pietro's staring reaction when the Sicilian woman had burnt her hand in his household before Christmas, the Bolognese still had a horror of fire.

'I'm sorry.' Words were inadequate. Julia thought of her present bleak search for justice. Justice was not the same as restoration. Knowing how she would feel if she had to give up singing as a career, Julia drew closer to Pietro.

Pietro wiped his nose on a bright hankie. 'Doesn't matter now. Look, here's another of those posters.'

Over a photograph of Mussolini, the poster revealed when the city would be celebrating the fiftieth anniversary of its wartime liberation.

'Evil man. He seduced a lot of people, including, I'm ashamed to say it, myself—Watch out!' Pietro jerked Julia back as a Vespa came roaring from an alley. 'Peasant!' He shouted after the driver.

'I'm all right.' Julia, amused by Pietro's indignation, was also grateful. 'I can't get used to them riding on pavements.'

'Rule of Italian traffic: he who hesitates is squashed.'

Chuckling, Julia walked into Atti's. 'I can't stay long,' she explained regretfully to Pietro. 'I've another appointment.'

The Dontini sisters lived in Via Farini near Bologna's watch-towers. The street, with iron grilles and peeling shutters, was blankly imposing, but once admitted through the automatic door Julia found herself entering a world of whiteness: sofas, easy chairs, linen cut-work cloths covering occasional tables.

In this setting the sisters' ruddy complexions, blue eyes and flaxen hair were shown to advantage. Both were dressed in brilliant colours: the severe-looking one in a red two-piece; her sister, seated on the sofa, in a turquoise dress.

Fraternal twins, Julia guessed, as the taller thinner sister came to shake her hand and express delight when Julia offered her the poinsettias as a traditional seasonal gift. The first surprise came when the woman introduced herself – from her accent she was certainly not Italian.

'Go make our drinks, Elsa.' The plump sister in the turquoise dress cut short Signora Dontini's gratitude. She struck the cushion next to her on the sofa. 'Sit down, Julia. You realise that we're German? Yes, I thought you did. Elsa married her Nino just after the war, but we've lived here since 1936. I'm the singer Karin Schmidt. I watched you win that competition before Christmas. You're not bad.'

'Thanks,' said Julia drily.

'Elsa's a flautist.' Karin waved towards the kitchen. 'We came to study music here and stayed.' She smiled, showing uneven teeth. 'We never had any desire to go back to Nazi Germany.'

Julia settled into the sofa, accepting a steaming mug of chocolate from Signora Dontini, who had reappeared. She pointed to the black and white photograph displayed on the main wall. 'Your husband, Signora?'

'That's Nino.' Karin answered for Elsa Dontini. 'Looks too small for a bass. And he would wear that goatee: I used to tell Nino it made him look ridiculous.'

Keeping a grip on her mug so as not to spill any chocolate on the immaculate tiles, Julia rose. Receiving a nod of permission from Elsa she went as close to the picture as a rug would allow.

'Nino was the Dontinis' only child,' said Elsa quietly. 'This apartment was his.'

So Nino was from Bologna, thought Julia. He could have known partisan or Fascist groups – groups which operated in those same snow-capped mountains she could see in the distance through the window. Julia ran her eyes down the rooftops and back to the picture. The smiling face did not look like that of a torturer's, but then how should a torturer look? Certainly Nino Dontini was not blond, had no earring in his left ear, nor a mole on his right cheek, nor a deep cleft in his broad chin.

Elsa drew her chair closer to the radiator. 'Unfortunately, I doubt if my husband is connected with your missing relative,' she said. 'Nino was adopted: there was some scandal concerning a nun at a convent; a young woman who came from Rome. The Dontinis offered to take the child . . .'

She sighed. 'So you see, Nino had no brothers or sisters, no nephews or nieces. And we never had any children: my husband . . .'

'I'm sorry.' Julia felt to be intruding on a private grief.

'Don't be sorry!' Karin shattered the reflective moment. 'You wouldn't want *your* relation to be connected to Elsa woodwind players are the worst.' She beamed her bright gaze on her twin. 'Julia hasn't come to hear about us, but to trace someone in her family. A singer, like myself.'

Julia resumed her seat.

'I knew all the performers who played at Bologna: Elsa's Nino of course, and Mario Felici, young Francesco Vincenti, Gina Respini.' Karin leaned sideways, scooped a plateful of marshmallows off a table and plonked it between herself and Julia. 'It's a pity the relative you're after isn't a woman.' She dunked a marshmallow in her chocolate and popped it into her mouth. 'Gina came from Castel, the sister village to Croce. Mind, she was always a touch paranoid.'

'Have you any photographs of Felici or Vincenti?' Julia asked, 'Or their autographs?' she added, glancing at Elsa. A picture might be a clue for Clara; handwriting a possible lead if any documents were discovered. Julia did not mention that she'd already received a letter from Felici.

Smoothly, with a wicked look at her twin, Elsa lifted a large envelope from the side of her chair and handed it to Julia. 'These are all the photographs I have of the singers I knew in the war and the 1950s, my husband included. You can take them with you when you leave, they're copies.' She smiled vaguely at Julia's thanks and glanced again at her sister. 'You said you could go one better than that, Karin.'

'I can and I have,' replied Karin trenchantly. With a grand gesture, something Julia could imagine doing herself on stage, she produced a cassette from her dress pocket. 'Recordings of Bologna artists in 1939. The quality's not good because I had to play it into this tape off a 78, but you can hear Vincenti on it as clear as a bell.'

'Thank you.' Pietro Terni had said there were no recordings: he was mistaken. Julia's interest was fierce again. 'Thank you.' She took the cassette. 'Are you on the tape, Signora?'

Karin shook her flaxen head. 'I had flu that day. Elsa's on it, though, along with the rest of the woodwind section.'

'There's a photograph of the full orchestra in the envelope, taken in 1952,' said Elsa quietly. 'I've written the names of those I can remember over their heads.'

Instrumental musicians were often good singers. The thought flashed through like lightning, making Julia wonder why she had been so blind before. Yet, if Scarpia or his second Spoletta were musicians, what instrument might they have played, and for which orchestra? The net of her search seemed to be widening, but this only made Julia the more certain that she must find something in one of these avenues. At least the photographs and names would save her from trawling through yellowing Bologna newspapers.

Elsa was talking about Gina Respini, who, along with Francesco Vincenti, shared a major part of the recording. 'Such a modest woman. She made me ashamed to be German.'

Karin sighed extravagantly.

Her twin ignored her. 'She used to tell me how German troops would harass her at their checkpoints every time she travelled between Castel and Bologna. She had a permit but they always searched her.'

Karin sniffed. 'Purest fantasy.' She reached for another marshmallow. 'Gina was really man mad.'

'Whatever she was, the soldiers searched the wrong Respini,' said Elsa mildly. 'It was Giovanni who carried the cartridges.'

'What are you talking about?' Karin gulped her marshmallow.

'The partisans of course. Nino used to help Giovanni to smuggle ammunition to them in the mountains. There was one group in particular; Nino called it the Red-Headed League . . .'

'Nino and partisans? You've never mentioned this before. Why didn't you tell me?'

Both sisters, in the manner of old people, seemed to have forgotten they had a guest. Julia sat rigidly, hoping they would forget her a moment or two longer.

'Nino asked me not to,' came the casual answer. 'He said you were a chatterbox.' Elsa smiled.

'But that's ridiculous! Anyway, *he* couldn't have done much, he had flat feet,' said Karin spitefully.

'Nino stood up for us on the night that Nazi officer dragged us in to their military headquarters to act as dialect interpreters. June 1944, Karin. Do you remember?'

They were glaring at each other.

'Do you remember that young officer who spoke such impeccable German?' Elsa went on softly. 'You said he had beautiful eyes. Do you remember what he said to you, Karin?'

Karin hugged herself and would not answer.

Julia was not long in taking her leave. Closing the door on the sisters, she was ashamed for ever going there. She felt like a carrion crow picking at a buried past, a bringer of bad luck. She walked into sunlight, and it was cold.

A Nazi officer with textbook German and no understanding of the local dialects. A man with beautiful eyes. Clara had mentioned beautiful eyes.

Krusak.

Skidding along frosty cobbles, Julia dived into a bar, thinking now about the Red-Headed League. The phrase was familiar. She said it in English and suddenly understood.

She knew then that she must talk to Giovanni Respini.

24

Krusak glanced at his platinum watch. Anna had said that Julia would be coming here by seven to meet Rita.

Krusak smiled. He had spoken to Rita, and paid her. The fat whore had lost her looks and was desperate for money, which was why she hung out in this grubby dance hall, partnering stumbling widowers for the price of a drink. For thirty thousand lire, Rita would tell him everything that Julia said to her.

Pleasant thoughts. Tomorrow at Lucca, Bazzini's crowd would be ready with their welcome of Julia onto the Italian stage. Whether this would be sugar or poison was dependent on his whim, which was itself dependent on this encounter.

The manager of the dance hall, provided with Julia's photograph, came bobbing over to the bar to say the lady had arrived forty minutes early and was asking for Rita.

'Take her coat and delay her until I've entered the hall,' replied Krusak. 'Did you tell the band to be ready?'

'As you instructed.'

'Go,' said Krusak. He finished his champagne – his own, brought from the car – and wandered through into the main room. Standing beside the manager, obviously asking the man to point someone out, was a small, dark-haired young woman.

She was beautiful but her clothes were a disaster. For their first meeting Julia sported boots, bluejeans, a white blouse and an incongruously long grey waistcoat.

Krusak, frowning, approached.

Ignoring glares from middle-aged mammas swirling round in lurex evening wear, the band switched from polka to waltz.

Coming beside Julia, Krusak opened his arms. 'Dance with me?'

The dark head twisted round. The grey eyes – Clara's eyes – widened. She smiled, and he was young again.

'Why not?' She entered his embrace.

The shock of pleasure was almost too much. Self-discipline came to the rescue. Krusak whirled his prize about the room, heart riding in his throat.

Her voice was richer than Clara's. She was saying that she had not danced for months; she admitted how much she was enjoying herself. He wanted her to be silent. He wanted her to stop glancing round the room, the couples, the single women, and look only at him.

The dance ended, he did not release her. She seemed amused rather than surprised. Krusak did not want that. This time, this second match between himself and a woman of the Scudieri clan, he was to be the one in control. The beats of the next number rang out: the manager was following instructions. Krusak tightened his grip, making her step closer.

She stiffened. 'I don't know the tango.'

'You will learn from me.'

She laughed. 'I'll tread on your feet and spoil your shoes.'

'Then you'll shine them.' Krusak swept her into position.

The tango began. The dance floor was almost empty. She moved less surely, her eyes questioning what he was. Krusak knew that she knew he was not Italian. He relished her bewilderment at the dance, her striving too for a connection when it was there literally in her face.

They glided over polished wood, Krusak aware of her concentration, her response to his slightest cue. She learned quickly, returning unprompted to his grasp for the final swirling steps. She was looking at him now, her head drawn back, eyes tightening slightly.

'The last part is a kiss.' Stooping, Krusak took what he had wanted for so long, then thrust her from him.

'Signore!' He felt the scorch of her anger, the frustration he had felt so often with Clara. It was better than the kiss.

'Next time we meet, Julia-Clara, you will wear a dress. A long white dress made of silk.'

The girl went rigid. Her face bloomed with sudden colour.

'Go to hell!' The whisper showed that she knew him now, but he would show her that their introduction had barely begun.

He had smudged her lipstick with his kiss. Repulsed and at the same time excited, Krusak put up a finger to wipe away the offending mark. Quick as a striking lioness Julia knocked away his hand.

The band was playing but no one was dancing.

'Keep away from my family,' said Julia.

This chit of a girl was too intense; it would be a pleasure to teach her that she was no one without him. The lesson could begin tomorrow night: he would have Bazzini's group boo – no laugh – her off the stage. To see Julia's face when he told her who was behind the laughter – and his price for silencing it – was a future delight he would begin savouring now.

'Remember, princess,' he said, 'I'll be in touch.'

With a mocking bow Krusak left.

'I danced with a murderer: he had beautiful eyes.' Julia uttered this surreal phrase before the cracked mirror in the ladies' toilet. Her mouth and body were still not working properly: shock, she supposed. This sick occasion was not something to share with Roberto; she did not want to tell anyone. She had met a killer, a torturer, and done nothing. She had said nothing.

Impeccable German. Beautiful eyes. Elsa Dontini and Karin had known the pleasure of Krusak's company. The twins had been dragged into Nazi headquarters to act as interpreters, perhaps on the night the Croatian had interrogated Pietro Terni. Perhaps they had been there when Krusak had burned Pietro.

Morbid thoughts. Julia rubbed her mouth with a paper towel. She had scrubbed her lips and hands, everywhere he had touched. She had not confronted Krusak with his crimes.

How had he known that she would be at the dance hall? Julia could not dismiss their encounter as coincidence; Krusak was rich. She had seen the whip of distaste which seared across his austere features as he took in her clothes. If a man like Krusak wanted to go dancing he would visit a select club. Had she been set up by Bianca Terni?

Considering Bianca, Julia yanked a comb through her curls. She could see no reason for Bianca to tell Krusak anything. So far as she knew they had never met. Nor were they likely to be allies after what Krusak had done to Bianca's father.

And Krusak had been so chillingly normal, dancing the waltz. His hands had been warm, his limpid eyes gentle. Remorse did not sting him even whilst he sought the past in the present, using her as a prop in his fantasies.

Julia opened her shoulderbag. Wearing stage make-up at night she did not bother with more than lip salve during the day. Now though she took out eye-liner and shadow.

Clara looked at her from the mirror. A fifty-year-old image for Krusak, which he pursued with the relentlessness of fading vigour. Such obsession was disturbing.

The instant she was sure Krusak had left the dance hall Julia had telephoned Andrea. He and Clara were safe. Warning Andrea to guard her grandmother, Julia had asked him to say nothing for tonight. Tomorrow would be soon enough to tell Clara that Krusak had returned to Italy.

When had he come back? Where and how had he lived in the years between the war and today?

'Dammit!' She had smeared her eye-liner. 'Slow down,' she told herself, removing the blob of make-up with a tissue.

Her watch said six-forty-five. She was to meet Rita by seven. Did Krusak know anything about her search? Krusak's narrow smile winked at her in the mirror. Julia began to hum one of the songs she would be performing tomorrow night. Bianca had said there might be trouble for her and Ruth. At the dress rehearsal yesterday, the atmosphere had been bad. Some stage hands even threatened to go on strike, and the costumes were still not ready.

Julia shrugged and brushed on her lipgloss. She looked different from Clara now, less of a princess, more of a tart.

Julia laughed and scooped her things into her bag.

Rita was as shiny and round as an olive, and a good dancer. Her low-cut dress and wedge shoes were a lurid green. She wore no make-up or jewellery and her grey-streaked hair was loose, in a style better suited to a young girl. As she talked she constantly brushed her long hair behind her ears. She was dying for a cigarette, she told Julia, but ladies were not allowed to smoke in the hall.

'Let's go out to the café across the street,' suggested Julia. To her surprise Rita agreed.

In the café Rita surprised her again by insisting on buying their coffees. She sucked the froth off her cappuccino like a child. Julia motioned to the waiter and ordered another coffee and four slices of pizza. 'For the lady with me.'

When the pizza came, Rita accepted it without thanks but offered Julia a slice. 'I don't like people watching me eat.'

Rita wolfed three portions down whilst Julia ate one, crumpled her napkins into a ball, then waited with poignant delicacy until Julia had finished before she lit a cigarette.

Julia let her chain-smoke two before she turned to business. 'Did the lady who set up this meeting tell you why I wanted to talk to you?'

'She said you'd pay,' said Rita flatly, with humour.

The precariousness of her living touched Julia. She counted out banknotes, held them out. 'That's half.' Smoke was stinging her eyes. 'That's for your time.'

Rita spirited away the cash and appeared to relax. Leaning forward in her chair, looping two grey-black streamers of hair behind her ears, she lit a third cigarette on the glowing stub of the second. 'You're a journalist. I wanted to be a writer.'

Julia nodded, glad that the café was crowded, that there was a cheerful backdrop of conversation. It didn't matter that Rita was lying, putting on an act. She was doing the same.

Suddenly Julia was tired of asking the same questions about singers, spinning the same half-truths. Let's change the entire opera, she thought. 'The man in the hall who danced with me. Have you seen him before tonight?'

'Very likely.' Rita's voice did not betray her, but the grinding out of her cigarette did.

'Has he paid you today, too?'

'What do you think?' Rita lifted her cup to her lips. 'All right!' She took a gulp of coffee. 'So he was one of my regulars back in the war. Used to call me Clara – the same name he called you. I'd strip and he'd look.' Rita's face was hidden behind the cup. 'We never did anything. I was glad.'

Julia let out a sigh of relief. 'How old were you?'

'About twelve.' Rita put down her cup, scooped her hair behind her ears. 'You know he's coming back tonight?'

'With a bigger bankroll, I expect.'

'Don't depend on my discretion then.' Again that kink of humour. Rita leaned into the window as a woman edged through the narrow gap between their table and the next: the café was growing more cramped and noisier.

'OK,' said Julia, 'During the war, where did you operate?'

'You mean what streets did I walk? Round the two towers there was an army post nearby where the men would let me take a warm by their fire.' She stared at the crumpled napkin on her plate. 'It always seemed to be winter then.'

Julia propped a photograph of the Bologna orchestra beside the table's lamp. 'Recognise anyone?'

Rita shook her head.

'Now?' Julia dropped a photograph of the Bologna chorus in place of the orchestra.

'No,' said Rita, studying one half intently.

Julia under the cover of the table, shuffled her final pictures. She decided to take a chance. 'How about these three?'

Rita handed Julia back the photographs of Francesco Vincenti and Nino Dontini, but kept the last, which showed Guy. Her shiny round face, blurred by cigarette plumes, grew sharper.

'Him!' Her finger stabbed the picture. 'I remember him

Saved me from being picked up when a client had kept me late and it was way after curfew. Dragged me into an alleyway as a dozen Blackshirts came marching round the corner: without him I'd have walked right into them.'

She was talking freely now, smiling at the memory. 'He gave me coffee afterwards for having been "a brave girl". Coffee in wartime! I sold it for a fortune. He was nice. Even though he had guns hidden in his coat – I felt those when he grabbed me – I wasn't frightened of him. I wish I could have seen him in daylight. I know he had red hair.' She laid Guy's photograph on the table and flicked it with her nail across the polished wood. 'Do you know who he is?'

'He was a war hero,' said Julia. 'I'm doing a piece on him.' She slipped the picture of her grandfather into her bag. Krusak could not hurt Guy. 'He died during the German occupation. Can you remember when you met him?'

'Sometime in winter 1943,' said Rita. 'He was nice. But he wasn't part of the partisan group I knew.' She laughed at Julia starting. 'That's what you want to hear about, isn't it? That's what your journalist friend told me, anyway.'

Julia reached into her bag for a notebook and pen.

An hour later Julia shot back her chair and stood up, coughing smoke from her lungs. With Krusak as final paymaster, everything she had learned from Rita tonight would be passed on. She had not been able to risk direct questions, except once.

Rita had been talking: 'When one of our messengers disappeared for three days we were frightened he'd been taken by the Blackshirts, and given to Scarpia.'

'How do you spell that?' Julia asked. She hoped Rita could not see the tremor of her hand as she wrote.

'You're the one with the education.' Rita was chain-smoking again and the air was lethal for a singer. Julia hung on, and after a moment's silence, Rita added, 'Scarpia was their top interrogator. He was notorious amongst partisans, especially after Mauro vanished, but that's all anyone ever knew of him: that nickname. No one knew why he'd got it, because hardly anyone got away from him alive.'

Mauro, the best forger in Bologna. He had supplied her grandfather with false papers and helped Pietro Terni escape the German round-ups by telling Pietro that Clara was someone who could help. Mauro was a man she had hoped to find. Julia jotted the name down, drew a circle round it. Too late now, she thought. An enquiry after Mauro's surviving family brought a long silent drag on her cigarette from Rita.

'When did Mauro disappear?' Julia asked.

'April '44. Ran out of his shop one day, never came back.'

'And Scarpia was responsible for his disappearance?'

'And murder.' Rita yawned. 'More than likely.'

'Was Scarpia from Bologna?'

Rita lifted her hands. 'Who knows? From what little I know, Scarpia was based at Blackshirt headquarters there, but I think he had a villa somewhere quiet as well, where his activities wouldn't be disturbed. Scarpia thrived on secrecy – I've had plenty of clients like that.'

A visit to the country was certainly in order, thought Julia, as she paid Rita the rest of her money and they parted.

As she walked away, Julia heard the clock in the main square striking nine. With three hours still before her final meeting, she thought of returning to the dance hall and being there when Krusak reappeared. But that would make him, and her conversation with Rita, appear important. She wanted Krusak to think she regarded him simply as a nuisance, like the man in the red scarf.

The man in the red scarf – who was he? Was he Krusak's man? Had he followed her here and told Krusak?

Julia blew on her hands. She felt stale now, sluggish. It was bitter outside, much colder than Florence. She didn't want to wait. Why not go early? Midnight was a crazy time.

After all, according to Bianca, Emilio Gucci had never hurt a woman.

25

Gucci lived in a modern high-rise within the noise pollution radius of Bologna airport. The taxi driver was unsure of the address and they cruised round four tower blocks before stopping at a fifth, near a bus depot.

Julia asked the driver to keep the meter running and wait.

On the way up the stairs – Julia disliked lifts and closed-in places – her bad timing made her laugh. Tomorrow she was to play in Italian opera, the thing she had worked for ever since deciding that she had to be a singer. Instead of resting, focusing on her role, here she was, on her first free day since Christmas, rapping on the door to an ex-Marshal's house, asking to be let in to talk about war crimes. To bring Clara's torturers to justice was vital, and yet . . .

'What do you want?' A wrinkled face appeared as the door opened a crack. Julia lifted her fake press card. It gave her name as Giulia Varisi.

'You're early,' the face spat. 'He's taking a bath.'

'Who the hell is it?' demanded a voice from inside the flat.

'That journalist who was supposed to be coming at twelve.'

'Fucking hell!' There was a series of loud splashing. 'Tell her to go—'

Julia thrust her foot in the doorway. 'Signore!' She shouted above the racket, 'I want to know about the Red-Headed League.'

There was a silence in which Julia prayed she had said the
right thing. Emilio Gucci was in his sixties, a retired Marshal
of Ponte Maggiore, the town in the plain beneath San Martino
della Croce. He had taken over from the Marshal who had
helped Clara and Guy. Gucci had lived in the region as a boy.
Surely he must have heard something of her grandfather's
group.

'Let her in, Rosa.'

Rosa's desiccated face disappeared from the crack in the
door. '*Campionissimo*'s on in a few minutes.' She named a
popular TV game show. 'You know I always watch it.'

'So watch.' The sounds of moving water increased as Emilio
Gucci obviously settled back in his bath, 'She can talk to me
in here.'

Rosa flung off the chain, tossing open the door. 'She's shy,'
she called over her shoulder. 'Hasn't moved.'

'Can't be that serious then.'

Julia walked into the cramped, three-room apartment and
pushed open the bathroom door. Clouds of scented steam,
the knocking of antiquated plumbing as more hot water was
run into the tub, greeted her entrance. Emilio Gucci grunted
and turned off the tap.

'So you're serious. Pass me my glasses, I like to see who
I'm talking to. You sit on the linen basket: it's buggered
anyway.'

Julia found a pair of metal framed spectacles under a heap
of towels and handed them across. She shrugged off her coat,
settling carefully on the cracked wicker lid of the linen basket.
They peered at each other through the steam.

Emilio Gucci – what Julia could see of him above a froth of
pine bubble-bath which lapped beyond his navel – was a dark,
thick-set man. Grey body hair coiled over his arms and chest,
swirled down his shoulders and back. He had hairy knuckles
and a boxer's cauliflower ear. His deep-set eyes seemed at
first glance to be remote, visionary, but the metal spectacles
which framed them gave him a tough look. A brawler, Julia
decided. He was frowning into his double chins, eyes
narrowing so much as to be almost invisible.

'Have I seen you someplace before?' And then he said, 'I thought everyone had forgotten the Red-Headed League.'

In the living-room *Campionissimo* was starting. Julia shifted on her wicker seat, trying to be comfortable. Talking to a pensioner in his bath was bizarre to her, but maybe not to a real journalist. She imagined Bianca in the same position, calm, amused, carrying off this meeting with sang-froid.

Julia cleared her throat. 'Mario started the group, didn't he?' she said, giving her grandfather Guy's Italian alias. 'Red-haired Mario.' She lifted the pictures from her bag. 'This man.'

'Yeah, that's him. Mario Scudieri. I can even forgive that man his relatives.' With that cryptic comment Emilio handed back the photograph. Stretching for ashtray and pipe balanced on top of the pink plastic bathrack, he raised the pipe questioningly.

Another smoker. So far as she knew, smoke didn't affect her voice, but Julia didn't want to discover otherwise tomorrow night. 'Go ahead,' she said. 'It's your bathroom.' Maybe the pipe would make him more forthcoming.

Emilio Gucci lit up and continued. 'The man got me interested in police work; used to tell me stories about an English detective called Holmes. That was in '42. I was about ten then, a kid.'

Julia nodded. 'There's a Sherlock Holmes story called the "Red-Headed League",' she said. Emilio Gucci gave a bark of laughter as he made the connection.

'Yeah, that would match his sense of humour, all right! He was the only guy I knew who could make our old Marshal laugh.'

That would be the Marshal Clara had known, thought Julia. He had lost his son on the Russian front. 'Was the old Marshal part of the league, do you think?' She smiled. 'Children see lots of things.' She leaned forward, inviting a confidence.

'Maybe. I used to run errands between them, orders for food: sausage, cheese, tomatoes. Mario sometimes worked a small-holding near Gasparini's place. I'd tell him what the Marshal wanted and he'd give me a list of the wines he needed in return: so many red, so many white.' Emilio tapped his mat of chest hair. 'I figured then that it wasn't groceries, but I never told anyone, not even the priest. Especially not the Croce priest.'

There was a new edge to the man's voice. Julia, racking her memory but still unable to think who Gasparini was, decided that she couldn't let it pass. 'Why him in particular?'

'Pah!' Gucci knocked out his pipe into the ashtray. 'Effeminate little snob. A *gentleman*, if you please, always keen to hob-nob with the quality.' He jerked a flannel into the froth and began scrubbing at his arms. 'I'd watch him and his fancy curate chatting to Nazi officers, showing off their German. Told my father about it but he just clipped me round the ear and said that was the priest's business.' He shot the flannel back under the suds. 'After the Germans' last big round-up of partisans in the region the priest and his curate disappeared. I can't say I was sorry.'

The priest of San Martino della Croce, thought Julia, feeling the loss of one more illusion. The man Clara had helped so that he could live like a gentleman. Had he been one of the six in the underground chamber? Was it possible her grandparents had been tortured by their own priest?

She flinched as Gucci struck the water with the flat of his hand.

'Christ's sake! Don't tell me you're shocked by a little collaboration from our holy fathers!'

Remembering what Bianca had said about Gucci and his brutal tactics in the police made the man's sudden burst of temper alarming. She'd rather he smoked: that kept his fists occupied.

'Who was Gasparini?' she asked hastily. Julia noticed that the bubble bath's potency was diminishing: gaps were appearing in the suds. Trying to ignore that, she listened to the ex-Marshal's explanation.

'As a kid I used to call him the Arab. Very dark, hooked nose, glowing eyes. Very solemn. He was one of the league – I know that for a certainty. Gasparini had a radio. He used to listen to the Allied broadcasts – you weren't supposed to, it was illegal. If he'd been caught he could have been hauled off to Blackshirt headquarters. Anyway, he used to pass on what he learned to Mario – I overheard them once talking in Mario's barn; I was hidden by the hay and they couldn't see me. They talked about the war and how it was going and then Mario said, "We need to move tonight. I'll tell the others." '

Umberto Gasparini: the farmer Guy helped when his vine crops failed. Julia wondered if he or any of his children were still alive. A question as to Gasparini's whereabouts after the war brought only a shrug and the answer, 'Everyone moved out of the mountains in the fifties, the land up there had turned sour. I've no idea where Gasparini wound up.'

Turning over her memory Julia came up with another name. 'What about Stefano? Was he involved with the partisans?'

'You must be joking! That crook-leg was a Blackshirt. He joined up in the 1920s and again in '44.' The sinews bulged ominously along Gucci's right forearm. 'The herbalist and the priest, two black vultures!' He wiped a finger under one of his spectacle lenses and stared at Julia. 'You know a lot already.'

'I don't want to waste your time, Signore,' said Julia smoothly. 'Did Stefano move with the rest of the villagers?'

'I heard a rumour he'd emigrated to America.'

'That's strange. I heard a rumour only last month that Stefano's son broke into a Bologna art gallery and created a disturbance. He claimed the owner was a Neo-Fascist.'

'Did he now? Good for him! The art world's nothing but a bunch of posers.' Gucci's smile broadened. 'Old Stefano was always getting into scraps. When I became Marshal of Ponte I saw his police file.'

So the man had been violent, thought Julia. 'It sounds as if his son might have an interesting story to tell,' she said.

'Leave it with me. He'll have an identity card on file and that'll give you an address.'

Julia scribbled down the number of the Lucca opera house. 'Thanks. You'll be able to reach me here.' She didn't want to give anyone a possible lead to her grandmother.

She put the paper by the towels, thinking about Stefano. Since the herbalist himself had been a Fascist, she wondered why his son had accused Pietro Terni of being a party member.

Francesco had not told her everything that had happened on the night Stefano's son had burst into Pietro's art gallery. Or perhaps Francesco had not been told everything.

'What did you mean about Stefano *rejoining* the Fascists?' she asked.

'Just what I said. But not everyone was as keen as him. There were call-ups in the spring of '44: men of military age were given a deadline, and if they hadn't signed up they were automatically suspect and could be arrested or simply shot. In our area, if you were *really* lucky, the Italian SS passed you on to Scarpia.'

Emilio Gucci surged forward in the water. 'That bastard!' Rearing up like an angry elephant seal, he hammered a fist against the side of the bath.

Julia was off her unofficial seat, her photographs strewn over the bathroom tiles.

'You're OK,' Gucci motioned stiffly with his hands. 'Come and sit down.' He waited whilst Julia gathered up her pictures. 'It's him you're after, isn't it?'

Was she that transparent? 'Torturers always make good copy.'

Gucci laughed and shook a finger at her. 'You're good, but don't try to fool an old policeman, girl.' He coughed sharply. 'Suppose we skip that for the moment and you show me your other pictures. This bathwater's getting cold.'

He recognised the blond Francesco Vincenti at once. Said he had been one of the first to join the reformed Fascist party.

'Vincenti thought himself better than everyone else because he was a singer,' Gucci complained. 'I remember how he used to swan through Ponte in his big car on the way to his mamma's house beyond Castel, waving at us as though he was royalty.'

So Francesco Vincenti, like Gina Respini, had come from Croce's sister village, thought Julia. Elsa Dontini and Karin her sister must not have known that, or else had forgotten.

Emilio Gucci's hand stabbed at the picture of the Bologna opera chorus. 'Who's that?' He turned the photograph round.

'Pietro Terni.' Julia recalled how Rita had stared at that

same half of the picture. 'Another singer.'

'Bianca's old man? No wonder his face seems familiar!' Gucci gave her back the photograph, then startled Julia by asking, 'How did you vote in the nationals?'

'Communist,' answered Julia. She received another smile.

'Good for you! We'll bring the swindling crooks down in the end.' Gucci rolled in his bath. 'Go on through and sit with the wife whilst I get dressed. That game show should be finished.'

'I didn't expect you to burst in like that,' Gucci said when he reappeared. Crossing to the TV, he turned it off without so much as a glance at his partner. 'Maybe that was a mean trick to play on you, but I was pissed off with your coming so early. Do you make a habit of it?'

'Before I answer that I'd like to ask you something.' Julia felt more steady now that Gucci was wearing a suit. 'Did you fix the time of our meeting for tonight?'

'No, that was Bianca.'

Julia didn't like to think about the significance of that. She was singing with Bianca's brother tomorrow night. She coughed Gucci's pipe smoke from her throat. 'Did she give any reason why it had to be midnight?'

'None at all.'

It could be nothing, but – Julia rose and walked to the window. 'Can I check my taxi's still waiting?' Drawing aside one curtain, her eyes scanned the streets. No one seemed to be lingering in the cold.

Behind her Emilio Gucci said, 'If someone's followed you they'll be waiting under the bus depot, out of sight.'

It took all her skill as a performer not to show fear. She let the curtain go. 'If anyone's followed me they're welcome to lurk wherever they like in this weather.' She turned back to view Gucci, seated at the flat's living-room table. 'I won't be stopping to talk to them.'

'You haven't answered my question.'

'No, I do not make a habit of turning up three hours early to appointments.' Julia did not enlarge on that answer. She was only slightly relieved when Gucci did not ask why she had made a special exception then in his case.

Instead the former Marshal of Ponte Maggiore placed his pipe and ashtray softly onto the table.

'Not in here, Emilio,' said Rosa Gucci warningly.

Her husband's metal spectacles flashed as he shot her a furious look. His fist banged on the table. 'Make us coffee!'

Rosa rose stiffly to her feet and stalked into the kitchen. Passing the table, she snatched the pipe and bore it off.

'She only lets me smoke in the bathroom,' grumbled the hard man of the carabinieri. He leaned back in his seat.

'I know who you remind me of now,' he said. 'Clara Scudieri, the Contessa of Croce. You heard of her, too, as well as Mario?'

Already uneasy at what was coming, Julia inclined her head.

'People called her the bitch of the mountains. Whilst her cousin was fighting to free Italy, she was snug in bed with the Germans: officers and aristocrats only, of course. When Mario disappeared in '44 and his group broke up she scarpered off south to the Americans.'

Gucci's face blurred for an instant as the image of Clara's hideous injuries flashed before Julia's eyes.

'She was a whore, that one.'

If she didn't move, she'd hit him. Fighting her anger, Julia swung her handbag over her shoulder and walked out without speaking, slamming the door.

26

Hours later, pacing the dressing-room she shared with Ruth, Julia was still furious. To have fallen out of the character she was supposed to be, walked away when she should have stayed . . .

'Fool!' Julia yanked the room's only chair from the back wall and sat before the mirror. So Gucci hated the upper classes and had nothing good to say about Clara because she was an aristocrat: that would have made no difference to his information about Scarpia.

'Grandmother, what did you do in the war?' Touching her face, Julia felt a surge of pity. Eboli, the character she was playing, was scarred, but the wounds were wiped away at the end of the evening. What choices had the war forced Clara to make?

Julia swung from her seat. It was going to be hard tonight, singing, but this was her job. She had snatched little sleep, her head pounded. She missed Roberto and was unreasonably anxious because she had received no letter from him that day.

A strange thing, this ache for another human being. Julia considered it as she hurried along the opera house corridors. She missed Roberto for absurd reasons. The way the hair curled on the back of his neck. The endearing lump his sleeping body made in a bed. She hoped Roberto was all right.

Of course he was all right. Why shouldn't he be?

Julia swept into a practice room. She was early for opening night to grab a piano to herself. Roberto was performing this evening in Naples. It was curiously comforting to know that they would be 'warming-up' at the same time, singing together although apart.

Music is often spiritual, but singing is physical, sweaty work. At the end of her practice, Julia admitted that she missed Roberto in more than just spiritual ways. She stroked a hand along the piano, remembering.

'Flowers for Signorina Marlow!'

'Don't move.' Julia put down the scissors and opened the door, taking in the bird of paradise bouquet.

Ruth glanced at the card with the flowers, the blush in her cheeks fading. 'My parents.'

Julia mentally cursed Francesco. He had sent her red roses, but nothing to Ruth. She was disappointed at his insensitivity.

She nodded at the orange flowers. 'Stunning.' She crouched to unpick another pleat of material. As she and Ruth had half-expected, one of the wardrobe staff had been uncooperative: she had delivered their costumes late and made no alterations. Ruth's costume was too short and hers too big. Ruth would play the Queen in bare feet, but with the hem let down the gown would be full length.

'Well, we suspected the lady was part of this anti-foreigners thing,' observed Ruth. For weeks, she, Julia and the American playing King Philip, the three non-Italian principals in the cast, had been made to feel unwelcome by this woman. And tonight they had no dresser, no one to help with costumes.

Ruth's calm voice belied her work as she added darts to Julia's gown laid out on the make-up table. Ruth sewed the quickest seam Julia had seen.

Julia nodded, continuing the simpler job of unpicking. Her eyes felt to be starting out of her head.

'They're playing politics with our lives.' Ruth frowned. 'Listen to that crowd.'

'I can't hear anything.'

'That's right.' Above, the audience were gathering in the auditorium. Where there should have been conversation, there was silence.

'There.' Julia sat back on her heels. 'Your parents here?'

'I've asked them not to come backstage. Mother fusses.'

Julia gave what she hoped was an understanding smile. Her mother and stepfather were in England tonight, and Clara at Julia's insistence had stayed away. No one except Francesco had sent any kind of good wishes.

Don't be childish, Julia told herself, as Ruth, finishing off, bit through her thread. *Why should he send flowers from Naples? It's not important. What matters is to find out who has turned Lucca opera house against us, and why.*

There was a rap on the door. 'Flowers for Signorina Marlow!'

Ruth surged forward. On the threshold, a handsome prince offered the fair soprano a bunch of orchids. 'You said they were your favourites.' Francesco stepped into the room. 'You're as lovely as Ophelia in your white gown.'

Murmuring about a vase, Ruth slid past him into the corridor.

Francesco watched her go, brown eyes busy. 'She looks sexy with her hair back,' he remarked in surprise. Ruth's long golden hair and calm, regular features were shown off by her deep blue headdress and high collar. The stage make-up, accentuating eyes, lips and cheekbones, also helped.

Slowly he turned to Julia. 'You're not in costume.'

'I'm not on for a while,' said Julia easily. She thought Francesco looked pasty; not surprising, given that crowd upstairs. 'Thanks for the roses. They've a marvellous scent.'

'Hey! I'm forgetting my deliveries.' Francesco held out his other hand. 'For you, from an admirer.'

A white rose. Julia accepted it silently, guessing who it was from. The thought of the man with the red scarf prowling round the opera house made her headache worse.

'This is from my father.' Francesco produced an envelope.

Inside the message: 'Good luck. Sorry to hear no luck yet with your stepfather's relative. If I can help, let me know.'

Francesco had asked Julia once how her search was going. If prompted by Pietro, he wasn't the most reliable of informants, Julia reflected. It was kind of Pietro to remember her.

'Beginners half hour!' The stage manager passed down the corridor, beating on doors.

'Oh God.' Francesco, careless of creasing his royal blue doublet and hose, slumped down on the chair. 'Bazzini's crowd's in tonight. They roast you if you make a mistake.'

'You're not going to make any,' said Ruth from the doorway. She was pale, but her voice was steady. 'I've marked where you need to stick the pins,' she said to Julia. 'Shall we go up to wait our call, Francesco?'

'You go,' moaned Francesco, tugging at his lace collar. Julia nodded, motioning with her eyes. Ruth was the prima donna, the first soprano. She was nervous enough without having to calm the tenor. Over their heads the orchestra were taking their places; there was no applause.

'We're dead.' Francesco clawed a hand through his straight blond hair. In a flash of insight Julia saw him as the youngest child, father's pride and mother's favourite, the one they would shield. Francesco, she realised, would know nothing about Pietro's flirtation with Fascism or the clubfooted Stefano's links with the party because Francesco would not have been told. The incident in the gallery with the younger Stefano had been passed on to him as an amusing story, nothing more.

That at least was reassuring: Julia hadn't liked the idea of Francesco being involved in this murky world of collaborators. Seeing him turn a bilious yellow she grabbed the wastebin and dumped it at his feet.

'Frankie, you'll be fine. The people know you here, you've already been a success.' Julia sloshed brandy into a paper cup and pressed it into his hand. 'Bianca and your dad will be cheering you on.' She slipped the miniature back into her bag. Dutch courage usually worked.

'Bianca won't be here till the second act.' Francesco tossed back the brandy, dropped the cup into the bin. 'It's easy for you, the mob never expects as much from lower voices.'

'And who insists on hogging the limelight? Tenors get the biggest fees – Get out and earn them.' Julia swirled round, checking make-up brushes and colours laid next to her costume.

'Hey, I'm sorry.' Francesco came behind her and rested his chin on her shoulder.

Julia took a deep breath and nodded. 'You can help if you want.' She handed him the big staple gun and safety pins she had bought some days earlier and shrugged off jeans and top: there wasn't time to be coy. Lifting the crackling gown off the table, she dragged it over her head.

'Start by lifting the shoulders where Ruth's marked . . .'

Under her instruction, Francesco pinned. The dress, its new darts added by Ruth, became less of a sack, and once the tenor hacked four inches off the bottom, it began to fit.

'You know, in a weird way this is fun,' Francesco admitted, as Julia stood on the chair for him to staple up the ragged hem.

Julia laughed, disarmed by his sense of the ridiculous, his essential kindness. He was a very attractive man, she thought.

'Beginners five minutes!' The stage manager pounded the door. In the corridor there was a flurry of coming and going: people singing scales, bodies racing for the stage.

'I can do the rest.' Julia, still balanced on the chair, gave Francesco a hug. 'Good luck.'

The feel of his body sent a jolting shock through her. Dismayed by the contact, Julia tried to pull away and slipped.

Francesco grabbed her. In the charged atmosphere, with the orchestra overhead tuning up and the opera house beginning to buzz, their sudden closeness was disturbing.

Francesco licked his lips. 'Feel what you've done.' He rocked against her. 'You are a naughty girl.' He grinned, releasing her as she stiffened. 'See you later, princess.' He bowed, leaving as the bell for the start of *Don Carlos* rang out above catcalls.

Julia sat in the chair to apply her make-up. Krusak had nicknamed her princess and now Francesco had done the same. Francesco's smell was on her flesh, his touch digging under her skin to set her mind off-balance.

'Why aren't you here when I need you?' she addressed the shadow in the mirror. A frivolous thought, she put it aside leaning forward to paint Eboli's scars onto her face, to think herself into character.

Again there was a knock upon the door. 'Come!' Julia called already becoming Princess Eboli. Adjusting her high collar she sped to the entrance and looked out.

No one was there.

27

'Roberto!' The stage manager grabbed his arm. 'You've got to help me.' With the force of desperation he hauled the bigger man through the first door along the corridor.

'You have got trouble.' Roberto flipped the light in the sluice room, crouching by the figure sprawled over the drain. 'Get a doctor.'

'One's on the way.'

'William!' Roberto shook the bedraggled lump of clothes. He found a clean handkerchief, wetted it and wiped the singer's sweating face. 'Bill, you sick?' he asked in English.

'Three times.' The American groaned, clutching his stomach.

'He was fine when I looked in on him in his room ten minutes ago,' protested the stage manager. 'Then I find him here. The conductor knows nothing.'

Music rang out above them. The opera had started.

Roberto turned back to the singer. 'You want a hand to your room, Bill, or do you want to stay here?'

In a gesture of panic, the singer clutched the nearest floormop, shaking his head.

'OK. The doctor's here.' Roberto backed away to let the man in, tugging the stage manager with him into the corridor.

The manager slumped back against the wall. 'What am I going to do? Bazzini's brought his group in. They've taken over part of the top tier.'

'Have they, now?' Roberto scratched a scar on his hand. He knew Bazzini and his claque. They were hatchet men, people you bribed if you wanted an opera to fail. Time to re-introduce himself to Signor Bazzini and remind the man of his dues, he thought.

'What shall I do?' The manager was shredding his programme.

'Well, you could start by telling the understudy playing Philip that it's his big night.'

'That's just it! He's disappeared!'

A fanfare from the orchestra made Roberto blink but he knew the opera and had been subconsciously prepared for it; the sudden noise didn't worry him. What made him stiffen was the barracking which almost drowned the trumpets.

'Holy Mother.' Two young singers were facing that reception. Ruth and Terni must be experiencing a whole new dimension of terror.

Roberto glared at the manager. 'I thought you back-room boys understood opera politics. Listen to that, for Christ's sake!'

'What are you doing?' The stage manager, attempting to stand in the bigger man's way, found himself flattened against the wall. 'Where are you going?'

'Top tier,' answered Roberto, without looking round.

'But the American, who will take his place?'

'Pay me cash,' said Roberto. 'And find me a costume that fits.' He made his exit, taking the back stairs three at a time.

Snug in the damask-lined opera box on the right-hand horseshoe curve, Bazzini was unaware of the whirlwind about to engulf him. At a nod from Krusak, seated in the royal box, he was allowing his group free rein to register pleasure in the soprano and tenor. It was the mezzo whom his patron wanted driven off-stage: Rochfort would feel the claque's sustained venom from the moment she took the boards.

Francesco Terni was lovely, Bazzini reflected. Of course Terni was known by the Lucca opera house's 'regulars', and the anti-foreign group who were in tonight had been mollified by the fact that the young male lead was being taken by an Italian tenor. They had begun to applaud the foreign soprano, whom Bazzini thought deserved praise. Ruth Marlow had shown courage, ignoring vulgar raspberries from the stalls, until the audience were shamed into silence. Bazzini had no doubt that by the end of the act the American would be taking her quota of curtain calls.

Behind him the door opened. 'This is a private box.' Bazzini disliked having to break away from looking at the pretty young singers, 'I must ask you to leave.'

'All in good time, Signore.' The stranger switched the inner light of the narrow box: on, off. 'We know each other now.' A murmur of disapproval from the nearby boxes brought a smile to the man's mouth: Bazzini could see his teeth glinting in the swirling lights from the stage. Ducking under the low roof, the man settled in the chair next to his, hands hung casually over the long drop into the stalls.

'Roberto Padovano.' Shock drew the name past Bazzini's lips.

'Signor Bazzini.' The singer appeared to be chewing. He smiled, taking a narrow silver packet from his pocket. 'I'm on tonight as the King, poor Bill's prostrate with food poisoning. Would you like some gum? Good for the nerves, I find, gives a singer something to do with his mouth before he has to perform. With me, it's either chew gum, or stuff down a mountain of food. On the whole I prefer gum.'

'Thank you.' Bazzini took a piece and mechanically unwrapped it. They chewed through the final bars of act one.

Any doubts that Roberto Padovano was not singing were killed by the bass's shout of 'Bravo!' before the music finished. Next moment he was on his feet, leaning out carelessly from the box and leading Bazzini's claque in the applause. In the gods above, Bazzini could see people rubbernecking into his box: the news that Padovano, a former player at Lucca, had returned for that evening, would be blazing through the house.

'So.' Roberto Padovano drew back, sitting on the bench seat at the rear of the box, 'How is Signor Putti?'

Few people ever remembered poor Luigi, his long-time

partner, reflected Bazzini. 'He couldn't make it tonight.'

'I'm sorry. I know this opera was his favourite.'

The curtain had come down. Bazzini stared at it, ignoring the gesticulations coming from the royal box. He twisted out of his seat. 'A pleasure to see you, my boy.'

'And you, you old fox.'

The singer rose and they embraced each other. Memories swept through Bazzini. 'I still remember it, you know,' he said. 'How you saved me from those ruffians of the San Frediano district. You were just coming out of that church—'

'The Carmine—'

'And when you dragged that big youth off me and smashed him against the wall, the other one shouted, "How about turning the cheek, pansy-lover? What about your religion?" Do you know what you said?'

Padovano raised his fingers in an openhanded gesture.

' "Complain to Christ – he beat up the temple moneychangers. Religion's for women. God is for men." Then you threw them both down the church steps.'

'You've a good memory, Signore.'

'I also remember,' continued Bazzini in a distant voice, 'that I promised that if there was ever anything I could do for you . . .' He resisted the desire to touch Roberto Padovano.

'Yes, Signore. I need your help.'

The door to the box burst open.

'I'm not paying you to cheer, get your group organised, she's on this next act.' Krusak stopped, obviously waiting for Roberto Padovano to leave.

Padovano stretched his long legs so that they touched the opposite wall and continued to chew. Krusak's deep eyes met the singer's gleaming eyes and they glared at each other. Without dropping his gaze, Krusak stepped back, lit a cigar in defiance of the 'No Smoking' signs and stalked away.

Roberto Padovano laughed and closed the box door.

Bazzini let out his breath. He was getting too old for this.

Catcalls started again from the anti-foreign contingent in the stalls as the orchestra played the opening of the next act.

Roberto Padovano turned his large head. 'What's Krusak,

a millionaire, doing hiring your services, Signore?' His voice glided easily above the raucous yammering from the stalls. 'It's more personal than those flag-waving idiots below us, isn't it? *They'll* change their tune the moment they realise Julia is Italian, but Krusak doesn't want your group to cheer. Why?'

'You've made a bad enemy there.' Bazzini slid along the seats to resume his place in the box front. 'Let it go, Roberto,' he added suddenly. 'Krusak always gets what he wants. For some reason, I swear I don't know why, he means to break the girl tonight, show her the power he has.' Bazzini dare not add that Krusak was using his influence by trying to force La Scala into casting the mezzo as and when *he* wished in their productions.

' "I swear I don't know why," ' mimicked Roberto. 'You're an old fraud, but we'll let that pass: Krusak's motives are obvious. I don't suppose you know anything about the carrot he'll dangle in front of her, once he's shown her the stick.'

'I— I—' Bazzini did not know what to say.

'Nothing will happen to Julia.' Roberto's hand slammed against the side of the box, making the older man start. 'Do you understand me, Bazzini? No firecrackers on stage, no eggs, no thrown coins. Nothing.'

Sweat appeared on Bazzini's bald head. The red walls of the box were suffocating. 'You've got to understand my position.'

'I'm calling in the debt, Signore. You pay tonight.'

Both stiffened as the door handle moved.

'Signore!' The stage manager was tapping on the antique pannelling, 'I need Padovano, have you seen him?'

'Here.' Roberto pushed open the door with his foot.

'You're on in ten minutes!'

'No,' said Roberto. 'It's a silent procession across the stage, get someone to stand in for me. I'll see you in a practice room. Bring my costume there, and a dresser.' Roberto set his hands on the manager's shoulders and turned him. 'We'll do fine.' He gave the man a push.

Raising his eyes heavenwards as though imploring some miracle, the man rushed off.

'Now,' said Roberto without closing the door. 'Suppose you tell me what hold Krusak has on you apart from money.'

'No!' Bazzini's cry was matched by Francesco's shout on stage as he poured out Carlos's grief at losing his betrothed to his father, King Philip. 'I can't tell you!' Bazzini whispered. 'He'll ruin me.'

'Signore, you've had a good career. Don't you think it's dishonourable to blight a beginner's before she's started?'

'God! You're the only man I know who talks to me about honour.'

'I'm old-fashioned,' said Roberto, and he winked.

The man could have charmed the serpent in Eden, thought Bazzini. The thought of defying Krusak or Padovano made his heart stutter.

'Listen to her!' Roberto pinned Bazzini's wrist against the front rim of the box. His free hand chopped down to the stage where the scene was changing. 'Look at her a moment.' His thumb and forefinger indicated that instant. 'Stop judging with your wallet. Look.'

A seemingly slight figure had appeared on stage. Bazzini heard the familiar rumpus from the stalls, but there was mostly silence from the gods and the highest tier of seats. His group, awaiting his signal, were doing nothing.

Ruth Marlow was pretty; Julia Rochfort was beautiful. Eboli's theatrical scars made no difference; she was the loveliest creature Bazzini had seen.

'English cow!' someone shouted, shattering the mood. At which a woman from the stalls jackknifed to her feet, shook her fist at the gods and yelled, 'Keep quiet, pigs! Let her try!'

Nodding to the woman, Julia Rochfort began to sing.

Bazzini was cheering. Roberto left him to it. Racing backstage, spitting his gum in the first ashtray he found, he tore off his jacket as he crashed into a practice room.

The stage manager was waiting. Roberto listened intently as the man explained the layout of the stage. Singing under this conductor would be no problem; they had worked together before. As for the part of Philip, Roberto had sung it for the last five years. He still had not caught every aspect of the character: tonight would give him the chance to investigate another layer of the role.

'We'll be fine,' he assured the manager again. 'Listen.'

The roof shook over their heads as the audience stamped. Lucca, Bazzini, and the Italian faction were united in delighted discovery of Julia as a new star.

Grinning, Roberto ushered the manager from the room and began a rapid vocal warm-up. He felt as excited as he had thirteen years ago, when he'd first appeared on Lucca's homely stage and thought it enormous. It would be hard playing a grim King when he knew that Julia would be on stage with him. He knew he looked grim but he didn't feel it, especially not tonight.

'A bit cheerful for Philip, aren't we?' asked the dresser, bustling in with doublet and hose. 'Good to see you, Signore.'

'And you, Giovanni. How's the family?'

The dresser answered, but Roberto forgot everything the man said as he tugged on his costume and the dresser prodded and tweaked and joked. As the dresser added a false beard and white flecks to Roberto's spiky brown curls, Roberto was thinking about Krusak, remembering the gloating look on that narrow face.

It was amazing how singers could change their moods, the dresser thought, watching the tall, black-hosed figure head for the stage. Padovano looked as grim as a tombstone.

Julia, coming off-stage at the end of a scene with the baritone who played Posa, stumbled as she reached the wings.

'What is it?' Posa caught her.

'Caught my gown,' Julia lied, head buzzing with adrenalin. On-stage, Ruth held onto a high note and Julia winced. She felt empty now, as if the applause had sucked her dry.

It was too far to go back to that colourless dressing-room to await her next call. Julia lowered herself by the black curtain onto cable-strewn boards next to the prompt desk.

A page skimmed past. The singer playing Philip was coming in from the opposite wing, Julia recalled, head bowed as a bead of sweat rolled down from her nose to her chin. Anxiously, hoping it was not a nosebleed, Julia wiped it away as Philip growled out his first angry lines of music.

Julia jerked her head up and scrambled to her feet.

His eyes had found her and blazed for an instant before Roberto resumed the character of Philip, stabbing a glare at his Queen. As the chorus and Ruth stared with horror at the stern, black-robed figure, Julia slipped out of the wings.

She felt to be walking through a light where every detail was picked out. The beard, jet earring, the grey hairs beneath the heavy crown: these were superficial additions, spice to their meeting. They had not changed to each other.

For Roberto it was the same. Julia was Eboli: beautiful in her golden gown, passionate with eyes, face and voice, and yet the energy was Julia herself.

As Philip, he pointed imperiously to a spot close to his side where she might remain until the Queen had taken her sad farewell of a disgraced lady-in-waiting. As Roberto his fingers brushed her wrist. His thumb touched the tiny hairs of her hand.

Julia's headache was blotted out in a pulse of pleasure. Explanations could wait: she and Roberto would be singing to each other. 'You're beautiful,' she said.

A smile lurked in the recesses of the King's greying beard.

'Where's Bill?' Posa glided past.

'Sick but improving,' answered Roberto, signalling with closed fist for Queen and courtiers to leave. As Ruth and the chorus sang, Roberto began to sing.

At the end of the evening, the conductor singled out Roberto and Julia to take a curtain call with him.

'I thought you were in Naples, you horror,' Julia murmured under the applause.

'I arranged with Naples opera to give my understudy a chance to sing tonight. He's a local boy.' Roberto bowed to the gods.

'Risky in this competitive business,' Julia murmured.

'In another five years, maybe. Tonight it was worth it.' To

ee the look of wonder on Julia's face, to be on-stage with
er, to make music together. Spirit and flesh, she was sexy.
he curtain swept down and Roberto tossed her over one
houlder.

'Stop it!' She was laughing, thumping his back. Laughing,
oberto pelted off-stage and jogged her down corridors.

'I'll sing a top A in your ear!' Julia pinched him.

'Ah.' There was a reception waiting for them outside the
ressing-rooms which Julia couldn't see. Roberto set her down
1 the corridor, shielding her with his body.

'Careful,' he warned, catching her hand as she tapped him,
There are fans waiting for you.' Krusak was there, standing
ehind a smaller man who seemed familiar to Roberto.

Julia looked round him. 'They're all men.'

'Yes.' Roberto glared at Krusak.

'What, you aren't jealous?' Julia detached herself from him.

'Of course not.' Roberto tried to sound amused, but with
rusak in the corridor he didn't feel like laughing. If he
ouches her I'll kill him, he thought. He wished the millionaire
ad not seen their horseplay.

Suddenly Julia stopped. He felt the start run down her body.
Red scarf. The man who had thrown her the rose at the
nd of the Galatea competition. Of course, Roberto thought.
le put his hands upon her shoulders, his lips near her ear.
'll be with you,' he said.

They moved forward.

28

Ruth recognised Krusak waiting backstage because Francesco kicked her in the shin. 'That's Krusak, the opera sponsor!'

Ruth, who often went to the movies, thought that the elegant man in the grey suit looked like an older Richard Gere, but not so decent. Krusak had ignored her and Francesco.

'Bellissima!' The head of Galatea made up for Krusak's lack of reaction by going down on one knee and kissing her hand. 'So pure. Remember the press call tomorrow, noon prompt.'

'Stop!' Julia's protest, Roberto's laughter, came sparking down the corridor. On-stage Ruth had seen her shaking yet the sound Julia projected and coloured so easily never wobbled. Ruth was glad Julia wasn't a soprano, otherwise she doubted that they could have remained friends.

What had been surprising was that Roberto had been nervous. Ruth had felt the slight tremor in his body when he had taken her hand on-stage and stared at the darkened royal box. It was reassuring to know that you never lost fear, that another singer's show of confidence, like hers, was a front.

That being so, Ruth reflected, smiling graciously at fans, she didn't have to *be* assertive, just *act* assertive. Which meant that as the prima donna she was going to grab the first shower.

Minutes later, costume and clothes tossed on the floor, Ruth was basking under a jet of hot water, sleeking sweat from her hair. Someone rattled the door. 'Beat it!' she shouted, delighted at the freedom *acting* the prima donna gave her.

The catch burst open and Francesco barged in.

'Little bitch!' he was shouting. 'Gone off with that bastard Padovano.'

Ruth adored swimming, felt less of a giantess surrounded by soft flowing streams. In water she was sure, certainly sure enough to deal with a jealous tenor.

'Face it, Francesco,' she said above the pumping water, 'I've had to accept that Roberto and Julia are, as the papers put it, "romantically linked".'

'But on-stage, she was . . .'

Ruth laughed, water tickling her breasts. The sensual pleasure of the shower made her tipsy. 'That's called acting.'

Francesco, still in costume, whipped open the shower door. He squinted through the spray, blond head level with her chin.

Ruth looked at him over her shoulder, hand on hip in Betty Grable pose. She had seduced the audience tonight, she thought, so why not the lead? It didn't matter if she was a stand-in for Francesco's dreams of Julia: she would show him right now that she was more than pure.

'Is that just your cod-piece, or are you glad to see me?' A revised quote from Mae West. Ruth covered half of the shower head with a hand and spurted warm water over the relevant part.

Francesco's prominent cheekbones flushed with shock.

'Ever made it with a mermaid?' As Ruth Marlow she would never have dared be so outrageous, but right now she felt beautiful enough to say anything. 'Close your mouth, Carlos, you're making a draught.' She wiggled her behind.

The fact that the outer door was unlocked, that at any moment one of the chorus might come wandering in for a dip only made this more exciting. 'Come on, lover.' A host of scenes from *Last Tango in Paris* whirled in her head as Francesco stepped fully clothed into the shower.

Beneath her shy, cool exterior was another reckless Ruth who didn't give a damn. As they made love half in and half out of the cubicle, stinging needles of water beating against their bodies, her toes levered against the tiles of the rear wall, lifting her hips, Ruth made a further discovery.

She loved playing the prima donna.

29

With Krusak staring at her back, Julia left the opera house.

Roberto was at the side entrance, signing autographs. As she came out, dark-suited men surged forward, waving pens.

Thirty minutes later, Julia was left with a programme she had signed but no one seemed to want. Roberto was talking patiently to two old dears out walking a dog: they wanted to know who he was.

Julia idly opened the programme, grabbing the note tucked inside before night air swept it down a drain. She read the typed message and her breath stuck in her windpipe.

'Plini's tonight, 4.00 a.m., for news of San Martino della Croce. Come alone.'

'What's going on? – Don't say "nothing", you hardly ate a thing at Plini's and you've scarcely said two sentences on the way back here.' Roberto brought a hand up to her bedraggled curls, lowered it without touching her.

He had told her about Bazzini's claque, but Julia wasn't disposed to be communicative: she didn't want Roberto involved in the ancient history of Krusak, Clara and Scarpia.

'I've no idea even who Krusak is.' She flopped onto the hotel bed, staring at the moulded ceiling, winding and rewinding a curl of hair with her thumb. 'How did those clowns outside the church know that Bazzini was gay?'

'They didn't: they saw an old man with a wallet. Anything they yelled was just frustrated abuse.' Roberto smiled then frowned. 'Seriously, Krusak's one of the richest men in Italy. He came to Milan in the sixties, made a fortune selling fridges. Bazzini says he gets what he wants. Right now that's you.'

And not only for desire. Roberto's painter's eye had caught another expression slithering across Krusak's smooth face. Incredible as it seemed, the millionaire was afraid of Julia. She threatened him.

Which meant that the pay-off, when it came, would be spectacular, something he couldn't match. Roberto yanked shut the hotel window, cutting down on the cheerful racket being raised by the dustbin men in the street. Krusak had the reputation of being a collector of women. As a successful singer he knew all about the aphrodisiac effect power had on many women; he knew too how big businessmen operated: intimidation and corruption. The bullying, then the bribe.

'Did he give you anything tonight?' He leaned his head against the cold glass. 'Promise anything?'

'You were with me. You heard what was said.'

Krusak, frowning, had offered his congratulations.

'Does Krusak know your grandmother?' Roberto rubbed the blipping pulse by his temple. Given the uncanny similarity in looks between Julia and her grandmother, maybe Julia was some kind of proxy for Krusak, another Clara.

'Oh, come on.'

Bull's-eye, Roberto thought. When he turned, Julia was looking him straight in the face – too good an actress to look away. He wanted to shake her. *'I'm involved!'* his mind was shouting. Julia looked terrible: hollow-eyed, white-faced, agitated. Like a junkie.

Julia rolled over and came at him with fingers crooked. 'Sit! You're the proverbial bear with the sore head.'

'And you look like Dracula's mother.'

'Thanks!' Julia tugged him onto the edge of the bed, began pummelling the back of his neck. 'Ruth and Francesco were pleased with each other at tonight's dinner.' The cast had returned to Florence to celebrate at Plini's. 'Be at Plini's,' the note said. Someone had known of her movements in advance.

Roberto's neck bones cracked under Julia's fingers as he turned. The top of his spine was damp where he had missed towelling after a hasty shower. 'Who's the red scarf man?' he asked. 'He seems connected with Krusak.'

'Maybe.' Trying to block out the man, Julia put her nose in Roberto's neck. 'You smell good.'

Roberto leaned against her. 'Missed you,' he said. He sighed as Julia slipped from the bed and stepped round to stand in front of him, cradling his head. Still he couldn't let go of the pictures in his skull.

'You've met Krusak before, haven't you?'

A Nazi who had shot and tortured Italian civilians in Emilia Romagna had been able to settle in Milan. Even as Julia grew angry at the idea she wondered how Clara had not known it. Of course her grandmother had never been involved with business.

'Answer me!' Roberto's anxiety made him clumsy. He seized Julia's wrists.

'Why should I? I don't have to pander to your suspicions.' Tearing away, Julia leaped from the bed and snapped on the TV.

'Don't do this,' said Roberto. 'Don't shut me out.'

Next instant they were sprawled on the carpet, Julia on top of him as they kissed.

'You're going to have to leave.'

It was three-fifteen. They were in bed.

Roberto stroked Julia's back. Tonight her lovemaking had been almost desperate, a denial of the world.

'Want the gossip columnists to find you here tomorrow morning?' Julia's voice was slurred. At least she was relaxed enough to sleep.

'I'm going.' Roberto rolled her off him onto her side and tucked the covers round her. His final action reminded him of his father. He needed to have it out with Simone about Naples. What had his father done, or not done, in the war which had made him so ashamed that he should lie for so long? Certain possibilities Roberto didn't want to consider. Talk to him. He had to talk to Simone—

'Night.' Julia's sleepy voice shadowed him as he dressed in darkness. Carrying his shoes, Roberto padded to the door. Letting himself out, he made certain it was locked behind him.

Julia heard the lock click and tore back the covers. Three-fifteen. She had to get to Plini's before four.

'Come on!' She couldn't fasten her trainers. Leaving one untied, Julia tugged on her coat. Alone, the message said. Come alone.

'That old trick,' Julia said aloud, disgusted with herself. She should have told Roberto. She had implied he was jealous, but she knew that was unfair. He was worried and frustrated by her secretiveness, as she herself would have been, had their positions been reversed.

'I'm my mother's daughter,' muttered Julia, fastening her watch. Why hadn't she told Roberto? And yet, what could she say to him? He wasn't the kind of man who would watch from the sidelines, and she didn't want him hurt. Maybe it was a false illusion, but she hoped that Emilio Gucci, or whoever it was who had sent her tonight's note, would hesitate to injure a woman.

Julia dropped back on the bed, attacking the laces in her loose trainer. She'd given Gucci the opera house's phone number. Gucci knew she was looking for someone from San Martino della Croce.

So did Rita, the Bolognese prostitute, but a typed note didn't seem her style and besides, how would Rita know that she, Julia, was a singer, not a journalist?

Which left Bianca and Pietro Terni, Krusak and the gentleman with the red scarf. Four in the morning matched Bianca's humour, but Julia couldn't see her being so dramatic. And Pietro would hardly wait around in the small hours with information he could pass on through his son.

Krusak might have paid someone to hand her the note. The man was a wartime murderer, obsessed and malicious: Julia shuddered at what could have happened earlier had

Roberto not 'persuaded' Bazzini to have his claque support her. Krusak had been furious tonight: he had spat his congratulations at her. If Krusak had sent that message, she would be a fool to go.

'Oh, God.' Julia pushed herself to her feet, walked wearily to the bathroom and splashed water over her face.

If not for mischief, why would anyone wish to meet her at four in the morning? *You are afraid? So am I.*

The man with the red scarf hadn't been afraid. He had said 'Hello, Julia.' He had spoken in English. He had smiled. He had been about to say more when Krusak had cut in, stepping straight in front of the man.

Remembering the stranger's knife, Julia hadn't known whether to be relieved by Krusak's rudeness or angered.

The man had known her name. Many people who were strangers knew her name and picture. Julia buried her over-photographed face in the hotel towel, wishing she had dropped that programme in the gutter after all. She sighed, rubbing her aching eyes. Maybe she should call the police—

The towel was a noose about her throat: a hand punched into her diaphragm. Even as she kicked out desperately behind, she felt the needle jab into her neck.

'You won't be so pretty when we've finished.' The voice felled her like a bolt of lightning, then there was darkness.

Roberto hadn't been able to obtain a booking at the hotel where the *Don Carlos* cast were staying; he was at the Florence Savoy. Going from one hotel to another, he could have taken a taxi but preferred to walk.

Stars were shining above the glare of the city. It was cold: breath spumed from his nostrils. His ears were raw. Frost slicked shop windows, ice exploded under his striding feet.

Usually he enjoyed walking at night, but not now. One tiny part of his mind was reviewing the evening's work, trying to wind down; another was still thinking about his father, whom he had not spoken to in any real way since Naples.

But those things were just surface. Pounding the deserted streets, Roberto's brain beat with questions. Why was Julia so frightened of the man with the red scarf? Was Krusak connected with her grandmother, or with the mystery relative Julia was trying to find? Why was Krusak afraid? What was he hiding?

Whatever Julia was hiding, he prayed it wasn't one thing. Since learning of Bianca Terni's existence he'd heard from his police brother about that journalist's connections with the Milan narcotics scene. Julia had visited the Ternis several times since Christmas to rehearse *Don Carlos* – nothing wrong with that. Just because he knew singers who 'did' drugs it didn't follow that Julia was one of them: her friendship with Bianca Terni was totally innocent. And he knew Julia's body as he knew his own; there were no needle marks on her.

But then, a small voice reminded him, pushers often don't 'do' drugs. In two months how well did he know Julia really?

Roberto grunted. A whole lot of rubbish was spinning through his head: he must be tired even to consider such crazy ideas.

Secrets he could accept: all couples have secrets from each other. What Roberto found hard to swallow was that Julia was badly scared and yet shielding him: though he knew she did so because she cared, it made him feel less of a man.

Maybe this was what Carlotta had meant when she accused him of being medieval, but he was still going to go after Krusak *and* that funny little man with the scarf. He'd have them both.

Jerking his head at the faded corner shrine, Roberto stepped round the dustbins blocking the end of the alley. Out in the small cobbled square a stack of Vespas below green neon reminded him that he would soon be passing Plini's.

Behind him a car was accelerating along one of the streets running into the square. Roberto kept on walking. When the car crashed through the two narrow wooden posts supporting the café's awning, he flattened himself against the wall, head down so the headlights would not shine in his face. The car roared by within a metre of him, the draught almost sucking him off the pavement, before it bumped to a screeching stop.

A drunk would have kept going or stalled the car. Roberto whipped away from the wall, diving under cover of the buckling awning. A house light opposite spotted the place where he had been then snapped off. The apartment above the café was deathly quiet. Roberto, prowling deeper into shadows, doubted that anyone would phone the police.

The Fiat's engine was still running. He wasn't surprised when the rear doors burst open and a body was shovelled onto the unlit cobbles sixty metres away – a live one, at least. Two men wearing harlequin masks, dusting down their light suits, clambered out and kicked the twitching figure.

'You stupid little creep!' muttered Roberto, hands clenching the stump of a splintered wooden post. He wasn't about to have his head kicked in for some pusher or pimp who'd kept back part of the take: the heavies would work the poor bastard over and, if they were feeling kind, leave him on the pavement not the street.

Yet there was something about that dark, curiously formless shape lying with its face turned from him on the road that raised the hairs on his back . . .

Cursing under his breath, Roberto wrenched the stump from the ground. Two and the driver, probably armed. Christ, by the time the carabinieri appeared it would be all over.

The cry sent Roberto crashing through the awning into the square. Piling into the attackers, he smashed the taller of the two heavies across the throat with the staff. The man dropped, but even before he had fallen Roberto had jabbed his fingers into the eye sockets of the second sharp-suited harlequin. As the man reeled back, roaring and clutching his face, Roberto hurled the splintered post into the car's rear window, then stamped on the groin of the taller man.

'Cry later!' He yelled at the huddled figure, ducking sideways as a knife jagged into his clothes, 'Run!'

His intuition was right. Even before the figure rolled over, raised its bloodied face in darkness, he knew her.

Shock froze him and the knife slashed again, probing for his liver. It grazed his flank and as Roberto twisted from the searing pain another blow, a fist, jellified his guts. Too astonished to feel anything at first, he staggered, then hit back.

His fist connected with something soft and as his blurred

vision cleared he saw the second harlequin falling, screaming
as his hand ripped down the Fiat's shattered rear windscreen.
In a smear of bloodstains the man clawed for the door.

'Move it, arsehole!' The driver yelled at the taller heavy,
who seemed to be trying to remember how to pick himself off
the cobbles. The Fiat's engine squealed as the driver stepped
on the gas. Through the cloud of exhaust fumes, Roberto saw
what looked like a funnel aimed at his chest.

'No!' Julia shouted, flinging herself in front of him.

The explosion made them start but the driver's shot went
wide, possibly because the taller heavy had tottered against
the car. As he slumped over the bonnet, the driver dragged
him inside the gaping passenger door and scorched rubber
out of the square.

Julia spun round. 'I saw you dead!' she was whispering,
her nails clawing at Roberto's back. She screamed when her
fingers caught in a rent of cloth and her legs buckled.

Roberto caught her, then discovered he couldn't even hold
himself together any more. Julia dead, Julia dying; his
grandfather dead and the blood: the images scored into his
eyeballs as the sound of the gunshot overwhelmed him.
Twisting his head, Roberto threw up over one of the chained-
up scooters.

Somehow they finished seated on the pavement, feet in
the gutter, Julia on his lap, both of them shaking. Roberto
knew he had to get her away from here, that it wasn't safe,
that the heavies could come roaring back round the block.
'It's over,' he kept telling himself. Over and over he heard the
gun shot. His teeth rattled in his head. Sweat burst from him
as his groin crawled with fear. He despised himself and his
weakness.

Julia still clung to him. She was shivering. Roberto took off
his ruined jacket, wrapped it around her. The gunfire echoed
in his mind but he clamped on it, forced himself to move. One
handed, he jerked on the chain of the Bravo parked next to
the Vespa he had baptised with most of his dinner. The chain
held for two tugs then snapped.

'Hang on.' He swung Julia onto the back of the moped,

kicked the motor into life and took them away from the square.

Julia was in shock. The only time she reacted was when Roberto slowed outside a brightly lit building. Her hands dug painfully under his belt. 'Keep going! Please!' Panic broke up her voice. He heard her sobbing with relief as they rattled past the police station into darker streets.

Roberto chose a pensione in San Frediano, a place which wouldn't remember faces. 'Keep your arm round me,' he murmured, as they entered the cabbage-smelling lobby with Julia pressed against his side, hiding the bloodstains. She tottered but managed to keep her feet until they reached their room, where she stumbled fully clothed onto the bed. Roberto piled blankets over her then used the phone.

'Not the police,' he explained, seeing Julia's eyes flicker as he lifted the receiver. 'A doctor.'

'Another old school-friend,' filtered a muffled voice from the covers.

She was right. Roberto smiled as his fingers jabbed the number, but instead of dialling, he wished he had his hands pressed round the taller heavy's throat.

Mild concussion, minor cuts on face, bruises on arms, legs, buttocks and lower back, said the doctor. He cleaned Julia up, gave her something for the pain, then strapped Roberto's side.

'She'll be on her feet tomorrow and able to sing at her next performance, if she's sensible.' The doctor picked up his bag and coat. 'Any idea who did this?'

'I mean to find out,' said Roberto.

The wake-up call Roberto had asked for prodded Julia from sleep. Groping the phone back onto its cradle she rolled over.

A sherry-coloured eye, bright as a cat's, blinked at her. 'Good morning.' Roberto lifted a stubbled face from the pillow. 'And how are you?' He smiled, showing that gap between the two upper front teeth which Julia found so endearing.

Julia rumpled his spiky hair, remembered him risking his

life for her in the street and started to cry.

'They took my good coat.'

Roberto drew her to him, wrapped his arms around her, rocked her as she wept against his chest.

'They beat me in the car. I came round and they were hitting me. The taller one slapped my face.'

It was coming out now. Julia couldn't stop it, didn't want to. 'They said I wouldn't be pretty when they'd finished. I'd never realised how much it hurts to be battered --not just the pain, which is terrible, what's worse is the feeling that another person can do what they like to you, that you can't stop them.' She shuddered. 'They could have killed me, I wouldn't have been able to stop them. I couldn't help myself.'

'Who are they?'

Julia squinted at the big muscular man in bed with her. 'What are you saying?' she whispered, her bright grey eyes puffy with bruises. 'What do you think I'm involved with?'

Roberto brought a finger up to her battered face. Pity and anger welled in him: he hated himself, his cynical suspicions. Yet the question which had kept him awake for the greater part of Julia's four hours' sleep remained: Why no police? What was Julia doing that made her scared of the law?

Roberto sighed: in the end it didn't matter. 'Whatever it is you're doing, I don't care. Do you understand?' He slowly wiped the tears from the grazed cheekbones. 'I don't care what you're involved in. All I care about is you. Let me help.' His arms cracked as he pulled her on top of him.

He was absolutely serious: his features were as white as the tundra; his arms locked about her were as hard as granite. His body was warm. 'Don't be angry,' he said steadily. 'I've been wondering about you and Bianca Terni, who I know was once charged for possession of drugs. And last night, when you didn't want the police—'

'What?' Julia almost gave a bark of laughter. 'You're not telling me Bianca's into illegal substances are you?'

'She knows some strange people.'

'Sounds as if you do, too.'

'Drugs are part of the music scene: singers use them to

ep going, or else they carry them – after all, learning to
ay opera is an expensive business, with the lessons and
stumes. I remember what a struggle it was for me in the
eginning. When I was starting out – as you are now –
meone approached me to see if I'd be a carrier. Who would
spect an international artist? I know one soprano who
veeps through customs with a cache of coke hidden in her
th crystals.' Seeing Julia's expression, Roberto stopped. 'You
ally don't know about this, do you?' Colour seeped into his
oad forehead, ran down his strong chin. 'Oh, Jesus. I'm
rry.' He made to slide from under her, but Julia pinned him
ith her arm.

'You haven't insulted me.' She kissed him on the mouth.
m not angry.' She did not feel angered by Roberto's concern:
w could she? *All I care about is you.* No one had ever said
at to her. If she weren't careful she would start crying again.
presume you refused to be a carrier: if anyone approached
e, so would I. For the official record I'm not involved in any
ay with drugs, drug trafficking or anything else that's
iminal. Except maybe this . . .' She tickled him until with a
ugh Roberto pinned her beneath him and gave her the
nbrace she wanted.

Both were too sore to make love: they fell asleep.

When they woke, Julia had half an hour before the Galatea
ess conference. Roberto slipped out and bought some dark
asses, fake tan, a plum coloured lipstick, and set to work.

'I'm the painter,' he said, when Julia protested. 'I know what
ople see. We'll need to pick up your long earrings from the
her hotel. Silver looks good with a tan.'

When lipstick had blurred the minor cuts round her mouth
d dark glasses the cuts round her eyes, Julia's lip began to
obble. Roberto, standing behind her, saw her expression in
e bathroom mirror and hugged where there was no bruising.
'You're doing very well.'

'No, I'm not.' To her horror Julia began to weep again. 'He's
to me. That's why his men said that I wouldn't be pretty
ain; it was to show he knows. He knows and I'm no nearer
ding him. What am I going to do? If he knows about me,

he'll know about my grandmother: maybe they'll take he
next!'

Roberto turned her to him. 'Who you talking about
Krusak?'

Julia felt herself weakening, snapped back her shoulder
and shook her head. This time Roberto had escaped with
slight knife wound, next time he might not be so lucky.

'You're my lover.' She stroked his chest. 'Not my minder

Roberto took her head between his hands. 'Julia, with m
I'm afraid that's one and the same. Now stop being silly.'

'I should be mad at you, Roberto. You imply I might be int
drugs, what next?'

'Why can't you go to the police?' asked Roberto softly.

'Because this is Italy.' Julia thought back just two month
when she had first come to Florence, her idealised view c
the country, and sank down on the edge of the bath. If bein
grown-up meant losing illusions she had certainly matured
'Probably has the cops in his pocket.'

'Who?' demanded Roberto, looming over her, very nake
very male. She too, apart from the dark glasses was naked.

'Don't we look absurd?' she said.

'Julia.' Roberto hooked the dark glasses from her nos
tilted back her narrow chin. 'Please,' he said, crouching b
her feet, 'give me his name.'

She couldn't say it. Julia took the lipstick from his fist an
wrote on the white tiles.

Roberto sat back heavily on his heels, cracking his hea
on the toilet cistern. He stared up at her. 'You too? We'r
looking for the same man!'

Julia started, closed her eyes. 'Scarpia tortured Clara.'

'Scarpia tortured my father,' said Roberto.

Their hands found each other's and locked together. Finall
quietly, they began to talk.

30

When Bianca had slipped into Gucci's home last night after
Julia, the retired Marshal had been waiting, answers ready.

Gucci had questions, too. 'Why was the kid interested in
Scarpia?' 'Why had Bianca fixed the meeting for twelve?' 'Why
did Julia walk out when he mentioned the Scudieri female?'

'Clara Scudieri is her grandmother,' answered Bianca,
amused when Gucci choked on his unlit pipe, 'Julia's staying
with her.' She left the second question unanswered: her whims
had nothing to do with Gucci. 'Who's Scarpia?'

'A bastard. He'd make police "brutality" look like a slap a
mother gives a toddler. Julia's after him.' Gucci scratched his
cauliflower ear. 'What's her real name?'

'Julia Rochfort-Scudieri.'

'Double-barrelled, eh? That figures. And living with the
bitch of the mountains – I'd thought she'd be long dead.'

'Clara lives in retirement in a villa outside Florence,' said
Bianca. 'Why do you dislike her?'

Gucci shrugged and hoiked off his spectacles, fixed his
eyes somewhere over Bianca's right shoulder. 'How come
Signorina Double-Barrelled knew the name of our region's
wartime torturer and you didn't? She a better journalist?'

Bianca shrugged herself, ignoring the question. Di Salvo
had mentioned Scarpia as a name – nothing more – when he
spoke of 'old pro-Nazi alliances' which could not be allowed

to surface in the public domain. She was to dispose of anyone who appeared too forthcoming or curious about Scarpia, and not ask too many questions herself. The less Bianca knew the better.

'Did you tell Julia about Scarpia?' she asked, reaching into her jacket.

'Never got the chance.' Gucci scraped his stubble with his pipe stem. 'She buggered off in a huff over grandmama. Don' know much, anyway: only what I've said.'

Bianca relaxed, taking her hand from the gun in her pocket. 'What's this "Red-Headed League"?'

'A partisan group started by Mario Scudieri,' said Gucci, polishing the lenses of his spectacles with his shirt.

Sitting at the table where he had spoken with Julia, the former Marshal of Ponte Maggiore told Bianca the story of Mario Scudieri and the old Marshal: how Umberto Gasparini had helped the group by listening to the Allies' broadcasts and passing on information. Gucci was equally forthcoming about his suspicions of the wartime priest and curate of Croce and of his dislike of Francesco Vincenti.

Bianca learned that Julia had acquired old photographs of the Bologna opera orchestra and chorus, and that she seemed to be trying to trace a particular man, or men, from the pictures.

Bianca nodded, scooping her black hair – dyed for her night at the opera – behind her ears in an echo of Rita's habitual gesture. She had dropped in on Rita at the dance hall. Rita had been shown pictures. Rita had her own story about Mario Scudieri. Rita had mentioned Scarpia.

Rita had been scared: Krusak's influence, Bianca guessed.

'Julia say why she was after these people?' Bianca wondered why Gucci kept fiddling with his pipe and didn't light it.

'Good copy, she said. I knew that was a lie – told her so.'

'Maybe Julia wants to find out more about her cousin Mario.'

'Not if she's shacked up with Clara the Contessa. Mario was a man of the people . . .'

Used to Gucci's politics, Bianca switched off until the man

laughed and thumped the table, almost crushing his spectacles.

'... here's the younger Stefano, ransacking some posy art gallery in Bologna, accusing them of being Fascist when his dad had been the most right-wing man in Croce! Your girl wanted Stefano's address. I said I'd get it.'

Bianca smiled. 'Think she'll come back?'

Gucci knocked the ash from his pipe. 'If she does, I'm not having her over my doorstep a second time!' The veins in his neck stood out like tree-bark.

Bianca nodded, satisfied. 'You'll let me know if she does?'

She had another call to make. She knew where Stefano lived: helping that drunk out of Papà's gallery into a taxi, making sure the driver had the address, had been one of her good deeds.

Ex-feds were the best, Bianca reflected, shepherding Pietro through Lucca's heaving lobby. Last night had been useful.

Scarpia. Gucci hadn't spotted the connection between the nickname and Julia's interest in musicians of the forties and fifties, but then opera to him was a waste of money.

Bianca squeezed her father's arm. Di Salvo didn't want her prying into Scarpia, but it wouldn't hurt to make some enquiries about Pietro's ex-colleagues, just to see if there were any leads – *Yeah, and curiosity killed the cat.*

'This way.' She guided Pietro out of the door. Papà was subdued tonight, Bianca thought, maybe he'd been racked up over how Frankie would perform. Not that he need have worried.

'Fabulous, huh?' She waved back at the opera house.

Pietro mumbled a reply, shuffling into the passenger seat of her car. Bianca shrugged and climbed in: she'd had a good time. On the Florence road, Bianca pulled in for petrol. Papà wasn't talking; she decided to discover why. Marching to the passenger door, she yanked it open. 'You want to drive, or what?'

Pietro turned a moon-face up to her. He tried to speak. His hand jerked and a used syringe dropped onto the damp forecourt, rolling under the car.

'Nice one, Pop.' Bianca slammed the door on her father's limpid smile. She drove slowly from the petrol station, and later even more slowly through the first toll booth of the Florence – Bologna autostrada. Her father was tipsy, she explained to the ticket man.

'Would you mind telling me why you found it necessary to mainline on a petrol station forecourt?' she observed, several kilometres after the toll. 'Why not at the opera house? That would have been even more public.'

Bianca drove faster, counting off makes of cars as she passed them. She didn't look at her father.

'You're shocked,' said Pietro Terni.

'Yes!' muttered Bianca, who had interviewed drug abusers in the course of her career as a journalist. She had contacts with pushers in Milan: had once been picked up by the cops for possession, but this was different. 'What is it you use, Papà?'

'Cocaine. A weak solution. I can take it or leave it.'

Bianca blinked as a four-wheel drive streaked past on full headlights. 'So for how long have you been enjoying the buzz?'

'Six months – that's all, I swear. Once I get this next year over, I'll give it up.'

His speech was less slurred. Bianca glanced at him. 'Be sure you do.' The risks for someone of his age indulging in narcotics were frightening. Where had he got the stuff? From those Sicilian street traders he chatted with in Bologna?

Bianca thought of herself as broad-minded, but finding a seventy-plus-year-old doing drugs in her car she could feel cracks appearing in her façade. What was Papà doing? With every 'fix' he risked heart failure or a stroke.

'What made you start?'

'You mean tonight?' Pietro deflected the question and Bianca let him; she wanted to know about tonight.

'Yes: here you are, having a pleasant evening, watching your son's triumph . . . What went wrong, Papà?'

'I thought I'd laid it to rest a long time ago. And the music, the plot: Verdi's *Don Carlos* is so different from Puccini's *Tosca*. But they've more in common than I realised. Both are about oppression, injustice.'

'Right.' This was something to think about later, when she wasn't having to negotiate traffic.

Pietro heard the doubt in her voice and realised he had said too much. It was his own fault, mainlining always made him feel invulnerable. It was that feeling of safety which Pietro had craved ever since the singer playing the Inquisitor – the one who questioned, who could demand answers by use of the rack – had mounted the stage in tonight's *Don Carlos*, bringing memories crashing round Pietro's silver-blond head.

Now he dug out a handkerchief, patting sweat from his temples. 'Don't know why you're fussing, Duchess. Drugs are accepted in the art world. Cash or coke – either will do.'

Bianca threw him a glowering look. Pietro closed his eyes, pretending to sleep.

Finally they were home. Finally Papà was tucked up in bed. Bianca walked through to the dining-room. Bracing her arms, she lifted down the fake Impressionist picture Julia had admired.

Pietro's safe. She doubted if her father had changed the combination that she'd overheard him telling her brother on one of those occasions when Frankie had been admitted to the macho inner sanctum and she'd been outside, listening at the door.

The numbers were the same: the door peeled back from the wall. Heart beating fast, as though she had won a race, Bianca placed her hands within the safe and drew out the papers.

31

Next day Bianca was summoned to Tancredi di Salvo's Venetian villa. At Marco Polo airport she was met by di Salvo's secretary, driven by Lamborghini to the Brenta Canal and escorted aboard a private speedboat. It was mild; the water sparkled. The air palpitated with scents: damp earth, a barbecue, Bianca's Chanel.

Bianca was scared. She was in disgrace: the secretary sat with his back to her in the boat. Once only did he turn his bearded head, removing his dark glasses.

'You are to go riding with Signor di Salvo. Suitable clothes have been provided. Leave your handbag with me.'

So. No gun. Bianca inclined her head. Riding meant a canter around the villa's grounds: private woods where anything might happen.

'Women should always ride side-saddle.' Di Salvo flicked Bianca with a gloved hand. 'The riding habit fits?'

'Perfectly.' Bianca's waist felt so nipped-in that if she took a deep breath she would probably burst the gold buttons down the front. 'Black is elegant.'

'Excellent!' Di Salvo's mouth moulded in a smile whilst his eyes were as ever opaque. Sun lit his once fair hair as he turned a noble profile to the smaller bridle path. 'This, I think. Then we'll have our talk.'

The subtlest movement of his fingers brought the white stallion to obedience. With a turn which would have graced a dressage competition, horse and rider cantered beneath an arch of chestnut trees towards a distant fountain.

To make her horse stir, Bianca had to use heels and crop, and then the mare's sideways lurch almost had her tumbling into a bay tree. Clinging on, wishing someone had provided her with a hat, Bianca galloped after her boss.

Di Salvo reined in his mount to a smooth trotting gait, allowing Bianca to come alongside.

'Pietro's business does well?'

'Yes Signore.'

'He has heeded my advice concerning the reproduction cartoons?'

Di Salvo made faking sound a legitimate enterprise. In the art world, almost the easiest work for modern artists to pass off as old masters were the cartoons: these drawings, preliminary sketches by painters, brought high prices. If a modern forger used old paper and inks, a cartoon was almost impossible to spot as fake.

Bianca wasn't surprised that di Salvo wanted her father to expand in that area. 'He's given the matter serious thought.'

Di Salvo nodded. 'Allow me to congratulate your father on Francesco's performance last night. Tell Pietro I am pleased with my godson; he is a credit to us.'

'We're proud of Francesco.' The pommel of the side saddle was a spike against her stomach. The mare, sensing her fear, was jumpy, bucking at shadows.

'Look at that fellow in the trees, Bianca. Squirrels are pretty creatures; it's a pity to shoot them.'

Di Salvo turned his head, a scar on his right cheek close to the jaw showing where a mole had been removed. Strange, how she had never noticed the mark before, thought Bianca, but today she was in a mood to see everything. 'Yes, it's a pity.'

He smiled: a fair-skinned, handsome man in his seventies, his well-honed body perfectly balanced on the stallion, jacket and cravat immaculate. Di Salvo wore clothes as well as did her father.

Bianca twisted her head away from those dead eyes, looking for some fauna to comment on.

'Black becomes you,' said di Salvo in his rich speaking voice, watching her as his hands gentled the living creature beneath him. 'Allow me to congratulate *you* on your disposal of Sprint: a neat operation.'

It was di Salvo who had called Cesare Celere by that nickname when he had ordered Sprint's 'disposal'.

'Does that mean that you'll consider using women in other areas of your organisation?' asked Bianca, shifting nervously on her horse as she tried not to appear too eager. Bianca was ambitious: she wanted to rise in di Salvo's powerful 'family' network. That was why she had undertaken to 'hit' Sprint for di Salvo: her first killing. A good clean job, except no one had warned her about the dreams afterwards . . .

Her companion chuckled at her presumption. 'Tell me, before Sprint died, did he mention any names of those he'd been involved with during the war?'

'No names. He said the group used code-names.'

'I see.' Di Salvo lightly snapped the reins. 'Still, better to be safe than sorry, I think, with these fiftieth anniversary celebrations stirring up such interest – and financial rewards for the unscrupulous. If Sprint had decided he could make money talking to you as a journalist, he would certainly have gossiped to the hack from *Oggi*.

'What do you know about this attack on Julia Rochfort?'

The question was whipped at her. For an instant, Bianca's shoot-from-the-hip style fell away. 'Julia?'

'Three morons kidnapped Julia from her hotel last night. They were only prevented from doing her serious injury by the intervention of Roberto Padovano, who despite being one against three drove them off.'

They were alive. Relief slammed like a fist into her chest: an emotional reaction which took Bianca totally by surprise. Coughing, she hung over the mare's flank. Di Salvo grabbed her reins, bringing both horses to a jolting stop.

'Control yourself! This is a serious matter, shots were fired. Did you know anything of this?'

'No!' The process which had begun for Bianca last night in her car when she had found her father taking drugs was continuing: the gap between herself and reality was shrinking, she was beginning to be involved.

'What's wrong with you? Was Padovano one of your lovers?' Di Salvo thrust his riding crop under her chin, tilted Bianca's head. 'According to my sources, my favourite bass is involved with my new favourite mezzo. It would not please me if that relationship were threatened.'

'I understand.' The man was crazy about opera, and singers.

Di Salvo appeared to relax, although he did not remove the whip handle from her throat. 'So you were not meddling?'

'No.' She could taste sweat on her upper lip.

'Yet you are agitated.' Di Salvo stroked the crop handle down her breast before lifting it away. 'Is there something you wish to tell me?'

Ah the gentleness of that voice!

'Scarpia! Julia is looking for him. Scarpia did something terrible to Mario Scudieri, one of her family. Julia wants revenge. She wants to find and unmask him . . .'

For an instant the urge to confess had been so overwhelming Bianca had actually believed she was speaking. She didn't want to mention Julia's interest in Scarpia: it wasn't scruple on her part, more an intuition that Julia, with her opera and partisan connections, was on the verge of turning up something very big concerning di Salvo's taboo subject. Information she, Bianca, would then extract from Julia by fair means or foul and have as a safeguard in case – just in case – di Salvo turned against her family. Yet if di Salvo found out about Julia's search from another source and she had said nothing . . .

'Julia is searching for details of her family history . . . her grandmother is an Italian aristocrat who appears to have been pro-German . . . Julia is interested in such alliances.' Bianca, hoping enough had been said, stared into the bare chestnut trees. She wondered how it felt to die.

'And you think those thugs could "deter" my mezzo?' The white stallion beneath di Salvo shifted, pawing gravel.

'Whoever sent the men obviously thought so.' Bianca believed that the attack would make Julia more determined. She risked her own forthright statement. 'Perhaps you sent those men yourself.'

Di Salvo pursed his lips. 'Why?'

Bianca, who had spent a night studying the papers from her father's safe, could think of a reason, connected with Julia's search for pro-Nazi alliances, but said nothing of that. 'As a favour to Krusak. The man would welcome the opportunity to pose as her protector.'

Di Salvo's jaw tightened. 'That role has been taken by Padovano. I count Jan a personal friend, but even for him I would not injure such a creature as Julia Rochfort.'

Di Salvo flung Bianca back her reins. 'Come!' He cut his heels into the stallion's side.

They galloped to the fountain, allowing the horses to drink at the marble basin beneath. Waiting, stirrups so close as to be touching, Bianca felt the tension seeping into her loins.

Memory swept through Bianca. Twenty years ago, as an impressionable sixteen-year-old convinced her long legs and spectacles made her ugly, she had been seduced by di Salvo. Her godfather had been her first lover. Since then, the seduction had been of the spirit: the attractions of power. And yet, lingering still, was this attraction for the older man, a concern which had sharpened her resolve when she had shot Sprint, who had dared to threaten *her* boss—

'Bianca.' Di Salvo's voice recalled her to danger. 'You have not asked if the three men have been caught.'

'I assume they've already been dealt with.'

Di Salvo snorted, but let it pass. 'Remember: I am fond of Rochfort's voice. The way to preserve such an instrument is to ensure it is not contaminated by grosser substances. Such substances are to be removed – permanently if necessary.'

'So I continue to use the same discretion as I have over Scarpia.'

Di Salvo's dead eyes sparked at Bianca's reference to the subject he had placed under anathema, but he nodded. Precisely! I want you to follow Julia, make her your friend, ensure her safety. She is now "family".'

'I understand.' Bianca was oddly relieved: Julia intrigued her. Bianca had already tested her by fixing the midnight meeting with Gucci, by telling Krusak about Julia's visit to Rita's dance hall and allowing him to move in first. Both times, Julia had shown courage.

Di Salvo leaned towards her. He kissed her on the mouth, placing his hands around her nipped-in middle.

'You're no horsewoman, my dear. Let's hope you are better at keeping Julia from danger.'

It was said lightly, but Bianca knew it was a threat.

32

Roberto had two more weeks in Naples singing opera, charity galas and recordings at Milan, then four days clear before he flew to Austria. Julia had performances of *Don Carlos*, then six days clear before new rehearsals.

Whilst Roberto was in Milan, he would call on Sandro and ask him to use his police contacts to look for Umberto Gasparini and the younger Stefano. Roberto would also talk to his father, find out why Simone had lied about living in Naples during the war when he had never left Castel.

Julia would write again to Giovanni Respini, as a relative of Mario Scudieri, but care of Roberto's address.

They would visit Emilio Gucci together to discover what he knew about Scarpia.

Julia now knew that Scarpia had murdered most of his victims. This made any suggestion by Roberto that she give up her search because of danger irrelevant. She had to find Scarpia in case he moved against Clara.

Julia hired a security firm to patrol Clara's home. Their rates were cheap to pay for peace of mind.

Into this whirl of strategies came a card from Angelica: 'You promised to come home for Enrico's birthday.'

'You must go,' said Clara throatily: she'd had a cold for a fortnight, but was on the mend now. Julia smiled as her grandmother added, 'English air will do you good.'

Her mother, meeting her at Leeds airport on a dank winter's day, was more blunt. 'I think you should remove those dark glasses.' Angelica also remarked that fake tans were common, and that Julia looked to be putting on weight . . .

And now it was the morning after Enrico's birthday. Her stepfather was tidying his garage and Julia was helping Angelica change the sheets in her own small bedroom.

'What are these?' Angelica picked the photographs off the bedside cabinet where Julia had left them: she knew a direct approach would be no use.

'Some snaps grandmother lent me.' Julia peeled off the bottom bedsheet, walked to the landing cupboard for fresh ones. Opening the cupboard revived unpleasant childhood memories and she shivered. Returning to the room, she found Angelica sitting on the bed, her back to the window, clutching a photograph of Guy.

'I didn't need a picture to remember him.'

Julia, warm scented sheets draped over an arm, settled on the bed.

'If I could have told you about him without mentioning *her* I would, but you were so curious. You wouldn't have been satisfied to know about my father. You'd have wanted more.'

Angelica laid a picture of herself and Guy on the bed. The shadow of the maple tree growing outside the Victorian terrace threw a pall over her hair.

'He was handsome,' said Angelica. She was like him, tall as Ruth, elegant. At fifty-seven she was beautiful, flawless skin, rippling auburn hair shining in an immaculate French knot. Her fingers closing round the pillow-slip were clever and strong. Painter's hands, thought Julia, thinking of Roberto.

Angelica used her old room as a studio: easel and paint tubes were pushed into a corner under the high moulded ceiling. She never let anyone look at her pictures.

'I was proud of him, but she made his life wretched. I remember them quarrelling.'

'You and Enrico argue.'

Angelica's cobalt eyes clouded at Julia's mild defence of Clara. 'Not, I think, as they did.'

Julia recalled how terrifying Angelica and Enrico's odd disagreements had appeared to her when she was seven years old. Because Guy died when she was a child, Angelica had kept a childish image of her parents' marriage.

'I suppose with the war being on . . .' she began, but her mother rose to her feet, brushing her spotless blue apron.

'Enrico will be coming for his dinner soon. Will you finish here?'

As so often throughout Julia's life, Angelica withdrew.

That show of her mother's feelings might have been all Julia glimpsed during her visit except for her accident. She fell asleep that evening in the bath.

After three weeks, her bruises had almost healed. Painkillers and adrenalin kept her going through her practice and performances, but until she felt able to relax Julia did not realise how much the beating had taken out of her.

Five minutes later, after a hammering on the bathroom door and a thump as Enrico's shoulder forced the lock, her mother's arms were around her.

'Breathe, Julia, that's right.' Angelica kneeling pressed Julia's wet head against her shoulder, careless of wetting her crisp cream blouse. 'Breathe. Enrico, please make us some tea . . . Now, do you feel steady enough to stand?'

Angelica had always shown some affection when one of her family was unwell, Julia reflected another five minutes later. Comfortably propped up in bed in her dimly lit room, she watched her mother stirring a cup of Earl Grey tea. She smiled at her hovering stepfather.

'Sorry, Papà. Had the water too hot.' She spoke in Italian.

'The main thing is you're all right.' Enrico, kept out of the bathroom, sent downstairs whilst Julia was staggering from the bath, and now unable to see much in the subdued bedroom light (especially since the covers were tucked around Julia's arms), had not spotted the faded bruising over his step-daughter's body.

Angelica handed him the china teapot. 'Would you like to slip downstairs and boil another pot for us?' she asked in English. 'I'll be down soon.'

Enrico closed the door. Angelica sat on the bed. It was difficult to tell if she was shocked. She did not at once ask what had happened. She cleared her throat.

'You were always independent, from being a child.'

How could I be anything else? thought Julia. *You were never interested.* Enrico had been the one who came to her school evenings, who listened, who talked. Angelica, wrapped in her painting, in her English reserve, had been remote, coming down to Julia's level only to criticise.

'Is it some man you're involved with?' Angelica leaned closer, peppermint-scented breath wafting a curl of Julia's hair. 'I didn't want to ask whilst Enrico was here: it would only upset him and he can't do anything, poor man.'

Julia nodded: she didn't want her seventy-one-year-old stepfather worried. She wondered how much to tell her mother.

'That man you talk to on the phone, Roberto. It's him, isn't it?' Angelica, as so often throughout Julia's childhood, had already decided what had happened.

'It's your life, my dear, but I think you would be wisest to break with him. Do it now while you're here with your family . . .'

Julia's mind began to burn. She heard a car turning in the avenue outside in a whine of tyres and flinched.

'Only you yourself can walk away from the brute who did this.'

'Run away, you mean. Like you did from Clara.'

Angelica gave an ironic laugh. 'Is that what she told you?'

'Grandmother didn't need to. You've been doing it all your life. Oh, don't worry,' Julia added as Angelica drew back, 'I'll be gone tomorrow. My face won't be around as a reminder.' Krusak and her mother, neither would see her, independent of Clara. Julia put down her cup. 'If you don't mind, I'm tired.'

Angelica, titian hair neat as an angel's wings, blue eyes never blinking, hands controlled in her lap, answered as though Clara had never been mentioned, 'You and men. Isn't it time you grew up?'

Julia slipped out of bed, showing her arms and legs. 'See this?' She seized Angelica's arm as her mother looked away. 'These are where two thugs worked me over three weeks ago. Roberto saved my life that night, so don't suggest that he could ever do anything like this! You don't know anything and you don't want to know, but someone's got to protect Clara from Scarpia!'

She felt Angelica start. 'What?' Suddenly her mother's face was rosy, she looked like the picture of herself as a teenager in Clara's gold locket.

For some reason that show of feeling, of vulnerability only made Julia more determined to wound. 'Scarpia the collaborator. The man who tortured Guy, or Mario Scudieri, if you prefer—'

'Stop it!'

Angelica writhed and Julia let her go, growing angry as she watched this tall, elegant woman backing for the door. Clara was in danger and her mother was retreating.

'Scarpia wants to finish the job he started,' she called after Angelica. 'You know, the facial surgery on the woman who got you away from danger? Your mother?'

A cheap victory. Julia was ashamed the instant she said it. Not expecting to see Angelica again that night, she sat on the bed, head in hands.

'Julia.' Her mother crouched by her feet in an elderly, stiff-jointed way which brought tears to Julia's eyes. Angelica held a faded leather-bound notebook in her hands.

'I never thought you'd need to know,' she was saying. 'I thought here in England you'd be safe from the past. I didn't want to have its shadow hanging over you, as it has over me.'

'What are you saying?' Julia whispered.

'This diary belonged to my father. I found it twenty-four years ago, in the ruins of the home where I'd lived as a child. I went back there, you see, to Croce.'

She was talking freely, as though once released the words were a relief.

'The old footman Luigi had died, the villa was boarded up. I decided to break in – this was my home. I had some romantic idea of spending the night there.

'I wandered round the rooms, sitting on the mouldy sofas and beds. It was under the master bed that I found the diary – such a clever hiding place! Just like Papà.'

Julia's breath caught at Angelica's use of the Italian word.

'So clever I almost missed it. The chamber pot – I picked it up to read the joke on the bottom and it slipped from my hands and shattered. It had a false base: the diary was inside.'

Angelica sighed. 'It took me a while to read it, because my father had written in English and my English then wasn't so good. Afterwards, I wished I'd never found it.'

She broke off, her fine eyes bright. 'I loved my mother. She was beautiful, charming – everything you are. But my father's words showed that she lied.'

Julia, accustomed to her mother regarding her as a rival, did not take in the oblique compliment. Remembering when Angelica had discovered her telling a lie, remembering the punishment her mother had meted out, she shuddered.

'She was a collaborator . . .'

'That's impossible!'

'Julia, sit down.' Angelica was tugging at her. 'My father heard her selling secrets to the Germans – he heard!' She shook the mildewed pages, the copperplate writing, in Julia's face.

Julia sank back onto the bed. *They called her the bitch of the mountains'*, Gucci had said. Now, here in her grandfather's own words, she listened to an account of the time Clara had entertained Nazi officers at her villa; the time she had told Guy she was staying at a friend's house for the evening and yet the friend, when questioned, knew nothing; the time Guy had overheard her telling a German officer where an English prisoner of war was hiding in a shepherd hut, and the German promising her a bottle of the finest brandy . . .

'She was tortured by Scarpia,' Julia muttered. 'She went out with Sprint that night because she'd been told Guy was hurt.'

'So she says.'

Julia raised her head. 'Is this the reason you left Italy so suddenly? Guy's diary? Couldn't you have talked with Clara?'

Her mother's perfect rose-petal mouth closed with a snap. 'There was never anything to talk about. She would only have lied.' Angelica shut the diary, clutching it in her fingers. 'I'm sorry, darling, that you had to find out. I wanted you to have a clear start, without shame. I thought our little family – you, Enrico, myself – would be enough. I'm sorry it wasn't.'

Julia bent her head, guilty at having failed to be satisfied with Angelica's 'little family', angry because she might have been satisfied, if only her mother had not been so critical, so secretive. She was still Julia Rochfort: Angelica, proud of her own father Guy Rochfort, had left her with that name. She still knew nothing of her real father.

But she had already been cruel tonight. 'May I see that?' she asked, nodding to the diary.

Angelica held the leather notebook out of Julia's reach. 'You don't need to,' she said, a touch triumphantly, Julia thought. 'The other entries are virtually the same: accounts of collaboration—'

'But Scarpia's still alive—'

'And what is that to me?' snapped Angelica. 'You say Clara is in danger – but why? Because of your meddling!'

Stiffly, Angelica rose to her feet. She stared down at her daughter, her blue eyes remote. 'Take care, Julia. Please don't be hurt again as you are now: I don't think I could bear it.' Her expression changed, becoming softer. 'It's a pity that you never could leave things alone.'

'Wait!' Julia started off the bed: Angelica was taking the diary with her. 'I need that—'

Too late. The door slammed in her face. Her mother was gone.

33

Andrea picked Julia up from Pisa airport. Ushering her to the Mercedes' front seat – they sat together now – he gave her a keen look. 'Bad trip?' he asked, blasting past a Porsche, grey moustache quivering with pleasure.

Julia shook her head. The trip had been fine, but last night had been immensely frustrating. Angelica had refused to relinquish Guy's diary, repeating over and over that Julia had already heard one entry. Since the others were almost all more of the same, Julia did not need to hear any more.

Going round that argument for the fourth time, Julia glimpsed her stepfather's harassed face over the top of his latest car magazine. Seeing Enrico brought her spate of angry words to a sudden stop: Angelica had always been impervious to requests for more information, Enrico was not, and there was nothing he could do. It wasn't *his* father's diary, and Julia was his stepchild. If he voiced an opinion, Angelica would no doubt accuse him of interfering.

Still Julia couldn't understand why Angelica had run away. No matter what was in the faded notebook, Julia felt that it wouldn't be enough to justify her mother's action. Whatever Clara had done, she had been tortured by Scarpia. Last night Angelica never questioned a word Julia said about Scarpia, and clearly already knew about him. Why had Angelica never tried to bring him to justice? *You say Clara is in danger – but why? Because of your meddling!'* Was that true? Julia wondered.

'The Contessa can't wait to see you,' said Andrea now. 'She's been listening to the tape you left.'

The German twins' cassette, thought Julia. For two weeks, Clara had been bedridden with a cold, unfit for anything. Maybe now Clara had heard something, recognised a voice.

Julia wished Guy hadn't kept a diary.

Andrea checked his steel-grey watch by one of the roadside clocks, sucking in his cheeks as he realised it was slow. Tutting, he put this right, driving one-handed.

Julia watched him rather than the landscape of train lines and potato fields. She was grateful for Andrea's devotion to Clara, particularly whilst Clara had been unwell and she herself tied up with performances.

'How did grandmother save your life?' she asked. A sudden question often provoked the truer answer, and right now Julia felt she had to know. 'What happened?'

Andrea's tiepin was glinting as a red light instructed them to halt. Julia knew she had caught him by surprise when he obeyed the traffic signal, stopping the Mercedes. He turned pale eyes on her, pushing back his chauffeur's cap with an oil-stained finger.

'Right! But this is brief. 1944, mid-July. The Germans were getting ready to pull out from Florence.'

Andrea slammed his horn at a lorry which had dared to accelerate away from the lights first.

'Now those German troops were jumpy – I mean jumpy! They knew they were losing, they knew they were hated by everyone in the country, so they over-reacted to *everything*.

'There was this small hospital outside Florence – a supermarket's there now – and I heard a rumour they had fruit trees in the grounds and that these luscious peaches were rotting on the trees.' Andrea coughed. 'You got a lot of crazy rumours then, especially about food.'

'So you went to the hospital,' put in Julia, as the Mercedes thundered past an iron-smelting works.

'I rode my bike there. It was midday. There was no shade, no trees at all, just the old noonday devil.' The drumming of

₁e road seemed to shorten Andrea's speech. He was talking
₁ster.

'A wasted trip, no peaches, nothing! And then this German
fantryman popped up: he seemed to grow out of the grass.
₁aybe he'd been hiding in the grounds. He walked right up
₁d grabbed the handlebars. He wanted my bike.

'I said no. I wasn't scared at first. He was only a few years
₁der than me, small and thin. We shook the handlebars
ᵣound between us like a couple of kids – that's what we were,
ᵣally – and then he slapped me across the face.

'I say slap but it brought me off my bike and flattened me
₁ the dust. I was mad and did the first thing I thought of –
₁nk my teeth in his leg.'

Andrea chuckled, changing down a gear. 'Sounds crazy,
₁t it wasn't, it was deadly. Both of us wanted that bike and
₁e German decided he was willing to kill for it. He could
₁ve taken it after he'd knocked me into the dirt but instead
₁ swung the rifle off his back. He smashed my head with the
₁tt.

'I must have blacked out, because next thing was the
ᵣerman boy standing over me with his rifle point on my chest.
₁aw his face – he was going to pull that trigger. I closed my
₁es and prayed quick to the Virgin that if she saved me I'd
ᵣrve her.'

Andrea glanced at Julia. 'That's when your grandmother
₁me. In a white hospital gown, with bandages round her face
₁d a black veil covering the bandages. When the German
ᵣy saw her he must have thought she was a ghost: he froze.

'She'd seen us from an upper window. Told no one, run out
ᵥer the sun-blasted grass in bare feet. I remember turning
₁ head, seeing nurses streaming down the hospital steps. I
ᵣmember your grandmother saying slowly to the German
ᵣy, "If you shoot him you must kill me also." '

Andrea sighed. 'He aimed the rifle at her. I'd like to say I
₁rew myself on him in that moment, wrestled the gun off
₁m, but I couldn't move. My heart was chirruping faster than
₁e cicadas and I could hardly get my breath. Not very heroic.'

'You were only a boy,' Julia reminded him softly. 'And if

you'd rushed him then, who knows? Maybe the rifle wou
have gone off and Clara killed for sure.'

Andrea nodded his curly grey head. 'The nurses ha
stopped rushing forward. No one wanted to do anything, I
noticed in any way – except for the Contessa.

'She walked towards the rifle. A step, another step. H
face was paler than the bandages: I could see that even wi
her veil. The breeze lifted the edges of her veil – so I thougl
until I realised the air was as still as glass. She was shaking
yet still she came.

'The German boy cocked the rifle. She took another ste
He lifted it to his eye: another step. And she said, slow
before, "You don't have to." '

Andrea drew the Mercedes in for a red light. 'It w
strange.' He fumbled in his jacket for a Toscana. 'That soldi
uncocked his rifle, lowered it, swung it over his back ar
marched away.'

He lit the Toscana, inhaled. 'I promised the Virgin the
lying in that baking field in the hospital grounds, that if
survived to the end of the war I'd serve the lady she'd sent
save me. I tell you this, too: the Contessa's been good to me

'Your grandmother was in there for plastic surgery, after beir
blinded and tortured, and yet she came out. Amazing.' Rober
was impressed. 'And for Andrea to keep his word . . .'

Julia frowned over the coals of the sauna. 'This rosema
hasn't much scent.'

It was evening. Roberto had met Julia at Clara's hous
they had driven to Bologna and were staying at a hotel. In tl
morning she and Roberto were going to the deserted villag
of San Martino della Croce. Tonight they were to call on Emil
Gucci.

Julia dropped another sprig of rosemary onto the coal
She tried to keep any censure from her voice. 'Maybe v
should try the cassette on your father.'

'Damn him.' Roberto vigorously splashed water over tl
coals; clouds billowed. 'All last week whenever I've tackle
him he's been evasive. He's hiding something, wants to te

ne yet doesn't.' Roberto shaded his eyes from the steam. 'If
e picked out Vincenti, as your grandmother did, that would
e interesting. Holy Mother! I make my poor dad sound like
scientific experiment: stimulus and response.' He shook
imself, frowning.

'I know,' said Julia. She didn't like it, either, but the thought
f war criminals still free, still violent and bloody – as the
ssault on herself and Roberto had shown – hardened her
esolve. If she gave up now Scarpia would have won.

'Vincenti was blond, with an earring,' she said, leaning
gainst Roberto's legs. He was sitting above her on the slatted
oards. 'And Vincenti spoke the Castel San Martino dialect.'

They looked at each other. Both said, 'I don't think he's
carpia.'

Roberto laughed. 'You first.'

Julia trailed a hand down the hairs of his calf. 'Clara said
is voice was too resonant.' Her grandmother, finally listening
o the tape, had singled Vincenti out because 'There's
omething familiar in the sound, maybe the underlying accent.'
But as for his singing, Clara didn't recognise it as Scarpia's or
poletta's.

'I think she'd have recognised those instantly,' said Julia.
Clara *wondered* if Vincenti was the guard who'd yelled that
he building was going to come down after the blast—'

'I say Vincenti was there,' put in Roberto. 'Vincenti had no
erformances in Bologna through May or June – I checked
ack via my retired pianist. And Vincenti had a truck as well
s a car.'

The night Guy was captured, Clara was taken by Sprint to
truck. Roberto didn't smile at Julia's raised eyebrow; neither
elt like smiling. 'In the late 1930s Vincenti drove some of the
Bologna opera company to his mountain home in a truck. The
ianist can't remember if it had tarpaulin sides, but talked
bout "flaps".'

'So why don't you think he's our star interrogator?' Julia,
espite the sauna's heat, shivered.

'He's too simple,' said Roberto. 'Look how he sings –
eautiful tone, little expression. I can't see Vincenti having

the imagination to whisper. And a man wearing an earring t
make him look tough doesn't sound sure of himself. Scarpia'
certain – he must have been, to act as he did.'

'I wish we knew for certain.' Julia squinted at Roberto.

'What about Pietro Terni? He's on the tape,' said Robertc

'That's suspicion gone mad, isn't it?' answered Julia sharpl
'After what Clara said about him helping her escape? And hi
experiences in the German headquarters?'

'He's blond. Clara and Guy knew he reported to th
authorities whilst living at Croce. He must have known th
dialect. And,' Roberto continued, 'Pietro begged Clara to hid
him at Croce because he was afraid of being rounded up a
an artiste and sent to Germany. If he was under threat, wh
not Vincenti or Dontini, two opera principals?'

'Pietro was running scared: Clara said he wasn't big o
nerve. Besides,' added Julia with a wicked grin, 'Vincenti wa
a baritone, Dontini a bass, but Pietro's a tenor. As we know
tenors are always in demand.'

They both smiled, but Roberto was not to be put off.

'Still, Pietro *reported* to Bologna: they could have shippe
him to Germany any time they wanted.'

'Round-ups were hit and miss affairs,' Julia pointed ou
'Maybe the Nazis found they valued him more as informe
than performer.'

Roberto nodded. 'OK, I'll accept that.'

'And Clara said Terni's voice was too high for Scarpia's
Men's voices usually darken over time, but when he sang a
Christmas, Pietro could still hit top C.' Julia spoke witl
confidence.

Roberto pushed her with his knee. 'Let's go and talk to Gucci

'Signor Gucci, I'm Mario Scudieri's granddaughter—'

'You're not coming in!'

Roberto thumped the door. 'Signore, we're on the sam
side,' he said evenly. 'Scarpia tortured my father, too.'

The door opened, Emilio Gucci appearing in a heavy coat
'We'll talk outdoors.' He jammed his pipe into his mouth
striding for the lift.

Julia pulled Roberto to the stairs. 'How did you know about Gucci's father? I'm about to suggest a paternal connection and you breeze in.'

'Masculine intuition.' Roberto rubbed the back of his neck and they laughed, releasing tension as they hurried after the retired Marshal.

An hour later, seated in the park – it had been closed but Gucci picked the lock – the ex-Marshal was finally convinced of Julia's and Roberto's stories.

'So Sprint was the traitor! God, if he weren't already dead I'd go shoot that bastard myself!' Gucci blew a smoke ring into the night air. 'My father once said that towards the end of May '44 he'd begun to wonder if one of the group was working for the Fascists: nothing he could put his finger on, mind, just a feeling. I wonder why the group wasn't rounded up at once.'

'Scarpia knew everything they did in advance,' said Roberto.

'Them, and through them possibly other groups,' said Julia. She already knew that in the fight for Italy's liberation, Guy's group was minor. That didn't matter. He'd still been a partisan.

'So the Red-Headed League was a kind of bait, eh?' Gucci, shrewd as Julia and Roberto, understood at once. 'To draw bigger groups into Scarpia's net? That figures. From what my old man told me, the League were mainly in the transport business, shipping and hiding small-arms and stores for other groups to collect. Only Mario and his second-in-command knew which groups: Dad and the others just stashed the guns where Mario told them.'

Gucci glared at Julia. 'Why didn't you tell me this the first time we met? Could have saved a lot of wasted time.'

Julia blushed, remembering the circumstances of that encounter. She threw Roberto an anxious glance. 'I didn't know if I could trust you.'

'She didn't trust me until recently,' said Roberto.

'Very wise,' said Gucci. 'I wasn't strictly honest with you, either. Over my years as a cop I've learned to be wary of reporters – or people posing as such.' To Julia's astonishment he tipped her a wink, then held out one of his brawler's hands.

'I've done you and your grandmother a disservice, particularly your grandmother.' His fingers caught hers, wringing his apology. 'What can I say? I was a boy during the war, seeing but not understanding. People were envious of Clara Scudieri's wealth: I picked up on their filthy names for her and being a child never questioned the rumours—'

'My grandmother's German lovers, you mean.' Julia did not feel any satisfaction when Gucci coloured. Guy's diary, still firmly in her mother's hands, remained heavy on her mind.

'How do Clara and Guy fit into your father's recollections?' Roberto was cool: Gucci's account would be painful for all of them; to preserve some distance was vital.

Gucci closed his eyes, folded his arms and began to talk.

Gucci's father had been one of the Red-Headed League. There was Mario Scudieri, Cesare Celere, Umberto Gasparini, the Marshal, a woman Gina and two boys, Giovanni and Pietro. Mario started the group in July '43, with Gasparini and the Marshal.

That was why the Marshal had helped Guy obtain false papers to change his name to Mario Scudieri after the German invasion in September 1943, thought Julia. He and Guy were already working together as part of a partisan unit: Guy probably already used the alias of Mario in the group. Julia wondered why Guy and the Marshal hadn't let on to Clara that they really knew each other quite well; probably her grandfather didn't want to worry his wife. Or was it that he hadn't quite trusted her? 'Go on,' she said quickly to Gucci.

Gucci had learned all this from his father years later, when Carlo Gucci was to go into hospital for an operation he might not survive. Emilio's father then explained to his son about the vendetta he had sworn to pursue against the Fascist known as Scarpia.

Carlo Gucci could not have known why Mario – Guy – had gone out on the night of 10th June, 1944, because Carlo had been picked up in the street in Ponte after curfew two nights before. With his hands tied behind him, he was thrown

indfolded into the back of a truck. Clawing for a hold in the
rching vehicle, his fingers closed on a scrap of paper caught
etween the side and floor of the truck. Gucci's father had
rabbed the paper and, lying on his side, managed to jam it
own his pants.

He'd been searched when taken, but not afterwards. Gucci's
ther had kept the paper. Emilio Gucci had it with him. He
noothed it out on his knee and handed it to Julia. 'I don't
now why I've hung onto this, it's meaningless.'

So it appeared. 'Entrance – Loud. Question – Soft. Waiting
– Loud. Answer – Soft.'

Julia brought her hands up to her mouth. 'That's Francesco
incenti's handwriting.' She recognised the club-handed script
om the autographed photograph she'd been given by Elsa
ontini. She surged to her feet. 'Can't you see they're
rections?' she demanded of Roberto.

'Music!' With a sweeping hand Roberto took the paper.
he horn gramophone Clara and Simone remembered
earing! Mother of God, you're right! Loud during Scarpia's
ntrance, soft during a question, then loud again . . .'

'So one of those bastards was Vincenti, who's already dead.'
ucci showed no pleasure at this, rather he seemed
sappointed.

'I'm surprised a singer needed directions,' muttered
oberto. 'Obviously not overburdened with brains.' He
anced at Emilio Gucci. 'This wouldn't count for anything in
law court.'

'No,' agreed Gucci, continuing with his father's account.

arlo Gucci was kicked down steps into an underground
llar. He was beaten, gagged, then left for hours before his
iptors asked any questions. He had the feeling they enjoyed
eir work, particularly with the boy they brought in later. At
ie point in the boy's interrogation Carlo recalled how he
mself had shouted out, screaming revenge on his captors.

Julia bowed her head. Roberto took her hand, his face
ardening. 'What was the boy's name?'

'My father never knew.' Emilio Gucci turned towards Julia.

'My father never knew about Mario or Clara Scudieri bei[n]
taken, and after his outburst the guards had beaten hi[m]
senseless. He was unconscious until after the air-raid.' Guc[ci]
tapped out his pipe into a flower bed and refilled it.

'I won't go into what you already know,' he went on heavil[y].
'My father, still unconscious, was saved because of the a[ir]-
raid. The walls of the cellar collapsed, burying him and th[e]
boy Scarpia's men had been holding: they were left for dea[d].
They would have been too, but the Fioretti twins dug the[m]
out.'

'Were they part of the league?' asked Roberto. Gucci smile[d]
and took off his spectacles.

'The only thing those twins were interested in was settl[ing]
scores with another local family called Patuzzi. All the time [I]
was Marshal of Ponte, ten, twenty years after the war, th[e]
Fiorettis kept up their vendetta. No! They dug my father an[d]
the boy out because their dog had been scrabbling aroun[d]
Davide Patuzzi's old farmhouse and they couldn't have a bett[er]
excuse than to go snooping after it. As I said, they got my ol[d]
man and the boy out and they brought my dad back to Pont[e].
He was hurt pretty bad and by the time he'd got word [to]
Umberto Gasparini about being captured, Mario was alrea[dy]
missing, presumed dead.' Emilio Gucci shook his hea[d].
'Mario's death broke my father. He never joined anoth[er]
partisan outfit.'

'I'm sorry.' Roberto clasped the man's shoulder.

Julia frowned. 'I thought Patuzzi was a coffin-maker.'

'But his father wasn't,' answered Gucci, brisk again. 'He'[d]
worked a farm farther up the mountain but the land was ston[y].
It was a long way from the hamlets, too. No one was surprise[d]
when Davide let the place moulder away.'

Gucci began cleaning the metal frames of his spectacles. [I]
often wondered if the Patuzzis knew what that old farmhous[e]
had been used for, but Davide was smooth; I never knew wh[at]
he was thinking. After the war the bombed-out shell was le[ft].
I went back there but found nothing of what had been don[e]
there. Most of it's fallen down the mountain.'

'Amazing,' murmured Roberto.

Gucci, reading Roberto's mind, was unimpressed.

'Scarpia couldn't have used the local police headquarters in Ponte. The SS hadn't taken it over, and the old Marshal wouldn't have let him torture anybody.' Gucci replaced his polished spectacles, hooking the frames carefully round his cauliflower ear. 'The Patuzzis live in Ponte now. Ardent neo-Fascists.'

'You never mentioned that,' said Julia.

'I thought you as a journalist could do your own digging.'

'Davide Patuzzi?' asked Roberto.

'Died last year – cancer. Couldn't have wished that guy a more fitting end.'

Julia rubbed her arms with her hands. She was wearing her duffel coat, her good coat had been ripped from her by the three thugs. She had not asked if Gucci had sent the note she had received care of Lucca opera house: after what one of the thugs had said to her, the threat 'You won't be so pretty when we've finished', Julia knew who had sent the note.

To Gucci, Julia asked a different question. 'The younger Stefano: did you find his address?'

'Queer thing that,' said Gucci. 'Last month I found a Bologna apartment in his name and soon after I read in the paper that Stefano's died in there: slipped on the stairs and broke his neck. Can't say I was sorry.'

Gucci had said the same thing over the disappearance of the priest and curate of Croce, Julia recalled. Perhaps the ex-carabiniere had even less faith in the law than she did and had decided to continue Carlo Gucci's vendetta to make sure his father's tormentors – and maybe even their families – were punished. A chilling thought.

Cesare Celere, nicknamed Sprint, had been murdered at his house. Now the younger Stefano, whose father had been a Fascist party member, had fallen downstairs in his apartment. Someone disposing of old enemies or allies? thought Roberto. As the attack on Julia had shown, Scarpia or Spoletta, maybe both, were still forces to be reckoned with.

As for the victims, Clara and Simone so far were the only ones still alive. Two witnesses, who had to be protected. And now Emilio Gucci knew about them.

Roberto threw the older man a hard look.

'I've never seen you tonight,' said the retired Marshal. He held out his hand to the taller man. 'Good hunting. I've kept an eye out for Scarpia all the years I was Marshal but all I found was Patuzzi.' He snorted. 'Even him I couldn't bring in: no court would convict a man for owning a derelict house, never mind that Davide wasn't the kind who wouldn't know everything that was happening on his land.'

Gucci's brawler's features contorted in frustration. 'If I can help in any way, call. Maybe you'll have more luck on your own, too many people remember me and would clam up if I came along.'

'Thanks,' said Roberto with a certain irony. 'By the way, I've taken out insurance. My brother's a policeman: he's been looking over your old case files. Several are very interesting.'

Gucci snorted. 'You don't need to threaten me, for fuck's sake,' he began, pausing as Roberto held up a hand.

'Just a friendly piece of advice,' said Roberto. It was all lies. Sandro hadn't been near any ex-carabiniere's records.

'I wish I could feel we could have trusted him without that,' Julia observed as she and Roberto parted company with Emilio Gucci. Roberto shrugged his broad shoulders.

'He knows Bianca. I'm uneasy about her. The drug connection, I suppose. I don't know why, really.'

They returned to the hotel in silence. When they reached their room, Julia laid a hand on Roberto's arm. 'Our trip into the country will keep until after tomorrow.'

Roberto nodded, thinking of his father.

34

Viola case under one arm, shopping under the other, Simone let himself into Roberto's apartment. His son was home: he was playing his cello to some recorded accompaniment. No, in opposition to it: Simone winced as cello and orchestra clashed.

He pushed open the living-room door. 'What's going on?' he demanded, when the singing began.

That voice – viola and shopping fell. Simone shrunk against the wall. He was back in the chamber, the wet walls, the music, the singing. That voice, laughing. The all-powerful figures you never saw. The Whisperer.

Strong arms were about him, holding him. Roberto's cello bow knocked the back of his legs. Simone blinked and the room was full of sunlight. The music had been stopped.

'Dad, I'm sorry. I didn't expect you back yet.'

Simone found his voice. 'What are you doing?' Roberto only played the cello with total concentration when deeply unhappy.

'Trying to make up my mind whether you should be put through something – only you've heard it now.'

'Yes.' No point in denying it. Simone moved and Roberto released him, tossed the bow onto the sofa, picked up the spilled bag and followed him into the kitchen. His son was dressed in black, like a priest. Like a priest he knew when to be silent, drawing up stools to the breakfast bar and waiting for Simone to settle. He poured two tumblers of wine, glinting liked stained glass in the sunlit kitchen.

Now Roberto was waiting, scarred hands resting in a pyramid on top of the bar. Simone remembered how his boy had got those white, hair-line scars when he was twelve, tearing through scrub to reach his younger brother who had fallen off a rope swing into thorny broom. In the end, Roberto, not Sandro, had been the one to be hurt, from deep and festering thorn cuts and from Simone's own penalty.

Simone gulped his wine. He had always known it would be this son he must tell.

In his memory Fiesole and Naples flicked by like stills from old movies. Then the picture sharpened and came closer . . .

Simone stepped into the frame.

9th June, 1944, Castel San Martino

Simone was fifteen. He was going to be a singer – Francesco Vincenti assured him. Better even than Cesare Celere, Vincenti's second private pupil, whom the maestro was grooming to appear at Bologna.

But now Simone was a partisan, fighting to free his country from the Germans. Captain Rodito was relying on him to warn the hamlets and village of Croce that a round-up of Italian deserters and partisans was to start in the area at dawn the next day. According to the charcoal burners – a reliable source – the round-up had already begun in the plains. Captain Rodito said that fifteen men had been trapped at one farm. The Blackshirts operated from trucks, swooping in on villages.

Simone was disappointed that the priest of Castel had also been assigned to this mission, but accepted without complaint the man's presence with him on the steep track. The youth hero-worshipped Captain Rodito, the dark young officer with the pencil moustache who had appeared at Castel three months earlier in the company of eight Italian soldiers. The Captain and his men had defied the Salò government's order to rejoin the army. They were deserters and could be shot.

Captain Rodito and his men were now the core of the partisan cell of Castel. Simone knew that Vittorio the mayor, the bell-ringer and his father Aurelio were also involved, but could name no others: the boy suspected that a great deal went on whilst he was shut in school in Bologna.

The Captain and his soldiers slept in Aurelio's barn during the day and at night ambushed or sabotaged the enemy – to his disappointment, Simone could find out nothing more about that. Instead, the young partisan officer admitted that sometimes he and his men gathered arms and supplies dropped by the Allies at a secret location – a flat outcrop in the mountains where men with torches would signal to the Allied planes. Simone had not been allowed to visit the place, but the Captain had promised that if he did this assignment well, then he would go with the soldiers on their next midnight trip.

The youth's only regret was that the Captain had called their unit 'Garibaldi' like so many others, instead of something more exciting like 'The Red-Headed League'.

Simone had only heard of that group. He knew they operated somewhere near Croce, the hilltop village he had never seen. There was a Contessa in Croce: she owned most of the mountain. If he could, Simone was going to persuade Father Angelo that they call at the villa and pay their respects to Clara Scudieri. Cesare Celere, who lived at Croce, said that she was beautiful. Simone had never seen a Contessa.

The youth knew he was lucky to be involved. Aurelio his father was sick, otherwise he would have been the one to take the long walk to Croce. Simone had begged to go in Aurelio's place, and the Captain, weary and preoccupied, relented.

Simone recalled the Captain's instructions. 'Go with Father Angelo – a priest and a boy travelling openly in the day should provoke no comment. If anyone asks, you're going to speak to the priest of Croce about this Sunday's mass for Our Lady of the Vines. Tell only those people Father Angelo points out to you about the round-up.' Captain Rodito clasped Simone's broadening shoulders. 'Today you will save lives.'

The Captain had been right. No one gave him a glance as they passed through the first hamlet, although the priest seemed to stop and chat to everyone. Between greetings he murmured to Simone. 'Tell the woman balancing the pole and two water-buckets on her shoulder. Speak to the man loading the cart. And the toothless old man with the walking stick. Those men playing cards in that shed: go past them and whisper to the girl with the flowered headsquare milking the black cow. Sneak a kiss – the men will think it's horseplay.'

Simone wished he could tell someone: 'The priest gave me leave to kiss a girl.'

They had started out in the cool of the morning. Now as they passed a fig tree dipping out of a hazel copse on the boundary of certain lands of the Patuzzis and the Fiorettis – the region's feuding families – noonday sun slicked off the shiny leaves. Heat steamed from a huge pile of donkey dung in the middle of the track. Away in the forests in the hills above hung the sweet smoke of the charcoal burners.

The priest of Castel, walking the rutted track a few paces ahead, held up a black-clad arm, motioning to Simone to keep behind. Simone, who was a tall boy, looked over the dent in the priest's broad hat. He laughed when he saw who it was.

'It's all right, Father. It's Cesare: he's one of us.' Simone tried to move round the stocky figure but Father Angelo, sweeping his hat off his scarlet forehead and using it as a fan, barged forward.

'Sprint!' The priest gave the youth his nickname. 'Little Sprint! I haven't seen you close in months. You've grown . . .'

They all laughed. Simone, who always felt sorry for Sprint because of what the Fascists had done to his father, was bursting to tell the older boy why he was climbing the track to Croce. When Sprint, shading his green eyes against the midday glare, asked what was bringing them up the mountain, Simone thought he would explode if he did not say something.

'We're here to see your priest. And the Contessa.'

'Well, I suppose we might,' began Father Angelo, and then pointed. 'Seems we won't need to climb to the third hamlet or Croce – look who's here.'

Simone's disappointment at seeing the small, neat figure approaching was compounded when he realised who was with the priest of Croce. Mario Scudieri in wide-brimmed hat, collarless shirt and baggy trousers was no hero. He might have reddish hair but he couldn't hold a gun, and all he talked about was wine.

Simone could hear him now, speaking to Father Angelo. 'I'm trying different herbs in this year's vermouth.' Mario patted the bulging sack by his booted feet. 'Gathered these from the roadside this morning.'

'From where he can watch comings and goings quite openly,' murmured Sprint. He nudged Simone in the ribs. 'Didn't put you down as an altar-boy.'

Simone saw a surge of red. 'I'm not,' he said through gritted teeth.

'So what's going on?' murmured Sprint, stretching up into the fig tree to pluck a just-ripe fruit. The three adults were huddled together, talking about the Contessa's feast for Our Lady, set for tomorrow. That was all priests and men like Mario Scudieri were interested in, thought Simone.

He glanced at Sprint. It wouldn't hurt to tell Sprint. 'There's to be a big round-up tomorrow.'

'By the bastard Fascists, huh?'

Simone nodded, turning over a pebble with his wooden clog.

'And your group's sent you and the priest to warn us in Croce. Big mission, I must say.' Sprint shrugged.

Father Angelo was handing Mario Scudieri a note from his breviary. 'This month's wine order for Castel church,' he said. Small concerns, reflected Simone. Captain Rodito risked his life every night so men like these could smoke their cigarettes in peace. Even though Sprint had already guessed he was a partisan, Simone still wanted to impress his young singing rival. 'I'm more than a messenger boy.' Recalling something the Captain had said, he added, 'A big Allied operation's due soon.'

Sprint smiled. Slightly taller than Simone, he regarded the younger youth with a patronising air. 'Don't tell me your outfit's involved. I thought it was only larger units.'

'Captain Rodito's is a larger unit.' Simone felt a thrill as Sprint's green eyes clouded.

'Well, you've a wasted journey up here.' Sprint was rubbing the fig on the seat of his pants. 'The Contessa thinks partisans are nothing but thieves, unless of course there's a soldier or two in the ranks. Then she gets interested.'

Sprint grinned at Simone. 'Maybe she'd be intrigued by your Castel group.' He bit into the fig, squirting juice onto his faintly stubbled chin.

'Maybe.' Simone wondered if the older boy was being serious or not. Now he sensed someone looking at them and glanced up the track. Mario Scudieri winked at him, swinging his sack over his shoulder.

'Back to work,' he said. As though his words were a signal, Sprint and the priest of Croce turned towards Croce.

Father Angelo tugged Simone's arm and they too turned and began walking back. 'Our message!' hissed Simone. 'What about the third hamlet and Croce?'

'Already in hand,' said the priest, placing his platter hat on Simone's sun-bleached hair. 'You should wear a cap.'

Mosquitoes began to hum in Simone's ears, or maybe it was surprise. The alarm call of a blackbird made him stutter on the steep road and for a moment the mountain screwed sideways. It took two scissoring steps before he was right.

'Our contact's the priest of Croce?' he gasped. 'But he talks to the Nazis!'

'Watch yourself, boy.' Father Angelo opened his breviary, squinting down into the valley bottom haze. 'Some are more fitted to the task than others.'

Father Angelo would not enlarge on that statement. Simone, feeling bored, cheated of setting foot in Croce, began to think his mother was right. He had argued against her, been granted a day off his senior school in Bologna, but instead of feeling like a man, playing a man's part, he still felt like a boy. Even school would have been better than this long, dreary march with a lumbering priest.

Later Davide Patuzzi, the coffin-maker, passed them in his cart. Simone wouldn't have minded sharing the cart with the man's coffins, but Patuzzi whirled by, lashing his horse.

'Death waits for no man,' remarked Father Angelo.

An hour later still, within sight of Castel, they heard a truck grinding up the hill. No one in Croce had a truck.

Father Angelo picked up his cassock. 'Run for the trees!' he shouted, sprinting awkwardly back up the track for the cover more than a hundred metres above.

Simone was faster but even he was not quick enough. The truck overtook them. Shots were fired. Behind him Father Angelo collapsed in the dust, clutching a bloodied leg. Two hooded men in black shirts, carrying clubs, leapt down from the moving vehicle and closed on Simone. The boy, who had whirled back when the priest fell, now rushed forward, zigzagging for the trees.

For one moment he thought he had succeeded, then something hard and heavy hit the back of his neck.

When he came round he was lying bound and blindfolded in a manger, straw piled over his head. Simone moaned, freezing when a voice somewhere beneath him said, 'You're alive. Too bad.'

The man was from Ponte Maggiore. Simone recognised the accent. Head spinning, the boy hung over the manger into nothingness. 'The Father?'

'The bastards are still working on him. Scarpia wants to know about your resistance group in Castel, and the Allied landings.'

'Who?' The stranger was making no sense.

Then Simone heard the music. It was a gramophone recording of *Tosca*, the distinctive chords which herald the entrance of the Chief of Police into the opera. Abruptly the sound was snapped off and a voice began to sing the part of Scarpia, only a few bars of music because then—

Then Father Angelo screamed. Simone could smell blood and burning. Had his stomach not been empty he would have been sick.

Music surged, blotting out the curses of the stranger.

Three times Simone heard the same sequence: music, singing, screaming, music. The man lying somewhere in the dirty straw beneath him was beating one wall of the chamber

with a fist: Simone caught the muttered words, 'No names.'
Over and over, like a prayer.

If Father Angelo's tormentors had spoken aloud, Simone
felt he would have been able to stand it better, but instead
all his straining ears could catch between the curses and
the screams were whispers, whispering voices, one in particular.

Then someone laughed, a ringing sound like a stage laugh.

Hearing it, Simone began to shudder. Francesco Vincenti,
his mentor, was a part of this. The man singing Scarpia was
not him, the main questioner – whisperer – was not him, yet
Vincenti was there. Vincenti, his teacher, was in that hidden
room somewhere in the nothingness, doing terrible things to
a priest.

Suddenly a shot blazed out. There was the sound of a heavy
weight being dragged.

'Oh, Christ,' said the man with Simone. Simone tried to
pray but the only word he could think of was Judas.

Vincenti had betrayed him and Father Angelo was dead.

'Bring me the boy.' The whisper wormed into his ear like a
maggot into a sheep's skull. Simone thought of a smiling
mouth with fanged teeth, like a wolf.

Booted feet marching over the unseen flags.

'Take me, you bastards!' The man from Ponte yelling,
kicking out impotently.

Hands seizing him . . .

Time was fluid. Hours between the torture ran by like
minutes. The pain, the fear of the music, the dread of the
single shot, were with him for ever.

They broke the smallest finger on his right hand with a
pair of pliers, a joint at a time, beginning with the top joint.
The Whisperer waited patiently whilst Simone's screams
subsided.

'The names of your group,' the voice would say, and the
gramophone would be wound up, 'Tell me!'

Vincenti laughed when he called for his mother. Vincenti
carried Simone back. 'Save yourself grief and speak, boy.' He
rumpled Simone's hair. 'It'll be over then.'

'Aye, and he will be dead,' said a new voice, speaking pure Italian with quiet purpose.

'You next, English!' Vincenti clashed the door behind him.

In the torture room the music began. They had started again on the man from Ponte Maggiore.

'Ah, the Whisperer's entrance,' said the new voice. A body scraped across the dirt to Simone, warm hands touched his face. The man began to chant something in another language, then he stopped and stroked Simone's cheek.

'You wouldn't understand the Lord's Prayer in English. Let's say it together, in dialect Italian.'

It was Mario Scudieri.

So began one of the strangest half-hours in Simone's life. Mario Scudieri, clumsy because of the handcuffs round his wrists, cradled the boy's head on his lap and began to talk.

Yes, Mario said, he was English; he had been born in Bristol . . . 'I married a local girl,' he said, a phrase which stuck in Simone's mind.

'What's going to happen to us?' he whispered.

'You're a brave lad,' said Mario – he said he had an English name, but not one Simone would understand – 'We must hold out for as long as we can.'

They were quiet. The man from Ponte was whimpering. The chords from *Tosca* were repeated.

'Try to ignore it,' said Mario. He laid his manacled hands across Simone's chest. 'Have you lived in Castel long?'

'All my life.' Simone flinched as the music stopped.

'Strange! I'd never noticed you before yesterday. Of course you lads from Castel are our rivals.'

'How can you fire a gun without fingers?' asked Simone suddenly, across the probing voice of the Whisperer. He felt Mario stiffen.

'You don't need guns or fingers to fight evil,' he replied, breaking off at the sound of footsteps. He bent his head and kissed Simone on each cheek.

'That's from your father, and that's from your mother.'

Simone knew then that the guards had come for Mario.

Mario – the Englishman – made no sound. The music

played, the Whisperer spoke, but the man said nothing. Leaving him – presumably bound and gagged – on one of their ghastly tables, the guards came again for Simone.

They beat him and then burned his feet. 'Tell me!' The whisper carried over the chords of music, over his scream, piercing the moment when he felt he could bear no more.

'Know nothing – please – don't.' His voice, begging.

Then the man from Ponte, shouting. 'I'll have you! I'll have your wives, your children . . . I promise you!'

'Make him shut up!' hissed the Whisperer, the voice without a body, who never touched. Two guards ran at the Whisperer's command and the man was silenced.

Simone was wrenched to his bleeding feet. He could hear water dripping into a butt, trickling from somewhere.

'Now Spoletta, my good lad, let's see if this boy from Castel can swim.'

Simone was thrust head-down into the water-butt, held in the icy fluid until he blacked out.

Hands pummelled him back to life, heaved him puking onto the table. A finger glided down the boy's twitching calf.

'We know the names now. Your precious Captain Rodito. You betrayed them, you see.' The Whisperer's voice was gloating. 'You've betrayed all your unit.'

Simone tried to speak. He wanted to tell someone he was sorry. 'Mario—'

'Ah, yes. We're taking him for a little trip to fetch his wife. When we come back we'll need *that* table. Oh, and I'll need more answers. After all, you might as well tell me everything.'

The Whisperer withdrew. Vincenti carried the boy back to the manger. This time he did not speak to Simone. Simone wept.

January, Milan.

'You know what happened next,' said Simone slowly. 'Mario the Englishman and the woman were brought into the chamber. Mario was thrown back in with me and the man from Ponte. His wife was interrogated to make him talk.'

Simone finished the wine, set his glass on the kitchen bar.

'Tell me the rest, Dad,' said Roberto. 'You want to.' When he had first admitted to being tortured, Simone had refused to say how he had been captured, where he had been taken and how he had escaped. 'I don't want to say any more, it's too terrible to remember,' he said when Roberto, very gently, tried to press him. Roberto, he knew, had not been satisfied, but had let it go for his, Simone's sake.

Now Simone realised he wanted to speak, to clear the guilt which had haunted him, on and off, for fifty years. And he had already admitted the worst.

'An air-raid started, and the place we were being held in was hit. Mario must have been near the metal doors in the centre of the blast; there was no shred of him left. The man from Ponte was in the manger next to mine; the blast covered us with rubble. I was too weak to dig myself out. The man from Ponte was unconscious; I wasn't sure then if he was even alive.'

Simone sighed. 'I don't know what became of the woman, or Vincenti that night. I don't know if the Whisperer escaped: I'd like to think he didn't, but at the time I didn't care. I'd betrayed my unit and nothing else mattered.'

He smiled bleakly. 'I heard later that Vincenti was staying in Bologna and that the Contessa of Croce had left her villa and moved to another estate in Tuscany. So I never saw her.'

'In a way you have now,' remarked Roberto. 'Julia is Clara Scudieri's granddaughter, and they're very alike.' He did not add that Clara Scudieri, the Contessa, had been Mario's wife.

Simone, hearing Julia's name, sighed again. Wary of any direct criticism to Roberto, he never the less regretted his son's relationship with that young woman. Considering whether he could take any indirect action to break up the affair, Simone heard Roberto clear his throat: a reminder he had not yet finished his account of his brief and tragic partisan career.

'I lay in the ruins. I woke to find a dog licking my face. The Fioretti twins of Castel had found me and the stranger from Ponte: they dug us out, took us back to their farmhouse. They wanted us to accuse the Patuzzi family of trying to murder us.

The man from Ponte refused: he said he couldn't be sure. After that the twins lost interest in us and let their womenfolk do what they could for our injuries. It was the women who sent word to my parents. My father came with a cart to take me home.'

Simone ran a hand across his mouth.

'The atmosphere in the village was terrible. I knew straightaway something was wrong. My father wouldn't say what but it was obvious: Rodito and his men had been rounded up by the Fascists.

'I knew then that the Whisperer had been right. I had betrayed them, me.'

'No,' said Roberto, with a cutting sweep of his hands. 'That's a standard trick of interrogation, to tell your victim that you've already broken him. It wasn't you, Dad. It was never you. Sprint was the one.'

Simone frowned. 'Cesare? But after what the Fascists did to his father—'

'Why do you think Cesare Celere was murdered just before Christmas? As you said yourself, these fiftieth anniversary celebrations are raking up memories. Sprint was about to share his with the newspapers.'

'Sprint collaborated?' Shocked by that idea, Simone did not think to ask how his son knew about Cesare Celere.

Roberto twisted his hands in assent, not adding that he believed Sprint had been one of the six in the torture chamber, and that Simone's own youthful desire to impress a rival had given Sprint – and Scarpia – Captain Rodito's name.

'But it was me who was spat at in Castel!' burst out Simone. 'A man spat at my mother! All the village knew what I'd done.'

'They assumed,' said Roberto. 'If Aurelio hadn't been hiding the soldiers in his barn then no blame would have been attached to you.' His voice darkened. 'Whatever you said or didn't say, no one in that village should have pointed the finger. Blame doesn't come into it. You were a victim.'

'That's what the priest in Naples said when I finally confessed.'

'And he was right.' Roberto folded his arms. 'After the war, your parents moved away from Castel because of the bad feeling. Why did they choose Naples?'

'My mother had a cousin there. We could live with her until my father got work.' Simone stared at his hands. 'We wanted to get right away. Make a fresh start.'

'You never wanted revenge on Vincenti?'

Simone shook his head. Roberto was more Old-Testament on such matters than he was. 'I was ashamed,' he said aloud. 'I knew that by my speaking I'd sent Captain Rodito to his death.' He cleared his throat. 'After those nights I never saw Vincenti again. I used to keep out of the way whenever I heard his car coming through the village. My father once asked after my lessons but I told him I'd gone off the idea. There wasn't any point in exposing Vincenti. It would have been my word against his.'

Roberto clasped his shoulder in benediction. 'Coffee I think. You deserve it.'

Simone shook his head.

'You did everything you could to resist those men,' said Roberto. 'I'm proud of you. I only wish you'd told me this years ago instead of letting Sandro and me assume that you'd lived in Naples through the war.'

'I was too ashamed.'

'But when you spoke to me before Christmas: why didn't you say it was Castel, and Mario Scudieri, instead of having me think all this had happened to you and some unknown Englishman in Naples in 1943, not '44?'

Simone ran a hand through his pewter-coloured hair. 'I don't know.' Roberto shot him a look.

'You were afraid I might find out more than you wanted to tell me then. But that doesn't matter. And you didn't betray anyone.'

'I'll never really know,' said Simone.

35

It was shame which kept him silent,' said Julia. 'Poor man, to
have carried that for so long. And this year's anniversary
brought it back.'

Roberto's gleaming eyes darted over her profile. He said
nothing, reflecting how relieved he was that it was nothing
worse than shame.

'Strange, how he never suspected Sprint.' Julia flicked a
glance at her companion. 'Did you tell him that the woman
who was brought in that night was Clara?'

'No – Dad only knows that Cesare collaborated. He was
pretty shaken, so I told him nothing more.' Simone still did
not know of the search for Scarpia.

'Will he be easier in his mind now, you think?'

'I believe so. Anyway, he's invited himself over to Sandro's
tomorrow. He'll be OK.' Roberto rubbed the back of his neck
with his pencil. 'We're invited.'

'Your family want a look at me, eh?'

Roberto only remembered the knife nick in his side when
he was tense. He felt it now, a puckering as he stiffened.
Sandro and Margherita were interested in meeting Julia,
yes, but the main reason for their visit was because he
wanted to show her off. Over the week spent in Milan,
Roberto had found himself hovering outside jewellers, staring
at rings.

'That's a grim expression.' Julia skimmed a hand at him. 'Can I look yet?'

'If you'd stop fidgeting I'd be quicker.' Sometimes, when she was still, Julia had the look of a Madonna. She would be a good mother, he thought. She probably wanted children: most women he knew wanted a family.

'There.' He added the highlights to the eyes and passed Julia the drawing, watching her glance at him, the notepad, then over her shoulder at the stone cross he had sketched her against.

He made himself smile. 'Behold, the Contessa of Croce.'

Julia leaned back against the cross, looked around the square. 'San Martino della Croce. Your car looks out of place, it should be a carriage.' Roberto's Alfa, blue as the sky, was parked in the middle of cobbles studded with daisies.

The houses round the square, stripped of doors, roofs sagging or collapsed, stood open yet secretive. Sun glazed the snow on the encircling mountains a pale crimson, like the flowers of the almond tree blooming, bowed over by the prevailing wind, beside the church.

Julia had hoped that seeing Croce, where Guy and Clara had lived, would provide some insight, some proof which would bring her and Roberto closer to finding Scarpia. Instead of which the deserted village, like the three deserted hamlets lower down the mountain, was stripped of resonance.

'Gucci was right about Patuzzi's old farmhouse,' she said, fingering the lichen on the stone cross. 'It's fallen away.' They had stopped the car near the fig tree growing over the road. Tramping over coarse vegetation, they scrambled round deep gullies for almost a kilometre before reaching a hollow, where, in the lee of the mountain, a building had stood. Nothing remained except a wall and a door with its lintel stone tilting at an angle, preparing to skid down the hillside to join rubble, gorse, and roof-beams sprouting fungus.

'No wonder Clara was confused about where she'd been held,' remarked Roberto as they stood looking over the wreck. 'The hill and trees would have hidden this place.' He put a rm around Julia's shoulder. 'To be so close to her home and ot know.'

Julia frowned. 'Would a truck have been able to get here?'

'Ah, I know it's difficult to imagine with this erosion, but it vould have been easy when there were terraced, level fields. 'robably crossed fields too, so that tracks wouldn't be seen eading away from the road.'

'Why did they bring their victims here, I wonder?'

'From what we've learned, I don't think these men were a ery official outfit,' answered Roberto. 'And as Gucci said, carpia couldn't use Ponte police station. Maybe this was the ext best secure place. Or maybe the group was in a hurry or results when they captured my father and Clara, and ragged them here, the nearest Blackshirt's house.'

'I'm amazed no one noticed anything.'

'Maybe they did but this was wartime; no one supposed to e out after curfew. Scarpia moved at night.'

'So did the partisans.'

Roberto squeezed her shoulder. 'Maybe the man was lucky.'

Julia stared at the cracked lintel stone. She hadn't nentioned Guy's diary to Roberto: she wanted to see more of first.

'And there was Sprint,' continued Roberto. 'With him in our grandfather's group, Scarpia must have known a lot of ne local partisans' movements in advance.'

'Drink?' Roberto brought Julia back to the village, to where ney were now, catching their breaths after exploring the uined houses and tiny church. In a vault near the altar Julia ad found a chest. Roberto had dragged it out into the square nd knocked off the lock with a stone.

Instead of the baptismal records they'd hoped to find the hest contained nothing but a rusty gin-trap. The boy Pietro, ho along with Giovanni Respini had been part of Guy's Red-leaded League, remained a mystery.

'Well, there were five Pietros in Croce,' Julia said then.

'But he'd have been one of the youngest.' Roberto hurled ne stone over the rooftops. 'We'd have found him if only the ecords had been here.'

If only: that summed up much of their search, thought Julia.

'Here.' Roberto set plastic bottle and two glasses by the base of the cross, removed his sketchpad from her unresisting fingers. 'We've another hour before Respini turns up. We can drink a glass of vermouth: toast your grandfather.'

Julia sat on the steps, poured the dark liquid into the glasses. Part of her was still absorbing the idea that Giovanni Respini had not only agreed to talk to the grandchild of Marie Scudieri, but suggested they meet at Croce. The man's about face was so absolute that Julia was suspicious, although Roberto had laughed. 'Typical Italian: anything for family and village,' he'd said.

'Wait.' Roberto's voice stopped her as she was about to take a drink. Julia turned.

'Not another sketch, surely?'

Roberto grinned. 'You're very sketchable, but no.' He swept the bottle and his glass up, held out his hand to draw her to her feet. 'That's where we should drink to Guy.'

Above them, its gardens long overgrown, was Clara's villa.

They settled on the steps to the old herb garden, looking across the orange orchard and the wizened apricot trees. The orchard was peppered with little oaks and a browsing herd of sheep which had come in over a broken wall.

Julia yawned: she loved mornings, but mornings were not a good time for a singer. Roberto caught the yawn off her. They laughed, then were quiet.

'The door's open,' he said after a moment. 'Want to look?'

Julia drew in a breath. She could not help this feeling of reluctance. Roberto lifted his head: she knew he knew she was keeping something back again. 'Listen,' she said quickly, putting her glass on a patch of moss. 'The angelus.' The monastery bells, faint with distance, seeped across from the opposite ridge.

Roberto drained his glass. 'Well I'm going to poke around Guy's cellar. Who knows, I may find more vermouth.'

He walked away with that flowing, deceptive stride.

Humming a tune, Julia took a music score from her bag.

he music blurring into shapes like the copperplate writing in
ier grandfather's diary. Yet nothing her grandfather could
say would alter what Scarpia had done to Clara, what Scarpia
iad done to her.

Practice was impossible. Julia set the score on the step.

'Julia.' The voice seemed to come from the bowels of the
earth. 'We've got something.'

It was a message in a bottle: papers hidden in a small cask.
Roberto, shaking the cask by chance to see if it held any
sherry, heard a rustling and removed the stopper.

'Ah, your grandfather had long fingers.' He reached inside
with his fingers. 'That's it!' He flicked the dry crackling rolls
onto Julia's lap.

Julia spread the first sheet on the herb garden steps.

'English?' asked Roberto above her, admiring her long
neck, his hand drawing in the air the curve of Julia's breast.
Her oval face took on the glow of the almond blossom.

'Code. Maybe I'll be able to break it.' She stopped.

Roberto heard it too, the sound of a car skidding up the
dirt road. Julia crammed the papers into the cask, he rammed
home the stopper.

'Back into the cellar with this,' he said. 'It's been safe there
for fifty years.' He returned before the car had stopped in the
square below.

'Dammit!' Julia watched two figures climbing out of the
Fiat. She felt a hand on her arm.

'Hide in the orchard!' Roberto spun her down the last three
steps. Julia ducked under his arm and darted back.

'We see them together.' She wrapped an arm about him.

The two men were looking round at the Alfa, the church,
the villa. 'Maybe this wasn't a good idea,' the stocky blond
was saying to the shaven-headed man, the one with the shot-
gun broken over his arm.

'Come away!' hissed Roberto, as Julia leaned over the villa
wall to look down into the square. Her long earrings flashed
in the sun: both men looked up.

The stocky blond's jaw sagged. Shaven-head lowered his
gun.

'Giovanni and our Pietro, I think.' Julia beckoned to the stunned figures. 'Sometimes my resemblance to Clara is quite useful, wouldn't you agree?' She smiled brightly.

Laughing softly, Roberto shook his head.

'Why the gun?' Julia handed Giovanni Respini a glass of vermouth. He sat with Pietro Masone on the herb garden steps. The two men glanced at each other, then at Roberto, standing behind Julia, arms folded.

Giovanni scratched his shaven head. 'Pietro better explain.' His companion hurled him an indignant look.

'Someone better explain,' said Roberto.

So the story came out. Giovanni and Pietro had been part of Mario Scudieri's group during the war, its youngest members, and had always kept in touch. Giovanni, receiving Julia's second letter, had driven from Parma to Castel San Martino, where Pietro Masone now farmed. Pietro had wanted to ignore the letter, but Giovanni had convinced him this was dishonourable to Mario Scudieri's memory. Besides, hadn't Pietro something he wished to say to the Contessa's granddaughter?

'You knew that Guy – Mario – was married to my grandmother,' said Julia softly.

Giovanni Respini said yes. Their marriage was common knowledge in Croce, although no one spoke of it outside the village: he had only known because Pietro, who was his best friend, had told him. But now if he could begin by apologising for the shot-gun . . .

'Last week the old people in Castel received the same letter saying that if anyone in the village spoke out of turn about what had happened in the area during the war then watch out!'

Giovanni Respini gave Julia a disarming grin. 'After that, even before I got your last letter I was ready to talk to you without lawyers present and for nothing: I don't like to be threatened, however indirectly.'

'Why then did you ask for money the first time I wrote?'

Respini shrugged. 'My daughter's getting married this year

t'll cost me a fortune. When I heard from you before Christmas, I didn't know you. You didn't say you were Mario's grandchild. I thought you were some rich singer searching for a distant cousin. Didn't think you'd miss a little cash.'

'We're after the man who captured and tortured Mario,' said Roberto. 'We know he's still alive.' He fixed Respini with an intense stare. 'His code-name was "Scarpia".'

Pietro Masone gulped his glass of vermouth, poured another. 'Don't ask about him!'

'If you know anything,' began Roberto persuasively.

'I know nothing!'

'Relax, Pietro,' said Respini. He glanced at Julia. 'The warning the old men got at Castel was signed "Scarpia".'

'That letter frightened my ninety-year-old father very badly,' put in Pietro Masone.

Yes, Pietro said in answer to Roberto, he had taken the letter to the police, but they said they could do little. There were no fingerprints; the typeface was common and the paper could have been bought anywhere. As for the postmark from Florence, had Pietro Masone any idea how large that city was?

'So you see,' Pietro went on breathlessly, 'I had to be careful.'

'And we wouldn't have got very far if we'd tried to talk to anyone in Castel,' said Roberto. 'Is that why you suggested we meet in Croce?'

Giovanni Respini nodded, then drained his vermouth. 'We also know Cesare Celere was murdered in Florence.' His black eyes scanned Roberto's and Julia's faces. 'Do you know who I mean?'

'Sprint,' said Julia. 'The youth Pietro tried to warn against when he threw my grandmother a bunch of corncockles.'

Pietro's jaw dropped again. 'That's right,' he stammered. 'I tried all the rest of that day to speak to Mario but could never be sure of catching him alone: whenever I saw him Sprint was nearby. I tried again early the following morning. I would have told the Contessa that the flowers held a message for her husband, but the German officer was right behind me – I dared not speak.'

'Clara told Guy about the flowers,' said Julia. 'They knew i
symbolised betrayal, but didn't know whom you meant.'

Pietro blushed. 'There was a paper with the flowers,' he
murmured, looking aside. 'A brown strip. That was Sprint':
colour. We each had a colour, you see,' he went on, 'corres
ponding to wine. Sprint's was dark tawny. Mine was ruby.'

'Mine was white,' said Giovanni Respini. Face to face, hi:
aggressive letter-writing style seemed not so muck
incongruous as out of character. He was calm, much steadie
than Pietro Masone. Someone who as a boy could have carriec
cartridges through Nazi checkpoints.

Julia rose to her feet, and walked along the terrace of Clara':
villa. Roberto was asking how Pietro had discovered that Sprint
was a traitor.

Pietro, it turned out, had missed school that day. He hac
been gathering firewood in the woods Simone and Fathe
Angelo had been trying to reach when they were capturec
Pietro knew that Sprint had a hand in it: spotting the pries
and boy unconscious on the road, he had seen Sprint get dow
from the truck to drag the bodies back onto the truck. Th
other men had been hooded, said Pietro, but Sprint wasn't
even though one of the group had shouted at him to stor
showing off.

'That was Stefano the herbalist. I knew his voice and ever
if he'd not spoken I'd have had a good idea who it was, hin
being so tall and thin.'

'For the love of Christ, why didn't you report Sprint and
Stefano to the police after the war?' asked Roberto darkly.

'I did!' came back the reply. 'I told our own carabinier
who looked after Castel, Giuseppe Patuzzi. He said ther
wasn't enough evidence to secure any kind of conviction unles
the boy and the priest were found.'

'The boy was my father,' said Roberto. He was white with
anger. His voice rose. 'You watched him being driven awa
to Scarpia, and all you could do was tell a Fascist policema
months afterwards? Jesus! And you didn't even have the gut
to tell your own partisan leader that one of your group was
collaborator—'

'Stop it!' Julia shouted. 'He was only a boy!' She clutched Roberto's arm, making him look at her. 'Come away. Please, for my sake.'

36

They drove towards Clara's Tuscan villa, Julia clutching the papers Roberto had found in the cellar.

'Coward!' Roberto's fingers bit into the steering wheel.

'Giovanni Respini's no coward. I was going to ask him if he knew why Guy had gone out on the night he and Clara had decided to escape to Switzerland. I was going to ask if he knew where Umberto Gasparini's family were living now. You made that impossible.'

'I lost my temper, you mean. As you did when you walked out on Emilio Gucci.' Roberto slammed his Alfa into top gear. 'Scarpia tortured my father and Masone couldn't even report it to anyone outside Castel. If Respini hadn't driven him, he wouldn't have turned up today!'

They sat glowering at each other, the Tuscan hills ignored.

Roberto snapped on the radio. The regional news was that Bazzini had resigned his box at La Scala because of 'financial irregularities'.

'Krusak did it,' muttered Julia. 'He's ruined poor Bazzini.'

'That's not all.' Roberto swatted a finger towards the glove compartment. 'I've been talking to a German singer this week: floating names such as Whisperer, Spoletta, Scarpia. His sister's got access to the Berlin Document Centre where the Nazi membership files are kept. Krusak had enough German blood in him to make him an acceptable party member.'

Julia opened the glove compartment, extracted two photocopies and began to read.

On 7th May, 1944, in the village of Mutta in the plain fifteen kilometres from Ponte Maggiore, 263 women, children and old men were gathered in the graveyard by Italian SS Sergeant Zellomo. He ordered his guards to pull out those families he named, stating that they were to be shot as traitors in reprisal for partisans killing three Germans in Ponte. One thirteen-year-old girl was hauled out from a group of children, screaming that she had done nothing, at which Zellomo answered, 'We know from Scarpia's men that your father has,' and he shot her himself at close range with a pistol. The rest of the families, fifty men, women and children, were then gunned down by the Italian SS. The surviving villagers were ordered to bury them without a priest.

That same morning large numbers of German troops entered the village and began looting and burning houses. When the troops reached the graveyard and found Zellomo's men overseeing the burying of the dead, the German officer in charge ordered Zellomo to have the survivors dig a trench in front of the mass grave. When this was done and the murdered pro-partisan families heaped into the grave, the remaining villagers, over two hundred people, were lined up alongside the trench.

The German ordered his men to shoot them. When his troops showed reluctance, the officer seized a machine gun from one and gunned down twenty women and children, ordering Zellomo's men and his own troops to 'finish it'. The officer watched as the rest of the villagers were killed, then he and his men left.

One boy survived this atrocity by falling down with the dead. Zellomo discovered he was alive and let him go.

From questioning the boy, Antonio di Stefano, the commission has learned that the German officer responsible for this barbarity was probably a White Russian or Croatian. The boy heard him swearing at his troops in a

strange language: not German. Di Stefano also said that
the officer was young and of solemn appearance: 'Like the
saints in the frescos in our church.'

ulia re-folded the papers, silently replaced them.

Roberto, saying nothing, switched on the car heater.

'lara, wearing a dark blue dress in their honour, was waiting
1 the panelled music room. One look at their faces and she
ut down the piano lid. 'No duets before dinner.' She extended
er hand for Roberto to kiss.

Julia brushed her grandmother's dry cheek with her lips,
elieved yet disturbed to see Clara. She kept thinking of the
iary entries Angelica had read out to her, of the English
risoner of war whom Clara, according to her own husband,
ad betrayed to the Germans. Julia hated the idea. Maybe
his was why Angelica had left: to escape these contorted
eelings of shame and affection. Yet when Clara embraced
er, Julia knew comfort.

'So, children.' Clara took Julia's and Roberto's hands in hers,
rew them towards the apple-wood fire. 'Tell me everything.
fter all – ' she flashed Julia a keen glance – 'neither you nor
ndrea have explained to me what security men are doing
urking in my shrubbery.'

Clara patted the two-seater sofa. 'Roberto, you're with me.
ulia, you've the rug.' She pulled the big man onto the sofa,
rinking at him. 'Hope you don't let my granddaughter boss
ou about.'

'All the time.' Roberto, flicking an indulgent look at Clara,
tretched his legs over the marble hearth. He began to explain
ow he and Julia now knew the identities of four of the six
nen who had held Clara and his father Simone on the night
;uy had died.

'Francesco Vincenti of Castel San Martino is a certainty.
3oth you and my father picked him out from the cassette of
ld singers. My father recognised his voice in the torture
hamber and Vincenti actually spoke to him. Vincenti was
he blond man with the earring and the Castel dialect whom

you caught a glimpse of under your blindfold.'

'But he wasn't Scarpia,' said Clara. 'He wasn't the singer.
Or the Whisperer,' she added.

'No. He was in opera though, and he had a truck with
tarpaulin "flaps" that an old pianist remembers being driven
in up into the mountains. As a singer with a good salary,
Vincenti was the member of Scarpia's group whose truck, you,
Guy and Carlo Gucci were bundled into when captured. We
know that because Carlo Gucci found a paper written by
Vincenti in the truck.

'Stefano the herbalist and Cesare Celere, known as Sprint,
are also certainties. Pietro Masone, the blond boy who threw
you the corncockles, saw Sprint helping several hooded men
to drag my father and Father Angelo, the priest of Castel, into
Vincenti's truck. Pietro recognised Stefano as one of the men
because of his height, thinness and voice. Stefano in the torture
chamber spoke either in whispers or not at all. That's why
you never recognised his voice yourself.'

'You said he was a greedy, grasping man,' said Julia. 'I think
he envied you and Guy your wealth.'

'He and Vincenti were long-standing Fascist party
members, according to Carlo Gucci's son,' said Roberto.

'And Stefano was often in trouble with the police because
of his violent behaviour,' said Julia.

Clara nodded. 'Very well, I'm convinced. But Stefano sang
like a crow. I remember him in Croce church, croaking the
responses in mass. So though he was there that night, he
wasn't Scarpia.'

Roberto cracked his knuckles. 'We've no direct witnesses
to the fourth man, but we both believe that the coffin-maker
Patuzzi was involved.'

'Davide?' Clara squinted at Roberto, turning her head
sideways. 'But why?' She brushed fretfully at her blue silk. 'If
I was a Fioretti, I could believe it, but Davide Patuzzi? He
owed me rent and I released him from the debt! And I knew
his voice.'

'Would you have known his whisper, though?' Julia, sitting
on the rug, twisted back as the fire scorched her side. 'All the

Patuzzis are right-wingers, even today.' She jerked a thumb at Roberto. 'The Fioretti twins found his father and Carlo Gucci in the ruins of Davide Patuzzi's old farmhouse: you were all held on the coffin-maker's land.'

Clara was shaking her head. 'Davide was dark: he could have been the man I glimpsed with the dark stubble – but still . . . I can't believe it. He owed me.' Her hands found one of Roberto's and clung on.

Roberto covered the narrow fingers with his. 'I think I know how it worked,' he said. 'Patuzzi had the deserted farmhouse, well away from other houses and the road. Vincenti had the truck. Vincenti brought you and Guy and my father to Patuzzi's house to be interrogated by Scarpia.'

Clara cleared her throat. 'Go on.'

'The day my father and Father Angelo were captured, they'd met three people on the boundary to Patuzzi's land: your husband Guy, Sprint and the priest of Croce. Simone my father had talked to Sprint and been indiscreet – he mentioned a possible Allied landing. I believe that Sprint slipped away to Patuzzi's to tell Davide what he'd learned, and Patuzzi, realising that my father and Father Angelo might possess vital information, hared off down the mountain with his horse and cart to Castel San Martino and Francesco Vincenti's.'

'That is why you and Guy were interrogated in Patuzzi's farmhouse,' said Julia. 'We believe Scarpia wanted quick results and didn't want to waste time taking you down to Bologna.'

'Are you saying that Scarpia usually operated from Bologna?' asked Clara, frowning.

'According to what Rita told me, I think it's likely,' said Julia. 'Rita did wonder if he also had a villa somewhere outside near the city.'

'From his base in Bologna – which may have been a room beneath Fascist headquarters but could have been a cellar anywhere – some sounds may have escaped,' put in Roberto. 'And not everyone supported the Fascists in 1944. From everything we know of Scarpia, secrecy was his obsession.'

Clara shuddered. 'I still can't really believe Stefano and

Patuzzi were involved in this. They were members of Scarpia's "cell" you say, but for how long?'

'That we don't know,' said Roberto, 'but since they were both party members, maybe for some time.'

'But how would they have moved about after curfew from Croce and Castel? How would they have got to Bologna?'

'Vincenti had a truck,' said Julia. 'They could have gone with him.'

'As Blackshirts, Stefano and Patuzzi probably would have had passes,' added Roberto.

'Then it seems crazier than ever that the group used Patuzzi's farmhouse at all,' said Clara decisively. 'Even if Scarpia had wanted Guy and me to talk as soon as possible.'

She closed her eyes. 'Tell me the rest,' she said. 'What happened on 9th June after Davide Patuzzi rushed to Francesco Vincenti's house to warn him about a possible Allied landing?'

'Vincenti brought Patuzzi back up the mountain in his truck, no doubt picking up Stefano the herbalist on the way,' answered Julia. 'They then captured Simone and the priest before the two of them reached Castel.'

'But you said Sprint was in the truck too.' Clara rubbed her forehead with her free hand. 'How is that possible if Roberto's father never saw Sprint pass him on the way down the road?'

'Because Sprint was hiding in one of Patuzzi's coffins,' said Roberto.

'Two men from Croce.' Clara sighed. 'Where are these four today?'

'All dead,' said Julia.

'Vincenti: May 1972. Stefano: December 1977. Patuzzi: July 1993. And now Sprint.' Roberto looked away from Clara to the fire. 'The dates are from death records.'

'So they are out of reach.' Clara straightened on the sofa, still clutching Roberto's hand. 'And the last two? Spoletta? Scarpia?'

Julia raised her head. 'Cesare Celere may have had two nicknames: Sprint and Spoletta. He was a singer, you see. One of Vincenti's pupils.'

'Ah,' Clara's mouth tugged downwards. 'Well I must say he never sang in church.'

'Your priest of Croce,' said Roberto. 'A man the ex-Marshal of Ponte and my father both mentioned as someone who'd talk freely to the Germans during the war. Had he a good voice?'

'No!' Clara whipped her hand from his. 'That's grotesque!'

'If you tell me his name we can find him through the church,' went on Roberto steadily. 'He may still be alive.'

'As may his curate,' said Julia.

'No!' said Clara. 'I won't tell you. He was my *priest*.'

Dinner was tense. Clara insisted on being told why she was being protected. Julia's explanation of the night she had been attacked took up most of the meal, and then Roberto, peeling each of them an orange from the Venetian glass bowl which Andrea had ceremonially carried in, told Clara about the written threats the old people of Castel had received.

Clara scooped teaspoons of sugar into her coffee. 'I think you should stop this, Julia.'

'So do I,' said Roberto. Clara jabbed her teaspoon at him. 'You should stop, too. Four of the men who tortured your father are already dead.'

'Scarpia's alive,' said Roberto.

'So are you,' retorted Clara. 'For the present.'

Roberto was asleep when Julia thought again about Guy's coded papers. Sliding out of bed, she was toying with the idea of taking the papers into the flower gallery to study when she heard a tapping at the door. Opening it she found Clara in a white fluffy night-dress.

'I've remembered something.' Clara did not give the man in the bed a glance: Clara was broad-minded. 'Come.'

Julia followed. In Clara's room the four poster bedclothes were turned down; Clara, walking to the bed, touched a hand to Guy's photograph hanging on the wall.

'Get in, there's no fire.'

Julia did so and Clara climbed into bed beside her, pulling

up the covers. In the pink glow of the bedside lamp they looked like twins, thought Julia.

'I didn't want to be alone tonight,' said Clara.

'I understand.'

'Can I turn the light off? My eye's sore.'

Julia nodded. When the light clicked off she could just make out Clara's profile.

'The priest's name was Abramo Coletta,' said Clara. 'He was a Roman, but he'd been at Croce for two years. The old priest before him married Guy and myself: when war broke out that priest brought us the records of our marriage; he foresaw trouble before it came.'

Julia heard an owl hoot, the sound of feet on the flags outside the villa. Security men patrolled at night.

'Do you have to keep going with this?' asked Clara and added, before Julia could answer, 'I suppose you must. Scarpia knows people are looking now.'

She turned towards Julia, her face in darkness. 'One more thing I remembered tonight: seeing Roberto again brought it back. The guard who strapped my arms to the table was tall; maybe taller than Roberto or Guy. He smelled of perfume.'

'What?' Julia had been reflecting on Angelica's claim that Clara and Guy had often quarrelled. If not happily married, would a woman widowed for fifty years keep a portrait of her husband near her bed?

'I know it sounds amusing, but the man had a distinctive scent . . .'

Next morning, Roberto was amused when Andrea, taking Clara her morning coffee, found Clara and Julia sleeping together. 'I've heard of a girl running home to mother, but to grandmother is a new one on me,' he said, when Julia appeared in their room in her dressing-gown.

Julia stuck out her tongue and went to snatch a bath. Today, their last free day for several weeks, she would meet Roberto's family. She wanted to shine for him.

She was in the bath when he walked in, his hands cutting and sweeping in emphasis of his satisfaction. 'You, Ruth and

erni are doing Verdi's Requiem in Venice next week. I've
st had my agent on the phone: the bass has cancelled and
n I step in?'

'But you'll be in Austria.'

'Your concert's between my performances. I could do it.
he fee's good.' He named a sum that made Julia whistle.

'That's double what I'm getting. Go away!' Laughing, she
rew the sponge at him.

Roberto tossed the sponge back, the planes of his face
rowing starker. 'Your grandmother's right.'

Julia slid back under the water. 'I'm not going to give up.'
hey were having this 'discussion' more and more of late.

Roberto's broad hands cupped in a plea. 'Vincenti, Stefano,
atuzzi, Sprint – all dead. What do you want?'

'*You* ask that? Are *you* going to stop? No, I didn't think so.'
lia stood up in the white bath, hands on hips. 'Clara told me
mething new last night.'

'Ah.' Roberto handed her a towel.

'Don't laugh,' warned Julia, wondering how to put this. She
ttled on how Clara had expressed it. 'One of the six had a
ry distinctive scent – and before you say anything it couldn't
ave been Stefano, Patuzzi or Sprint. Clara met those men
gularly; she'd have noticed something so obvious.'

Roberto smiled, not needing to observe that this still left
incenti, as well as Scarpia and the final man. 'What's this
rth-shattering scent, then?' he asked indulgently. 'Something
e can use as evidence, you think?'

'All right, it's probably nothing.' Julia shrugged, slightly
nnoyed. She wasn't going to be patronised, and she wasn't
ing to tell him.

'Any luck with Guy's papers?' Roberto helped her out of
e bath.

'No time.' She sensed Roberto's eyes narrowing.

'What is it?' Roberto, grabbing the towel, snared her against
m. 'Watch what you keep to yourself, Julia.'

He would not let her go. Desire and irritation joined forces.
ig!' Julia laughed, pressing herself closer.

'We've time.' Roberto lowered his dark head.

* * *

'Vincenti, Patuzzi, Stefano and Sprint are dead,' Roberto sai to Simone.

'That still leaves the Whisperer, and one more.' Simone watching Roberto fiddling with his cufflinks, snorted when his son dropped one and it bounced under a bookshelf. 'I' better get that: you'll have the lot down.'

'Allow me.' Julia detached herself from the window in blue swirl. Kneeling, she retrieved the cufflink and playfull tossed it to Roberto – only part in play: she wanted to show Simone that his son was not as clumsy as he claimed.

'My thanks.' Roberto caught it with a flourish an disappeared into his bedroom for his jacket. He and Julia ha stopped off at the apartment for him to change and to collec Simone, who to Julia's irritation, seemed incapable of makin his own way to Sandro's home and meeting them there.

Now she and Simone looked at each other, Julia wondering why she could not like the man. He had suffered in the war she could pity Simone when he wasn't there. Present Roberto's father set her teeth on edge.

Yet in many ways Simone was like his son; tall, with the same nose, straight eyebrows. Simone's eyes though were hazel, more prominent than Roberto's. His carefully combed grey hair, his presence, the way he wore his black suit reminded Julia of a candidate for a right-wing party.

Simone had not offered her his hand to help her up. 'You're staying here tonight at the flat, whilst I'm at Sandro's.' H made it sound as though Julia were throwing him out, althougl Simone had already arranged to stay at his younger son's.

Julia, kneeling by the bookcase near to the window of the music-living-room, saw by a shaft of sun that Simone had cleft in his chin. 'That's right,' she answered.

'And Roberto with you.'

Yes, and we're having the orgy tonight. Julia gave a brillian smile. 'That's right.'

Grudgingly, Simone extended a hand. Julia expected hi touch to be cold, to reveal his obvious dislike of her. To he surprise his fingers were warm.

'Hold it!' said Roberto from the doorway. A flashgun spat as he snapped a picture of them holding hands. 'And another – Julia next to you, Dad.'

'*No!*' Simone wrenched himself free and stalked from the room, pushing past an astonished Roberto.

'What's with him?'

Julia shook her head, turning to look out across the park opposite Roberto's apartment. Her fingers trembled as she touched the glass. 'Tall,' her grandmother had said last night. 'Tall as Roberto . . .' Other snatches followed, Clara's voice blotting out the skid of Milan traffic. 'One had a cleft in his chin . . . The man who strapped me down had a distinctive scent: lavender, would you believe – I can't think how I forgot that; it's such a queer smell on a man.'

Lavender. Close to, Simone had that same scent.

37

Four days later, at the start of the Venetian carnival, Julia was pushed down the stairs of La Fenice opera house. Coming down a deserted staircase, she felt a hand on her back shove her forward: she missed her footing and plummeted.

A man caught her at the bottom of the stairs. A man in a harlequin mask. 'Next time, there'll be no one to stop you breaking your neck!' He thrust her back and ran off.

Tom was delighted to have made it to Julia's concert. He stood, clutching scarf and trilby, waiting to go into the wooden amphitheatre picked out in blue, gold and white; panelling studded with painting, and dominating it all, the obsidian shimmer of the stage.

Attendants were clearing a path for VIPs proceeding to their boxes. Tom turned and recognised Jan Krusak with two men: one tall, one small and portly, both grey-blond. The taller was saying to his companion, 'The first expression of an artist's creative intent, the cartoons, Pietro! We must see more cartoons on the market. Those are what people who appreciate art are buying, the drawings are what they *want*.'

To Tom, it sounded like a command that the luckless Pietro manufacture these cartoons. He wasn't surprised when the smaller man shook out a handkerchief and blew his nose to cover any need to enlarge on his murmured, 'Yes, Signore di Salvo.'

Jan Krusak, tall as di Salvo, dark-complexioned where the older man was fair, said, 'Your son is performing tonight, Terni?'

'Why, yes.' Pietro Terni coloured in pleasure.

Tom, moving to let them by, knew how the man felt. Tonight, he hadn't a rose for Julia, but he did have something. How would she react to him this time?

He wished he hadn't used his knife in the street. He wished he hadn't followed her in Florence. He'd meant to talk to her at Lucca, except Krusak had made it impossible.

Tom scowled. Krusak, sensing someone watching, turned. Deep-set eyes, blinkered as the beam of a lighthouse, passed over Tom in dismissal. Krusak didn't remember him.

And then Tom's plans were reduced to shavings when di Salvo, touching Krusak's and Terni's arms, reported in a conversational manner, 'I learned today that Julia fell down the stairs here – an "accident". I have told the management of this house that if any other "accidents" happen to my mezzo, the people responsible will answer to me.'

Tom watched di Salvo's hands tighten on the men's arms. 'To me personally,' he added. 'I will not have her damaged.'

Tom had a sudden vision of Krusak and Terni floating in some Venetian lagoon, equipped with a pair of concrete waders each. He shook himself: he wasn't superstitious.

Besides, why should Terni or Krusak want to harm Julia?

The question preoccupied Tom throughout Verdi's Requiem. Despite La Fenice's famous acoustics he didn't enjoy his evening.

By the end of the concert Tom had reached a decision. Tonight he was going to talk properly to Julia.

Tom waited by the artists' exit. An hour after the concert he was there, wrapping and re-wrapping himself in his scarf, wishing he had brought his gloves.

Pietro Terni, Jan Krusak and di Salvo were already gone. Tom had seen them being whisked into the velvet cold on a private lantern-bearing gondola. Now he watched the fireworks bursting over the city from St Mark's square. Sun

nd moon, symbols of the carnival, picked out by stars of
unpowder.

Two couples, the women in delicate silver moon-masks,
he men in golden sun-masks covering their faces from the
op of the head to below the nose, swept out in long capes.
Revellers in fancy dress coming into the opera house from
he carnival, thought Tom, ignoring them as the tallest said,
You go on ahead, I've left something in there.' The man
ashed back, moving surprisingly silently considering his size.
he theatre lights flashed on his sun-mask.

An attendant came to the narrow door and began to close it.
'Julia Rochfort?' asked Tom hurriedly. The attendant
quinted at him, bearded face purple in the nova of a firework.
'Long gone.' The man's arm pointed over the lapping canals.
'ipes, drums and rattles pulsated from every tiny square.
Glancing where the attendant had signalled, Tom saw a
rocodile of bodies in ermine costumes doing the conga along
n alley.

Tom swore, kicked the wall. He might as well start making
is way back to the station.

He began weaving towards the Grand Canal. At this hour,
e wasn't sure if water taxis were operating, but it was worth
chance. A door banged; he glanced back to the opera house,
aw only a vague movement in the shadows.

Tom turned and carried on walking. His rapid footsteps
hrew up a muffled echo. He moved crabwise past another
yrating group of people; one moon-masked woman devouring
slice of pizza reminded him that he was peckish.

A chrysanthemum exploded overhead, making Tom start
orward a pace, where he collided with the shadowed arm of
statue. The arm spun him round like the lid off a jar, a hard
old hand worried his throat, killing cry and struggle together.
Choking, Tom was hoisted into a dark, windowless alley.

'I expected you to turn up,' said a voice marbled with
menace. 'Now you're going to tell me exactly who you are.'

ulia, darting back to find Roberto, saw him striding from the
opera house in the opposite direction, clearly following

someone. Dodging a youth who tried to dance a rumba with her, she elbowed through tourists oohing over the fireworks. Taller than many Venetians, Roberto was visible a few metres ahead until suddenly, just past a lighted doorway, he disappeared.

Julia dragged off her moon-mask. Roberto had produced masks and cloaks at the end of the performance, suggesting that he, she, Ruth and Francesco wear them to enter the carnival spirit. Except now he was going away from the restaurant they'd agreed to eat in after the concert. 'Roberto!' She punched her shout above the roar of firecrackers and trumpets.

'Julia!' An agonised cry somewhere to her left drew her to the end of an unlit street she had missed and sent her pelting along its flags, her cloak slapping the walls. Glad she had worn jeans and trainers, she jumped over the lethal shards of a broken bottle, slowing before she reached the two figures. The taller one had pinned the other man to the wall.

'She's here now. If you speak politely I'll let you talk to her.' Roberto caught the smaller man's sagging head, jamming it back. His fingers left weals across the man's chin which were visible even in the dim alley. 'Nicely, mind.'

'Don't!' said Julia. Roberto ignored her. The man with the red scarf who had followed her in Florence whispered something.

Roberto lowered his masked head. 'Didn't quite catch that.'

A group of party-goers, waving balloons, laughing each time a firework went off, passed the end of their alley.

'Stop it,' said Julia: she did not like this Roberto. 'Let him go.'

Roberto's arm tightened across the man's torso. 'How does it feel to be afraid?' His palm cracked quicker than a whiplash into the man's ribs. Julia screamed and ran forward.

'Stop!' She tried to help the man up: a hand pushed her away, held her at arm's length.

'Leave her alone.' Roberto kicked the wall by the cringing figure. The man leaped up and fled, leaving his trilby in the middle of the alley.

Roberto peeled off his sun-mask, hurled it into a canal.
Don't say anything.'

Both were drained after the concert, but when Roberto held
the door for her on the first open restaurant they found, Julia
shook her head.

'I'm not hungry.'

'I am.'

'What about the others? We arranged to meet them—'

'I've to fly out tonight. When I get to Vienna, you know
what I'll be doing? Going straight to rehearsal. I think we can
forget Terni and Ruth.'

They walked into the Chinese restaurant. Yes, Roberto told
the smiling waiter, they were happy to wait.

He and Julia settled in the small lounge area beside the
tables, Roberto looking at the painting of the celestial dragon,
Julia looking at him.

She could see how exhausted he was. Every free moment,
Roberto was pushing himself to find out more about his father's
tormentors, trying to squeeze more into an already busy list
of engagements. She heard him humming scales and vocal
exercises as he drove them hundreds of kilometres to see
people. He practised roles whilst she was relaxing in the bath.
He studied scores and learned parts in odd corners during
family reunions and mealtimes. As more of a newcomer, Julia
had a schedule which, although full, was not so hectic.
Nevertheless, since calling in at Clara's the previous week
she'd had no chance to study Guy's coded papers in any kind
of detail . . .

'God, I'm tired.' Roberto yawned, one hand picking into
the pocket of his new black denim jacket. Julia stopped him.

'Don't bother looking at your music tonight, let it go. Here
– ' Julia pushed the menu at him – 'Study that instead.'

'You're right.' Roberto, with a rueful smile, thrust the
miniature score back into his jacket and took a drink of grappa:
Julia, more conventional, had ordered a sherry.

'What are you doing? What's that you've got?'

Roberto opened the wallet, began to remove the cards.

'You took his *wallet*?' Julia snapped down her glass on the top of the tropical fish tank. She could hardly believe it.

'You didn't want me to question him: this is the next best thing.'

'Do you like what you're becoming?'

Roberto frowned, rubbed the back of his neck. 'That man frightens you. I don't like him prowling round.'

'And I don't know him,' retorted Julia. 'I don't know why he's interested in me. He's probably just a fan: after all, he gives me roses.'

'You think I shouldn't have gone after him.' Roberto sat back in his easy chair, every line in his face gone hard. 'But when I see men like him and Krusak sniffing round—'

'Don't be revolting. Krusak's in his sixties.'

'And he's dangerous.'

'Tonight I didn't see much difference between Krusak and yourself. What about loving one's neighbour, Roberto? If you're like that with a stranger who's never actually injured me, what are you going to do when we find Scarpia?' Julia's face as bright as the celestial dragon, leaned forward, scooping her glass off the bubbling fish tank. 'What will you do to the man who tortured Simone?'

Roberto's features seemed sunk in on themselves. 'I feel as though I'd like to do to Scarpia what he did to my father. That's the main reason I've not gone to the police.' His eyes lost their shine. 'But then how can I? That will make me as bad as he was. And Scarpia's an old man now. It's complicated.'

'It didn't look complicated tonight. It looked absurdly simple.'

'I could have hurt him much more than I did.'

'You think that makes it right?'

'No!' Roberto's hand sawed the air. 'But if he touches you . . . If any man touches you . . .'

They were both still partly on a performance high – every mood stretched and overwrought – otherwise what followed next might not have occurred. Now though Julia's eyes glittered. 'You don't own me.'

Roberto's eyes gleamed. 'I won't have them prowling

round.' His hand shot out, grabbed her wrist. 'Understand?'

'Perfectly!' muttered Julia, draining the last of her sherry in a single, burning gasp.

'Keep away from the Ternis, too,' Roberto's fingers tightened on her wrist. 'Bianca writes a regular column in an ultra right-wing paper. And Pietro Terni's involved in some shady business in the art world – the authorities suspect he's dealing in fakes but can't prove anything.'

'Sandro been spying for you, has he?'

'I asked him about Bianca, yes. He came up himself with information about Pietro. Listen!' Roberto lunged closer. 'Krusak's been seen in Terni's Bologna gallery: their relationship is kept out of the papers but the art police know the two men meet regularly. Pretty strange for former enemies, don't you think?'

Stunned, Julia was silent. After what Krusak had done to him, how could Pietro bear to be in the same room as the man? She recalled how Roberto had asked questions before about Pietro, questions she had dismissed. Yet she, unlike Roberto, had actually met Pietro: she knew the man. All her instincts told her that Francesco's father was as innocent as his son.

'I'm serious, Julia. You should keep away from all of them – including Francesco.'

'That's it, isn't it? This isn't anything really to do with Bianca and Pietro – you're talking about Francesco!' Julia, hurt that Roberto might think she wanted her easy friendship with the tenor to be more than that, wrenched herself free. 'I can't believe it – after Venice – after what we've shared.'

'Sharing's more than sex.' Roberto was furious that she should think him jealous of Francesco Terni. 'You've lied to me from the very beginning. How do you think that makes me feel, when you didn't trust me enough to say openly who you were searching for? And that night you were set upon – you wouldn't have told me anything then if you hadn't already been beaten up!' Roberto glared at her. 'You could put this Scarpia stuff into the police's hands now. The police would give you and Clara protection. This not wanting the police, not wanting to talk: have I been wrong about you? What is it you're hiding?'

'Was that all Venice was to you, sex?' Julia met accusation with accusation.

'You know it wasn't—'

'But you don't trust me around Francesco.'

'Are you saying that I should, Julia? Or that I shouldn't?'

'What about when you're in Vienna? What about you and the opera groupies?'

'It isn't the same thing.'

'So it's OK for you to flirt and kiss, but not me. You were right, Roberto, when you said the first time we met that you were a pig. You are!'

Julia threw the menu at him, tossed over a packet of chopsticks as a garnish, and blazed out into the street.

38

When Julia stormed from the restaurant, Roberto stuck the 'borrowed' wallet into his jacket, forgetting it until he was on the plane to Vienna. Unable to work, he decided to look at the cause of his first real row with Julia.

The business cards gave the man's name as Thomas Jessop, funeral director. His residential permit gave his place of birth as England.

Tom Jessop had six photographs in his wallet. Four showed him with a fragile woman and three lean boys – Tom's wife and sons. Two showed a woman whom Roberto dubbed in his own mind a pre-Raphaelite 'stunner': tall, athletic, cobalt eyes, auburn hair. In the first picture she was alone, standing before Michelangelo's David, her glowing femininity challenging the masculine block above her.

In the second photograph, she cradled a baby. Her figure was fuller, still rounded from pregnancy. The infant was tiny, dark.

On the back of the picture, a dedication written in the same hand Roberto had seen on the postcard Julia had received from Tenerife: 'From Angelica and Julia to Daddy, Florence, 1969.'

Two days later, Tom stared at the opened parcel on his work-bench. A new trilby, his wallet, an airline ticket, a hotel booking, a ticket to a recital at the Musikverein and the note 'Meet me here, backstage.'

Tom looked at his apprentice. 'I'm flying to Austria today.' He brushed shavings off his apron, breath tight in his bruised chest. Wise or not, he needed to talk to someone who had Julia's interests in mind. And he'd look round his rivals in Vienna.

Roberto came out of a Vienna sweetshop and saw Tom peering into a window across the street. He jogged across tram lines in the snowy road, candybag in one hand, music score in the other.

They did not shake hands. Still wary, the two turned to take in the shop window: headstones of every size, stone angels, marble crosses. 'Austrian funeral directors are traditional,' Tom remarked, 'but use good materials.'

'And do you work alone, Signore, or as part of a group?'

The question wasn't about headstones. Tom scowled, then reflected why he was here. 'Signor Padovano—'

'Roberto.'

'I think you've good reason to be uneasy.' It was hard not to step back when Roberto's eyes narrowed. 'I'm uneasy.' Tom told what he had overheard in La Fenice. 'What's going on?'

'Why should I tell you anything?' shot back the demand.

'What kind of person do you think I am?'

'Julia's being watched. Someone got into that opera house and stalked her.'

Tom coughed. 'That night in Venice. Was Julia as angry at you as she seemed?'

The singer's features did not soften yet he looked younger, uncertain. His spiky curls brushed the top of the window frame.

He and Julia were no longer easy with each other. He wanted commitment, but was wary of appearing possessive. Besides, there was still his problem in fathering children: that humiliation he'd yet to confess to her. Julia was tense: worried about his safety, Clara's safety, her own career.

And now Francesco Terni was helping Julia and Ruth find

furnished apartment in Milan. Whenever he was away, reflected Roberto with rising irritation, Terni was right in here, hovering around Julia.

Roberto ran a finger down the glass. When singers quarrel 's often a long time before they see each other again. Things an fester.

He shook himself. This wasn't helping. Heavy as a boulder, is hand came down on Tom's shoulder. 'Come, Signore. We an talk on the way to the opera house.' Roberto left Tom's uestion unanswered: any quarrels between him and Julia were personal. 'Tell me why I needn't suspect you.'

Tom found himself being marched between Vienna's quietly etermined shoppers towards the Gothic spire of St Stephen's athedral. As the older man explained how he had impulsively ollowed Julia in Florence, how her turning on him had ntrigued him, the sun disappeared behind the cathedral's reometric-patterned roof tiles. A drizzle of sleet splashed om's hands.

'You started coming to her concerts.' Roberto's flowing tride matching the rhythm of the booming cathedral bell.

'I wanted to see her.'

'Why didn't you telephone, or if you didn't know where ulia was staying, try an approach through her agent?'

'Telling family business to her agent isn't my idea of ommon sense,' snapped Tom. Roberto chuckled.

'Well said! But you'll admit your behaviour's been bizarre.'

'Bizarre?'

'I doubt if a professional would have followed Julia with a ed scarf around his throat. And in Venice you didn't know vhen I was hot on your trail.' Roberto, reflecting on these hings, was amused and relieved: Tom was one threat less.

Tom scowled. 'My wife bought me my scarf just before he died. It's a good warm scarf. Why should I throw it away?'

'No reason, Signore. Just as there is no reason why you hould not give Julia a white rose when you see her.'

Tom, embarrassed, stared at a Turkish street cleaner.

'What you overheard at La Fenice makes sense,' Roberto vas saying. 'Krusak wants Julia but he's also scared of her.'

Roberto stepped into the gutter to give a barrel organist money. 'This di Salvo is a new player, though. I know the name: he's a big opera sponsor. Dislikes publicity. Loves singers.' Roberto was wondering if this was the new secret Julia was hoarding, wondering too – again – about Pietro Terni. How much of his unease against Pietro was because Pietro's son was so clearly interested in Julia? Unhappy at what that made him, Roberto glanced at his companion, noting the bouncy step, the neat ears. Julia's ears were the same shape.

'What's going on?' demanded Tom again. Roberto thought him over-concerned for someone who'd not involved himself before now. Yet the man had taken the trouble to come to Vienna.

So, weaving between svelte Austrian women in tailored suits wielding lethal umbrellas, Tom heard of Clara, Krusak and Scarpia, of the search for war criminals, of Simone's capture and torture, of the beating and threats Julia had endured. Roberto told it bluntly, meaning to shock.

Tom heard with astonishment, then with anger. When Roberto finished, Tom spat out: 'Why, if your father was tortured, aren't you being threatened? Why does it have to be my Julia?'

'Steady!' Roberto caught Tom back as the man was about to step into the path of a white-haired youth carrying a box of Dresden table ware. 'That's how it's turned out. Scarpia knows about Julia and Clara, but not about my connection.'

Roberto drew Tom into a shop doorway as a column of school girls passed along the pavement. It was one worry off his mind, at least, that Simone was safely unknown. But Julia wasn't.

Tom watched the passing girls. 'Maybe if I talked to her . . .'

'You should, Signore. You owe it to Julia.'

Tom's lean face was as grey as his coat. Singing at the Musikverein that evening, Roberto had already run through his recital programme and today's rehearsals at the State Opera House were taking place without him. His afternoon had been free – but no longer, he decided.

'Here.' He ducked into one of Vienna's coffee houses, where

he and Tom were ushered to a window-seat and served with coffee, mineral water and chocolate gateaux. Roberto waited until the waiter had gone. 'How did you meet Julia's mother?'

Tom, dropping his red scarf onto the seat, began to explain.

39

Their time at Lucca over, Julia, Ruth and Francesco, as part of the Galatea opera 'prize', were based at La Scala. Julia and Ruth were now cleaning their newly rented Milan flat.

Julia was polishing the wooden floor, her thoughts far from opera or the new flat. Angelica was still refusing to send her Guy's diary. So far, she had found it impossible to decode Guy's papers, or to trace through the Church the present whereabouts of Abramo Coletta and his curate.

She shook her head. With the demands of her normal singing training, the concert at La Fenice in Venice, the move to this flat, then new rehearsals at La Scala, she had been able to snatch only the odd free moment.

Roberto, trapped into recitals, rehearsals and performances in Austria and Germany, could do nothing for the moment either. He had hired a researcher to dig into the Berlin Document Centre files, to see if there was more evidence against Krusak. The researcher found only the account of the massacre of Mutta.

'It's not enough,' Roberto said on the phone.

'I know that!' Julia answered, frustrated by his absence.

'Fair enough,' Roberto said briskly. 'Tell your flat-finder about it – I'm sure he'll have some better ideas.'

'Who?'

'Terni – I notice he's always around these days, bubbling with advice.'

'Don't be ridiculous!' One of those awkward silences had followed, a silence heightened by the phone line. Venice and the accusations made there was always between them: both were inhibited by it, by separation, by their inability to bury fully their quarrel. And with Roberto in Vienna, and Julia tied up in Milan, the whereabouts of Umberto Gasparini, the final partisan of Guy's Red-Headed League, and of Scarpia himself looked likely to remain a mystery.

Neither could Julia understand the motivation of her mysterious protector, di Salvo. When she'd read Roberto's letter, Julia had been furious. Never mind that here was someone who wanted her safe: to Julia, this di Salvo was another obsessed stranger. Nor did she know even what he looked like. Snatching time when she was supposed to be practising, Julia spent backbreaking hours poring over newspapers, but to no end. Di Salvo, who most recently had been involved with Krusak himself and another man in a thousand million lire art deal, was never photographed.

Camera-shy, concluded Julia wryly, like Simone.

The elder Padovano was another mystery. He had lied to Roberto for years – by default, Roberto said in his father's defence, but Simone had not willingly admitted that he came from Castel San Martino. Had he kept silent solely through shame? The war trials had been the trigger for his nightmares – did Simone feel threatened by what might emerge?

According to Clara, Spoletta was young, with a good voice. Francesco Vincenti had two singing pupils in the 1940s, Sprint and Simone. Simone, the younger youth, had been the one with the greater promise. Simone had told Roberto that himself.

'You should hear Francesco and me sniping at each other.' Ruth's words reminded Julia of where she was, what she was doing.

Julia applied more floor polish. 'How do you get on with Bianca and Pietro?' Julia had not forgotten what Roberto had told her about Pietro. She was still trying to reconcile the idea of Pietro associating with Krusak. It was a business relationship, but even so – Julia shook her head.

'Fine.' Ruth brushed back her gold hair. 'Bianca makes me laugh with her "more American than American" routine, but Pietro's rather cute.' She crouched to move her kneeling-pad forward. 'Have you met Elizabetta Terni? Weird woman. When Francesco mentioned that he and I were thinking of sharing an apartment she took to her bed. Francesco had to promise to find a separate flat before she got up again.' Ruth's long hair fell past her face again. 'Francesco's mother has to know that we sleep together, but it must be done *secretly*.'

'Tell Francesco I'll take the single flat off his hands,' suggested Julia, glad that she could help someone.

'That won't do, some busybody in Milan would be on the phone in two minutes sharp – about you and him swapping flats.'

'Ugh!' Used to Ruth's puns, Julia threw her polishing rag at the taller girl.

'Roberto's dad any easier these days?' Ruth slid the cloth back across the floor. Julia had said nothing, but Simone's hostility could be read like an open score.

Julia put her tongue between her teeth, then grinned. 'I don't think he cares for mezzos.' She began to buff as far as her arms would reach. There was no point in thinking about Simone, who was implacable.

Without any kind of direct confrontation, Roberto's father made it clear he disapproved of her and Roberto's relationship simply by never mentioning Roberto. At La Scala where he and now Julia were based, Simone treated her as a stranger, and only acknowledged her when she was with other musicians.

'I don't like him. He leers.'

'Ruth!' Julia laughed as Ruth added, 'Well, he does. And how come when he's at La Scala *you* can never find a pianist? Francesco and I do all right; there's always one for us. And look at that blowup a couple of days back, when a missing prop turned up in your coat pocket: a prop Simone just happened to notice there ...'

Julia shrugged. 'It was only Cinderella's fake diadem; no one could possibly have thought I'd want to steal it.' Still, principal or not, she'd been called up to the main office and asked to give an account of how the diadem had come to be in her pocket: difficult, since Julia didn't know how herself. Also, whatever her own suspicions, she could hardly accuse a respected viola player in the La Scala orchestra – Roberto's father! – of palming the thing onto her.

'I still think Simone's trying to turn the stage hands against you,' said Ruth decisively.

'How are you getting on with your part in *Cinderella*?' Julia wanted to change the subject, and she was genuinely interested. She was fond of Ruth, delighted to see how every day the American was growing in confidence – even while rehearsing as Tisbe, an Ugly Sister.

Just a month ago, Ruth would have accepted Julia's changing the direction of the conversation. Now she said, 'Nuts to Tisbe. I haven't got Roberto's father glaring daggers each time he sees me – nor psychotic fans trailing after me.'

'No need to be envious,' answered Julia easily. 'You will.' She had passed off her brush in La Fenice as a misunderstanding with an over-ardent fan. Ditto when Ruth mentioned the man with the red scarf. Weird fans were nothing new.

The intercom buzzed. 'Julia? It's Frankie. Can I come up?'

'Sure! Ruth's here,' Julia called back. She grinned at Ruth. 'I'll make some tea.' She disappeared into the kitchen.

Ruth went into the small lobby to open the door, pleasure over Francesco's arrival blending with disappointment. *Julia? It's Frankie*. Not *Ruth? It's Francesco*. She thought she and Francesco were going out – staying in, more like – but Francesco has flexible ideas when it came to fidelity. 'Hey, I'm a man,' he replied, when Ruth became upset at his courting of Julia, 'what's a little flirting?'

Except it wasn't flirting. The kisses, the rapid-fire Italian jokes Ruth couldn't quite grasp, the presents: flowers for her, yes, but a red rose for Julia. He made no secret of his admiration, bordering on infatuation, for the Anglo-Italian.

'How's my glorious girl?' Francesco wrapped his arms around her hips, lifting Ruth right off her feet. 'I love you in dresses.' His hand stroked.

When he touched her like that Ruth wanted to drag him off to bed. The smiling devil knew that.

An arm round Ruth's waist, Francesco drew her into the main room. 'Here.' He tossed Julia a parcel. 'This came for you, care of me.' The tenor gave his most appealing grin.

'Pour the tea,' said Julia absently. Hoping for a package from her mother, this small parcel rang a peal of alarm through her. 'I'll hack this with kitchen scissors.'

The parcel was malleable. No scent. No wires. Julia turned it over. Surely explosive wouldn't be this soft. Keeping her hands steady, she dug the scissors into the padded bag.

A globular mass wrapped in cling film spilled onto the kitchen sink top. 'Good appetite!' the message stuck on the red mass read. 'Next time, the heart could be yours.'

Fighting nausea, Julia shovelled it into the bin and escaped Ruth and Francesco by saying someone had sent her a fantastic shower gel and she couldn't wait to try it.

Someone had known she could be reached through Francesco.

Bianca Terni.

Pietro Terni.

Jan Krusak.

Simone Padovano.

The names came to Julia at once. Others followed: di Salvo. The unidentified man with the red scarf. Naturally Roberto and Clara, although they could be discounted.

Ten minutes later, Ruth rapped on the bathroom door. 'Come on, Cinders! We've five minutes to get back to La Scala!'

Feeling vaguely unclean, Julia turned off the shower, dressed and sprayed herself with the first perfume she found.

A man entered the practice room and held out a card. Julia glanced at it. 'I won't see him.'

'If this is inconvenient, Signorina, the gentleman will call on your grandmother.' The stranger held the door open.

* * *

The silver car was the first stretch limo Julia had been in, but she was in no mood to luxuriate over the personal bar, black windows, or gleaming interior. On the back seat lay an open box, a white dress pleated between sheets of tissue paper.

Nosing the car over cobbles and tram lines, the driver put up the barrier between himself and his passenger and bore them away through twilit Milanese fog towards the Sforza Castle.

As that symbol of domination towered out of the mist, a voice issued from hidden speakers.

'Good evening, Julia. I use your first name because of the difference between us in age.

'Open the cabinet beside you: inside is a poster. "Julia Rochfort to star every night as Rossini's *Cinderella*." This can be your future: not the three or four nights you have been offered. You have the talent, I supply the impetus.

'What can be given can also be withdrawn. My company supplies La Scala with sponsorship. Remember Bazzini? Those who betray me are always punished. Wear the dress, Princess.'

'Go to hell!' muttered Julia, punching the dress box. The tape faded away as Julia, coiled in the seat farthest from the driver, waiting the moment when she could strike back.

Krusak's offices overlooked Milan's stock exchange. His penthouse was a showpiece of classic design. Julia and the driver – who retrieved the dress box she left in the car – waited in a vast room complete with an Adam fireplace and eighteenth-century Chinese wallpaper. Seated on an elegant chaise-longue, Julia was offered champagne by a male secretary.

Julia refused to be a puppet. No thank you, she would keep her coat. Could she have a cappuccino instead of champagne? When the coffee was brought she sipped it, aware Krusak was making her wait.

Twenty minutes ground by. Julia studied her music. The driver was called into Krusak's suite. Tapping her feet, Julia waited. The driver emerged.

Ten minutes later, Julia rose from the couch. Placing her cup and saucer on the desk, she nodded to the secretary.

Too late, the man realised she wasn't about to powder her
ose. 'Signorina, you mustn't . . .'

Krusak's office was a shrine of high Catholic baroque. An
namelled crucifix hung on the wall above a heavy spiral-
egged gold desk which seemed to stretch to infinity.

Spread on the desk was the white dress.

The walls were studded with ikons, the armchairs opulent
s a cardinal's throne. Cigar smoke billowed like incense.

Krusak was standing at one of the room's lancet windows,
tained glass haloing the grey in his hair.

'I wondered how long it would be before you barged in.'

Julia spoke quickly. 'Keep away from my family.'

'Certainly,' Krusak was amused. 'You think I admire the
rune when I can have the peach?'

Revolted, Julia stepped back. She dragged one of the heavy
rmchairs from the huge desk and sat on it. 'You're as arrogant
ow, Signore, as you were as a young man.'

The shaft went home, but another draw on his cigar
estored Krusak's colour. 'I am disappointed, Princess. You
orce me to be strong where I would be gentle.'

'Don't delude yourself,' replied Julia. 'You enjoy it.'

Krusak glided to the long table, stubbed his cigar out on
he silk dress. 'Very well! Let us keep it strong. I will put you
ut of La Scala. I will see that you are withdrawn from every
roduction. I will take all my business sponsorship from that
pera house and inform everyone – musicians, singers, stage
ands – that you are responsible. You know I can do this.'

Julia said nothing, struggling to keep her temper. The
eople Krusak had so casually dismissed, the employees of
a Scala, why should they suffer because of a man's obsession?

'I don't understand, Signore. You're rich, well-bred,
andsome –' she said the word without inflection – 'Why me?'

Krusak, every contour of his body accentuated by the tight
rown suit, came weaving round the chairs. His sinewy arms
hot out, gripping the arms of Julia's seat.

'The pleasure of your company is all I ask. And one more
hing.' His fine eyes blazed. 'Stop probing into matters which
o not concern you.'

Julia lowered her head. She was trembling with anger. Krusak wanted her to be his mistress, to give up the search – how did he know about that? She wanted to break out, threaten in return, although she knew it would be a fatal blunder. Until she or Roberto obtained more evidence regarding Krusak's involvement in the massacre of the villagers of Mutta, Krusak himself should know nothing.

Krusak leaned down, brushing her forehead with cold lips. 'Passionate anger, passionate love . . .' Krusak's mouth sought hers.

Julia lashed out, catching Krusak in the chest, pushing him out of her way. Scarpia sang those exact words in *Tosca*.

Krusak as Scarpia – could it be?

'Walk out and you will regret it.'

Julia turned. Krusak settled in the chair, long fingers draped over its gold arms.

She walked towards the seated figure. Somehow, she had to buy time. Antonio di Stefano, sole survivor of the Mutta atrocity, had so far been impossible to trace, but she knew where Pietro Terni lived. Reluctant as she was to stir up old memories for Pietro, she must talk to Francesco's father, persuade him to speak about the night Krusak tortured him. And discover once and for all, why Pietro had been willing to meet the Croatian after the war.

If not Pietro, there were Elsa Dontini and her sister, the German twins forced to act as interrogators.

Krusak as Scarpia – could it be?

Here was a man who had shot Vittorio at a party, who had ordered his troops to murder two hundred people, who had burned Pietro Terni, terrorised the German twins. Oh, yes, it was possible, thought Julia, shuddering.

Clara and Guy had been driven around for some time in a truck. What if the truck had passed Nazi headquarters and Krusak – as 'Scarpia' – had been taken aboard? Perhaps he had been in two places that night . . . Yet why would Krusak not want to question Clara and Guy in the official headquarters? Had his obsession for Clara prompted him to take them somewhere even more private?

That left the singing. Clara had told her that two live singers were in the chamber that night, but perhaps she had been mistaken: her grandmother had been interrogated, she had experienced intense fear and pain, where all difference between illusion and reality had been distorted. A record, then. A record and Spoletta to sing live. Vincenti or any of the others could have whispered Scarpia's questions in the local dialect.

Or perhaps it could be that Krusak, with his impeccable German and precise Italian, his flair for language, had been equally impressive in the San Martino della Croce dialect.

Swift thoughts, rushing through Julia's head as she walked towards her enemy.

'I apologise, Signore. You startled me. I was once shut in a cupboard as a child, a punishment for lying: I don't like to feel trapped.' She held out her hand. 'With your permission, may we continue this discussion outside? I've yet to see the Brera Gallery.'

Krusak, smiling, buzzed down to the lobby. They were leaving.

40

Bianca dragged on an American cigarette as she settled at her computer. She kept sensitive material at home in her bedroom, on floppy disks which appeared blank, their contents hidden by a simple command.

The most dangerous files were on the third disk from the back of the box. Bianca slotted the unmarked disk into her computer, typed the 'check disc' instruction which would reveal any hidden files on it.

The disk was blank.

Bianca sagged in her swivel seat. Di Salvo! His men had been sent here and they had removed the disk. They could break in and out of the houses and the occupants be none the wiser.

'Wait a minute!' Bianca sat up. Di Salvo's men would have taken the goddam box. 'Let's be systematic about this.'

She found what she was looking for on the fifth disk. As she typed instructions to bring up her hidden 'Scarpia' file, Bianca coughed in relief. She'd put the thing back in the wrong order.

It was a mistake. No one else knew what she was doing. Sure, Papà had computers at his gallery, but he didn't know how to use them. Pietro left technical stuff to the younger staff.

Just a mistake.

Right now life was unsettling. She talked to Francesco most days, a way of checking on Julia. She was meant to be protecting di Salvo's mezzo: following and making Julia her friend.

The following bit Bianca had already tried, especially after Julia's Venice concert. Di Salvo had phoned Bianca about that one, demanding to know why she hadn't been around when Julia 'accidentally' fell down a flight of stairs in La Fenice.

'Signore di Salvo, I knew you'd be there.' She was forgiven, but next time would be different.

A tedious week ensued, trailing Julia in Milan. Opera house, flat, shops, newspaper records – Bianca wished she could have seen what records. The flat Julia shared with Ruth, the opera house with La Scala employees. She wasn't alone long enough for any attacker to strike.

Bianca decided to take a chance and leave Julia to her own devices. Bianca was trying to trace people Emilio Gucci had mentioned. So far Umberto Gasparini, who had risked death to listen to Allied radio, remained unaccounted for. Gasparini had moved from the Croce region during the fifties. Where had he gone? Bianca's contacts in the tax and emigration offices were working on that.

'Friendship' would have to wait – Julia was preoccupied. Lately, Francesco had been full of how Julia and Padovano seemed to be going through a rough patch. Frankie hadn't exactly gloated, but his voice had been alive with hope. Crazy Francesco, when he had Ruth.

As for Julia being preoccupied, Bianca could appreciate the feeling. The more Bianca dug for Scarpia, the more compelling the search became. Julia with her opera was continually having to break off, restart. Bianca, with her journalism contacts, had more time and opportunity.

The crazy thing was that when she had interviewed victims and suspects, this file would stay in its box. The file was insurance, protection for her family.

Bianca blew smoke into the cupid wall-light above her head. Living at her parents' meant rent-free living space without questions: Elizabetta fussed over Francesco.

Bianca rose, crossing to the window. Papà might call her 'duchess' but he too had tagged her as wild: weird clothes, odd working hours, strange men.

Strange men. Bianca turned to the flickering screen. She'd called on Emilio Gucci. No, Gucci assured her, Signorina Double-Barrelled hadn't been back. Scarpia? His father had mentioned him, but Gucci couldn't enlarge on what he'd already told her.

Flapping photographs round Gucci's neighbours in the high-rise, Bianca found no one recognised Julia, but several women said 'Yes, that was definitely the man they'd seen a week or so back with Emilio. Striking, isn't he?'

Bianca dipped down to the keyboard and typed: 'Roberto Padovano – searching with Julia for Scarpia?'

She stepped back, lobbing her cigarette stub out of the open window. She'd known Emilio Gucci for eight years but until this year had known nothing about Scarpia –despite Scarpia's impact on Gucci's family.

Emilio had already given her something, though: two more to trace and these suspects: villains not heroes. The priest and curate of Croce, whom Gucci suspected of informing for the Germans. Using Vatican press contacts, Bianca had traced them. Both were alive.

Abramo Coletta was a Dominican friar. His curate had left the priesthood after the war. Bianca's contact mentioned the curate undergoing a 'spiritual crisis' which had left him unable to take his final vows.

Something had happened in Croce during the war. Something which had, according to Gucci's wilder implications, not only involved but divided members of Julia's family, set Clara and Mario Scudieri against each other. Something which had drawn in Gucci's father, the priest of Croce, and his curate. Something which affected the curate so deeply he had left the priesthood. Something which always came back to the man Julia was looking for, the man di Salvo wanted to keep hidden, Scarpia.

The curate was Michele Bozzi. Bozzi had gone to America and vanished, but Bianca's Vatican contact came up with a photograph. It proved what she had begun to suspect.

A robin twittered outside her window, making Bianca start
Her hair was now as red as the bird's breast: she'd dyed it a
few days ago, hoping the colour would give her new
confidence.

Confidence is a tough thing to lose when you're thirty-six
She and Pietro were members of the 'family', but that wouldn't
prevent Tancredi di Salvo from dumping her father if Julia
released some juicy details of Scarpia into the world. Pietro
was the perfect fall-guy: similar in looks to di Salvo, the same
age, living in the same village through the war, and bound by
the 'family's' code of silence.

Bianca shuddered. One fading photograph had made her
world even more of a lie than it was already.

'The Abbot suggested I see you as an act of charity. Tomorrow
I leave for a closed order in Rome, so this is the last opportunity
I will have to speak to anyone regarding those unfortunate
events in Croce.'

Had she not been entering church Bianca would have
cheered. Abramo Coletta was the perfect witness; willing to
talk and then silenced, with no guilt on her part.

Dipping fingers into a stone scallop shell, she crossed
herself with holy water. Her hair was covered by a headscarf
To the Abbot and to Coletta, she was a relative of one of
Scarpia's victims. The Abbot had treated her gently. Coletta
now Brother Abramo, was regarding her with a humility close
to reverence.

The former priest of Croce was small, neat, white-haired
A beard covered his cheeks, hiding the mole on his chin. From
an old seminary photograph her Vatican contact had sent
Bianca knew that at Croce Coletta had been clean-shaven.

'The Abbot told me your name was Maria, but I know
nothing more of you. Will you tell me something of yourself?'

His voice, muffled from disuse, was still melodious. Bianca
hesitated, astonished to find her reluctance stemmed from a
childhood scruple about lying in church. Alarmed to find
another chink in her cool armour, Bianca turned towards the

high altar with its six gold candles and golden crucifix.

'I will tell no one of our conversation.'

There it was, thought Bianca, an invitation to spin any yarn she liked. If Julia or Roberto spoke later to the Abbot he would not be able to tell them any more than that Maria Stella, a red-headed woman with horn-rimmed spectacles, had already spoken with Coletta about the suffering caused to her family by a wartime Fascist.

Around her the church, the resting place of Saint Dominic, smelt of pear drops from the burning candles. Outside, power drills and sirens, the bustle of Bologna. Inside, sunlight slanting through the upper windows, crystal chandeliers and vases of white lilies. A strange place to speak of torture.

Yet – here the irony which freed Bianca's tongue – part of the Dominican order had developed into the Inquisition which had used the rack against suspected heretics.

'I'm the granddaughter of Mario Scudieri.' Bianca lifted her head, looking at the marble tomb of Saint Dominic.

She sensed Brother Abramo start, saw his hand lift towards her dyed red hair. She guessed no further explanation would be needed, and fell into step with the former priest as the man wheeled about, marching from the church.

They sat on a bench in the pebbled square. The day was fine; Bologna smelt today of baking bread. Brother Abramo began to speak.

San Martino della Croce had been his first and last ministry. The Contessa, Clara Scudieri, treated him kindly. Mario Scudieri came to church but never to confession.

Then came the day sacred to Our Lady of the Vines, 10th June, 1944.

Bianca learned what Krusak had done at that feast. Even to her, shooting a man at a feast in the midst of a host of onlookers was extravagantly grotesque. No wonder that her father, present at the feast and witnessing Vittorio's murder, disliked Krusak. No wonder Krusak wished to keep his wartime past hidden.

When Coletta apologised for recounting what she probably already knew, Bianca demurred. 'Go on.'

Coletta sighed. 'Everything which happened then comes under the seal of the confessional.'

'Scarpia confessed to silence you? Why, if you knew nothing before this?' Brother Abramo suddenly took on new possibilities as a suspect, Bianca decided. During the war, many priests worked against Fascism, but a few had been followers of Mussolini, often spurred on by rabid anti-semitism. Perhaps the priest of Croce, who 'chatted' to the Germans, had been one.

'Me?' The man stabbed his fingers into his chest. 'You think I was involved? No! The man confessed because it suited his vanity: he took a delight in spreading evil.

'He came to me the next day, seemingly in great spiritual distress. I did not know then what he had done. The village was reeling with the disappearance of the Contessa and Mario Scudieri – no one knew where they had gone, what had happened in the night after the feast.

'He confessed too because of the involvement in his group of someone close to me, someone whose night-time absences he believed I might suspect. He told me this himself, and corrupted my innocence also.'

'The person close to you – that wouldn't have been Michele Bozzi?' asked Bianca. Coletta blinked.

'That too is under the seal,' he muttered.

'Your curate confessed to *you*? Why did you hear it? You could have refused and gone to the police.'

'He was in distress; I thought him repentant. I could not refuse, do you understand?' The former priest of Croce shuddered on the bench. 'He was dear to me, like a brother.'

'So they duped you.' Bianca was sickened by the man's naivety: a few tears and the priest of Croce was gagged by his own calling. A neat trick, one she could almost admire, but not quite. This wasn't clean and quick, like a gun. Scarpia had used and then warped Coletta's faith, his wish to do good, his feelings for his own associate.

Coletta lowered his tonsured head. 'When my curate had told me everything, I knew how much I had failed as a priest, how tainted the village had become. Envy, cruelty, vanity –

all had played a part. The worst to me was that the man you
know as "Scarpia" had found the ground ripe. Even those in
my closest care. It had been going on for weeks. And Father
Angelo . . . but I can say no more.'

'Why did you leave?' demanded Bianca. 'Why didn't you
stay in Croce to fight the good fight?'

Coletta's narrow shoulders jerked at her mockery. 'The
shock, the betrayal, my failure . . . I had a nervous breakdown,
and was transferred to a monastery. After the war, the church
decided I was unfitted for pastoral work.'

Scarpia had accomplished that too, thought Bianca. 'What
kind of man was Scarpia?'

'He was a small-natured man desperate for glory. He wanted
respect: more than that, fear. Like others, he was a hanger-
on of the Fascists: almost anyone could set up or be part of
any of the private "special police forces" which existed then
in occupied Italy. He was also bewitched by the glamour of
the Italian–German SS. I think they used him in their minor
operations, to spy for them. He recruited for them in various
localities in and around Bologna. Other things he did come
under the seal, as does his name.'

Abramo Coletta interlocked his fingers, watched an escaped
balloon drift away from a wailing child in the square. Vespas
cutting across corners nibbled at the territory of this
pedestrian island.

'So Scarpia as the region's "Top Interrogator" was
propaganda?' Bianca fought flippancy and then decided it didn't
matter; no one else would see Coletta. 'He was only a part-
timer?'

'If you like. Certainly there was some jealousy in branches
of the Italian SS for the more notorious activities of the Koch
gang in Milan: I learned that myself from German officers,
who were amused by it. As propaganda, your "Scarpia" will
have been useful. But let us not forget that the man caused
real suffering to his victims.'

The reproof made Bianca blush.

'He always wanted to be other than what he was,' Coletta
went on. 'If he had been a full SS member, he would have

wanted to be a spy, bound by no routine. As it was, I believe he sensed the military men's contempt for their own informers. Besides, most of the "special police" relied ultimately on high-level protectors. He would have done anything to win their recognition. When the chance came to impress, as he thought it, that desire turned him into a monster.'

Always on the fringe, thought Bianca uneasily. She didn't want to identify with Scarpia. More importantly, would any of her new knowledge show in her face the next time she met di Salvo?

'And Mario Scudieri? What did Scarpia do to him?'

'You must not ask what I cannot answer: the secrets of the confession are inviolate.' A muscle jabbed in his face. 'He died quickly,' he muttered.

'Was he tortured?'

'Talk to Claudia and Nuccia Rasella,' Coletta finished abruptly. 'They are not bound by the confessional.'

A phone call to her source in the tax office traced the Rasellas. Both were living in Ravenna. Phoning each sister, presenting herself in her genuine occupation as a journalist, Bianca found Claudia and Nuccia eager to talk. Both refused Bianca's offer of money, they only needed the chance to tell their story, to be believed. They had tried to speak to the nuns at the orphanage, but the nuns had accused them of lying like Judas, like the Jews they were . . .

That night, Bianca transferred Nuccia's and Claudia's telephone conversations from her pocket recorder onto her secret file. What she saw on the screen shook the foundations of her life, her clean and violent solutions. Money and the getting of money were no longer real.

Nuccia Rasella: 'I was ten when Davide Patuzzi denounced my widowed mother to the authorities. We were the only Jews in the second hamlet near Croce. In the past the Contessa had helped my mother, but the Contessa did not help us then: maybe she did not know what had happened; many people "disappeared" during the war. And Davide Patuzzi hated us because we were Jewish.'

Claudia Rasella: 'Men in the black shirts of the Fascist militia took us to Bologna. They had meant to hand us to the Germans, but one officer said, "Why not let Scarpia have them? He's based near Croce these days: it'll be home from home for them. Scarpia'll get rid of them quicker than the Germans. Tell him the mother's withholding information: that'll keep him and his group happy." So we were blindfolded and hauled into another truck.'

Nuccia Rasella: 'We were blindfolded, Mamma included. Claudia was eight, the youngest. They started on her first. And all the time there was music and between the music whispered questions. Asking where the Allies were going to drop weapons and food for the partisans, where and when they were going to parachute in troops, who the other members of Mamma's group were. If Davide Patuzzi was obsessed with our being Jewish, the Whisperer was convinced we were working for the resistance.'

Claudia Rasella: 'It didn't matter what our mother told those people, the same questions kept coming back. When she gave an answer they didn't like, someone burned me with a cigarette.'

Nuccia Rasella: 'We heard the shot which killed Mamma. Then we heard them arguing softly. One man wanted to save us because we were only children. "Do they know us?" he hissed. "And which of you wants to do it?" '

Claudia Rasella: 'The man who spoke for us won. They gagged us and gave us to him. He took us on horseback to his home. He gave us medicine to make us sleep.

'When I woke, my blindfold and gag were gone and I was lying in the nave of Ponte church. My sister was with me.'

Nuccia Rasella: 'We were taken to a convent in

Bologna. The nuns hid us from the Nazis – although the nuns didn't believe our story, they looked after us.

'Because of what had happened to her, Claudia would not talk for months. We were too frightened to show anyone our injuries and so hid them.'

Simple, direct language, as though they were still children. Sitting on the edge of her bed in her darkened room, Bianca thought of herself at eight years old, and began to cry.

41

Julia and Krusak were strolling through the Brera gallery. Outside, rain streaked the pavements, collecting in huge puddles in the gutters.

A word from Krusak had opened the gallery. The man was accustomed to being obeyed. She must play on that assumption, carefully. Krusak would recognise fake emotion.

The secret of acting is not artifice but reality. That was the thing Julia shrunk from – she had to find something she genuinely admired about Krusak. Yet if he were Scarpia, he had blinded Clara, tortured and killed others.

'Tell me what you are thinking.' Krusak put his hands on her shoulders. Well-shaped hands, Julia noted.

'That the popes in this room look so marvellously shifty.' She turned her head as though it was Roberto behind her, glimpsing a night porter switching off lights in the long room they had passed through.

Krusak pursed his lips then unexpectedly grinned. Humour was a start, thought Julia, suppressing her revulsion. 'Show me your favourite picture.'

Krusak's choice was a surprise. Two small paintings by Bernardo Bellotto. Serene blue light and country landscapes.

'Astonished, Julia?'

'They are what I would have chosen.' A dimple quivered in her cheek. 'But which is it? You can't have two.'

The lustre in the man's eyes deepened as he suppressed a

smile. Julia suddenly found herself wanting to make him really laugh; thaw him out a little.

'You see, I am not so bad.' Krusak took her wrist, pointed her rigid fingers to the left-hand picture. 'That one.' His fingers traced round the curve of her thumb. Julia's hand twitched, fingers closing for an instant around his.

'Dance with me?' asked Krusak. 'Clara and I learned a different dance together, but this kind, Julia, can be our own.'

He laughed now, as Julia recoiled, dragging her against him. 'You're not the first Scudieri female to find me attractive.'

Cold fury blasted through Julia at Krusak's smug implication that he and Clara had been lovers; fury followed by disgust, but she managed to restrain the first, basic impulse to strike Krusak's hands away. She had to buy time; justice took longer than vengeance. Yet her skin crawled at the implications of the man's claim: that Clara had ever been attracted to *this* man. And if it were in any way true, and if Krusak were Scarpia, then he had tortured his own lover . . .

The memory of walking out of Gucci's, the wasted chance there, saved Julia, gave her the control she needed. Besides, she could do better than that with Krusak. 'Really, Signore?' She relaxed in his arms. 'Wish fulfilment at your age?'

His saturnine expression did not change, although Julia sensed she was drawing blood. Lower, his head came, his breath hot, glowing eyes dominating his features. Heart hammering Julia waited, suspended on a breath.

'Dinner, I think.' Krusak suddenly put her from him. Deftly he refastened the button of her blouse which had slid open. 'One of the advantages of age, Princess, is that you wait patiently for your goodnight kiss.'

Julia ate little. She and Krusak dined in Milan's most exclusive restaurant, and the food on her plate was tasteless and slimy. Feeling exposed in her jeans, she sat amongst women dressed in designer gowns and men wearing their ulcers on their frowning expressions. Krusak had done that on purpose. He spoke of opera in a raised voice, as though expecting diners at other tables to listen. Which they did, to Julia's seething anger.

For her, the climax of this wretched evening came when, at the moment Krusak presented her with a freesia corsage – goodness knows from where he had obtained it – and kissed her hand, Simone Padovano walked into the room. Witnessing the scene, Roberto's father settled at the first empty table and demanded a waiter to bring him a telephone.

'Who's that?' Francesco darted out of Ruth's bedroom as Julia entered the flat. 'Hey, what's he done to you?' Fizzing with anger, Francesco bounded out of the door. As he was naked, Julia didn't think he'd be long in scrambling back.

Krusak hadn't given or received more than a goodnight kiss and the thing she had been dreading all evening – how to answer Krusak's demand that she stop her search and become his mistress – hadn't arisen. Never had one of her nosebleeds been more propitiously timed. Krusak had backed off instantly.

'Does this often happen?' His features warped in revulsion.

Julia, nose sunk in her hankie, nodded. Ever since Simone had entered that restaurant her head had started to pound. She couldn't even feel much relief when Krusak muttered, 'I'll bid you good night then,' and disappeared. Any other time, any other man, and Julia would have laughed.

Francesco slammed the door, prominent cheekbones pinched with rage. 'If I'd caught him,' he was saying, Bolognese accent more pronounced than Julia had ever heard it. Julia, grateful for his swift leaping to her defence, even when not needed, found herself staring. He was naked, and in his concern for her had forgotten he was naked, and she did not want to stop looking at him. Francesco was a blond negative of herself, compact, vital. She wanted, just for an instant, to touch the vulnerable fuzz on his chest, to feel its softness.

Frankie wasn't possessive: life was a limpid, sparkling surface to him. And she, Julia, was solemn enough for them both.

To live with that easy smile would be simple. And Francesco would marry her.

Was that what she wanted from Roberto, marriage?

Julia blinked, astonished and alarmed by her own thoughts. Francesco touched her arm and she wrestled with two immediate conflicting desires: both to throw off his hand and to bring that hand and its warm, obliging body closer. Francesco was young; he was her age. Krusak's maturity was sour in her mouth. She didn't want to be alone tonight. In the dim lobby Francesco glowed like a stained glass hero. The pull of his attraction was never tauter than now.

Julia closed her eyes, opened them. 'Go to bed, Francesco,' she murmured, sweeping the tenor a swift downward glance to remind him of his condition.

Clamping hands belatedly over the relevant parts, mumbling apologies, Francesco made as stylish an exit as was possible.

Julia walked to the fridge in the darkened kitchen. She couldn't stop thinking about Simone, his childish maliciousness in calling for a telephone: no doubt to inform Roberto about seeing her with Krusak.

'Oh, God!' She'd dropped the carton. Frozen, Julia watched it pump over the floor, disappearing into blackness where the fridge light did not reach. That was her and Roberto at present, in the darkness, out of reach. Francesco was a fantasy, a temptation. The commitment she wanted from Roberto was altogether tougher.

Julia groped to the sink for a cloth. Somewhere in mopping up black sheens of orange juice, the trembling began.

It was morning. She'd fallen asleep at the kitchen table poring over Guy's papers – anything to stop thinking about Roberto . . . Francesco . . . Krusak . . . Roberto . . .

'Julia?' Ruth, peering through gold hair, pink dressing-gown undone, was concerned when she saw the figure hunched over the table. When Julia remembered what she had felt about Francesco last night, she couldn't meet the American's friendly blue eyes.

'Stay home,' said Ruth. 'You don't look too good.'

A day alone in the flat, jumping every time the phone went, hoping it was Roberto, wondering what he would say. Today,

s bad luck would have it, she couldn't contact him: he was
oing a recital on a barge-cruiser in the Danube. Simone would
ave made the most of what he had seen at the restaurant last
ight. And then there was Krusak, who, sooner rather than
ter, would remember that he had yet to receive an answer
om her.

Julia nodded, resigned. 'I'll stay home,' she said.

ow she was back at the kitchen table, Guy's notes spread
at in the hazy light. Painkillers had drawn the teeth of her
eadache, a shower her tiredness. She raised her head,
lancing at the lobby phone, wondering if she should ring
ietro Terni, ask if she might speak to him about Krusak. In
ıe end she decided to keep the phone line clear, returning to
er reading.

She had finally broken her grandfather's code last night.
nce she had realised that the recurring words 'YME' and
K' were the English 'the' and 'of' respectively, the five-letter
ıift in the alphabet which Guy had used became clear. The
tter 'E' made no sense in this scale of fifths – A becomes F,
becomes G, and so on – because her grandfather had left it
ith the same meaning.

Now the opening 'LZD AFQESYNSE WTHMKTWY', made
ɛnse as 'Guy Valentine Rochfort', and the first sentence read:
iuy Valentine Rochfort writes this account of the resistance
the hope that one day it and other personal papers will
ake sense of the strange, distressing and contradictory
rents which can occur in war.'

More disturbingly, the next paragraph observed: 'Things
man may say to no one, even his wife, are recorded here. I
ake no apology for this being an intimate memoir: the other
ırtisan groups, the way we and they operate – those details
can carry easily in my head. Being vital, they will remain
ere. But for more personal matters . . . There is no one else
can trust as much as these mute pages.'

She read at random, where the entries were short, so a list
stantly claimed her attention. The names were abbreviated;
e first three letters, and an initial. As with the code it was

not unduly complex, Guy had clearly been concerned only t
buy some time for word to reach his group if he or the diar
were taken. Julia was sure that written in full the list woul
be:

Masone, Pietro – Good	Dontini, Nino – Good
Stefano, herbalist – Doubtful	Respini, Giovanni – Goo
Patuzzi – No	Respini, Gina – Good
Father Angelo – Good	Gucci, Carlo – Good
Fioretti (twins) – Possible	Mauro the forger – Goo
Gasparini, Umberto – Good	Vincenti, Francesco – N
Father Abramo – Wavering	
Celere, Cesare – Good	

Guy had divided the list, with, on the left, ordinary villager
from Croce and Castel. On the right, Nino Dontini, Francesc
Vincenti and Gina Respini, singers, had been listed separatel
So had Carlo Gucci and Mauro the forger, the man who ha
provided Guy with false papers as Mario Scudieri. Mauro mu
have helped many partisans, yet Julia continually forgot hi
because the forger had not been a member of Guy's group.

Yet Mauro had disappeared in Bologna in April 194
probably tortured and murdered by Scarpia.

Further down the page were two more names, given almos
in full, and with fuller descriptions.

'Bozzi is dangerous. He is not fitted for the church. H
prowls around Croce, clamped down like a champagne cork
What wine will emerge when that cork is drawn? He could b
a great asset, but he has no ties here; he could sacrifice himse
and many others for the grand gesture.

'Simone P. – Strange and rather sad. What can one mak
of him? I sense more than the public face. His youth make
him appear simple. He has been honest with me, and yet . .

'He has not been seen in the other villages. I will wait. Ther
is probably nothing to fear.'

Bozzi. The curate's name. From Guy's brief portrait Juli
shivered. Bozzi had been a coiled spring. Great good or grea
evil. Clara had said she couldn't remember much about Fathe

bramo's curate; he had merely been a presence behind the
riest. Now Julia had a name.

And the last, Simone P. A youth. A strange youth. What
id Guy mean 'he has not been seen in the other villages'? Of
ourse, strangers in a wartime Italian village would be noticed.

Julia sat at the kitchen table, head in her hands, her thumb
wisting at a black curl near the base of her neck. Her mind
itted over two scenes from a family reunion before Venice.

Margherita Padovano, Sandro's wife, tossing her red hair
nd exclaiming in tones of mock-horror at the dinner table,
'apà was frightfully strict, especially to Roberto. No supper
nless he'd practised the cello well, eh, Papà?' And the glowing
edhead had tickled Simone under the ribs whilst Roberto
ughed and accidentally knocked the pepper mill flying in a
arge gesture of denial.

Sandro, Roberto's brother, walking with her in the back
ard of their flat whilst Roberto played there with the baby, a
trange haunted expression flickering like a trick of light
cross his face. Sandro, smaller and chunkier than Roberto,
ith his mother's passive features, saying softly, 'Dad was
retty hard on Roberto when he was a boy. Roberto could
ever do enough for Dad, you know? Whatever he did, it was
ever enough. And Dad probably caused Roberto's, you know
later problem.'

Seeing she didn't know what he was talking about Sandro
ad backtracked: 'It doesn't matter, you're not a Carlotta-type.
on't for God's sake mention this to Roberto, he'll go nuts.'

Julia hadn't mentioned it to Roberto because of lack of time
their perennial difficulty – and also a shyness when it came
discussing Carlotta, Roberto's ex-wife.

Thinking back, Julia admitted there was another reason.
he did not like Simone, did not like to hear Roberto talk
bout his father gently, as though Simone were someone to
e pitied. Yes, he had been taken by Scarpia, but he'd lived
ith that quite successfully for the last fifty years.

Simone: tall, with his lavender scent, and a cleft in his chin
ke one of the men who had blinded Clara. Simone, who unlike
erself, had not been threatened by Scarpia. Simone, who had

a history of unkindness against Roberto. Simone, whose recen nightmares had been sparked not by shame but by othe modern war trials.

Simone P. . . . Simone Padovano?

Julia, bringing her hands from her hair, counted off on he fingers. 'He never was in Naples during the war: he lied abou that. He lived in Castel San Martino and spoke the dialect. H was a pupil of Francesco Vincenti and better than Sprint. H has presence.' Julia pushed herself from the pine table. 'Mayb Sprint wasn't Spoletta!'

Now she was walking up and down the kitchen. Simon was in the music business, but earning far less as a viola player than he would have done if he'd continued his voca training.

'He'd be fifteen.' Guy had spoken of Simone's youth. Sh knew boys as young as that had been involved in military outfits during the war. In February 1944 the Blackshirts furthe north had established a battalion of young soldiers from fiftee to eighteen years old at Vercelli.

But Roberto's father, a boy sadist?

'It's not possible,' said Julia. Roberto had spoken of scar on his father's feet. But there again, she had read that in certai Fascist groups there were often brutal initiations.

'Stop it!' Julia put a hand up to her mouth. This indeed wa suspicion gone mad: she was allowing her dislike of Simone her distaste at his underhand spitefulness against her, t colour her judgement. Roberto did not suspect his father, why should she? Yet Roberto did not know about the entry in Guy' papers, nor the scent.

The day Simone and Father Angelo had walked to the three lower hamlets on their way to Croce, warning people of the Fascist round-up . . . Father Angelo had spoken to her grand father Guy, but Simone had talked to Sprint. He had mentione Captain Rodito's partisan unit. Unwisely, Roberto had said but supposing Simone's 'indiscretion' had been deliberate: Had he, like Sprint, been two-faced, a member of a partisa force whilst at the same time informing for the Fascists?

Perhaps Simone really had betrayed Captain Rodito

'erhaps the villagers of Castel had been right to spit at him: eople knew things in these small villages—

The intercom chimed and she jumped at the intrusion of ormality. 'Julia? May I come up? We need to talk.'

The voice was English. She recognised it instantly, and lmost as if the man with the red scarf could see through alls and up stairs, ducked down behind her chair.

'Julia?' The voice sounded hesitant. 'One of the orchestra players said you were here, sleeping off a late night . . .'

That would have been Simone, making more trouble for er at La Scala, as with the palmed costume jewellery, thought ulia. The chair scraped on the tiles as she prowled from the itchen into the sitting-room.

'I want to help. I don't like Krusak either.'

Mention of Krusak put Julia back in the cold fury she had elt with the Croatian. Furious, she stabbed the release button n the outer door.

Tom, who had intercepted the postman on the way in and uggested he take the parcel up with him, mounted the stairs 1 a hurry. Thirty second later, he found himself pushed onto plush sofa, the parcel he'd brought in with him dropped etween heaps of music scores. Above him, one angry aughter with brilliant grey eyes. White blouse, grey skirt, ow shoes, good legs.

'Well? Don't you think you've caused me and yourself nough trouble? You owe me an apology as well as an xplanation.

'And what exactly do you mean by help? Can *you* stop Krusak throwing me out of La Scala any time he feels like it?'

'Yes.' Tom was surprised at the firmness of his voice. 'Yes, can. There are others who together are as powerful as Krusak, and several of these have been my clients. Bazzini, or instance, I buried his mother.'

There was a pause. 'Do go on.' Julia's hand invited.

'I'm a funeral director. Here's my card. I moved my business rom Britain to Italy in 1992; my bid for the European market.'

'And you've lots of powerful clients.' Julia's tone was cathing.

'Who would support you if I asked them to.'

Julia tilted her head of black curls on one side. 'Why should
you do that? I know you send me roses but to take on Krusak
is of a rather different order in the scale of admiration, isn't
it? What would you want in return? Don't forget I saw you at
the Bologna dance hall where Krusak just happened to arrive
to tango with me.'

'Bologna? I've no business there. When was it you thought
you saw me in Bologna?'

'January 7th. The night before my first *Don Carlos*.'

Tom scowled. 'This is a trick. I've never been to Bologna.'

The telephone started to ring. Julia heard the answering
machine click on. 'Julia, Bianca. I'd like us to meet, soon as
possible. Reach me at this number. Ciao.'

Julia lifted her head. 'I'd like to believe you,' she continued,
as though the phone had not sounded. 'Certainly your offer of
help is interesting, and I will consider it.'

Faced with that dismissal, Tom reacted before she could
say more. 'Here.' His arm jerked forward. 'This came for you.'
He held out the parcel as though this would persuade Julia to
let him stay, watching her eyes scanning the English
postmarks, the masculine writing.

'Ah, yes, I've been waiting for this.' She took the package
in her right hand, gripping it possessively, moving her arm
slightly as though testing the parcel's weight. Her face,
thought Tom, showed not satisfaction but a fleeting suggestion
of alarm.

'Thank you.' She smiled, her poise returning. 'Now, if you
will excuse me, Mr Jessop . . .'

Politely but firmly, Tom found himself escorted to the door,
no nearer to giving an account of himself today than when
their paths first crossed in Florence.

42

lia stared at the opened parcel on the kitchen table. Guy's
ary, and a letter from her stepfather.

'Your mother did not want to trust her father's papers to
e Italian mail, but when I suggested that I bring the diary to
u in Milan myself, she relented and said that would not be
:cessary. The man in the British post office assured us that
u would receive this within a week – he was more confident
the Italian postal system than myself or your mother.'

Julia smiled at that. The parcel had taken eight days to
ach her.

She touched the diary with a finger, brushing the clammy
ather. She was reluctant to open it, although she knew she
ust.

Not yet though. Not just yet. Putting off the moment, Julia
andered back into the lobby to telephone Bianca.

Too soon, her call was answered, an arrangement made.
lia was meeting Bianca at the Milan flat.

Bianca still hadn't said why they should meet. Roberto said
anca knew strange people and could be into drugs.

Bianca certainly knew Emilio Gucci, whose father had been
ptured by Scarpia. After agreeing to act for Julia to trace
e son of the herbalist Stefano, Gucci had admitted that soon
ter he'd found the man, the younger Stefano had fallen
wnstairs in his flat and broken his neck.

Julia put down the telephone. When she first learned of the younger Stefano's death, she was horrified at the idea of the ex-Marshal of Ponte pursuing some private revenge. Further reflection had dismissed this hasty judgement.

When she, and later Roberto, had talked with Gucci, they had known that Stefano's father was Fascist but hadn't known then that the herbalist had been a member of Scarpia's cell. For all his bluster, Gucci didn't strike Julia as a murderer. For years, he had suspected Davide Patuzzi of being involved in his father's torture, but never moved against the man because there was no proof. Gucci pursuing a family vendetta was simply wrong: Gucci wanted justice within the law.

So what was she missing here? thought Julia, returning to the kitchen. *Bianca* had set up her first meeting with Gucci and her meeting with Rita. *Bianca* had been the one to tell Francesco about the younger Stefano bursting into his father's gallery: Francesco had confirmed his sister had been there that night.

Bianca and Gucci. Bianca and Rita. Bianca and the younger Stefano. Bianca reporting on Sprint's murder. Bianca and Krusak, maybe? Tom Jessop had denied being at the dance hall where Julia had gone to talk to Rita and had run into Krusak as well. Jessop's denial seemed genuine, which left Bianca . . .

But why, after what Krusak had done to Pietro? Could Bianca be involved in some deadly game with Krusak? Supposing Bianca was the one continuing a vendetta?

Journalists don't go round shooting people, or pushing them to their deaths down steps. Krusak had hurt her father badly in the war yet Bianca had made no move against him. Perhaps, like Gucci, she wanted more proof.

In which case, the younger Stefano's death was an accident and she and Bianca were allies.

Again the telephone rang.

It wasn't Roberto as she hoped, but Andrea. Clara was worried: Julia hadn't been in touch for days.

'I'm sorry,' Julia began, but Andrea interrupted.

'Listen! Last night the security men spotted two masked

intruders trying to climb in through one of the lower windows. The guards chased the men away but didn't catch them.'

'Grandmother?'

'Knows nothing. Can you come?'

'Soon.'

The line went dead.

Suddenly, violently, Julia kicked the door jamb. Scarpia was toying with her. This outrage against Clara was his way of saying 'I can get at anyone you care about.'

'I'm not going to stop until I find you!' She had to go on, or Scarpia would have a hold over her and her family.

She had the morning before Bianca arrived. It was time to put aside reluctance and study *all* her grandfather's writings.

Forcing herself to look at the war diary Angelica had found at Croce and which she at last had received that morning, Julia discovered that it and the coded papers often related identical *personal* events, although the papers gave more detail.

Disturbing detail.

The diary entry which had been read to Julia by her mother, referring to Clara's betrayal of an escaped English prisoner of war, was brief.

December 24th, 1943. Clara returned from another evening spent with 'friends', but the 'friends' know nothing of her visits. Nazi officer called to be entertained. Typical aristocrat, looked right through me. Heard him and Clara talking in the dining-room above the cellar: if I put my head against the water pipes, I can hear everything in the room above.

I heard Clara – my wife! – selling our English prisoner of war, telling the German which shepherd hut to search. For a bottle of brandy, the finest Armagnac, one bottle . . .

Why did she do it? Why does she go out at night to the German headquarters? To cling to what's hers? I will never understand what she has done.

The coded entry for that day read:

* * *

December 24th, 1943. Airdrop successful. Giovanni delivered more guns. Mauro forging the group's passes: I'll collect after Christmas.

Christmas. Croce villagers bowing and scraping, Clara dealing with creatures like Stefano and Patuzzi, men I want to hit. How can she stand what the Fascists are doing to Italy?

She thinks I do not know. Those evenings with friends. The opera, concerts, dances . . . false. I've watched her glancing at Krusak. I cut across country on horseback one Sunday, followed her to Bologna where she said she was going to mass in the cathedral. She and Krusak in the car, with that poor stupid German aristocrat as cover. They drove into Nazi headquarters. They were there two hours.

I feel I shall go mad. This afternoon that German fool strutted into my house, demanding to speak to my wife. He wasn't Krusak, but what I would have given to have kicked him down the garden steps!

She betrayed me. After swearing she would say nothing of young Broadbent, our English POW. I hid that boy for six weeks and Clara gives him away like a pair of old socks. Where he's hiding. Whether he's armed. Seven years we have been married, and I feel I don't know her.

And then two vital entries in the diary, spaced a month apart:

May 9th, 1944. Heard today about Mutta. When I told Clara what her smooth Croatian officer had done, she answered, 'I know.'

The question is – how? Krusak has not been here for a week. How did Clara learn the news that the Germans and the Italian SS had killed over two hundred people? No one in Croce knew anything. Gasparini has only just brought word from the priest who visited the sole survivor of that massacre.

But Scarpia the torturer knew – and so did Clara.

And then the second, final entry in the diary:

> *June 8th, 1944. Clara entertained a German SS Major and an Italian SS Captain at our home today – and naturally the ubiquitous Krusak and the Munich fool. I was banished to the cellars: 'Cousin Mario' looking over wine barrels . . .*
>
> *Clara is leaving now with these Nazi officers, missing the village feast of Our Lady of the Vines which, as the Contessa, she is supposed to attend. To stay with the Captain's wife, she tells me. Four days she'll be away in the Italian lakes, a holiday . . . I do not believe anything she says.*

Julia quickly closed the diary. This was what her mother had read. Angelica too had remembered that Clara had said she was at the villa in Croce on the night of 10th June, the night Guy was captured by Scarpia. Guy's entry made Clara's account a lie. She had not been at the festival. She had not been there when Sprint had come to the villa. She had not gone out that night because Guy was in danger.

Yet Vittorio's murder and Clara's injuries, her account of what happened in Scarpia's torture chamber – what of those?

'No!' Julia muttered. 'Look – look at what else he says.' Quickly, she found the final entry of Guy's loose papers, hurriedly decoded it.

Word for word it was identical, the same. *The same.*

A tremor ran through Julia; the papers in her fingers twitched. She was beginning to understand why Angelica had never attempted to bring Scarpia to justice. She realised now what Angelica had thought, how her mother's mind had worked towards a horrible conclusion. Clara had lied to them, had lied to her husband.

Julia thought of the singer Felici, who had recounted how Clara came to his performance at Bologna in the winter of 1943, *accompanied* by German officers. Felici hadn't made a mistake, Clara had lied.

She and Krusak. Clara had implied that she had met the

Croatian no more than three times; Guy's diary and notes showed that to be another lie: Krusak had been a frequent visitor, over many months. Krusak's obsession made sense, now. Also his claim that he and Clara had been lovers. If that were so, Krusak might have told Clara about his shooting Vittorio.

Krusak instead of Guy. No wonder Angelica, loving her father, had been repelled at the idea. And Angelica ran from things she disliked.

Clara and her German officers, whom, as Guy's papers made clear, had been welcome at her villa as early as Christmas 1943. Clara's trips to German headquarters. Clara dealing with Patuzzi and Stefano, known Fascists. Clara who had said dismissively that Guy had been killed by his own idealism. Clara who had been thrown the corncockles, symbol of betrayal: perhaps not on the feast day as she had claimed, but on another, earlier day. Clara who now wanted her, Julia, to stop searching for Scarpia.

Clara who knew before anyone else, *except Krusak and Scarpia*, about the massacre at Mutta.

Clara had said she heard singing in the torture chamber, live singing from two men. Vincenti and Sprint were both trained – had Clara lied about not recognising Vincenti's voice on the tape supplied by the German twins?

A whisper can disguise the sex of a speaker. Luisa Ferida, the actress, had been a member of the Koch gang.

'No! That's not possible,' muttered Julia. 'There are the injuries . . . and she saved Andrea's life . . . and what about last night's prowlers around the villa?' What better smokescreen though, than to be under threat?

And then the injuries. Patuzzi's old farmhouse had been bombed. Could she, Julia, say for certain that the hideous disfigurement recorded on one small hazy photograph was the result of a knife, or of blast?

'But why would Clara have me search at all?' Julia raised her head. Rita's voice gave an answer: 'Scarpia thrived on secrecy.' With the fifty year anniversary approaching, that secrecy was being threatened. Scarpia might want to find out

y how much. Sprint, one of the few who could have identified
carpia, had already been murdered. Julia remembered how
lara, hearing that Vincenti, Stefano, Patuzzi and Sprint were
ead, had remarked, 'Then they are out of reach.' Now her
'ords took on a sinister meaning.

Simone and Clara were so far the only surviving 'victims',
nd if Simone was the Simone P. of Guy's notes, then it wasn't
urprising if the man disliked her. She would remind him of a
ast he would prefer to be kept buried, thought Julia, hugging
er elbows.

If Simone Padovano were Spoletta, then who was Scarpia?
'Krusak,' muttered Julia. But why should Krusak as a
erman officer need people like Francesco Vincenti or Davide
atuzzi: local Italians, who by custom would have been loyal
o the Contessa of the region? The Contessa, who according
o Sprint, disliked partisans but was still interested to know if
ny were in *her* region, particularly if there were ex-soldiers
a these outfits.

'The bitch of the mountains.' Gucci's filthy name for Clara
ounded hollowly in Julia's head. Was she being used? she
ondered. So far, she had told Clara everything she had
arned in her search for Scarpia. Now she thought of the
reats against herself: terrifying, not fatal. Yet whoever had
urdered Sprint would be ruthless enough to dispose of her.
. single bullet fired whilst she was on stage would be enough.

One thing was painfully clear. Angelica had been right when
he remembered her parents quarrelling. Guy's diary and
apers showed a marriage under tremendous pressure,
erhaps strained beyond breaking point.

How well in just a few months did she, Julia, know Clara?
Vhat would Clara have been capable of, if her love for Guy
ad turned to hatred?

'Scarpia' a woman, not a man?

'No,' said Julia.

ulia didn't want to read any more. One last entry, she thought, hoosing any at random.

The date was 15th April 1944. 'Mauro finished false papers or myself, Clara and child. Gasparini collects tomorrow, will and over in church.'

So, even as late as April '44, Guy's anger and misgivings ver Clara had not yet reached a point that it had destroyed is marriage, thought Julia, oddly thankful. Had Gasparini anded over these papers? No, it was here: Gasparini had ome with news of Mauro's disappearance. The documents vere too risky to use; Gasparini had destroyed them.

'RIP Mario Scapone,' Guy had written.

Bundling Guy's diary and papers together, Julia recalled ow Gasparini had left the Croce region in the fifties. Could art of that move have been to assume a new identity?

'ietro Terni had driven to Milan with Bianca. 'To collect a ortrait,' he said, standing, illuminated by sunlight, in the nusic-cluttered flat.

'Papà, quit posing and go.' Bianca flitted with a toss of red air, gold chains and green leather into the bathroom.

'See how she treats me!' Pietro's face set in tragedy.

Clara hadn't lied about this man's acting, thought Julia. His ound features seemed to have two performing expressions:

smile, hands on breast for joy; frown, hands on breast fo
sorrow.

'How's the search?' Pietro broke his pose.

'Continuing.' Julia swung to the window, admiring th
rainbow arching over the classical front of La Scala. Pietr
was reflected in the glass. 'Unfortunately, I've discovered ₴
relationship between my family and Jan Krusak.'

Pietro's jowls slackened.

'My father detests Krusak,' Bianca, hands dripping
tapwater, glided into the room.

Julia turned to Pietro. 'Yet you associate with him.'

Again Bianca answered. 'Because we must. Krusak know₴
Papà collaborated during the war. It was nothing,' sh₠
continued, ignoring the drooping posture of her father. 'Some
POW hiding in a shepherd's hut. Giving him up, Papà did th₠
guy a favour.'

The story sounded uncannily similar to her grandfather'₴
account of Clara's betrayal of an English soldier, but then afte₨
the Armistice of September 1943, thousands of prisoners o
war had been set free by the Italians, only to be retaken by
the Germans. Julia looked again at Pietro.

'He was English,' he murmured. 'Called Smith.'

Clara's prisoner of war had been called Broadbent. 'Wha
happened to him?'

'The Germans took him. He was starving. I don't know i
he survived the war; there are so many English with that name

'I have English buyers,' he went on. 'Most are my age.]
don't think they'd understand what I did.'

Bianca put an arm around him. 'Satisfied?'

Her aggression provoked an answering response in Julia
sympathy for Pietro gave way to renewed anger against Krusak

'No I'm not satisfied. Krusak should have been tried fo₨
war crimes. I'd have thought that more important than the
loss of business contacts.'

'Don't be a fool!' Bianca's voice snapped with her cigarette
lighter. 'One man's word against another . . .'

'There are other witnesses,' said Julia, thinking of the
Dontini sisters.

Pietro raised his head. 'Have you asked the German twins?'

Disconcerted, Julia said nothing. Before she answered, Pietro continued gently, 'I'm afraid you'll be disappointed. Both are terrified of the man and will not appear against him. I know because when Krusak first surfaced in Italy after the war and came to my gallery demanding cut-price old masters as the price of his silence to my other clients, I went to see the sisters and asked for their help. They refused.'

Julia's recollections of the sisters dovetailed with Pietro's account. She remembered Karin's trembling silence when her twin Elsa Dontini had spoken of a young Nazi officer with beautiful eyes and impeccable German. She recalled Krusak's office, the Adam fireplace, Chinese wallpaper, ikons. Krusak had a passion for art: his motive for approaching Pietro.

It all fitted.

'The night you were taken. Was Krusak there the whole time?'

Bianca started to speak. Pietro held up a hand.

'I can't tell you. I was blindfolded.'

'Gasparini owes millions in tax,' said Bianca. 'He was deep in debt when he left his farm near Croce.'

A compelling reason to change his name, thought Julia, although not necessarily to Mario Scapone, the unused alias invented for Guy by Mauro.

Unless Gasparini hadn't destroyed the false documents.

'I don't think we'll find him.' Bianca yawned away tension.

The last hour had been difficult. Julia had gained no fresh insights into the night of Pietro's interrogation by Krusak. Pressed by Julia, the Bolognese's twinkling eyes had clouded. He had begun a see-saw rocking on the sofa.

'Did you not say when we met at my house before Christmas that people's wishes should be respected if they prefer to forget certain wartime experiences?' he remarked. After that, questions were impossible. Julia felt his departure as a relief.

Jokingly asking to see where Francesco lived 'in sin', Bianca flopped onto Ruth's bed and opened up about Scarpia.

It was interesting to Julia that Abramo Coletta, with the

added insight of the confessional, viewed Scarpia as she did: vain, secretive, ruthless and opportunistic, seizing chances, turning each situation quickly to his own advantage.

In these, except the secrecy, Julia recognised Krusak and said so. She also admitted that the person she was looking for was not a missing relative but a war criminal responsible for the death of her grandfather and – possibly directly, certainly indirectly – Krusak's killing of the two hundred villagers at Mutta. She mentioned Sprint, Francesco Vincenti and the other dead members of Scarpia's 'cell'.

'I can't pretend to understand the envy, or hatred, or spite, or defective personality, or even idealism that motivated these people,' Julia observed.

'The greatest attraction of evil is that it gives justification for the most irrational hatreds, grants permission to act upon our darkest fantasies,' said Bianca.

Julia watched her hugging Ruth's pillow.

'Why not write like that about Vincenti and the rest?' she asked. 'You've already written about Sprint's murder. This could be a follow-up piece. It might stir things up, cause Scarpia to make a mistake that'll bring him into the open.'

'Maybe.'

Julia, settled on the floor, elbows resting on the end of the bed, said, 'You're not in this for the story at all?'

'That comes at the end. Krusak's been a vampire on my family. I've been waiting for a chance to nail him without dragging Papà's name into it. I don't want to mess up by giving any warning shots in the papers.'

There was something missing in her answer. When Julia had heard what Claudia and Nuccia Rasella had endured as children, she had been horrified, but there was more to Bianca's jerky agitation than distress for the victims. Beneath the Chanel perfume, Julia caught the stench of fear.

She too was scared – it was a relief to tell how she'd been set on, threatened, pushed down steps, sent revolting packages. Her respect for Bianca increased when the woman commented:

'All that could have been Krusak, I guess. Like you say,

ch time he knew where you were and he did hire Bazzini to
eck your first night at Lucca. But again – ' Bianca shook
r head – 'it doesn't feel like him.'

Julia didn't admit that she agreed, nor that her suspicions
r some of the more spiteful attacks involved Simone
dovano, who made no secret of disapproving of her
lationship with Roberto and who could have his own strong
asons for wanting her to stop delving into wartime events
ound Croce and Castel.

Yet would Simone have known how to hire the three men
ho had roughed her up outside Plini's? Memory flashed
rough Julia, an image of Clara the first time they'd met,
rusting wire into oasis. Clara, who lived in seclusion, who
dn't troubled to pursue the men responsible for her
sband's death until fifty years later. She'd once engaged
vestigators to try to trace Angelica, why not other private
perators?

If Scarpia *were* a woman, might she, Julia, be searching
t for the torturer but for the victims, perhaps the only people
ho had seen Scarpia and realised it was a woman?

'Mad,' muttered Julia. With her grandmother seeming to
ve so many guilty secrets, it was a relief to quiz Bianca.
he night I saw Rita. You set me up with Krusak at the dance
ll.'

'No!'

'Come on.'

'I swear I didn't.' Bianca blew her nose.

'Why did you fix my meeting with Gucci for midnight?'

Bianca shrugged. 'That's the time I always see him.'

'Do you know anything about a man called Tancredi di
lvo?'

'He's a client of Papà's.' Bianca licked her lips.

It was these gestures which revealed her agitation, Julia
ought. She pushed herself up from the bed. 'Why's he
terested in me?'

Bianca rippled a finger through her hair. 'He likes opera.
e's particularly fond of you, and your boy Roberto.'

'I'd like to meet him.'

'I'll tell Papà to ask next time he sees di Salvo.'

Julia caught the ease with which Bianca used the man's name. 'You know him well?'

'Me?' Bianca implied the question was absurd.

'Strange, how he's also friendly with Krusak.'

'The super-rich are a club. They stick together: use the same tailors, accountants . . . art dealers.'

'Give me his address and I'll believe you.'

Lifting a pen from her green leather catsuit, Bianca scribbled on the flyleaf of one of Ruth's scores. 'Here.' She ripped out the flyleaf.

Julia put her tongue between her teeth, then decided to ask. 'Why did you want to see me? To pool resources or to check how far I'm away from unmasking Scarpia?'

The challenge did not ruffle Bianca. She jingled her gold.

'Like I said, I've been after Krusak for years.' *Had she said that?* 'When I met Coletta and he told me about Krusak shooting Vittorio at your grandmother's dinner table I knew I had to talk to you. Papà says the German twins won't go into the witness box against Krusak, but maybe your grandmother will. Her testimony and Papà's would put this man away.'

A prepared speech, thought Julia, reflecting that as a journalist Bianca had taken a long time to trace the priest of Croce. Bianca's distress when speaking of the sadism employed against eight-year-old Claudia Rasella had been palpable, but in other parts of her narrative there were things missing. But then she herself hadn't mentioned Simone or Carlo Gucci, Emilio's father. Wherever Bianca was death had a habit of following. Someone seemed to be using Bianca without her knowledge, perhaps this di Salvo.

'Did Coletta tell you before he disappeared into monastic seclusion where we might find his curate Michele Bozzi?'

'America. I checked with emigration.'

'Dammit,' said Julia under her breath.

'Will you talk to your grandmother about testifying?'

Julia shook her head. Despite their both being after Krusak she could not really trust Bianca. 'Clara's too frail. It'll have to be another way.'

Bianca watched Julia carefully. Bringing Krusak to trial would rid Papà of a thorn in his side, since any collaboration the Croatian accused Pietro of in court would look like muck-slinging. Although she'd have to ask Papà about these mysterious German twins and the night Krusak had dragged him to Nazi headquarters. Bianca congratulated herself for keeping cool when that surprise popped up in the conversation.

Krusak deserved to go to jail. Next time he phoned, Bianca decided, she'd tell him to keep his commission. Time for 'Anna' to retire.

But Julia was getting too close to Tancredi di Salvo and his ambiguous war record. She hadn't told Julia everything that Coletta had said about Scarpia: she wanted to keep Julia suspecting Krusak. There was Julia now, standing in the window, winding di Salvo's address round her finger. One shot and that quick determination would be gone.

'What's wrong?'

Bianca glimpsed herself in the wardrobe mirror, taut and pale. Her mind was clear: her handbag was in the next room but she knew how to get Julia to the gun. This was what she had half-expected to happen in the beginning, follow Julia's trail then at the close show her the gun, make her talk, kill.

Julia's brilliant eyes were looking at her with sympathy. Julia, who wouldn't talk. In the killing clarity of her mind Bianca knew that instantly. She could waste Julia but that's what it would be, waste. There was still Roberto Padovano, interested in Krusak/Scarpia, and in God knew who else.

Bianca shuddered, thinking of Claudia Rasella.

'Ghost on my grave,' she answered.

44

Ruth had an arrangement with Francesco in a self-service pizzeria off the square by Milan cathedral. In the break allowed by La Scala she'd grab a place and Francesco would get the pizzas. Like everything they did it worked, but today, just for once, it would be great to queue together, even if it meant missing a table and standing by the TV wall.

Milan fog got her down. Leaning at a 'table', Ruth turned from the window and watched Francesco calculating which line of bodies to join so as to be served *now*. Jean-hugged hips thrust forward in the swagger Italian males adopted, he had the neatest behind. And those brown eyes, that smile, the sensational . . . Ruth smiled.

Was it enough? On their walk to La Scala, what had she heard? How worried Francesco was about Julia. Yesterday it had been 'Where had Julia gone?' The day before, 'Wasn't Padovano's father appalling?' Then a remark about English roses.

She liked Julia, was happy to share the flat with her. Julia liked her.

Julia liked Francesco, too, at times rather warmly. Ruth could understand that: love one man, you usually like all. At least Julia wasn't calculating.

Francesco was. It hurt Ruth to admit it. Under the charm, the kindness, was one cool European.

He was ordering their food, pretending to the girl behind the counter that he'd said extra mushrooms, not extra cheese, so their pizzas finished with both. Usually, his sleek tricks made Ruth shake her head but not today.

Last night, after guess-who had come home, Ruth had woken to a gentle stroking. The embrace was warm, Francesco considerate as always, but at the moment of climax he'd called her Julia. Eyes closed, handsome features racked in bliss, he'd not been aware of it.

Ruth had left him sleeping and taken a long shower.

She wanted more love than she was getting. Maybe it was time to break with Francesco. Ruth went cold, then hot at the idea. To do it, she'd need to turn herself to stone.

Francesco crossed to the drinks counter, balancing paper plates on spread fingers. He didn't so much walk as bound from place to place. It didn't matter that she was taller, he made her feel cute. She'd been out with men bigger than Francesco and felt less protected.

But she could turn to stone. It would shatter her for a time, a long time, but she could live without Francesco. She wasn't the understudy. She was the prima donna.

'Julia Rochfort . . .' She couldn't get away from the fan club, thought Ruth, glowering at the stately, grey-haired gentleman standing by the TV wall. Simone Padovano, without viola but with pizza and coke, was holding court with a quartet of string players. Accidentally knocking the straw from his drink onto the carpet, he imperiously kicked it under a table and continued with his analysis. 'Superficial, temperamental, immature, unprofessional. Undoubted talent but no dedication.'

'Maybe your boy has something to do with that,' remarked the cellist, drawing a snort from Papà Padovano.

'She's already fixing the horns on him with a man old enough to be her father.'

Ruth felt her jaw sag. In Italy, one of the worst insults was to say a man wore the cuckold's horns. For Simone to accuse Julia of being unfaithful to Roberto in those terms was gross.

The cellist protested. 'I think that's uncalled-for, Simone.

Unfair on your son and the young lady.'

'Bravo!' said Francesco in a loud undertone, appearing at Ruth's side and pitching their pizza-filled plates onto the table. Mortified, Ruth motioned him to be quiet. It would help neither Julia nor Roberto if Simone were drawn into a public slanging match about their personal affairs with another member of the Scala company. Heads were turning.

'When I want your opinion, I'll ask for it.' Simone's features took on the same stark planes as his son's. That was what he was to Francesco, thought Ruth suddenly, a proxy for Roberto, his rival. Nothing else would explain Francesco's reaction as he strutted up against the taller man.

'Take that back.'

'Please, don't!' said Ruth. Francesco totally ignored her.

Simone stared down his nose. 'Which part have you in mind?'

'Everything about Julia.'

That's it, thought Ruth. *I'm out of here.* Francesco's interest in Julia had clearly developed into full-blown infatuation. Ruth began to nudge her way through onlookers.

Behind her Simone said, 'I imagine someone with your "hands on" experience will describe her differently.'

Ruth took a deep breath. 'You're a disgrace to our profession, Signore.'

Her voice cut through Francesco's half-formed reply and continued, cool and devastating, her Italian at its most formal. 'What is totally unprofessional is your conduct in accusing a fellow musician who is not here, who cannot reply to your ill-mannered, cowardly and inane suggestions. If you continue with these slanders I shall resign from La Scala, and tell the management exactly why I am leaving. I will not work with anyone who spills such garbage in public places.'

Ruth's cheeks bloomed with anger. Her blue eyes were level with Simone's. Roberto's father looked like a man who'd had cold water poured over his head.

'Bravo! Julia'll be—'

'Be quiet, Francesco.' Ruth was sick of him, sick of foggy, smelly Milan. 'I'm leaving you. Don't follow.'

She advanced regally to the street, men jostling to hold the door for her.

She was cold. Bundling clothes into suitcases, her scores into her trunk, ordering a taxi to take her 'Anyplace,' she was frozen. Not numb. The wrench hurt like the time she'd been water-skiing and had broken her arm. All around her, Ruth remembered, the water had been warm, the air balmy, and she had shuddered with cold.

She was doing it, though. She was leaving this flat with its associations of Francesco, starting afresh. She was leaving him.

'Julia, always Julia,' Ruth muttered, dumping her sewing into a plastic bag. As Francesco said, she sewed, Julia *embroidered.* 'But who fixed most of her Eboli costume at Lucca?'

She was being unfair. 'So what?' Ruth stopped in the middle of the flat, fabric scrunched in a sweaty hand.

Francesco opened the door and heat blasted through. He jumped over her suitcases and kicked the rug aside. Her heart leapt with sympathy when she saw his anxious swallow as he came up and kissed her. His fingers roamed in the way she liked. He cared, but she knew that already. The question was how much.

She laughed at him and stepped out of his arms. Inside she was fighting herself and fighting him, but also fighting for him. Self-respect and Francesco: she wanted both.

'An apology would be nice.'

'I thought this would be better.' He produced a small gift-wrapped parcel. His sureness gave Ruth the whip of anger she needed. She shook her head.

'Don't you want a peep?'

'I'm not some doll to be dressed by you.'

Francesco put the box on the sofa arm. 'You don't have to move out,' he said, doing his down-trodden-liberated-man act. 'Give me a break,' he continued in charming fractured American-English. 'Please?'

'Your sincerity lacks conviction.' Ruth resumed her packing.

'Wait.' Francesco snatched the box from the sofa, following her into the bedroom. 'Look – one look.'

'Get lost.'

'It's a ring.'

'Give it to grey-eyes. And I hope Roberto sees and rams it through your fat nose.'

Ruth processed to the bathroom, scooping shampoo and cosmetics into another bag. The handle broke under the strain, and Ruth's temper spouted. 'Don't just stand nobly in the door, get on your knees and wipe!' She threw a towel and swept past, letting camomile lotion spill onto the blue tiles. 'My taxi will be here in thirty minutes. I'm not impressed by your acting. I'm not your mamma.'

The rest of what she was saying was lost on Francesco. He sank to his knees. Here was the real Ruth, this glorious, beautiful woman he'd lived with yet not really seen. Faced with her fire, all the blurred feeling, hopes, infatuation he once had for Julia vanished like puffs of incense; sweet but not real, nothing to grab hold of.

'I love you.' Francesco lurched forward. Every step took him closer to where Ruth had stopped, a score rolled in one capable hand. He loved the way her hair fell over her ears. 'I love you.'

Ruth moved forward; she was smiling. 'I guess I'd better look at this ring,' she said.

45

'*Roberto – are you OK? How did it go tonight?*'

Julia's anxious voice. Roberto wanted to touch her, hold her, reassure her, make her laugh. He missed her.

'I'm fine, and it went superbly.' Roberto motioned to a waiter to unlock the door to the unfinished terrace outside this vast, stunning private apartment. After appearing as Don Basilio all evening and being persuaded up here for this reception, he reasoned that Max and his Viennese glitterati could spare him five minutes of privacy. He swept the phone outside with him, closing the door on the crowd of party-goers.

'How are you, Julia?'

'Fine. Where are you?'

'On a millionaire's new terrace, looking over Vienna.' Roberto glanced through ghostly polythene sheeting which would soon be replaced by reinforced glass. 'Very impressive.' Before him the black ribbon of the river, the distant Danube Tower, city lights, snow blurring every cornice of the baroque palaces.

Impressive and freezing. Despite polythene draped from ceiling to floor outside the waist-high safety barrier, the terrace was bitterly cold.

'Roberto, about the night before last. I don't know what your father's told you—'

'I know rubbish when I hear it. He won't do it again.' Roberto

squeezed the receiver. 'Krusak didn't touch you. That's all
that matters.'

To his relief, Julia didn't ask how he knew. The fact was
he'd contacted Emilio Gucci and asked him to look out for
Julia. Roberto understood that she would be furious if she
knew, yet dealing with a man like Krusak even Julia might
need help.

Frustrated by not being with her, Roberto rubbed the back
of his neck with a fist. He'd learnt more about Krusak. Wary
of speaking over an open line, he decided his news would
keep.

Roberto wondered if she would mention Francesco Terni.
Gucci had spoken of 'a naked blond guy' bursting from the
flat two minutes after Julia had been left there by Krusak. No
doubt Terni had been staying the night with Ruth, reflected
Roberto, aware of the funny side of Gucci's account, but still
frowning. Julia thought he was jealous of the tenor.

'I spent yesterday with Bianca.'

Another Terni, thought Roberto, scraping ice off the door
sill with his foot. Bianca in particular kicked his fighting
instincts into gear, although he couldn't say why. Nothing
more maybe than the battle of the sexes: she was an attractive
woman.

'We talked. She's after the same man as we are.'

Behind him the reception suddenly bubbled more loudly.

Instinct saved him. Roberto jerked sideways, crashing the
receiver onto the gun. As the pistol bucked down, he lunged
forward but his attacker was gone in the mass of party-goers.
'Julia!' He called anxiously into the phone, trying to reach her
but the connection was dead.

Breathing hard, Roberto leaned against the doorframe. He
understood what his unknown assailant had been trying to
do: a gun at his back, a few steps to the safety barrier; a push.
Accident or suicide? No court would be sure. And he had been
attacked the day after Julia had told Bianca he was searching
for Scarpia.

Frowning, Roberto stepped back into the reception.

*   *   *

Next day was free: Roberto flew to Milan. Walking out of the airport terminal, he saw Julia.

'I've skipped rehearsals,' she was saying. 'When I finally managed to reach you again at the hotel, when you told me about the prowler around Sandro's house, I had to come.

'We have to stop this. We can't go on searching, Roberto, not when it puts a child at risk—' Julia stopped abruptly, then continued strongly, 'I couldn't stand it any more: you in Austria, me in Milan. If you hadn't said you were flying home, I was coming anyway.' She shrugged.

Roberto dropped his bags and wrapped his arms around her. It was as though they had never quarrelled in Venice. Questions were stilled: this moment was theirs.

'Say something,' Julia murmured, black curls against the crook of his arm, arms tight around him. She ignored onlookers; the businessman, the cleaner, the nun. He could feel her heart beating through the flesh of his own body.

Roberto brushed her forehead with his fingertips. 'Love you.' Bending his head, he kissed her.

'Tell me again.' Roberto stretched his arms above his head. They'd made it as far as the sofa in Julia's flat. Gardening books, her substitute for a garden, were all over the floor.

Julia ran a thumb across his diaphragm. 'I love you.' She twitched a black eyebrow. 'I see you feel the same.'

'I do, but you know that wasn't what I meant.' Roberto, running a finger down her nose, across her mouth, dismissed the rest. His news of Krusak must wait. He took her in his arms, hugging her fiercely.

A day in bed is a luxury, sometimes essential, for a singer. A day in bed with Julia –Roberto had to fight against it.

'We mustn't go to bed.' Julia too knew the temptation.

Roberto, breaking from her reluctantly to pad into the kitchen, repeated his earlier question in full. 'Tell me again what you told Bianca, what she told you.'

Over coffee, Julia explained how Bianca and Pietro had appeared at the flat, how Bianca had found Coletta, how Bozzi

the curate was in America, how Bianca was looking for som
way of bringing Krusak to trial. Bianca had also said that
Salvo was concerned for Roberto's well-being as well as Julia's

'I told her about my being roughed up and threatened bu
I never mentioned you or Simone.' Julia drained her coffe
and refilled her cup. 'I think the note you got at the hotel afte
I talked to her was just coincidence.'

'Maybe.' Roberto, considering Bianca, remembered Tom
Jessop. 'Did anyone else come to see you yesterday?'

'Yes, the man who's kept following me. He's an Englis
funeral director: Tom Jessop. Harmless.' Julia laughed. 'I sen
him off with a flea in his ear.'

'I can imagine,' remarked Roberto drily. So Tom hadn'
been able to give an account of himself. Perhaps he shoul
say something. But no, Tom wanted to tell Julia himself, an
until these threats were removed from them, he and Julia ha
to concentrate on finding a way to unmask Scarpia.

'Can I see the note?'

Roberto dug in his jeans pocket, slid it across the table
'It's written in Serbo-Croat: a hotel cleaner translated it.
says "Unless you and Rochfort stop meddling in affairs whic
are not your concern, your nephew Paolo will pay." This wa
pushed under the door after I got back to my hotel last night

'And you phoned Sandro.'

'Sandro had noticed strangers hanging around the flat an
wanted to know what was going on. I told him about you an
Clara, who you were after and why; said I was helping. Whe
I mentioned Krusak he said the police wouldn't dare mov
against a man like that without serious proof: in fact the cop
couldn't move at all until any threat became fact; deeds no
words. I could tell you I was going to kill you, but until I did
the police could do nothing.'

Roberto, reflecting on this, recognised that here was th
most compelling reason why Julia had not wanted the polic
involved: all the carabinieri would have done was to aler
Scarpia the sooner. He had been harsh in his judgement o
her in the Venice restaurant, too simplistic.

'Just when is your brother going to learn the full story

And when is Simone going to learn *you're* searching for Scarpia?'

'I'm not telling Dad anything until I've found proof; take the thing through to the end.'

You never finish anything, Simone had often remarked through Roberto's childhood. Now, Roberto snatched up the salt cellar from the table, began sliding it from hand to hand on the polished pine. 'Dad should be the one to tell Sandro,' he added. 'I think that side of events will be better from him.' He cleared his throat. 'Sandro's taken leave to look out for Margherita, Paolo and Dad, but it can't go on for ever.'

'We must stop, then.'

'No. That means they've won.'

Julia seized Roberto's shoulders. 'It's a child's life!'

Roberto shook his head. 'We can't stop. We know too much.'

Julia released him, tossed him a penetrating look. 'That's all that happened last night? A note appearing under your door?'

It had been in his mind to say nothing, but that was impossible. For her own safety she must know.

'Someone tried to kill me.'

Slowly, Julia settled in her seat, colour slipping from her face. Once started it was kinder to go on. 'I think it was opportunism,' Roberto continued. 'The man – if it was a man – saw his chance when I walked onto that unfinished terrace.'

'He would have made you jump.' Julia covered her mouth with her hand.

Roberto thrust back his chair, walked rapidly round the table. 'I'm alive.'

'That's what Clara said.' Julia pitched forward, embracing him tightly, as though convincing herself of his reality.

Roberto knelt, drew her head against his shoulder so Julia could not see his face. He would have died outside Italy. An accident, maybe. Di Salvo, Julia's protector and apparently his own, would have been able to blame no one, especially not Jan Krusak . . . Or Pietro Terni?

Roberto frowned. Now he knew how Julia would feel if she

found out Gucci was 'looking after' her. Having di Salvo a: his protector was useful but humiliating.

Di Salvo, the opera sponsor. Tom had heard him warning Krusak and Pietro that Julia was his personal concern. I that were so, was Bianca playing a double game, pitting Krusak and di Salvo against each other? But why? Maybe fo her father. Then what was Pietro's role in this tangle? Or d Salvo's?

'Bianca told me about di Salvo.'

Roberto drew back. 'You a mind reader?'

'We're hunting the same quarry.' Julia smiled. 'Tancredi d Salvo. Lives near Venice. Bianca gave me his address. Sh was going to see him after we met: wouldn't say why.'

'That's interesting.'

'Yes, I thought so too.' Julia nodded to the paper on th table. 'Why a note in Serbo-Croat? Krusak's too careful to mak a mistake.' She was back on the trail.

'We're getting close,' said Roberto. 'We're starting to pusl him.' He leaned forward, kissed her. 'My researcher in Berlir finally came up with more. On 10th June, 1944, the night you grandfather was captured by Scarpia, an order went ou transferring Krusak to the front line. It was a punishment: th text mentions vicious acts against the civilians of Mutta.'

'Krusak's involvement in the atrocity,' murmured Julia.

'He was removed from command until he reached the fron line, then demoted a rank.'

'So when Guy was taken, Krusak had no troops.'

Roberto nodded. 'If he moved against the partisans tha night he must have used Patuzzi and the rest. He would know remember, that they were members of the Fascist party from records. He would probably have talked to them when he an his men came snooping round Croce and Castel. Here' Krusak's motive, too: a desire to win back his command. He' ambitious and ruthless: today he's a millionaire.'

'But, Roberto, your father was taken the day before Krusal was removed. And what about Pietro Terni, interrogated a German headquarters? And the Rasellas' testimony?'

'I've thought about this. The Rasella sisters don't mentio

date and they were children: their attention was focused on their mother; they might not have noticed other prisoners. As for Dad, well, he was picked up on the 9th by Patuzzi, Vincenti and Stefano but he may have lost a day when he was racked on the head. Maybe Vincenti and the others were thinking of doing some independent interrogation when Krusak as Scarpia appeared.'

'But from what we've learned these men were used to operating as a team. Surely in just a few hours Krusak wouldn't have had time to mould them into a unit?'

'He was used to command. These men were volunteers, all believers. By what the survivor of the Mutta atrocity said about Scarpia's men, it seems likely that Scarpia recruited locals in these places to do his work: they'd understand dialects.'

'But if Krusak is Scarpia and he had used informers in Mutta, why kill all the villagers?' asked Julia.

Roberto shrugged. 'Maybe he felt the spies there hadn't done enough, maybe it was a reprisal. What we do know is that this year Krusak ruined Bazzini because Bazzini didn't obey him.'

'And Pietro Terni?' asked Julia. 'Is he a suspect again? He claimed to be in the Nazi headquarters on 10th June when Krusak was no longer in any official position.'

'You said Pietro wouldn't say whether Krusak had been there the whole time he was being interrogated?'

'He told me he wasn't sure. He was blindfolded.'

'As with the rest of Scarpia's victims.' Roberto shook his head; he wanted to be fair to Pietro. 'The order is dated 10th June. Krusak couldn't have received it when he and several German guards gate-crashed your grandmother's midsummer feast: I think he got it when he was at German headquarters with Pietro. After that Krusak is on his own, smarting after being demoted. He wants to redeem himself. Feeling out of a job, maybe he goes to Blackshirt headquarters. In come the Italian SS with the Rasellas: someone makes a joke about handing them to Scarpia and Krusak thinks why not? Of course he can't hold them in official headquarters so he takes them to Davide Patuzzi's home. Krusak knows Patuzzi's loyal as he denounced the Jewish family.

'There he finds my father and Carlo Gucci already being held and he hears from Sprint about Guy's partisan group. Krusak might have known about Guy's activities for some time but that night he decides he's nothing to lose if he brings Guy in: he needs an information coup. Sprint is sent to lure Guy out of the villa by a false message and the whole night's events are set in motion until the air-raid which kills your grandfather, but not Krusak or the rest of the merry crew.'

'And the music? The singing?'

'Recordings. At Croce it was different because he had two live singers, Vincenti and Sprint. I think using Sprint would appeal to Krusak's vanity.'

'Then why didn't your father recognise Sprint?'

'Concussion, terror. Maybe Sprint sang differently. You know how a trained singer can alter his voice. That's maybe why Clara didn't instantly know Vincenti from the German twins' tape.'

'Which leaves us with Pietro, and whether Krusak did or didn't interrogate him on 10th June,' said Julia.

'You see now why I want you to be careful around the Ternis.' Roberto gave her a knowing look.

'Yet Clara saw Pietro's injuries: they were real,' said Julia slowly. 'And why would Pietro help Clara get away from Croce to Florence unless he was a friend?'

'To go over to the winning side, maybe?'

'No.' Julia shook her head. 'Pietro as rogue and art thief I can see, Pietro as Scarpia I can't. I've met him, you haven't. He simply hasn't the force of command, of personality.' She frowned. 'We have an awful lot of "maybes".'

'Not quite. The order transferring Krusak gives the name of his superior, Anton Wolf.' Roberto whistled softly through the gap in his teeth. 'My researcher has found him living in Munich. I'm going to call on him, next time I'm back over the Alps. If Wolf talks—'

'Krusak's finished.'

'We'll finally get the truth about Scarpia, too.'

Julia sighed, rubbed her arms. 'Can we go to the cathedral? I'd like to be somewhere peaceful.'

They knelt at a side chapel, Roberto to pray, Julia to think. She watched his keen grim face, wondering what he would say if he knew about Guy's papers, her lurking suspicions of Simone and Clara. Krusak, with these new revelations, seemed at last within reach by the law, yet did that make Clara and Simone innocent? According to her own husband, Clara had been Krusak's mistress. And Simone had been Francesco Vincenti's star pupil, who strangely hadn't recognised his singing rival, Sprint.

If Simone was as good an actor as his son, might he have pretended to Carlo Gucci and Guy that he had been captured – a trick to get Scarpia's victims to talk?

'No,' whispered Julia. Simone would hardly move against Roberto and Paolo. Roberto was lighting a candle. She loved his steady wrists. 'I love you.' It was marvellous to say it.

'I love you.'

Marvellous to hear it. Julia licked her lips. 'Those faint scars on your fingers.' She had often being going to ask. 'How did you get them?'

By the candle shadows, she couldn't be sure if Roberto's expression darkened. He said nothing but held out his hand. They walked through the echoing nave, out into the pigeon-infested square, settled on the cathedral steps. The sun was pretending it was summer: a warm breeze wound through Julia's hair, tufted Roberto's spiky curls.

'I was twelve – a big, older-looking twelve – and my voice had already broken. People tended to expect more of me than others my age. Sandro was eight. There was this rope swing: if you ran one way you swung out over a two-metre drop full of thorny broom. It added the kind of risk kids like. On one swing though, Sandro couldn't hold on – I watched him disappearing into this sea of spines.'

Roberto glanced at his hands. 'When I reached him he was crying, more from shock than hurt. He wasn't badly cut. He'd had sense to keep still until I reached him. I was thoroughly scratched when I carried him out.'

'What did your father say when you brought him home?' asked Julia. Sandro, she knew, was Simone's favourite.

Roberto drew in a breath. 'He was furious. Kept talking about responsibility and letting others down. None of it made sense to me then. It's only now, when I've learned how Simone thought he'd betrayed his unit, that I can understand why he acted as he did. He must have felt that, being the eldest, I should have taken more care of Sandro, stopped him going on the swing, acted more responsibly. So he decided to toughen me up – make a man of me.

'We set out next day on this long walk – him and me. I carried our food but Dad said when we could stop, when we could eat or drink.

'It was blazingly hot. Dad kept us going through the heat of the day. Neither of us had water. I was starting to feel bad by then but said nothing. I didn't want him to call me soft. Between my legs, under my arms, I felt strange.

'We plodded on. I was burning all over and my cuts were festering. The pain between my legs, too, grew worse, but I was determined to keep going, to be as good as he was. Dad marched on ahead, never looked round.

'When we reached home I collapsed. Next thing I remember was mother sponging me down, and the doctor telling me I'd mumps. The doctor was furious with Simone, demanded to know why he hadn't noticed, why he'd made me stay on my feet all that time in the heat. Of course the doctor didn't know that Dad was hopeless when it came to illness. Mother looked after us when we were sick.

'I mended and it was forgotten. I met Carlotta, we married. Once my career was settled and I could support a family we both wanted children. When none came Carlotta went for tests.

'By then, our marriage was starting to fall apart. I think we both hoped that children would bring us back together. Carlotta adored babies; I wanted to give her a child.

'This time, I went for tests. On the day I was given the results, Carlotta announced she was leaving me. She had a lover and wanted to make what she called a proper life with him.

'During our separation and divorce Carlotta went public for money with her version of my fertility test result. All of Italy learned that, possibly because of mumps caught as a teenager, Roberto Padovano was unlikely to have children.'

Roberto motioned to the cathedral behind them. 'The church has plenty to say on contraception, but, like many young couples, we ignored it. When all of Italy learnt about me, though, the church said nothing to help me. I've hardly been to church since then: after the divorce I went mad for a time. Trying to prove myself, live it down, ignore the glances from men who could parade their kids to show off their potency. I felt castrated. And I still had to go on stage and perform.'

Looking at his taut features, the look of shame in his gleaming eyes, Julia wanted to hit Carlotta. A person might choose not to have children, but when choice is almost impossible and the world knows it . . .

Seven years Roberto had lived with this. Seven years in Italy, where family is considered essential. Years in a competitive profession where some rival could remind him that, in certain creative areas at least, he was almost a non-starter.

A yellow taxi squealed round the corner of the square.

Looking out from the steps, all Julia seemed to see were men with pushchairs. She picked the children out in the surging crowds, bright little jewels in their colourful clothes.

The irony that Roberto should admit such a personal affair to her in so public a place did not strike her until later.

Now she reached out, put her arms around the big man crouched on the step by her. Roberto tensed, she could feel the shame, anger, sadness in him. 'I'm sorry.' She did not insult him by claiming it was not important, that it changed nothing between them. She and Roberto were unlikely to have children of their own. It took a moment to absorb.

'I should have told you sooner. I know right now you've your career, but you're young.'

'I'm a mature woman of twenty-six,' said Julia. 'I know what I want. I want to be the best mezzo on the international circuit.

That takes time and no interruptions.' She took his head between her hands. 'I haven't been honest with you, Roberto. I know it might seem strange, you coming from the land of the Italian mother, but I don't want the hassle of children. My work is too important.'

She meant it. Her work was vital, her voice too special to be ignored or eclipsed under a family. It was not that she would never miss children, only that she did not need them to feel complete.

She would miss Roberto. She did not need him, she loved him.

'I love you.' Roberto took her hand.

They sat in sunlight on the steps, watching Milan traffic.

46

La Scala was on strike. The news reached Julia and Roberto at Milan airport as Roberto was returning to Vienna.

'Now that you're free, come,' said Roberto at once. 'We can visit Anton Wolf together, settle this Krusak business for good.' He touched Julia's cheek with his fingers. 'Then we'll have time for ourselves. I want you to live with me.'

'Steady!' Julia laughed. 'This is sudden—'

Roberto shook his head. 'Not soon enough.'

'Too much.'

Roberto smiled. 'Give it a try.'

'There are the threats to you and Paolo and—'

'Gone once Krusak's arrested. Meanwhile I've still to work.'

'Your family. Won't they be shocked? Suppose they regard you as still being connected to Carlotta?'

'They don't, Julia. More to the point, *I* don't.'

'What about your father?'

'Now La Scala's on strike he'll be under Sandro's eye. And he's settled in himself; hasn't had a nightmare in weeks. I think the worst's over. Anyway, he and Sandro have put their heads together: they're pooling cash to buy a villa on the city outskirts, a base for Simone, a house for my brother's family. They all get a new home and Sandro and Margherita a toddler-sitter. I don't expect Dad'll be in my flat for much longer.'

'I see.' Julia wound a curl round her thumb. Was Simone a

war victim, or a war criminal? How would Roberto feel if she
found proof of his father's guilt? What would he think of her
when Clara's true story finally emerged?

'So, what do you say?' Roberto scooped her up, gave her a
vigorous kiss, set her and his bags down beside him on the
airport's moving trackway. 'Munich first. Will you come?'

'Can't. I've promised to see grandmother.' Even though
she hadn't had sufficient time or opportunities to decipher all
Guy's papers, she had to face her grandmother with his diary.
Julia, watching grey airport walls glide past as the trackway
took them to the departure area, shivered slightly as she
considered what Clara might tell her when they met. Putting
such ideas aside, Julia focused on her next tasks. After she
had finished Guy's papers, she needed to see di Salvo and
trace Gasparini.

Roberto squeezed her hand. 'As I've said, watch what you
hide. Be careful: no private research. After Vienna I need to
find you in one piece to answer my second question.'

For me that's answered already, thought Julia, pulling a
cheerful face at her departing partner. *Definitely yes.*

Packing, Julia discovered a note stuck in the fruit bowl from
two days ago. Ruth was going to live at Francesco's: they were
defying Mamma Terni. About time, too!

From the train, en route to Clara's, Julia spotted an
advertising hoarding in a maize field outside Parma. 'Mario
Scapone, specialist in agricultural machinery: phone . . .'

Scapone, the alias invented by Mauro the forger and never
used by Guy. Julia snapped her fingers at the tattered billboard:
Gasparini was finally found.

The train was pulling into a station. As she scrawled the
number in her diary, the carriage door opened. A Florentine
gypsy, clutching posies of lilies of the valley, smiled and
bowed. Julia reached for her purse.

The old man, handing her a posy, remarked, 'I hope
everything goes well for you and your little one.' Closing the
carriage door, he left Julia amused and disconcerted. The old
boy was crazy; she couldn't possibly be expecting. In formal

religion she had lapsed somewhat. Roberto's belief was stronger, but pragmatic. They'd used protection.

Every time? Oh, no – not on the first *Don Carlos* night: they'd been too involved. But after what Roberto had told her, was it likely? Was she seriously considering the ramblings of an old man?

Stations flipped past. Julia hummed scales. Would it hurt to check the date of her last period? she thought, fishing a second time into her shoulderbag for her diary.

About six weeks, said a wiry Sardinian doctor in the Florentine clinic. If the Signorina wanted to do anything about it, now was the time. It would be safe, discreet.

'Don't think too long,' the doctor warned, as Julia left.

Feeling dazed, Julia walked into a lingerie shop on Via de'Tornabuoni. She'd always wanted silk underwear; today she was going to buy some.

The assistant recognised her and fussed agreeably. How long would it be before she was forgotten? Julia wondered, as an array of slips was laid out for her inspection.

She chose black. Shimmering, sexy black silk. Strapless, plunging bra, snug panties. In another two months she would not be able to wear these. In another three she would not be able to sing opera. Recitals, if she was lucky, she might be able to continue for four months.

This would take two years from her career. Other newcomers would have moved in. She'd be nearly thirty: great for a male singer, not so good for a woman with a career to build.

'Dammit! Why now?' muttered Julia.

Silk petticoat ... waist-slip ... short top ... pure silk stockings. Feeling slightly mad, and wildly extravagant, Julia chose three suspender belts, knowing she would soon be unable to wear them.

She watched the assistant wrapping her purchases, her thoughts chaotic. Music had always been her goal. Would her voice be the same afterwards? Would motherhood diminish her, absorb her? Singing scales whilst ironing cot sheets? Studying a role whilst rocking baby to sleep?

Her baby. Hers and Roberto's. Unaware of what she was doing, Julia hugged herself. She smiled as a gold bow, perky as a cherub, was fixed onto the carrier bag. Other singers had children and came back . . .

Hurrying out, she had to be called back for her change.

Please let him be happy. Ashamed of her sudden feelings of vulnerability, that thought still recurred as Julia dipped on and off Florentine pavements around tourists and Vespas. If Roberto, faced with the reality of parenthood, discovered that he didn't want to be a father, what would she do? Whatever she decided, could they still be lovers?

Her instincts shrank from Roberto needing to know, which made Julia want to confront him with the news at once. But she must not tell him over the phone, or by letter. This was too important, too personal. It must be face to face.

Two weeks, and Roberto was due to play at Florence opera. She must wait two weeks. By then perhaps her feelings would be settled. By then, surely, the last two members of Scarpia's cell would be exposed. She would know Clara's full part in the war.

Until then she would tell no one.

Thinking of Clara, Julia quickened her pace. She had questions to ask, and Clara's answers had become more urgent. Angelica's attitude to her had been coloured by her mother's mistrust of Clara. So too, Simone, seeing himself in Roberto, had treated his elder son differently from Sandro. She did not want to fall into the trap of looking for 'bad blood': to avoid that, she must know the worst.

Clara picked up the diary from the table and smiled. 'Guy was a great one for keeping accounts.'

'Angelica found it.' Julia watched her grandmother's bony hands flipping pages. She did not want to look at Clara's face.

It was noon, the following day. Sitting opposite Clara at the villa's dining table, light pouring in through the open window shutters, the chandelier above fresh with golden candles, to be lit tonight to celebrate her return, Julia felt her misgivings to be absurd. She was carrying the future, and did not want to be enmeshed in the past. Nor did she want to hurt Clara.

The window ledges were full of sprouting pots of bulbs: iris, jonquils. Life, thought Julia, pressing a hand to her stomach, feeling a secret pride along with her sharp anxiety as she heard the dry pages being turned.

'My mother found this in Croce. I believe she read it.'

'I believe you're right.' Clara, reading the last page, sighed. 'I wish I'd known. I should have guessed: Guy always wrote about his feelings. He proposed by letter, you know, delivered to me by himself.'

'I'm sorry.' Julia wanted to touch Clara, cuddle her. Seated in the spring sunlight, she had never looked more frail. Glancing now into Clara's face, like her own but more drawn and lined, Julia thought she understood why her grandmother and Angelica had never pursued Scarpia. To do so was to admit Guy was dead, to go back instead of forward.

'Angelica would have left me anyway.' Clara closed the diary with a careful hand. 'We both realised her life had been drifting for some time, and after you were born she was no longer content to be an aristocratic play-girl. This – ' Clara rapped the leather-bound book – 'This evidence of my "treachery" gave her a final push, that's all.'

Clara rose to her feet – suddenly she looked her age, thought Julia. She had expected to confront her grandmother, perhaps accuse her angrily of wartime collaboration. That would have been an easier part for her to play, but real life was more complex.

'Guy wrote papers too, in code,' she said, feeling pity as Clara briefly closed her eyes. 'Angelica hasn't seen those.'

'And you have.'

Julia did not answer at once. Lifting the crackling sheets of paper from her bag, she pushed back her chair and stood up. 'I haven't had the chance to decode all of these, but I did make a point of looking at the last sheet. The final entry there is the same as in Guy's diary.'

Clara sighed. Her long black dress rustled as she leaned to a window box, picking off a dead leaf from a pot of basil. The sweet fragrance coiled in the still air. Outside the windows, dimly Julia could hear Andrea cutting the grass and chatting to the security guards.

'I wish Angelica had come to me as you have done.'

Her words were a bridge between them. Crossing the gulf of age, of suspicion, Julia was direct.

'Angelica told me you and Guy often quarrelled. What about?'

'Not what he wrote about in these diaries! We did argue, yes, ridiculous quarrels about small things, about Krusak . . . I thought it was because we were tense with the war. I never guessed Guy was really arguing with me about *us*.'

Clara turned and pointed to the door.

'Walk with me in the gallery. I will tell you.'

47

Roberto, unshaven, in denims and bare feet, warm after singing practice, and now working out refinements of stage moves in his hotel suite, was disconcerted. 'I understood we were meeting in Munich.'

'I'd business in Vienna.' Anton Wolf walked through to the piano-dominated sitting-room. 'I regret we meet in such circumstances. But then, the officer of whom you spoke on the telephone was part of my command. I have always regretted that I did so little to prevent his excesses in your country.'

Meeting the thick-set man's steady eyes, recognising shyness beneath the abrupt manner, Roberto asked in his careful German, 'Have you returned to Italy since?'

Wolf, tweaking up corduroy trousers before settling in an armchair, answered, 'I made a promise to someone: not to return unless invited.'

Silence followed. Roberto leaned across the piano, took pencil and paper and sketched two heads. 'The younger I'm trying to persuade to live with me, but she's as stubborn as her grandmother.'

Wolf took the paper, black brows working in a square, red, wrinkled face. He glanced at Roberto, seated on the piano stool.

'Her name was Clara,' he began. 'I met her in Bologna Cathedral.'

* * *

'I met Anton in October 1943,' Clara said to Julia. 'He was an officer in the force occupying Bologna.

'I can see him now: thirty years old, solid frame, brown hair, dimpled smile. He approached me in the cathedral, requesting a tour of the building. Anton was abrupt, proud, shy.

'My refusal pricked his pride. He demanded to know why. I was posing as a widow since the occupation and said that it wasn't seemly. Anton went to the cathedral door and summoned a junior officer to be a chaperon – so I met Krusak.

'I didn't pay Krusak much attention, although he made no secret of his interest in me. I gave Anton his tour and rushed off.

'Two weeks later I was in the city again. I was queuing for meat when Anton appeared and handed me a parcel of rations. I knew what people were thinking and wanted to hurl it back at him, but he grabbed my elbow and whispered that he couldn't find any records of my English husband's death.

'After that I let him draw me out from the queue to his car. Krusak was driving. I was whisked round the city, my face burning when I saw Italians staring. Anton talked about books and music: he was very polite. I saw that he was lonely, that he missed his own kind.

'He asked me to an evening concert. He told me, out of Krusak's hearing, that he *personally* had found out everything about me. He mentioned Guy by name.

'I was frightened for Guy, too scared to refuse Anton's invitation. Krusak was commanded to take me home. He was flirtatious in a heavy-handed way in Guy's presence, and when Krusak left, Guy was irritated with me. He thought I should have refused the invitation and said I was over-reacting.

'At the concert, Anton commented that my cousin Mario could be sent to Germany to work. That was the threat he hung over me: that my "cousin" might be taken away.

'I didn't know if Anton had guessed that Mario was Guy. Anton never claimed my "cousin" was English, he merely dropped hints about Mario's usefulness as a vintner, how such skills were needed in Germany.

'So it began. After that concert there were others, then the opera in December '43, when Felici saw me. I told Guy these were social outings. I dared not tell him the truth: Guy was afraid of no one. I was terrified he might confront Anton.

'At first Guy believed me, but as the weeks went on I could see doubt entering his face. Not for me and Anton – Anton was so stiff and pompous in Guy's presence that Guy thought him no threat – but about Krusak and me. To me, Krusak was a boy, but I admit that I flirted with him.

'Anton was becoming increasingly affectionate. At first it was no more than a farewell kiss, but I was terrified that Guy would find out. I knew he would not be able to tolerate Anton's friendship with me, if he knew that was the price of Anton's silence about "my cousin" Mario.

'More than once I tried to tell Guy the truth, hoping I could persuade him to go along with the charade for the sake of us all as a family, but there seemed no good time to tell, no time to explain. He was going out almost every night by then: black-market deals he said. During the day he shut himself in the cellar. I did not realise Guy's mistrust of my association with Krusak. I told myself that I would deal with Anton: as a wife it was my duty to protect my husband from being deported, or worse, shot as a spy.

'By then, it was spring, February '44. For the last three months Anton had wanted us to be lovers. I had fended him off, given him different sops for his pride: dinners for him and other officers, entertainments at my villa in Croce. When he came once in December, with his persistent demand and his usual threat, I gave him information instead. There was a young English prisoner of war hiding on the estate. I gave him to Anton – it sounds terrible, and was, but at that time I believed it was either the English prisoner or Guy, and I knew the prisoner of war would not be shot.

'Anton was pleased; he promised me brandy for the prisoner. He would often bring presents, or send them with Krusak. At Christmas I gave his gifts of food to Stefano and Davide Patuzzi: I knew they supported the Fascists and thought they would take them. They knew too, as the rest of the village, that Guy was my husband.

'Of course, I could threaten both men with my godfather Prince Zeno, who was still alive then and a power in Bologna. Guy was popular in Croce, anyway: certainly more liked than the herbalist or coffin-maker. And I had something on Stefano: his hoard of illegal "English gold".

'Still, I found it wise to offer inducements to those two, as well as threats. Stefano I hoped to bribe with the food, to keep sweet . . . I did not think it as necessary with Davide, since he owed me rent, but then he and I had quarrelled before Christmas over the only Jewish family in the area: Davide wanted to know why I hadn't denounced them.

'But that's past now: minor village politics. At the time my sole concern was for Guy and Angelica. I would have done anything to keep us together.

'For Anton, now that he had eaten my dinners, danced with me, been admitted into Bologna society through me, that meant going to bed with me.

'He took me to his rooms in German headquarters. Krusak was kicking his heels outside, his fine mad eyes bright with envy. I make Anton sound heartless, and so I thought him, but I was wrong.

'At first I detested him and despised myself. But then I was also naive – I, who had been married twice. I thought because Anton did not touch my heart he would not move me.

'I was so wrong! His hands gave new caresses. His body knew mine more intimately that I did. That was the worst shame, that he gave me pleasure.

'Now more than ever I wished to deceive Guy. I flirted more with Krusak. I asked other German officers to my villa.

'Guy demanded a promise of me once – this was in April – that there was nothing between Krusak and myself. He made me swear it. I did, knowing it was the truth whilst making me still a liar. By then Anton's strong body was beautiful to me. I was grateful to him, too, that he was so formal in others' company, so seemingly oblivious. Guy called him the Munich fool, and I wanted both to laugh and cry and yet be angry with him.

'That month, April, I was often angry with Guy: he seemed
o remote, untouched. Even though I was terrified he would
nd out, in a strange way I wanted him to know, to throw
nton out. There again I didn't want Anton hurt, I only wanted
im to leave so that maybe Guy and I would be as we had
een before the war.

'Things had been easier between us for a time following
y promise, but then towards the end of April Guy became
ore withdrawn. Anton by contrast was more demanding.
[e too had changed, the war had changed him. He talked to
e about what his commanding officers wanted to do to the
ivilian population – there were rumours about a "scorched
arth" policy being used if the Germans had to retreat. Anton's
mily were in land; he knew what that would mean. The idea
led him with horror and he turned to me for comfort.

'In early May Anton met me in the cathedral on the day of
y godfather's funeral. I knew instantly he was not himself:
is square red face was white. Before the mass began he
hispered that something terrible had happened in the village
f Mutta: two hundred people had been butchered as a
eprisal. He suspected Krusak, saying that he had misread
nd underestimated the Croatian, that he had made a terrible
istake in giving Krusak any active command. Anton felt partly
esponsible for what had happened at Mutta: he wanted to
ake sure nothing like that would happen again, but had no
vidence against Krusak.

'That night Guy mentioned the massacre, speaking
cathingly of Krusak. I was tired from the funeral, from worry,
om thinking about Pietro Terni – a new face to hide – from
ying not to think what could happen in Croce if men like
rusak had their way. I can't remember what I said to Guy.

'By then I had so many secrets to hide. Anton added one
ore, when he told me he could hardly bear to look at Krusak,
at he was determined the Croatian would pay, and yet until
omeone talked he had to act normally with the man.

'Anton wanted me to go away with him. A few days, he
aid. Four days, then cousin Mario could have me for good . . .

'I said yes. Anton was kind then, he made a charade for me

with some officers and a Captain's wife: I was supposedly staying with her. He came to take me away on 8th June, Krusak along with him as usual. Anton wanted to keep an eye on him

'We drove to the German headquarters again, where Krusak got out. An officer drew Anton aside. I knew from Anton's face that it was about Krusak: I learned later from him that one of the soldiers had finally confessed to the massacre. The soldier's testimony would be ready for Anton when he returned from leave. The Italian SS and their German commanders were also involved, and the matter would probably only be settled after a great deal of inter-military rivalry. To have Krusak punished would take days to settle.

'Anton said the thing was a mess but that it needed doing. Then he bustled me into his private car and we set off for the Italian lakes, weaving past German army transports.

'I thought about Guy and Angelica and started to cry. Anton kept on driving. I scrubbed my face with a handkerchief, told myself that it was only a few days. I made myself turn to Anton and tried to smile.

'He did not speak but suddenly swung the car round hard. We drove straight back to Bologna, through the checkpoints, through Ponte, Castel and the rest. It was midday when we reached Croce, and Anton had never said a word. He brought me to the villa, took down my case, helped me out of the car and only then did he speak.

' "I promise you now, Clara: you will not see me again unless you ask," he said, and he hammered on the cellar door.

'Guy opened it. Anton gave him the case and pointed to me. "She's yours, Englishman," he said. "She always has been."

'Anton turned on his heel, walked to his car, reversed it in the square and roared off down the track. I never saw him again.

'I sat down on the garden steps: my legs wouldn't work. I watched Guy striding towards me, the June sun flashing on his red hair. He looked at me with those startling blue eyes of his.

' "It's all right," he said. "It's all right." '

48

Clara's account rang true: there were no gaps, no mysteries. Her grandmother had never betrayed Guy. Whatever last written 'message' Guy had left, his final hours with Clara had been happy. They had been preparing to begin a new life in Switzerland.

Julia's eyes filled at the poignancy of that unrealised hope. 'I'm glad you and he were reconciled,' she remarked, when she was sure her voice would be steady.

Once more aware of the rolls of paper in her fist, papers she had been gripping fiercely throughout Clara's account, Julia relaxed to allow Guy's coded sheets to slide from her grasp onto the small coffee table in the flower gallery.

Letting go of the past, she stretched a hand to a camellia in the gallery, touching it gently. 'I'm going to write to Angelica today, tell her the truth.'

Clara looked uncertain. 'I've been ashamed of the truth. I never told Angelica because I thought I wouldn't need to. I didn't tell you everything because I wanted you to like me. I never thought you would accept it so calmly, as Guy did. He stopped me from explaining, said it didn't matter. Everything after that – the wedding dress, the feast, Vittorio – you know. We did talk that night about Mutta – what Krusak had done here – and the added threat of the Blackshirts' promise to burn villages unless aliens were handed over, but Guy changed his mind about fleeing to Switzerland partly because of Anton. He was worried Anton might decide after all to report him to the Germans.'

'But Anton kept his promise.'

'Yes – and as you know, only Krusak appeared at the feast of Our Lady. He never knew Guy's true identity: only Anton suspected, because he had taken the trouble to search local Italian records for a forty-four-year-old Englishman, forgotten by even the Italian Fascists in Bologna, who had lost three fingers, couldn't shoot a gun, and had never been considered as a spy. That day, 10th June, I think Krusak had assumed Anton and I had fallen out and was determined to seize his chance.'

'Whilst Anton was arranging to have Krusak removed,' said Julia. Clara had returned to Croce on 8th June, and the order transferring Krusak to the front line had gone out two days later.

'You've admitted that you knew about Krusak ordering the murder of the villagers of Mutta, so why did you never mention it when you told me about Scarpia?' Julia asked.

'I didn't see how to, without revealing that I knew Anton.'

'And you didn't want to do that because you were ashamed.' Julia released the camellia blossom. The truth was a gift to her: she felt lightheaded with relief. Now her only fear concerned Simone.

Clara, gliding up to the coffee table, lifted one of Guy's papers and squinted at it by the light of the gallery windows. 'You can understand this?'

'The base language is English.'

Clara peered at another of the coded sheets on the table.

'Here – ' She handed Julia the paper. 'Decode that.'

It was an entry Julia had not studied before. Several minutes passed before she spoke.

'He's describing someone he calls "Simone the Collaborator": Guy's mentioned him before. "Young, stocky, fair. Visits Fascist headquarters regularly. Makes a point of telling me what he's going to tell them. Rather a sad case. Prone to exaggerate. When we first met, Simone almost fell

ver himself to let me know how he'd been approached by
Mussolini *personally* to join the party . . ." '

'Oh, he's talking about Pietro!' Clara smiled. 'He was called
Simone, to distinguish him from the other four Pietros. Simone
Pietro, that was his name in Croce.'

Simone P. The name in Guy's papers stood for Simone
Pietro, not Simone Padovano. Julia frowned at her own
slowness and read:

' "No doubt I'm a middle-aged cynic. Simone's reports certainly seem to keep the Fascists from our doors. Yet each
time I see him setting out for Bologna I'm uneasy . . . he's so
naive and could be tricked into talking more than is good.
Sprint will have nothing to do with him. The others are careful,
but then, with Stefano and Patuzzi in the region, one is always
careful." '

Julia was about to continue when there was an interruption.
Andrea pushed back the gilded doors, admitting two security
guards and, marching between them, brawler's face dark
under glinting spectacle frames, Emilio Gucci.

'What on earth?' began Julia, but Clara, mistress of her
villa, touched her granddaughter's arm and beckoned Andrea.

'This man was picked up in your grounds, Signora. He
claims to know you.'

'I should hope Carlo Gucci's son does know who I am. You
two – release him. Andrea, escort the guards back to wherever
they were patrolling and then please bring us some tea.' She
indicated a small round table and chairs where they might
sit. 'Now, Emilio, what can we do for you?'

Gucci, confounded by Clara's assurance, eyes darting
between grandmother and granddaughter, sat down in a heap
on a wicker chair. Julia couldn't control a burst of laughter,
and Gucci started on her.

'Don't know what's funny: I lost you in Florence and it's
taken me a day to find this place. Then I'm just ambling up
the drive when those two beauties jumped me.' Gucci shook
his grey lapels. 'I'm absolutely buggered.' He drew in a great
breath. 'Roberto says Anton Wolf will testify against Krusak. My
wife passed that message when I phoned her an hour ago.'

Julia goggled. 'Roberto told you?'

Gucci removed his spectacles, examining the lenses by the sunlight. 'He told me not to say anything but now I guess it makes no odds. I'm working for him by keeping an eye on you.'

Julia, expecting to be furious, found herself dissolving into another bout of laughter. Relief, pure relief. Roberto was all right, Wolf would testify, and Clara had no connection with Scarpia, none.

'What's so – funny?' Gucci, stumbling in speech as he stopped himself swearing, glared at Julia and Clara. 'Jesus, you are alike.'

Andrea had materialised with the tea. Four cups: he was staying.

Gucci handed Julia a drawing. 'This was done by my father. Thought I'd chucked it away years ago. That's the boy he was held with: my father had a good look at him when they were both at the Fiorettis.'

Simone's youthful face, stark with fear: terror beyond the simulation of acting. Julia nodded, passed the drawing to Clara.

'Who is it?' Clara demanded.

'Roberto's father,' said Julia.

'They're not really alike . . . maybe around the nose, but the eyes are totally different.' Clara returned the paper to Gucci.

'This boy would have heard you shouting in the chamber,' said Gucci, staring at Simone's anguished features.

That was why Simone disliked her, thought Julia. Not because she looked like Clara, but because she sounded like her. True, her voice was lower, but there were enough similarities to remind Roberto's father: a sound, a voice associated with horror. His dislike was probably quite unconscious.

And the scent?

Julia twisted towards Gucci. 'I know this seems a strange question, but did Francesco Vincenti wear cologne?'

Gucci snorted. 'Naturally! Expensive stuff too, but it smelt to me just like lavender.'

Julia and Clara exchanged a glance.

Again the feeling of having been given a gift came over her. Simone looked less and less likely as Scarpia's second Spoletta. Cesare Celere – Sprint – looked more and more as though he had been known by two nicknames. Julia rested her empty teacup against her stomach, yawning with satisfaction.

Gucci stayed overnight at Clara's villa. Next morning, he visited a magistrate to find out how and where they should present evidence and witnesses to bring Krusak to trial. Julia phoned Mario Scapone, leaving a message on his answering machine.

'Mario Scudieri was my grandfather. I know about the Red-Headed League. Please call.'

Telephoning Tancredi di Salvo, Julia learned he had left his Venetian villa. There was an art fair running over several days in Florence: di Salvo was there.

'And if di Salvo's in the city, then so are Pietro and Krusak,' said Julia to Andrea, on her way upstairs to fetch her coat. 'I'm going to take a look at them. Tell Clara I've gone shopping.' Her grandmother would worry if she knew Krusak was in Florence. She was worried too, about Krusak spotting her, but art fairs were busy public places. She'd be OK.

After her usual vocal practice Julia took a bus into Florence that afternoon. The art fair was being held in one of the fortress-palaces near the Uffizi gallery. Passing fashionable cafés on the Piazza della Repubblica, Julia noticed UPIM's window display. She cut through a knot of harassed tourists to take a closer look.

Baby clothes. She was going crazy. She hadn't even decided yet if she was mad, sad or glad about her 'condition' and here she was, misting a department store's windows, comparing the prices of pram accessories with a blonde younger than she was but with a conspicuous bulge.

'Does Roberto know?'

Julia turned, the smile dropping from her face. In the sun Bianca looked old; her spring and laid-back charm were gone.

She had lost weight. Her eyes and skin were dull, quenched

'This mousy hair is my own.' Bianca didn't give Julia a chance to answer. 'The brown suit's my mother's. Though I'd give it an airing since Papà and di Salvo are into masters of classic design.'

She stepped closer. 'Krusak's here.'

'Thanks for the warning.' Julia squeezed Bianca's arm which felt alarmingly thin. Her companion, stripped of any spare flesh, had a fragile perfection. She had never realised how brittle Bianca was, beneath the polish. 'Come and have a coffee with me,' Julia coaxed.

Bianca glanced behind. 'Here's Papà. Have a drink with him if you want, I need to get back to report on the art fair.'

She started off in the opposite direction, dipping into the crowds, and was gone.

'My dear!' Pietro's face was as rosy as ever. 'Not looking for cribs so soon after Christmas, surely? You're as bad as Francesco and Ruth – they're engaged!' He gave her a kiss on both cheeks.

'Oh, lovely! – I am pleased.' Julia was delighted. As she moved, the image of Bianca's bare, unhappy face hovered an instant before breaking up in a swirl of city starlings.

Pietro patted her arm. 'Let's have a proper Italian coffee at Plini's, eh? I've been thinking over what you said about Krusak, you're right, something should be done about him.' He lowered his voice. 'As you see from Bianca, it's affecting us.'

'Shouldn't we follow her and make sure she's all right?'

'No – I don't think she's too pleased with her parents right now. I'm afraid my wife Elizabetta made a tactless remark at breakfast concerning Francesco's engagement. Don't worry, Bianca's rejoining Tancredi. She's comfortable with him, he's her godfather. He'll look after her.'

Pietro wheeled Julia round in the sunlight towards the covered Straw Market, making a detour to the bronze statue of the boar. Surrendering to superstition, Julia threw a coin and stroked the boar's nose; Pietro laughed.

'I know I'll return to Florence again, with or without the boar's blessing,' he said.

A couple of sparkling silver coins pinged against the base of the statue. 'On the other hand it's always wise to propitiate he local spirits,' said a deep warm voice. A long powerful rm reached past Julia, stroked the sun-warmed metal then wrapped around her middle.

Julia leaned back. 'You were in Vienna this afternoon.' Thinking of what she had to tell him she blushed.

'You were hard to find this afternoon.' Roberto squeezed hen let her go. 'Is it Plini's?' he asked, glancing from Julia to Pietro. 'Yes? Shall we go? Since jetting in I'm parched.'

On the way, Roberto explained why he was no longer in Austria. A neo-Nazi rally had taken place two nights ago outside the Vienna State Opera house. The Jewish conductor ad been heckled and pelted with eggs on the way into the ouse. In protest the conductor and principals had refused to lay the last two performances.

'Rather unfair on your customers,' observed Pietro.

Roberto shrugged. 'If we don't protest about how our fellow usicians are treated then who will? That rally shouldn't have een allowed near the opera house.'

'That's called democracy,' said Pietro drily. 'What all these d partisans are supposed to have saved.'

Julia left them to it. Roberto was here. She could tell him. Vhat would his face show when she spoke? Pride? Relief? by? Please let there be joy. Walking beside Roberto from the traw Market she watched him talking to Pietro; saw Pietro iving her and Roberto the occasional speculative glance. rustrated and anxious, feeling unable to speak, Julia turned er head aside.

oberto was free of the opera but was already committed. earning that he was available, a recording company based Pisa had insisted he fly in that evening: Florence was a atched visit. 'I shouldn't really be here,' was the singer's niling conclusion. 'But there again, Pisa's not far.'

'You're recording at night?' Pietro asked.

'Less traffic noise.'

'How is it, singing in the small hours?' asked Julia.

'Like singing through jet-lag.' Roberto drained his red win[e] and rose. Both had waited in vain for Pietro to move. 'Mus[t] go – no, you stay.' He leaned across the table, kissed Juli[a] 'I'll see you the day after tomorrow at Clara's, OK?'

He was gone and she had not told him.

'I should be leaving too.' Now, when it was too late, Pietr[o] Terni finally rose to his feet. With Roberto's unexpecte[d] appearance, they had not mentioned Krusak. Julia opened he[r] mouth to speak, but Pietro shook his head. 'I ought to b[e] getting back to Tancredi and Bianca. You're at Clara's? I'll b[e] in touch.'

He bustled out, leaving Julia alone.

invited him. He came this afternoon.' Clara threw Julia a challenging look. 'I've told him *everything*. As we're the only two adult victims of Scarpia who survived, we decided it would be an excellent idea if we saw Krusak together.'

Simone, seated at the dining table, inclined his grey head. Julia thought him less remote, higher-coloured, definitely more at ease. Still, there wasn't a smile on those fine features when he remarked, 'I only wish Roberto could have found it in himself to give me all the facts sooner: I'd like to have had the chance to be involved.'

Masking her astonishment at Simone's unexpected appearance, Julia drew Clara from the doorway. 'Is Gucci back?'

'No.'

'You're going to see Krusak at the art fair?'

'A public place? Certainly not! I've invited Krusak, di Salvo, Pietro and Bianca to dinner tomorrow. They have accepted. It makes sense.' Clara overrode Julia's disbelief. 'I told Bianca Pietro was out when I telephoned – that I'd love to see her father after all these years. I told di Salvo that my granddaughter would be honoured to meet a patron of the arts. As for Krusak – ' Clara tilted her curly head on one side 'I said you had an answer for him.'

'What!' Julia plummeted onto a chair, staring at Clara.

'I had to tell him something. The carrot of seeing me and hearing from you was just what was required. I must say,' Clara continued, 'it was quite simple to talk to Krusak. He sounds as he did when I first knew him. He'll be easily handled.'

'Grandmother, sit.' Julia was out of the chair. Ignoring Simone she made Clara settle and look at her. 'Listen, this man is dangerous . . .'

'We have the security guards. What could be less threatening than a dinner party of old acquaintances and new friends?' Clara's good eye gleamed in her wrinkled face: a youthful look.

The two older people were inordinately pleased with themselves. To Julia's chagrin, Simone seemed to have hit it off with Clara at once, despite – or because of – their mutual involvement with horror. Her narrow fingers snapped at Simone and Clara. 'Something's happened. Come on, give.'

'Mario Scapone has been in touch,' answered Simone from the table. 'I listened on the extension.'

'We talked in the Croce dialect.' Clara patted Julia's hand. 'You were right: Scapone was Umberto Gasparini. He'd never destroyed the fake documents. When tax demands overwhelmed him in the fifties, Umberto dug them out and used them.' She smiled. 'He said my voice hadn't changed; he knew me at once. He's fit and as quick-witted as ever, though in a wheelchair because of arthritis.' Clara rubbed an elbow. 'Makes me grateful my aches are minor.' She pulled a face. 'Getting decrepit's no fun.'

'Don't tease,' said Julia, smiling. 'What did you find out?'

Clara's smile faded. She glanced at Simone, who spoke.

'Gasparini was woken by your grandfather, the night following the feast of Our Lady of the Vines. Guy wanted to tell his second in command that he had decided to leave Croce to take his family to safety in Switzerland, and also warn the man about the wreath of corncockles, suggesting there was a possible traitor in the partisan group. Umberto thinks Guy may have been spotted by Patuzzi or one of the others on his return to the village and they picked him up then.'

So her grandfather hadn't been lured out, thought Julia. It had been opportunism on the part of Scarpia and his men.

Simone sighed. 'Even if Guy had not gone out of his own accord that night, I think Sprint would have been sent to summon him. I'd hinted about a big Allied operation to Sprint and suggested that the Red-Headed League was involved. Sprint naturally knew nothing about this and he must have decided that his intelligence-gathering days were over: either the group had guessed he was a double-agent, or Guy didn't trust him enough.

'I imagine that Guy had been allowed to continue his small-scale activities whilst every move he and his group made was known by the enemy: now, though, that seemed to have changed. To Sprint and Scarpia, Guy, as the head of a partisan outfit engaged in assisting a major Allied invasion, suddenly became more valuable captured and interrogated than left free.'

'Yes, I see that,' murmured Julia, not looking at Simone. She was trying not to blame Roberto's father, trying to ignore the feeling of disillusionment.

Because now her grandfather's brave efforts in the war looked futile. Scarpia – Krusak – had not considered them important enough to move against until the very last moment: presumably with the idea of having a small partisan unit free as bait to attract larger-scale outfits. Worse, her grandfather had never suspected anything until too late. 'Poor Guy,' she said.

'There's more,' warned Clara. 'Next day, Gasparini had to travel to Bologna. He spotted Krusak in a bar, nursing a hangover. The barman told him that Krusak had been there drinking all the previous evening, from about nine.'

Julia stiffened. 'He didn't return to Croce that night?'

'No.'

'But that means he can't be Scarpia! And what about Pietro?'

'Yes, it's interesting isn't it? Pietro told me that Krusak had returned to Croce to haul him off to German headquarters. Now it seems that Krusak never moved out of Bologna on the night of 10th June.'

'So how did Pietro get his scars?' said Simone.

Roberto's father was animated, open; different from the underhand Simone she'd seen, thought Julia. She liked this man.

'You see now why I've invited them all?' said Clara. 'Somebody's lying and sooner or later they'll make a mistake. Then we shall know.'

Roberto, standing by a wall phone in a recording studio corridor, address book in hand, time to kill until the Pisa traffic lessened, was considering Sprint. When and why had Sprint decided to turn traitor? Had he been approached by Francesco Vincenti, his singing teacher?

Singers. Since Krusak had entered the frame as the main suspect for the man he and Julia were after, they had tended to forget the opera connections.

Scarpia's voice. Too clear for Vincenti. Too developed for Sprint – who in any case looked a certainty as Spoletta, the junior singer in the wartime torture chamber. Stefano the herbalist had no voice, according to Clara. Patuzzi's would have been untrained.

Roberto clapped a hand to his head. 'I'm going crazy! It's been staring me in the face – Scarpia was a young singer, the voice might not have settled . . .'

Feverishly, he leafed through addresses. It was a long shot, but if the German sisters would talk to him . . .

How had he been so blind? Of course, the idea may not have occurred to Julia: women's voices generally go through less dramatic fluctuations than men's. At sixteen he had been a bass and remained so, but still he should have thought of it.

Rapidly Roberto punched the number he wanted. When the call was answered he began to talk.

Hours later, after two recording 'takes', Roberto was called back to the same wall phone. It was three in the morning. 'Yes?' He yawned into the receiver, hoping whoever it was wouldn't keep him long.

'How many lies has she told you?'

The voice, a sibilant whisper, killed Roberto's yawn, raised
: hairs on his arms.

'She's had an abortion—'

'What are you talking about?'

'When you met her in Florence it was already done.'

'Who is this?'

*'Listen! Julia Rochfort's killed your baby for her singing career.
d she goes with other men. What do you think of that, eh?'*
e line went dead.

Roberto dropped the receiver, crouched in the corridor.
had to catch his breath, everything around him seemed to
slipping away. The world had become suddenly unreal.

'I don't believe you, Whisperer,' he said. 'I mustn't. I can't.'
ground his knuckles fiercely into his eyes. Somehow he
l to get through the next few hours. From somewhere he
l to drag the resources to sing well and joyously.

How many lies. Even as he struggled to dismiss the call,
berto's mind flashed back to their quarrel in Venice, and
fore that to the time Julia was roughed up in Florence when
hadn't wanted the police. She hadn't wanted to tell him
thing either, done so only reluctantly. She had been hiding
nething from him again recently: he'd assumed it was to
with di Salvo but perhaps he'd been mistaken. And Gucci,
t Julia, had been the one to tell him about Francesco Terni
shing naked from her Milan flat.

Secrets, always secrets. Carlotta had been a great one for
:rets, especially towards the end of their marriage when
: was deceiving him with the Piedmontese. He'd been taken
once; he wouldn't be made the fool twice. Whatever he did,
his father, for his ex-wife, now maybe for Julia too, it was
ver enough. 'Stop it!' he muttered, disgusted by this self-pity.
Julia knew what *her* having *his* baby would mean to him.

'Mother of God, it's impossible!' Roberto smashed a fist
unst the wall. Anger blasted through him, fiery and swift
a meteor, leaving ashes. His baby. The idea ran through
head like water through his fingers. Blinking, Roberto
nd that his eyes were wet. Tiredness, nothing to do with
: call, nothing—

Julia was young, ambitious, blessed with exceptional talent. She had said she didn't want the distraction of children – he understood that, respected it. But surely, if she had been pregnant by him she would have told him? Did he not even have the right to know, that however briefly, he had been a father? Yet she had said nothing when they met. Not a word. Not a hastily scribbled note. Not a single look. She had been easy, happy. Pale, dark shadows under the eyes, but that was nothing; it did not mean what the caller had suggested.

The anger, hurt, jealousy, were coming for him again but this time he was ready: he couldn't let the Whisperer win.

'. . . *killed your baby . . . she goes with other men.*' Whoever had phoned him had fed him exactly the right lines to let him hang himself, and that was what he was doing. Roberto began to laugh.

'What's funny?' asked a technician, stepping round him.

Roberto, crouching, hid his bleeding knuckles. 'Nothing. A bad joke.'

50

ulia!'

Stepping from a florist's into midday rain, Julia turned. 'Do you often follow people?' she demanded, amused. Her eyes ashed over Tom Jessop's black jacket, cropped brown hair, gitated expression, empty hands. 'No knife today?'

'We must talk.' Tom ignored shoppers and rain. He witched to English. 'I need to talk to you.'

'Not right now.' Julia briskly cut him off. She'd enough to ink about without having to deal with this persistent fan.

'If you'd just let me explain—' Tom pushed in front of her, n act of calculated rudeness which ignited Julia's temper.

'Mr Jessop.' She stepped close to drive her words home. 'ven singers are entitled to privacy off-stage. I'm getting sick seeing your sharp little face bobbing up round every street orner. If you want my autograph, fine, you can have it, but ve anything else for the opera house. Just at this moment, d like you to grow up and stop pestering me. Try to be a entleman, can't you?'

Huddled under a shop awning, tourists in brightly coloured mpsuits and sandals looked up from their guidebooks to atch.

'Julia, please.'

'Leave me alone!'

She was going away, striding out in her jeans and trainers,

black curls bouncing as she sped towards the Ponte Vecchio.
He was losing her again, thought Tom, and in sudden panic
he blurted out: 'But I'm your father!'

That stopped her dead. The scent of the Florentine violets
she was carrying swirled in Julia's head. Tom's resonant voice
echoing in her skull, she whipped round to confront him, the
sight of that wiry frame with its dull black jacket and straight
brown hair making his claim totally improbable.

'You've got to be kidding!'

'I've a photograph.' Tom snatched his wallet from his jacket,
thrust out the second picture Roberto had seen. Rain splashed
down on Angelica and her baby. Tom saw Julia's brilliant eyes
widen then narrow. She made no move to take the photograph
from him. Above them the shadow of a building crane blinked
across her face as a brief shaft of sun scudded between grey
clouds.

Encouraged by her stillness, Tom hustled closer. 'And I've
a letter at my home from your mother, written when she must
have been pregnant with you.'

Julia thought of her own baby: hers and Roberto's – whom
she still had not told. She looked at the picture again, turning
slightly sick as she caught a sour whiff of the rain-swollen
Arno ahead. The woman was certainly Angelica, and the
child—

Tom's hand suddenly snapped onto her wrist, yanking her
aside. 'Watch where you're going!' he said sharply to a tourist
with a grey bag bulging with camera equipment who had
almost cannoned into Julia. 'Come on. We ought to find
somewhere to sit.'

Tom: drawing her towards the old bridge. The touch of his
warm fingers, his gesture of protection, above all the swiftness
of his reactions, made Julia admit it: Tom could be her father.
No hero, no handsome charmer, no tall dark stranger, Tom.

Even as her childhood fantasies drizzled away in the rain,
childish resentment followed. 'Let go!' She wrung her wrist
from his hand, pounding off into the crowds on the old bridge.

'Steady on!' Tom, striding out with the same rapid step as
her own, caught up. 'If you'd only let me explain—'

'I don't want to know.' Swerving round for another go at
is man – her father! – Julia almost knocked a briefcase out
a tall blonde woman's hand. 'In any case, where've you been
til now? Where were you when my mother "suggested" I
ep my "nice voice" as a hobby and learn to teach music
stead of sing it? Or when she came right out and said my
aining was a waste of time and money, and that I was
luding myself? Where were you when I was starting my
ofessional career, wondering always if my next performance
audition would be my last? And all the while pretending to
y mother and my stepfather that I was doing well when I
ten had to decide whether what was left of my fees was
ing to buy me another singing lesson or a decent meal?'

'Julia, we can't discuss these things in the open street, come
d sit in the loggia, please.'

'And where were you after that picture you've got there
as taken? My grandmother knows nothing about you. You
ok off when you realised my mother might need your help,
dn't you? Just left her in the lurch—'

'That is *not* true.'

'Dumped her and disappeared. Until I start to make a name
r myself, start earning steadily, and then look who pops up
ain like some fairy godfather, all ready for a serious family
lationship . . .'

'If I might just get a word in edgeways?'

'No, I haven't finished yet. Not by a long way. Did you expect
e to fall weeping onto your neck?'

'Will you be quiet for two seconds and give me time to
xplain?'

The sudden spike of volume was astonishing. His voice
verberated on the wooden roof of the old bridge. People
ering into jewellers' shops on the Ponte Vecchio turned to
are at Tom, who had gone quite red.

'Honestly!' he muttered. 'I've never had to shout at the boys
ke that.'

The boys: Tom's words sent another shock singeing through
lia. Not only the prodigal father's return, but brothers too
/ the sound of it. Suddenly her mind was empty of whatever

else she had been going to say. Silent now, passing the
jeweller's who had repaired her watch, Julia stepped with Tom
under the loggia. It was crammed with people sheltering from
the weather.

Not the ideal place to try to explain to his daughter why he
had not been in touch before now, thought Tom, but then life
was often like that, with great personal dramas played out in
packed bus stations, dirty noisy streets, teeming public
squares. He rested a shoulder against one of the loggia's stone
pillars, watching Julia watching the rain, violets gripped tightly
in her hand. His youngest child, but already a grown woman,
a stranger. For an instant Tom hated both Angelica and his
wife, two women who between them had kept Julia from him.

That wasn't strictly true, thought Tom, and he sighed.

Julia was still watching the rain: giving him time, Tom
realised, to collect himself. Now that the first flush of her anger
was gone he saw a keen yet forgiving nature in that strong
face, those laughter-lines that were just beginning. Perhaps
her nature was more generous than he deserved: she wanted
to like him, he knew. The knowledge gave Tom confidence to
speak.

'I met your mother here in 1968, during a conference. She
stopped me walking under one of the more dangerous of the
flood-damaged buildings, and in thanks I took her for a drink.
She knew more English than I did Italian and I asked if she'
be my guide for the week. Angelica said yes. That was the
start of our affair.'

Even in the shadowy loggia, he glowed at the memory. In
that instant Julia understood how her mother might have been
drawn to him.

'I was here two months – seven weeks longer than the conference. I told Jean, my wife, that I was after Italian suppliers
for cabinet wood. I hired a car and drove Angelica to Rome.

'Rome in midsummer. We sat on the Spanish Steps and I
asked Angelica to marry me. I said I'd get a divorce. In Rome
in that intoxicating heat anything seemed possible.

'Angelica shook her head. "Come back next summer, i
you feel the same," she said, smiling. When I asked how would

keep in touch she said, "I've your business address: that's ough." That was all she said. Soon after, I drove her back Florence and we parted.'

'And the following year?' Julia asked. After so many years wondering who her father was, she wanted to know erything, instantly. Impatient, she watched Tom fiddle with s black tie.

'That summer I'd a letter from your mother – my first and t. She said that if I still wanted to see her, it must be in ptember, not June. She gave no reason.'

Angelica, secretive as ever, thought Julia, winding a curl hair as she listened. Around them people coughed and attered softly. She and Tom were private in a public place.

'In September I went to the bar where Angelica had said should meet, on the day she'd suggested. I knew if she ln't come I'd lost her: Angelica had always refused to tell e her full name, or where she lived. She said that didn't atter.

'She walked in that evening – with you. She didn't have to l me you were mine. Those two months, your mother was th no one else but me. You were about six months old then, ry dark and quick. You had my ears—' Tom was about to d 'still have, in fact,' when he decided that would make him und like a sentimental idiot. And he wasn't sentimental: uldn't afford to be in his job.

Tom was silent, staring at the dark, wood-stained little gernail on his right hand. He was right about the ears, ought Julia, looking him over.

'Your mother showed me your birth certificate: Julia lentina Rochfort. It said father unknown. I was angry. You re mine – Angelica said that made no difference.

' "It won't work, Tom," she said. "Go back to your English fe and sons: I won't be the cause of breaking up a family. lia is mine. I wanted her, I had her. I'll find another man, meone to trust. I've watched you all day in this bar, ndering what to say when I came in. I didn't expect you ck, you see. I can't trust you, Tom: you had an affair with e. Go back to your wife." '

Enrico, thought Julia. An image of her stepfather, dar
stocky, kind, trustworthy, flickered on the river. Angelica ha
chosen Enrico, who had loved both mother and daughte
Julia is mine. I wanted her. Angelica's words rang in her min
She admired her mother's courage, her proud independenc

She glanced at Tom. His lips moved as he talked quietly
himself. Suddenly he jerked his shoulders back. He was quic
as she was. And he could shout just as loud.

'May I see that picture again please?' she asked.

Tom sighed, not sure if the sigh was exasperation or reli
'That was all Angelica let me have of you.'

Julia took the photograph, wiping it carefully clean of rai
water. 'Go on,' she murmured.

Tom scowled, disliking this next part, uneasy as to ho
Julia would react to it. 'Back in England, I told Jean everythin
She said she'd have me back, but only if I promised never
see Angelica again. I wasn't to get in touch with you, either.
agreed. It was hard for a time, but we rebuilt our life. Whe
Jean died two years ago I hadn't really thought of you in year
The boys were growing up; I had my hands full with them.

It was true: she did have brothers. Delight burst in Juli
and gratitude. She was someone's sister, she wasn't alon
She had always wanted brothers. How many? she wondere

'Three older brothers.' Tom guessed her thought. 'Nige
the youngest, is studying at Perugia. The middle one, Stephe
is working in Milan – for a subsidiary of Galatea, would yo
believe. Alan, the eldest, is married and managing the busines
in England.'

An English father. English brothers. Julia's eyes blurre
as rain, trailing off to warm drizzle, bounced off the stone wa
of the loggia and splashed her hand. People were moving awa
colourful in their holiday clothes, opening onto the cobbles
the Ponte Vecchio like the petals of a flower after a storm.

Now that they had space to move farther apart from eac
other, she and Tom exchanged glances. 'So you rebuilt you
life without me. What made you decide to get in touch thi
year?' Julia asked, turning slightly aside.

'I spotted an article about you in *Oggi* just before Christma

It gave your name and there was a picture. I recognised the name at once and when I looked at your photograph . . .' Tom smiled and shook his head. He didn't want to say she hadn't changed a bit since infancy because that was obviously wrong, and yet the essentials, the essence, remained the same. In an opera cast of thousands, he would have picked her out at once, recognised her as his.

Hesitantly, he touched her arm. 'I'm sorry I scared you the first time we met here. Only seeing you like that, by chance, put any last doubts from my mind.' Tom recalled the shock of mingled pleasure and alarm that encounter had given him. Julia, darker than anyone else he knew in his family, and yet who moved like him, nimble and quick. Jean, his wife, had always wanted a daughter. So had he, thought Tom, although he had pretended to Jean that he wasn't bothered. So strong had been this deception, he had almost deluded himself, until he spotted Julia skimming down a Florentine street, alive with that energy, that presence. His little girl, this amazing young woman who made him feel both protective towards her and just a little in awe. 'I wanted to know you. I wanted you to know me.'

The rain had stopped and the sun came out.

'Will you tell me about Alan and Stephen and Nigel?' Julia asked. 'Not right now,' she added hastily. 'Perhaps when we next meet – that is, if you want to?' Suddenly she was afraid that having made himself known to her, Tom would think that enough and disappear. And she didn't want that, Julia realised.

'Of course I want to see you, Julia – Do you think I go chasing opera singers as a general thing?' Indignant, Tom's lean features reddened. 'And I'll not only tell you about your brothers – you're going to meet them, too.'

His fiery belligerence touched Julia. She stood looking at Tom, the man with the red scarf who had frightened her so much; and who had been frightened in turn by Roberto. *Poor Dad:* the thought rose quite naturally, with no sense of drama or shock. Instead, Julia considered how – even after having been slammed against the wall of a Venetian alleyway and told in no uncertain terms to back off – Tom had still kept trying to talk to her. And she had been so difficult.

Their eyes met, Julia reflecting that now she understood why he had thrown her flowers, and why she had kept them.

'Hold still.' Surprisingly, her voice was breathy: trained as she was, Julia was finding it difficult to draw in a proper lungful of air. Carefully, still holding her breath, she tucked a slender spray of violets into Tom's buttonhole. 'There. That's in return for all those white roses.' She patted his jacket, colouring slightly.

Tom lifted his lapel to sniff the flower, touching the petals gently with a finger. He swallowed, then in a sudden jerky movement, bent his head and kissed her forehead.

'Julia.'

51

Roberto was waiting at Clara's villa when Julia returned. Meeting her in the lobby by the old walnut wardrobe, he silently opened his arms. Julia went and put her head against his shoulder and sighed.

They said nothing.

'How long you think they're gonna stay like that?' snorted Gucci, peering through from the flower gallery. 'Couple of statues.'

'They're young,' said Clara.

'Roberto and I need to get going: I told them in the city that we'd be down before six.'

'Have another coffee first.' Clara raised her handbell to summon Andrea. 'I think you'll find that when those two finally move they'll have an interesting story to tell; something you should stay to hear . . . Where are you going?'

'To fetch Simone from the music-room. If it's that interesting I think everyone better listen.'

Ten minutes later, flanking Andrea with his tray of cups and cakes as he entered the flower gallery, Roberto and Julia appeared.

'Someone phoned me in Pisa last night,' Roberto said. 'I was told that Julia had just had an abortion because of her singing career . . .'

'Pregnant!' mumbled Simone, shaking his head. Clara exchanged a nod and a secret smile with Julia, Gucci shrugged.

'So?' he demanded.

'Whoever telephoned knew where to find me, knew Julia and I were close and knew of the scandal about my divorce.'

'So?'

Roberto's hand made a cutting motion over his cup, then he smiled at Clara. 'It certainly did cause mischief. Especially as the first few times I phoned Julia I kept getting your answering machine. At six this morning, after being up all night recording, I could just about accept the idea that Julia might be with someone else, but even if I had believed the caller it would have made no difference.' He glanced at Julia.

Julia, snug in her wicker chair, winked at him. He motioned in case she wished to continue but she shook her head. She felt much too comfortable, and tonight's dinner party would be very different from this friendly gathering.

So, between drinks of coffee, Roberto went on to explain that when Julia had telephoned *him* at seven that morning in Pisa, and he had learned about tonight, everything the caller had said became irrelevant. With Krusak and di Salvo in her grandmother's house, Julia might be in danger. Roberto had to be there, too.

He frowned. 'Besides, I'm not a hot-blooded fool who believes one malicious telephone call.'

Julia decided to speak. 'Maybe it was just malice.'

'But why?' said Gucci. 'And who?'

'We will know soon enough,' said Clara.

Di Salvo, tall, grey-blond, in glossy black dinner jacket, kissed Julia's hand. Behind him in the ante-room, waiting to be admitted into the flower gallery by Andrea, was Krusak, eyes fevered with anticipation. Clara was with him, looking years younger in her dark blue gown and a pair of Julia's long earrings. She was staring at di Salvo's back.

'My dear!' Di Salvo straightened. 'Will you and Roberto sing tonight?'

Julia touched her throat. 'I've a cough, and Roberto's
'sting,' she answered, 'but I'd be happy to play for you or
gnor Terni to sing.' She smiled at Pietro, who was talking to
anca and Roberto by the small table laid out with a tray of
erries. Pietro did not appear to hear her.

'Ah, my dear, I've no voice. That is why I'm filled with
Imiration for you.' Di Salvo had not yet released her hand.
ell me, are all the guests here now?'

Julia shook her head. 'We're waiting for Roberto's father
d a friend of his.' Hearing the front door bang and seeing
nilio Gucci walk in, she smoothly detached herself. 'Excuse
e.' Retrieving the sherries, Julia walked through into the
te-room to Clara and Krusak.

'You have an answer for me,' said Krusak, taking a glass.

Julia, forcing herself to touch him, put a hand on his arm.
ater.' Her cocktail dress sparkled as she moved to Gucci.

'That di Salvo's familiar,' said Gucci, refusing a sherry.

'He tells me he can't sing.'

Gucci's double chins buried themselves in his collar. 'That's
t right.' He stopped. 'Why am I so sure about that?'

'Emilio!' Clara, hands outstretched in welcome, joined them.
reeting the ex-Marshal she murmured, 'Who is that man?
n sure di Salvo isn't his real name. You know him too, don't
u?'

Julia glanced at di Salvo, talking to Krusak in the gallery.

'Michele Bozzi!' Gucci leaned against the door with a thud.
he curate of Croce.'

Even though Julia had often wondered at di Salvo's interest
her, this news, this sudden linking of the man to San Martino
lla Croce was utterly unexpected. Finally, it seemed the
st person she had needed to trace, was here, now, in her
andmother's villa. Her heart hammering, the sherry searing
r throat, Julia twisted round to look again.

Tancredi di Salvo, now recognised as Bozzi, the curate
nom Guy had described as dangerous. Michele Bozzi. The
an had changed his name after leaving the priesthood. Why?
d again, since it was obvious that Bozzi had emigrated to
nerica and then come back, why had Bianca implied that

the former curate of Croce was still in the States?

'She knows his real name,' said Julia under her breath. Bianca, slim in her mother's suit, sipping her drink and listening politely to the men in the gallery. How long had she known that Bozzi and her godfather were one and the same? Julia wondered. Not long, she decided, glancing over the woman's dowdy brown hair and suit. Bianca still had not recovered from the shock . . . or was it that she now knew too much of this curate's wartime exploits? What else did Bianca know about Tancredi?

'Bozzi looks different,' remarked Clara, the first to speak after this revelation. 'Not simply older, more than that. Something's missing.' She reached to tweak a windowsill flower arrangement to her satisfaction. 'It's so long ago. I wish I could remember.'

'Give it time,' said Julia, drawing Clara and Gucci forward as the door rattled again. 'Bring Simone straight through,' she said over her shoulder to Andrea. 'We'll be in the gallery.'

'Watching faces,' muttered Gucci.

Fifteen minutes later, Andrea asked the guests to step into the dining-room. Roberto, Clara and Pietro, chattering about the Galatea competition, led the way in, followed by di Salvo and Bianca. Krusak was waiting to appropriate Julia, but Gucci deflected his attention with a question and she entered on Simone's arm.

'I was wrong about you,' Simone murmured without looking at her. 'You're right for Roberto: these last few months I don't think I've seen him happier.'

'You still tried to make it hard for us – or for me.'

Simone's hazel eyes looked confused. 'Can't explain why I was so unreasonable.' He cleared his throat. 'Ruth Marlow showed me what an idiot I was being: I wasn't proud of myself after she'd laid into me in that Milanese pizza parlour.'

Julia had no idea what Simone was talking about, but smiled reassuringly. Simone, as far as his nature would allow, was apologising. She could even forgive that petty trick with the costume diadem.

'I know my behaviour's been shabby, especially whilst you've been at La Scala.' Simone frowned, rubbing his breast bone. 'It seems so childish now.'

'Putting fake jewellery in a fellow musician's coat in order to make trouble?'

Simone drew back Julia's dining chair for her, his face hot.

'Thank you.' Glancing at him, Julia decided he'd probably been abject enough, and tonight she and Simone were allies, with more important things to resolve than their ridiculous dispute.

'Any joy with our other guests?' she asked softly.

'Krusak and Pietro Terni didn't appear to know me. Di Salvo wasn't sure.'

Gucci came alongside Julia as he walked to his seat, muttering, 'Bozzi in his twenties had a large mole on his chin. Where's that gone?' He picked up an ashtray. 'Courtesy of your grandmother, she remembered,' he said aloud.

Julia nodded, looking anxiously at Clara. One of her grandmother's tormentors had had a mole on his chin. Clara's face was pale as they walked to their seats.

Clara sat at one table end, Julia at the other. Pietro was on Clara's right, Roberto on her left, Bianca on his left, Gucci next to Bianca. Bianca, in her mother's brown suit, scarcely spoke. Listless under the burning lights, she toyed with her wine.

Julia had Simone on her right and Krusak on her left. Under the guise of studying the floral arrangement in the unlit fireplace she watched Simone. Clearly, Roberto's father wasn't sure if Krusak had been one of the men who had interrogated him. And what of di Salvo/Bozzi? Eating her Parma ham with melon, Julia considered the former curate, comfortable between Pietro and Simone. She coughed, ham catching in her throat. Beside her Simone, nervous, ate only melon.

Someone around this table had tortured Clara and Simone, set thugs onto her in Florence, sent an assassin to Roberto in Vienna and threatened his nephew Paolo.

Between courses, Gucci pushed back his chair and excused

himself. When Roberto followed suit, Julia slipped from her seat. Walking from the dining-room, she found Roberto and Gucci in the flower gallery.

'Bianca's father is on something,' said Roberto. 'His eyes are as big as dinner plates. Bianca's going quietly crazy about him.'

Julia, tongue between teeth, nodded. 'I'd better get back,' she said. She and Roberto touched hands briefly before Julia turned on her heel and went back inside.

Pietro and drugs. She and Roberto had assumed it was Bianca who was connected with the narcotics world, but with Bianca 'going crazy' as Roberto put it, was it likely that she had provided her father with anything? Wasn't it more reasonable to conclude that Pietro had his own supply? Julia recalled Pietro being approached by the Sicilian street trader in Bologna: the trader had asked if Pietro wanted his 'usual'. And if Pietro had contacts with pushers and other drug users, here was a steady pool of labour who would do almost any job in return for their fix, including assault and murder.

Julia resumed her seat, picking up her napkin. Pietro was talking to Clara, genial face shiny in candle-light. She thought of his poor acting, the way he had saved her from being mowed down by a Vespa in Bologna. Pietro as a villain just didn't fit.

Krusak touched her wrist. 'A pity La Scala is on strike. I was looking forward to your dress rehearsal of *Cinderella*.'

Julia, trying not to think about the massacred villagers of Mutta, made herself smile. 'It's given me these days in Florence with Clara, so I'm not complaining.'

'And Roberto here with you, too,' put in Simone.

That brought in the neo-Nazi rally in Vienna. Over the main course of lamb, the dinner party began to discuss politics and the right wing in Europe. 'You'd think, after Mussolini, people wouldn't be taken in twice,' said Pietro.

'Many idealists have been trapped that way.' Julia's mouth dried as she met Clara's gaze over the table centre-piece of violets. 'Absolute power to do good.'

'Whose good?' growled Gucci, back in the room.

'I think that's why Sprint turned traitor,' said Roberto. 'He

aw the Fascists *doing* things, saw they had power. Even the
iove against his father, making him drink castor oil, was
ctive, and Sprint would see it brought results: his father was
roken. To a seventeen-year-old that twisted logic can be
iewitching.'

'The Fascists were organised,' observed di Salvo. 'The
artisans were a rag-bag collection with no control.'

Gucci punched his chair arm, saying nothing.

'Sprint was impressed by strength.' Pietro leaned back in
iis chair. 'The same as his teacher, Francesco Vincenti.' He
iodded down the table to Simone. 'Vincenti was your tutor
io: I know who you are now, the boy from Castel. I must say
didn't recognise you at first, but then your son has
ivershadowed you.'

Simone frowned but Pietro smiled reassuringly.

'I remember Francesco telling me on an opera night in April
4 how he had a promising, but very young, pupil who was
:udying the part of Schaunard in *La Bohème*, and doing
irprisingly well with it.'

Simone's finely shaped chin took on spots of colour. 'That's
:range,' he replied, with a steadiness which reminded Julia
f Roberto, 'I didn't touch that part until June '44.' His hazel
ies darkened. 'No one except Vincenti and I knew about it.'

'I expect I've mistaken the dates – my memory isn't what it
as.' Pietro smiled. 'Francesco must have mentioned it in June.'

'But where was this, Signore? In June '44 my tutor was not
the Bologna opera house, neither were you.'

Simone rose to his feet. 'Vincenti ran through the music
ith me at his house on the evening of 8th June, the day before
was captured by Scarpia, after which I never went back to
incenti as a pupil. So when did you learn of this, Signor
erni?'

Clara too had risen, gripping the chair for support. 'And
ow did you know what impressed Sprint? In Croce you and
e avoided each other.'

Pietro gave a shaky laugh. 'Does all this matter?' he asked.
's fifty years ago – one forgets things. Clara, you know me,
this fair?'

Clara fingered the crucifix round her neck. 'I don't know you any more, Pietro,' she said slowly. 'Not at all.'

'It seems your friends are deserting you, Pietro.' Roberto glanced at Bianca, pale and silent opposite her father. 'Will you blame your daughter next for the phone call to me last night? Someone rang up trying to make mischief – no name, just a whisper. Apart from Julia, only one person knew exactly where I was in Pisa and that was you.' Roberto took a step closer to Pietro. 'What did you hope to gain?'

'I shall not answer your offensive suggestions.' Pietro jerked back his chair. 'Come, Bianca. We're leaving.'

'Not just yet,' said Julia. 'I know Signor Krusak would be interested to hear what he did when he interrogated you at Nazi headquarters during the war.'

Krusak's features took on the clarity of a woodcut. 'What am I supposed to have done?'

'Brought Pietro in for questioning on 10th June, 1944,' said Julia. 'You must remember that evening, when you were transferred.'

'After you'd murdered Vittorio,' said Clara, 'and massacred the villagers of Mutta. We know, Krusak! Soon Italy will know.'

'I executed those people as traitors. I was following orders.' Krusak's thin lips quivered. 'The rest is a lie!' He flicked a contemptuous hand towards Pietro. 'Why should I touch him? An informer, and not a very efficient one.'

Pietro laughed. 'If you believe an ex-Nazi—'

'Not quite,' said Roberto. 'I've spoken to the German twins, Elsa Dontini and her sister. They told me an interesting story about one evening in early June 1944 – neither could be sure of the exact date – when they and Nino Dontini were called upon by the Nazis in Bologna to act as dialect interpreters. Both remembered Krusak vividly, but neither mentioned you – which is strange, considering they would have known you from the Bologna opera chorus. Did you look into one of the interrogation rooms and see the two sisters and they not see you?'

'There's a simpler explanation. I wasn't there.'

'But then how did you know about the German twins?' asked

berto reasonably. 'You told Julia that Elsa and Karin were
rified of Krusak.'

'Opportunism,' muttered Julia. She pointed at Pietro. 'When
u realised I was gathering evidence against Krusak you
entioned the German twins as though you and they had been
ld together, in order to vindicate your own story.'

'Don't forget the threat to me, which just happened to be
itten in Serbo-Croat, Krusak's first language,' put in Roberto.

'Are these suggestions put for any purpose?' broke in di Salvo.

'Patience, Signore, I'm coming to it,' said Roberto evenly.
ter Elsa Dontini had finished talking with me, I had a long
at with her sister. Karin was a singer. I asked her about the
cording the Bologna opera company had made in the late
30s, particularly a tenor solo by a young singer called Pietro
rni. Karin said that Terni had been very proud of that solo,
eing he had started as a baritone and was just now
veloping his upper range.'

Clara stared at Pietro. 'You said you were a tenor.'

'I was! I am!'

Training can extend a singer's range, higher or lower. Julia
ndered how she and Roberto had not considered this simple
a sooner. But then, how could they have known that Pietro
rni had begun his singing career as a young, unsettled
ritone who had trained upwards into a tenor?

She leaned towards Roberto. 'How did we miss so obvious
act?' she asked softly.

'Easy. We didn't look,' Roberto murmured. 'You because
a regard for your grandmother's "friend", me because I
nted to be fair to the father of a young man who made no
etence at being interested in you. We were blinded by our
n prejudices.'

'Guy was right when he wrote that you were strange,' said
ara to Pietro. *You* were in the chamber. *You* were the singer
t would be easy for you to sing deeper than I'd heard in the
hedral or in church at Croce.' Her features set in loathing.
u! All this time, it was you!'

'You're making a terrible mistake,' began Pietro, but Clara's
ce cut across his.

'That morning after the air-raid, you came looking for m
at the villa – you wanted to know if I'd survived, and if I had
would I recognise you as Scarpia. When you found me, Pietro
on the track alone, were you tempted to shoot me too? O
had you decided even then that the Fascists were losing an
you needed cover to get away? What better than to travel wit
the widow of the man you had tortured?'

'Clara, stop it!' Pietro commanded. 'You're becomin
hysterical.'

With something of her old calm, Bianca rapped on the table
silencing everyone. 'Papà was good, I tell you. He fooled eve
me. All this last month I never suspected him of reading m
secret "Scarpia" file, but he did.'

'Last month.' Julia glanced at Roberto. 'That's when yo
were attacked in Vienna.'

'Sorry,' said Bianca ironically. 'I'd just noted in my file tha
Roberto too was looking for Scarpia.'

Krusak turned to Julia. 'Is that who you were looking for?
thought it must be me.'

'You're as bad as Papà,' Bianca observed. 'Always thinkin
people are after you. With him I used to think it was jus
paranoia, I never expected guilty secrets.'

'At your home before Christmas,' said Julia to Pietro, 'whe
you asked me what I thought of the war trials, you weren
sure then who I was after.' Julia's eyes sparked at the memory
'You were sounding me out!'

Pietro shrugged. 'You were very interested in old singer
as I recall.'

When he had mentioned Vincenti her face must have show
something: disquiet, excitement. For a man with guilty secret
that would be enough to alert him. Annoyed at herself, Juli
said nothing.

Bianca gave her a sly look. 'When Papà ran into you i
Bologna, the day before your opera début, he figured ther
must be more to what you were doing than my kid brothe
had said. Let's face it, no singer's going to waste time lookin
for a long lost cousin when they're performing the next day—

'Bianca, be quiet,' said di Salvo, but Bianca smiled.

'It's over, di Salvo. If my father's going down then so are you.' She glanced at Roberto, then Julia. 'Who do you think disposed of Sprint? I did, acting for di Salvo, who wanted his own role in Patuzzi's farmhouse kept hidden. I shot Sprint.' She touched Gucci's arm. 'Can you arrest me? I don't want to be taken by strangers.'

Gucci clasped her shoulder and nodded, asking quietly, 'And the younger Stefano? Did you kill him, too?'

Bianca shook her head. 'I wasn't worried about him at first: when he burst into Papà's gallery, I thought he was accusing Krusak of being a Fascist, not my father. Later, after I'd talked to you, I went to see Stefano, but he was already dead. I suppose someone got to him first.'

Gucci nodded, his jowls slack then stiffening as he looked at Pietro. 'That's why when Julia showed me those old pictures I picked you out,' he remarked in a wondering way. 'When I was a kid I'd seen you round Ponte and Bologna.'

'Rita must have seen him in Bologna, too: she lingered over his picture,' said Julia. She and Gucci glanced at each other.

Roberto, interested in pursuing the present, walked round to where Bianca was slumped in her chair, her head leaning against Gucci's torso. 'Go on, Bianca. Tell us about di Salvo.'

'He was the curate of Croce and, yes, his name then was Michele Bozzi. Ask the Vatican if you don't trust me, there are records and photographs. He was one of the final gang.' She smiled. 'And you were right about Sprint, the Fascists' power attracted him in the end.' Bianca glanced over Roberto's shoulder to Julia and Clara. 'Sprint changed sides in May '44, after he'd heard about Mutta. He didn't want his parents shot in a German-Fascist reprisal. Still, he didn't like the idea of turning Judas, so he paid a visit to his parish priest.

'He didn't see the priest but he saw the curate. Michele Bozzi helped him to decide: "Partisans," he told him, "are Godless Communists." Michele put him on to the main local Fascist sympathisers, including one who was a leader of his own "cell". After that Sprint was totally converted. He'd always wanted to be second in command in Mario Scudieri's partisan group, now with his new friends he was.

'Sprint was Spoletta.' Bianca lowered then raised her head. 'Sorry you have to hear this,' she said to Clara. 'He sang to you.' She flashed a look at Simone. 'Not to you, though. You just had Scarpia.'

Simone, gaunt in the candle-light, edged closer to Clara. He and Clara had been tortured by Spoletta.

Julia looked at di Salvo, revealed as also being Michele Bozzi. 'And you were a torturer in the chamber that night.'

'No, not me,' said di Salvo. 'It was—'

'Quiet!' commanded Pietro Terni. Simone and Clara started. Gone was the blushing, nervous fellow who hid his face in his handkerchief. Here was another man.

'Who *is* Scarpia?' Krusak broke in.

Di Salvo leaned across the table to Bianca. 'Could I have one of your cigarettes?' he asked calmly. 'Thanks.'

As tobacco smoke curled over the ruined meal, di Salvo spoke.

'Scarpia was the code-name for a Fascist informer who worked for the Italian and German SS. He began his career in the 1940s in Bologna, where he recruited other informers from outlying villages such as Mutta who would report to him in the city. The interrogation of suspects arose from that work and gradually became more compelling, particularly once the war started to go badly for the Fascists.

'In Bologna itself, Scarpia's greatest achievement was to remove Mauro the forger. It was from Mauro that he heard of a partisan group in the mountains called the Red-Headed League. That became his next target. Francesco Vincenti, Stefano and Patuzzi were already part of his network of informers – Vincenti he'd recruited through meeting him at the Bologna opera, and Vincenti then put Scarpia on to two more like-minded men from his own home area.

'Yet, despite Stefano and Patuzzi coming from the region, in Croce they could make little headway. Scarpia became convinced the League must be important, so vital that only his personal involvement would ensure any results. So he thought of a ruse to convince the Contessa to allow him to live on her estate where, living in the house of a simple-minded

arrier, he could come and go as he wished. And Davide
Patuzzi provided a secret place where Scarpia could indulge
his love of drama whilst he interrogated suspects.'

Secrecy and vanity: Scarpia's twin obsessions, thought Julia.
Here were the reasons why Patuzzi's deserted farmhouse had
proved so appealing to the group.

But di Salvo was speaking.

'Still the breakthrough he hoped for, the recognition, the
political protection he craved from the authorities for his own
kind of "special police force", did not come. Thanks to Patuzzi,
a Jewish family – the Rasellas – were handed over to him but
they knew nothing.'

Di Salvo drew on his cigarette. 'I persuaded the group to
let the children go. I left them in Ponte church. By then I was
part of the group: as Bianca said, the Communists were my
fear. I justified my role by saying the last rites over the dead
victims, by not being part of the interrogation process itself.
Still, the torture of children, of one's own Contessa . . .'

He coughed sharply. 'Sprint and I were the last to join
Scarpia's group. There were three long-standing members
who had been with him in Bologna: Vincenti, Patuzzi, Stefano.
They knew Scarpia's real name, as well as his code-name:
Scarpia didn't worry about these men knowing, since they
were his death squad – Vincenti, Patuzzi and Stefano all took
turns to execute victims. That's why Stefano's son kept quiet
until after his father died and Sprint was murdered: if he'd
talked earlier, then Stefano would have gone to prison.

'But in war this was all in the future. Once Sprint came in,
Scarpia realised the Red-Headed League was only a minor
operation, but it was gratifying to know that one of his people
had infiltrated a partisan outfit. That pride kept Scarpia from
moving against the League for several weeks, until June '44,
when Sprint met a youth and the priest of Ponte coming to
Troce and heard from the boy about a big Allied push. Scarpia
was always obsessed by the fear that the Americans would
overrun Italy from the north. After that, it was only a matter
of waiting until after the feast of Our Lady before Mario
Scudieri, the head of the League, was picked up.'

Simone swayed slightly on his feet.

'Mario Scudieri as head of the League was a surprise in more ways than one. Scarpia had earlier discounted him because the man was a non-combatant – no fingers to shoot. Also Scarpia, his henchmen Stefano and Patuzzi, had assumed Mario's main concern would be to lie low, since he was the Contessa's foreign husband.

'But Mario was tough – and Mario wouldn't talk. Scarpia knew from Sprint and Stefano that Mario was married to the Contessa, so a way was devised to bring her to Patuzzi's old farm. It was thought the Contessa's interrogation might encourage her husband to speak.'

Di Salvo looked at Clara. 'When the bomb hit the farm, it was I who released you from the table and tore away your blindfold. To allow you to escape the fire.'

'Should I thank you for that, curate?' demanded Clara. 'When you and your creatures murdered my husband and have since threatened my granddaughter?'

'Such attacks were nothing to do with me, Contessa. I have only the greatest admiration for Julia.' Di Salvo bowed his head to Julia. 'The war wrought two great changes in my life. It showed the priesthood was not for me and awoke my love of opera. When Bianca told me for whom you were searching, I was genuinely torn: not for a fortune would I have damaged your superb voice, yet I knew if you found Scarpia you would also uncover my part in his group. So I waited to see what you found. When I heard – from Bianca again – that you suspected Jan Krusak of Scarpia's war crimes, I was relieved.'

'What!' Krusak was on his feet, but no one looked at him.

Clara was touching her face, staring at Pietro. 'It was *you* who did this, Pietro, not Spoletta. Why?'

'It was an accident. The knife slipped! When the bomb dropped I was startled, the knife slipped.' His expression became aggrieved. 'Spoletta wouldn't touch you, his Contessa. He failed me, they all did. They left me to fend for myself in that inferno. All that heat: my shoes burned, one of my feet got burned – it was agony. Not one stopped to make sure I got out of that farmhouse; they all failed me. And this year:

oletta, ready to betray what he knew for money, and
efano's boy, accusing me *in public* of being a Fascist.' Pietro
opped.

'Nice confession, Papà,' said Bianca, trying to sound cool
d failing. 'Why not tell them what di Salvo told me?' Bianca
iiled at Julia. 'Mutual self-interest and knowledge, that's
iat's bound together my father and di Salvo all these years.
pà's description of Mauro the forger's workshop gave di
lvo – Bozzi – the idea of the fake cartoons: his family had
e money and contacts for him to make a success in the art
orld. After the war, Papà needed a new occupation—'

'Afraid your disguise might slip, Pietro?' asked Clara. 'That
u would sing and someone recognise you?'

Pietro looked her in the eye. 'The ones who'd heard me
ig solo were all dead – except you and the Rasellas.' He
ked his head at Simone. 'I didn't know he'd survived until
is year. Never knew his last name, and his face wasn't
emorable.' Pietro smiled again. 'It's hard to remember
ndfolded faces.'

Clara and Simone shuddered at the man's bland reply, but
etro was still talking.

'After the war, Vincenti and I were gradually edged out of
e Bologna opera company as collaborators – nothing said
ectly, just hints. That was a good way then for middling
ices to get on; to accuse rivals of having worked for the
scists . . .'

'Except that in your case it was true,' said Roberto.

'They were all against me,' Pietro said bitterly. 'Working
th such fools was a waste of my energy and talents.'

'Besides, there's a simpler explanation for Pietro not
rsuing an operatic career,' put in Julia. 'No voice.' She smiled
Pietro. 'That's right, isn't it? Your voice is too small for a
loist and your vanity would prevent you from rejoining the
orus: you'd had a taste of being a principal at Blackshirt
adquarters and even more at Patuzzi's farmhouse, and
cided you liked it. I suppose, too, after that reality the fake
od and drama was rather tame.'

Pietro's round face coloured with anger, but he said

nothing. Instead, Bianca spoke.

'Papà had papers showing that Bozzi/di Salvo was a member of the Fascist party: as a curate, he shouldn't have been. Di Salvo was doing well by then as a patron of the arts and Papà decided that role would also suit him. He went to see his former "cell" member, reminded him who had been in command there, hinted at his evidence of di Salvo's involvement with right-wing politics. Di Salvo set Papà up in business.'

'It seemed the wisest thing,' said di Salvo. 'And Pietro had a flair for it. He became my junior partner. After Vincenti's and his own unfortunate experiences at Bologna opera in the late 1940s he was glad to take a public back seat, as it were.'

Di Salvo dropped his cigarette into his half-filled wine glass. 'In many ways, Pietro put off the mantle of Scarpia and assumed it,' he continued reflectively. 'Those sessions in the deserted farmhouse: they showed me that people respond best to terror.' He shrugged. 'After I had assisted in the interrogation of infants, the intimidation of business rivals was easy.'

'I knew of di Salvo's methods,' said Bianca. 'And when I talked to Coletta, the former priest of Croce, everything pointed to Bozzi as Scarpia. I put my evidence in a safe place and went to see my godfather, letting him know that if anything happened to me, the evidence would come out. He then filled me in on a few new details that rather changed my attitude to my father.'

Smiling wryly, she said, 'It's hard for me to know that Papà's a war criminal. I wish you'd never started this, Julia.'

'I didn't kill Sprint,' said Julia. 'You did.'

Roberto stepped forward. 'Scarpia.' His hand shot out, hauling Pietro to his feet. He put his face close to Pietro's, then abruptly, he thrust the smaller man away.

Gucci, speaking with surprising coolness, said, 'I suppose your contacts in the drugs world were useful when it came to getting rid of the younger Stefano and harassing this young woman and her partner.'

Pietro coiled back into his chair. 'I really thought Clara'

granddaughter would back off after a little physical persuasion. When you're out of the interrogation business for so long, you get soft. I considered my son's love for Julia, my own personal regrets over Clara.' His voice faltered, then became spiteful. 'One of my junkies pushed Stefano down a flight of stairs: it would have been easy to arrange another accident. I should have let the boys kill the pair of them outside Plini's, but then I'd have had di Salvo on my back. I knew he'd find out. He has contacts with professional hitmen, not just ambitious amateurs. He would have gone after *my* family.' His brown eyes darted over Julia. 'It's a pity you ignored the warnings, a shame your lover didn't react more to my phone call to him last night – I expected a more full-blooded reaction from an Italian male.' He smiled maliciously. 'But then Roberto had already got lucky in Vienna – that should have been an easy hit. Of course that's how it is when you use junkies: they're willing but inefficient. Still they don't talk – unlike some I could mention.' He glared at his daughter.

'You knew about me,' murmured Bianca, almost shamefacedly. 'All this time – you knew.'

Pietro made a gesture of impatience. 'You're my child. Besides, di Salvo made sure I knew.'

Casually, he lifted a small handgun from his pocket. 'Everything I did in the war was necessary. Without men like me there would be no order. I regretted your blinding, Clara, I truly did,' he added softly. 'But then, I got you away to safety. I've lived a decent life – why should I be judged on just six months of it? I forgot the past, why couldn't you?'

'You hypocrite!' Heedless of the gun, Julia started forward. 'Your life's been nothing but a pretence! The bad acting, the Communist newspapers, your offers of help to me – all false. You've wanted to bury Scarpia, and you and di Salvo don't care how many corpses it takes to keep him buried!'

Roberto snatched at Julia's arm as the shots rang out. Pietro Terni slumped sideways onto the table, a small red hole in the middle of his forehead, another through the neck. The dining-room was suddenly full of armed men.

'You took your time,' snapped Gucci. 'Jesus, we spent two

hours today sorting out when you'd come in.'

Roberto closed his eyes, shuddering with the sound of the rifle. Julia put her arm around him.

'What now?' asked di Salvo, as he, Krusak and Bianca were handcuffed by carabinieri.

'Ask the magistrate,' said Gucci. He was the only one in the room who smiled.

52

Roberto shook his head. 'Do you think we'll always be like this?' he asked. 'You singing here in three days' time whilst I'm jetting to Russia. Then, when I'm back in Milan you're recording in London.'

A month had passed. He and Julia were walking arm in arm in the park off the Via Manin, relishing the scents of an April morning. Julia grinned now and licked her lips. 'Probably,' she answered. 'Do you mind?'

'Only the separations.' Roberto's jaw tightened slightly. 'Are you happy with the way things have turned out, Julia?'

Julia raised an eyebrow at him and laughed. Still laughing, she caught his head of spiky brown curls between her hands, pulled his face down to hers and kissed him.

Roberto kissed back, wrapping his arms tight around her, loving her warmth, smelling her scent, feeling those superb breasts pressing against his body. 'God, I wish we were still in bed.'

Julia gave him a wicked smile before turning Roberto's wrist so she could see the time. 'Angelica and Enrico will just be touching down at Pisa airport.'

'Are you sure you don't want to be at Clara's tonight?' asked Roberto.

'I'm sure. Mother and grandmother have things they need to say to each other.' Julia coiled a hair curl with her thumb.

'Angelica's written to Clara, saying she understands now, but a twenty-year separation takes time to bridge.' She smiled, her grey eyes bright. 'Still, I don't think it will take long.' Angelica and Clara were attending the Fiftieth Anniversary commemoration service next week, when Guy would be amongst those honoured.

Angelica had written to Julia, too, confirming Tom Jessop's story. Since learning of Julia's pregnancy, her mother had been telephoning every week, warm with advice and anticipation. They would be easier together now, Julia knew. The knowledge delighted her.

Roberto rubbed the back of his neck. 'Are you sure you're up to the drive to Florence this afternoon?'

'Worried about meeting my three big brothers?' teased Julia. She and Roberto had arranged to call in on Tom, who had promised that Julia's half-brothers would also be there.

Roberto snorted at the idea. One of his hands swept tenderly down her back. 'I just don't want you to get over-tired.'

'Roberto, I'm expecting a baby not an elephant.'

'I still can't quite believe it. My baby.'

'Don't take all the credit: I deserve some applause.'

Roberto laughed but then his black brows drew together. 'I know the way I learned wasn't what you intended: I'm sorry.'

'And now I've no more secrets.' Julia kept it light.

'I did trust you, Julia.'

'I know. Don't worry, Roberto.'

They were quiet a moment, walking steadily past the wind-blown fountain towards the outdoor café where the carabinieri dropped in for a morning coffee. Seeing the blue uniforms reminded Julia of Gucci.

'Emilio says that Bianca was lucky to get only ten years.'

'I think he's right,' said Roberto grimly. The courts, noting Bianca's conflict between the demands of di Salvo and the needs of her father and family, had been lenient.

As for di Salvo and Krusak, their trials were to come. But, with Bianca's confession, Anton Wolf's testimony, and the conversations recorded on police equipment worn by Roberto and Gucci, the papers were demanding that they be sent to

rison for life. That was even without di Salvo's involvement
dealing with art fakes, or Krusak's attempted intimidation
f Julia.

Julia's voice interrupted Roberto's thoughts. 'Did you know
hat Ruth and Francesco are planning to get married at the
nd of this year? A stage hand at La Scala told me.'

Inevitably the two couples, Ruth and Francesco, Julia and
oberto, had avoided each other since Pietro Terni's death.
ith Pietro's war crimes sure to come out in Tancredi di
alvo's trial, the constraint between the four singers looked
kely to continue for some time.

'I hope they do: they're good for each other.' Roberto,
oking back over Julia's head, saw the fountain dazzle and
out, the water rippling like applause, like a whisper.

Roberto shook himself. No part of today belonged to
carpia. Today Pietro Terni belonged finally in the past.

A couple were approaching on a bicycle, bride and groom.
he groom was pedalling slowly so that everyone could admire
is bride balanced gracefully on the crossbar, her long white
ress and veil rippling in the warm air. Julia and Roberto
opped to watch the couple wind slowly down the gravelled
ath until they were hidden by the trees.

When bride and groom had finally vanished, the two singers
oked at each other. Roberto touched one of her long diamond
arrings, one of his gifts to her.

'Dad's decorating his bedroom with the brightest red I've
ver seen,' he said against Julia's ear. Simone had moved out
Roberto's flat before Julia moved in and now, free of
ghtmares and stomach pains, fired with enthusiasm for his
ew home, he looked and acted younger than Julia would have
ought possible. And he was much easier with her.

Julia looked up. 'Do you miss Simone in the flat?'

'No,' said Roberto decisively.

'You've got me.'

'I've got you.' Roberto turned her to face him, his features
olemn. 'And I mean to keep you.' He touched her hand,
eling heat on the back of his neck, his heart thumping. 'Will
ou marry me, Julia?'

She smiled at him with brilliant grey eyes, her lips curving
She touched the two lines running from the side of his nose
to his mouth. She loved his gap-toothed smile.

'Ask me tomorrow,' she said.